A COVENANT KEEPER NOVEL

FOREVER

THE CONSTANTINES' SECRET

S.R. KARFELT

INDIGO

Livonia, Michigan

Published by Indigo
an imprint of BHC Press

Library of Congress Control Number:
2017945127

ISBN-13: 978-1-946848-46-8
ISBN-10: 1-946848-46-8

Also available in ebook

Visit the publisher at:
www.bhcpress.com

ALSO BY S.R. KARFELT

The Covenant Keeper Novels
Kahtar—Warrior of the Ages
Heartless—A Shieldmaiden's Voice

Other Novels
Bitch Witch

Non Fiction
Nobody Told Me—Love in the Time of Dementia

Multi-Author Collections
A Winter's Romance
In Creeps the Night
Through the Portal
Call of the Warrior

*Dedicated to my wild things,
I know for sure.*

FOREVER
THE CONSTANTINES' SECRET

THE LAWS OF BEING

The First Law
Love. It is your purpose. ilu is love.

The Second Law
Honor. It is the path. Dishonor breeds death.

The Third Law
Obey. The Covenant will lead you.

The Fourth Law
Heart. Open and trust it.

The Fifth Law
Truth. You must know truth in word, deed, and law.

The Sixth Law
Seek. Find ilu in all.

The Seventh Law
Be. It is who you are.

The Eighth Law
Protect. The earth tethers you.

The Ninth Law
Join. Be with your own as your heart demands.

The Tenth Law
Giftings. They belong to your people.

Keepers of ilu's Covenant, keep the Covenant

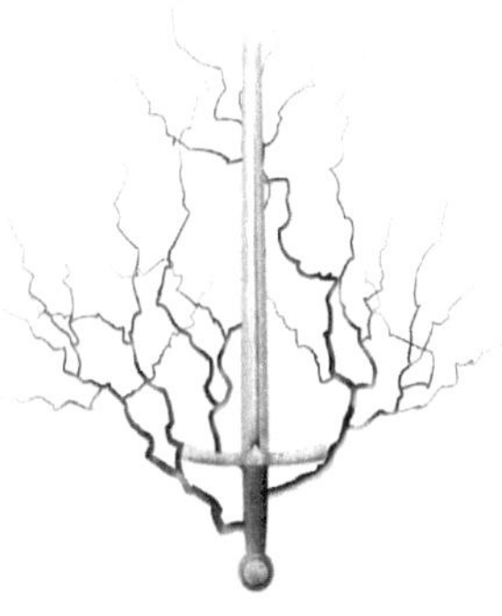

CHAPTER

ONE

Bloody Surprise—All Hallows' Eve

DURING THE THOUSANDS of years Kahtar had lived, died, and lived again, he'd never once employed corporal punishment on a female. A glance in the rearview mirror had him rethinking that.

Delphine Green sprawled across the backseat of his squad car chewing a fingernail like lunch, her legs spread wide in a short black skirt. Red and white striped tights gave her a well-deserved witch look. She glanced up, met his gaze and winked, running her tongue over full red lips. An angry flush crawled up Kahtar's neck and he resisted the impulse to pull the squad car over and teach her respect for their clan's warrior chief.

I'll have the Old Guard cane her. He tried to remember if they'd cane women. Surely they would. Sexism wasn't an Old Guard problem. They were equal opportunity punishers.

Giving her fingernail a break, Delphine slid to the edge of the seat and pressed her forehead against the metal divider. "Look, Kahtar—"

"Excuse me?" he interrupted. "What did you call me?" Even as a young girl Delphine had been disrespectful, just like her father.

"Sorry. Warrior Chief. Or do I have to say Police Chief, even though we're alone now?"

Kahtar ignored this. "Last I recall you were sent away. Imagine my surprise when the criminal I was asked to escort turned out to be a member of my own clan, one who shouldn't be on this continent, let alone arrested in the world of seekers! How is it you're back in town but not inside the Arc?"

"I just got back."

"And you missed the Arc by an entire city? Nobody mentioned you were coming back, and after the way you were practically thrown out of the clan I'm a bit surprised by that. I suspect they have no idea you're here. You seem to have only graduated from stealing to defacing public property." If memory served, and it surely did in this case, these were the same type of petty crimes Delphine's father had engaged in during his teens.

"Stealing? Are you accusing me of stealing?"

"Don't pretend you don't remember," he said, glancing back at her. Delphine had the same innocent expression and deep dimples that had kept Warfield Green out of the mists until he'd broken six of the ten laws of being and nearly exposed the entire clan.

"I never stole anything! They were library books and I was only fourteen years old!"

"You not only stole them, you snuck them inside the Arc! What about today? I saw photos of your graffiti! Symbols sacred to Warriors of ilu spray painted for the outside world to see! What have you been doing the past eight years? Making a pact with the forces of darkness? The apple doesn't fall far from the tree, does it?"

Delphine made a noise that sounded half-laugh, half-sob. "Maybe the apple doesn't, but seeds can be carried far and the seedlings unrecognizable!"

"I'd hardly say that is your case. I don't understand how you can be so irresponsible with a father like yours!"

"One might ask you the same thing."

"Excuse me?" said Kahtar. Instead of answering the young woman looked out the window, tangled dark hair hiding her face. "What does my father have to do with yours?"

"Whatever," muttered Delphine. "Who am I to call mammoth plop on the warrior chief? But if you think your *father* is in anyway superior to mine, I'd say you're the one who's delusional. Mine might have been a fool, but yours—well, it takes more nerve than I have to pick an adjective and criticize his son."

She wasn't making sense. Kahtar tightened his grip on the steering wheel and changed lanes. His biological father in this repeat had died long before Delphine was born, and Levi Constantine had been a good man. Perhaps all Delphine wanted was a father-figure's attention, but going about it with the smart mouth she'd inherited from Warfield wasn't the way to get it.

"Kahtar, do you know who your real father is?" Delphine asked, her voice pitched low. Kahtar opened his mouth to condemn the use of his name again, but as her words sunk in he shut it, swallowing a sigh.

It surprised him the love child rumor hadn't died by now. This happened in most repeats. Any time his new parents looked nothing like him, some clan members would assume his mother had taken a lover. But his biological parents in this repeat had died so long ago. He couldn't recall the last time someone in Cultuelle Khristos had even mentioned him looking nothing like the wiry, dark Constantines. Why did the girl care if he was a love child, anyway? Maybe she wished she'd been one.

"Your father was Warfield Green. You look just like him."

"I'm talking about your father, not mine."

"You shouldn't listen to rumors, especially old ones."

"What rumors? Do other people know about you? Does The Mother know?"

Kahtar glanced into the mirror. Delphine sat on the edge of her seat, her face still pressed against the divider. She had red indentations on her forehead. He tried to think why this topic fascinated her. "You need to worry what The Mother is going to say about the fact that you were arrested. Whether or not my long dead mother had a lover is absolutely none of your business."

"I'm not talking about your dead mother. I'm talking about your real father!"

"My father was Levi Constantine."

With an impatient groan Delphine threw herself against the backseat and a possibility hit Kahtar. *Maybe that's what her problem is.* He focused his attention on the touch of her heart before asking such a personal question. It seemed tense, tight, and worried. *No, not worried. Reckless.*

"Did you take a—I mean, are you pregnant with a love child?"

"Ha!" Delphine snorted. "You are so thick!"

Scanning to avoid an accident, Kahtar cut across three lanes of traffic to the shoulder of the highway, leaving screeching tires in his wake. Slowing as quickly as he could, he stopped the car and twisted in his seat to glare at her. "You watch your mouth or I will cane you myself!" The tears streaming their way down her face stopped the rest of his rebuttal.

"There is only one man I'd ever want to father a love child with, and apparently you are the only man in the clan who doesn't know who that is."

Surely she didn't mean him.

Delphine smiled, but the deep dimples and quivering lips made her look more wretched. "Far too late, he finally notices," she whispered.

The way her blue eyes watched his face made him uncomfortable. The only eyes that looked at him like that were Beth's.

"I've joined," he said.

"Do you think I didn't notice? I remember your heart."

He frowned at her. Women didn't talk to him like this. In all his years the only ones who did were ones not to be trusted, ones who wanted something from him. Big merciless warrior chiefs weren't popular with the opposite sex, or with anyone for that matter. His frown deepened, but he steered the car back into traffic and proceeded down the highway.

Delphine wasn't finished. "You know, I worked so hard to become worthy. I'm Tener Mulier, you know? That means I completed *all* the teachings Avalon offers. And I did it in eight years, not ten. I suppose I knew you'd never consider me because of my father, but I thought maybe if I did something impossible and honorable like that, you'd notice and really look at me. It never occurred to me you'd find someone else. If I'd told you I wanted you before I left, would you have waited for me?"

The question so distracted Kahtar that he veered the squad car onto the painted line and bumped over the hundreds of little ridges put there to keep drivers from doing that very thing. "What on earth are you talking about? You were a little girl when you left."

"The ironic thing is I could never be good enough for you, but apparently a half-seeker chick is."

"Watch what you say about my wife. How do you know about Beth?" If nobody knew Delphine was back, where was she getting her information? Her knowledge that he had joined with a Covenant Keeper who had a seeker father only proved that Delphine had been sneaking around the clan.

A very liquid sniff sounded from beneath the length of messy hair. "You and I would have made a good match."

Kahtar looked in his rearview mirror and nearly rolled the driver's side tires over the rumble strip again as her heart touched his. She meant every word and it didn't make any sense. Until Beth, no woman had ever talked to him like this. Throughout his centuries of existence, women never wanted to spend much time with Kahtar. Delphine Green needed her head examined if she did.

Stepping on the gas pedal, Kahtar hurried to take the next exit. If he dumped her off with someone at Cobbson Clinic they could figure her out, and she wouldn't be his problem. He barely paid any attention when Delphine again scooted to the edge of her seat and leaned on the divider to talk.

Thirty minutes later the entrance to Cobbson Compound came into sight. Kahtar shifted his big body inside the seat of his squad car and glanced into the mirror at the empty backseat.

The sight startled him, but he couldn't think why. For that matter, he couldn't think why he'd decided to go to Cobbson at all. He needed to get back to the police station. What had he been thinking? Halloween was possibly their busiest night. He shouldn't have wasted time transporting a prisoner today.

A memory of standing inside the neighboring town's police station while an officer told him someone else had picked up the prisoner floated into his mind and he frowned. They had called him to the police station, and then sent the prisoner off with someone else at the last minute.

Something pestered at the edges of Kahtar's mind, and for the first time in years the memory of Warfield Green's troublesome daughter intruded. She had been sent away years ago, and Kahtar hadn't thought of her since. The hair stood up on his arms and he physically turned to look into the backseat. *I hope this isn't a premonition she's coming back.* He tried to think how long Delphine had been sent away for, but couldn't recall the details. Little girls weren't often his jurisdiction.

The police radio crackled to life and a polite female voice demanded his focus. Kahtar responded automatically, shaking his head and shoving away the niggling feeling of having forgotten something. The message from dispatch required his attention and he pressed the gas pedal harder and headed to the local university. Far to the east he sensed an ambulance racing toward the university and forced his attention on scanning ahead. Trying to read what had happened at the local campus with his mental radar, he ignored the slight shiver rippling up his spine.

IT COULDN'T BE called a costume. The kid in the doorway of Beth's parents' house looked like any other unwashed teenage boy.

"You don't look like a rock star to me," said Beth with her usual candor.

"Like I said, Alternative Rock Star." Looking anything but, he held out an oversize Steelers t-shirt like an apron, exposing a bit of hairy underbelly.

Beth snorted, but her father tossed a handful of Snickers bars into the makeshift receptacle as he greeted the surly teen. "Happy Halloween! Good thing you came when I'm here, because this one," Ted White shot a thumb toward Beth, "would've given you organic apples and dark chocolate! She had to come here to try and peddle it because no one will take it from her health food store."

"Like I care, old man," said the kid in a bored voice.

Anger made cold hackles rise on Beth's neck just as her mother, who'd spent the last hour perusing organic gardening magazines without looking up, suddenly appeared at her side. The boy backed quickly down the steps, dropping candy bars with Carole White's finger shoved in his face. He nearly fell, but Carole twisted a handful of his shirt into her fist, skimmed the last few steps and lowered him to the sidewalk. The kid crumpled to his knees, but nabbed a couple Snickers bars off the concrete before scurrying away.

Carole jogged up the steps, slammed the door shut and flipped the porch light off. She took a cursory look at her husband's Halloween costume. Beth had to assume her father was supposed to be some sort of grizzled Girl Scout, but hadn't wanted to ask. Her face impassive, Carole adjusted the blue beanie on his head. It had once belonged to Beth during a brief stint with a Japanese Troop.

Ted leered at his wife and Carole ran the back of her hand over his ample belly in a decidedly sensual gesture. Beth averted her eyes and wished she could somehow un-see the private parental moment. Her mother returned to the couch and picked up her magazine, leaving Beth feeling awkward and scrambling for something to say.

We're like the Addams Family.

Although Beth had never seen the show, she knew it was true, the same way she knew when anything was true. But she played her role when she visited her parents just the same; ignoring their strangeness the same way they ignored hers.

Okay, Dad was making fun of my apples and good chocolate. I can work with that.

"Organic apples are expensive, Dad, and my chocolate is imported!"

Ted leaned past her to flick the porch light back on and grinned. Trying not to focus on the curly blonde wig beneath her old blue beanie, Beth noticed for the first time ever that his five o'clock shadow had gray mixed in the stiff red bristles.

"Yeah, well, today's Halloween. Nobody wants anything imported—besides, I give out full-size candy bars, and they're expensive. That's why our house is so popular!"

"It's nine and that was only the second kid. And isn't this the first year you've ever done Halloween? We never did it when I was growing up," said Beth.

"Yeah, well, we never lived anywhere we could 'til now." Ted nabbed an apple from the bowl by the door, tossed it to Beth, and unwrapped a candy bar for himself.

"Bet Mom never would have let me even if we had."

Across the room thumbing through her magazine, Carole made no comment. Beth hadn't really expected one. She took the candy bar off her dad and handed him the apple. "Did you notice neither of those kids had on a costume? I would make my kid wear a costume."

"You don't make your kid do anything," Carole muttered from the couch. "Someday you'll find out your kid will do whatever—" She stopped speaking mid-sentence and looked up at Beth, who stared back at her. Carole rarely spoke unless forced, and she never participated in small talk.

Ted stood frozen in position, his apple before his lips, as though moving would ruin any chance of another rare word. After an uncomfortable silence, Carole flipped another page on her magazine and returned her attention to it.

Beth gave up and headed for a chair, wishing Kahtar had come with her. Not that having her Covenant Keeper warrior chief husband with her, using an alias and disguised as the Police Chief of Willowyth, would make things any less weird. She couldn't imagine what he'd say about her dad's costume, but she already missed him. Kahtar—alias Kent Costas to the outside world, including her parents—hadn't been to visit his new in-laws since the wedding, and

Beth had a bad feeling he never would. The thought of sleeping without him made her lonely.

Settling back in the comfy chair, Beth noticed her father staring at her, still frozen in place.

"Beth's pregnant!" Ted shouted. "Isn't she?"

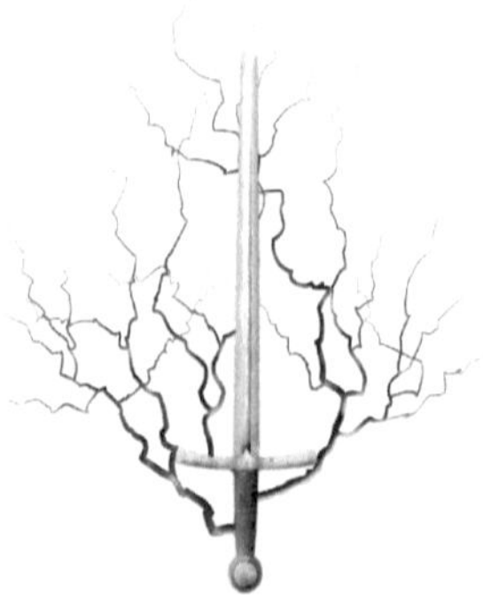

CHAPTER

TWO

Bloody Strange—Halloween

BETH LOOKED AT her mother, as though she could confirm her father's outrageous claim. The faintest of cryptic smiles quirked Carole's lips and Ted whooped as though it were medical confirmation of an impossible pregnancy.

"What?" Beth demanded.

Ted shot across the room and hauled Beth out of her chair, engulfing her in a hug.

"No, Dad. What are you guys talking about? I just got married! I didn't even get my wedding dress preserved yet. There's no way—"

But Beth couldn't seem to deny it. The words wouldn't come. She didn't have the ability to lie; something she saw as a handicap, but the Covenant Keepers told her was a gifting. *How can this be true?*

About a month after their wedding Beth had mentioned children and Kahtar had gone quiet for half the day. Finally Beth had pressed him, and Kahtar had announced that whatever kind of immortal repeating freak he was, he was a sterile one. So her mother had to be wrong. Shifting under her father's stranglehold Beth asked, "Mom, what makes you think that?"

Across the room Carole settled more comfortably against the couch. "You're pregnant, Beth."

It settled against Beth as truth, but she persisted, determined to oust the impossible. Kahtar had said with equal conviction that pregnancy was impossible, at least without the help of the clan doctor. "Even if I am, how do you know?"

Carole shrugged. "Mothers sense stuff."

It bounced against Beth like a lie, causing a stir of nausea in her belly and raising her hackles, like the boy being rude to her dad had raised Carole's. Beth wanted to call her mother out, to demand she explain how she could possibly glance at her across the room and know she was pregnant, but a familiar sparkle of light outside the window glinted dangerously and she kept her mouth shut. The Old Guard watched her to ensure Covenant Keeper secrets were kept. There were questions she could never ask.

Besides, the one she really wanted to have words with was Kahtar. He'd said he couldn't make babies.

Still smothered in her father's big hug, Beth realized he was talking, going on about the power of mother's intuition. Her thoughts were too scattered to listen. *If Kahtar's wrong, what does that mean?* Despite his centuries of experience Kahtar wasn't infallible, and with his murky origins, maybe he didn't want a child of his own. *What if this is a bad thing?* The thought made her shudder.

"Aw, come on! Babies are the best thing that can happen, you'll see!" Ted's hug tightened and bones in Beth's back cracked neatly into place. Usually she loved when he did that. It made her feel even taller and Dad seemed so safe and capable then. But right now Beth wanted to burrow into his chest and hide. "Hey, Bethy, focus on the wonderful even if you think its bad timing." After kissing both her cheeks, Ted grabbed Beth's hand to haul her upstairs. "I know what to do! Let's get on Amazon and order stuff for my grandchild."

"Dad, no!" Beth tried to plant her feet as he tugged.

"Don't slow me down! I have to baby proof this entire house, make the spare room into a nursery, get a bigger car, start a college fund, and build a swing set!"

"No!" Beth scrambled for an excuse, her thoughts on Kahtar. When he'd told her he couldn't make babies he'd been apologetic, but confident she'd have joined with him even if he'd told her before their marriage. It was the truth, so she'd accepted it.

Beth shivered now, certain he'd left something unsaid. Some part of her brain managed to come up with an excuse to curtail her father's sudden need to shop. "Don't waste your money until we know something for sure—at least until I pee on a stick or get some other scientific confirmation!" *Or talk to my husband! What didn't he tell me?*

"Your mother's always right," Ted said with a chuckle, tucking her arm under his and patting it as he marched her up the stairs. "And don't worry about my money. Even if you spent all yours on your big house and imported chocolate, Carole and I have invested wisely. We're real life thousandaires. If you play your cards right, someday you and your child might inherit literally up to hundreds of dollars from us."

Despite everything Beth laughed. At least she'd made her father happy.

"What's nine months from now? Carole! When do you think the baby will come?" Ted shouted to Carole from the top of the stairs, as though she were an obstetrician instead of retired military like him.

"For sure a long time from now!" Beth interrupted, desperate to divert him so she could go panic in the spare room by herself. "Besides, the cute stuff is gender specific! Let's wait!"

"We'll get boy stuff and girl stuff and I'll just return what we don't need!" Ted grabbed his wallet from a stand by the railing and dug out a credit card.

"I thought you spent your money wisely," Beth tried.

"No. I said I invested wisely. I spend foolishly. Didn't you see my blow-up Halloween decorations out front?" Ted grinned.

Beth had an urge to hug him and tell him he'd make an even better grandfather than he had a dad, and he'd been the best father she could imagine. *But what kind of father will Kahtar make?* She had a really bad feeling he'd never planned to find out. Beth widened her eyes, hoping tears wouldn't spill.

"July or August. Buy girl stuff," said Carole from downstairs.

Ted squeezed Beth's hand, his grin growing wider.

A girl? How can she possibly know that? I swear she can scan inside me like a clan doctor! How can anyone know the sex that soon? From the railing Beth stared down at her mother. Carole kept her eyes on the magazine, but Beth knew perfectly well she wasn't reading it.

We are definitely the Addams Family. Only weirder.

Somewhere deep in Beth's heart the thought of a baby girl sparked something new and hopeful, surrounded by a fear that Kahtar could somehow crush it.

THREE POLICE CARS pulled into the small lot in front of the Willowyth Police Station and parked. Doors opened and Warriors of ilu dressed as officers exited and hauled out an assortment of young perps. In the last vehicle Kahtar sat alone watching the subdued frat boys clutching sheets of clear plastic around their naked essentials.

Dressing as a pack of hot dogs no longer appeared to have been a good idea to the young men. The design flaw in using a vacuum cleaner to suck the air out and hermetically seal a giant plastic bag around a group of human beings had become apparent to even the dullest of them. Kahtar wondered how the boys from the ends of the pack were responding at the hospital. Helping them with his giftings was forbidden, but mouth to mouth resuscitation wasn't. Their blue color had faded by the time the ambulance loaded them in. Kahtar figured other than losing a few thousand brain cells—that they'd obviously never miss—the boys would be fine. He wiped his mouth off, still able to taste their alcohol. *Imbeciles!*

He had no intention of following his men inside the station. As chief of police he had no obligation to book intoxicated students into jail for the night. He'd rolled out of bed over twenty-three hours ago; it had been a long day. Kahtar rubbed a hand over his face and tried to turn his mind from the drunken rave.

Fifteen students is hardly a rave.

The thought popped into his head in Beth's voice, and he could picture the way she'd try not to smile when she said it.

"It's a rave in Willowyth," he said out loud, banishing images of his wife from his mind. Tonight she was at her parents, their first night apart since the wedding, and he needed to get some sleep not tempt himself to go see her. He put his car in gear, but before his foot touched the gas pedal, Francis Snickerbacher, Cultuelle Khristos Warrior of ilu and one of the newer cops, pushed through the doorway and waved, heading in his direction.

"Now what?" Kahtar groused, throwing the car back into park and yanking the keys out of the ignition.

Kahtar met Francis halfway across the lot. "Thought you'd want to know Beth called for you four times tonight. She didn't want to leave a message."

Kahtar paused briefly. Maybe she just missed him as much as he missed her, but as warrior chief and as her husband he certainly wasn't going to ignore it. He glanced back at his squad car, jiggling the keys in his hand. *It's a long drive.* He handed them to Francis. "Put these on my desk."

Hurrying to the back of the parking lot where he wouldn't be noticed, Kahtar scanned quickly, then closed his eyes and disappeared.

FOR A BRIEF moment Kahtar thought he'd appeared inside the wrong room. Lit by the light of an alarm clock, the guest room at the White's had changed from peace signs and the preservation of Beth's childhood to a king-sized bed with navy and gold draperies. Beth lay nestled under the blankets, sound asleep with cell phone in hand. For the first time in hours Kahtar relaxed.

Scanning gently through the house for any sign of trouble, Kahtar tried not to wake his shieldmaiden mother-in-law. However, it was the seeker Ted White who turned restlessly in his bed as the scan whispered around their bedroom. All seemed well enough and

Kahtar pulled it back, unbuckling his duty belt and silently settling ten pounds of gun and accessories on the nightstand.

Leaning over the bed, Kahtar eased the cell phone out of Beth's hand and put it on the nightstand too, pausing to plug it into the charger. They'd been apart not even twenty-four hours and even in sleep the touch of her heart raced for his as though they'd been separated for years. Relishing the taste of that heart, like diving into clear water on a summer day, Kahtar bent lower and pressed his lips against hers. Beth opened her eyes immediately. The touch of her heart lightened his mood despite the anxiety in it.

"You came!" Beth patted the bed beside her. Kahtar sat cautiously, expecting the protest of bedsprings from his weight, but the only sound was the rustling of Beth pushing back blankets to invite him beneath.

"I can't stay."

"My parents would be thrilled. Dad super-sized this bed just for you."

Kahtar was glad the dark hid any expression in his eyes, and even gladder Beth didn't press him. She didn't need to know that he'd never be allowed to visit with her parents. Maybe she already knew. She scooted closer as though seeking comfort and Kahtar couldn't resist sliding down beside her, outside the blankets, and dropping his head to the pillow next to hers for a moment.

Threading his fingers through hers, he held their hands against his chest. Since being joined with Beth, night had become his favorite time, and after two thousand years of night terrors that was a welcome first.

"My night was so strange. You should have seen my dad dressed as a Girl Scout." She grinned in the dark and her perfect teeth shone white. Kahtar lifted her hand and pressed his mouth against it in a lingering kiss. It felt thinner against his lips, somehow frail, although he'd kissed it goodbye just that morning. "It's been a weird visit," she continued.

"Did you say anything to your parents you shouldn't have?"

"No! You don't need to worry about that. I never will!"

"What do I need to worry about then? Why did you call the station four times?"

Beth took a deep breath. "Remember when you told me someday you'd love to love any baby I'd have with a little help from Welcome Palmer?"

Whoa. Kahtar extricated himself and sat up so Beth wouldn't see his eyes. They'd been married only two months; he hadn't expected this so soon. He ran a hand over the top of his bristled haircut and sighed. "I remember. Are you thinking about babies so soon, love?"

"Yes." It shot out of Beth's mouth as truth even he recognized.

Kahtar nodded into the darkness, again taking her hand in his. "Maybe it's for the best. This is the oldest I've ever lived to be in any repeat. I'd pass from this life easier knowing you had a child to fill your heart."

A smile quavered on her lips. "Don't assume you won't be here for thousands of diapers and the painful teenage years too."

"One can only hope, but longevity isn't often in the warrior chief job description."

Beth kissed his fingers. "Neither was marriage until this time around."

He smiled. "So you already want a baby?"

She nodded.

Kahtar wondered if she'd change her mind once she realized what it would entail as a Covenant Keeper. "Do you really want to talk about this right now?"

"Yes. It's why I kept calling. We need to talk about this. Tonight."

Tightening his grip on her hand he angled to face her in the bed, hoping to read her reaction in the faint light of the alarm clock and charging electronics. "Cultuelle Khristos believes all babies deserve to be conceived in love." When Beth returned his smile, he continued, "Even if it's just the love of a friend or acquaintance."

The smile faltered. "What?"

"There are no petri dishes or artificial insemination involved with fertility problems. This wouldn't involve Cobbson Clinic or even an Arc doctor. I would like it to involve Welcome Palmer though. He would be my first choice as a father. He's a good man. I could well love a child the two of you created." The last sentence came out hoarse and Kahtar cleared his throat. When he'd first considered this, it hadn't seemed as painful as the reality of it.

"Wait," said Beth. "What?"

Kahtar licked his lips. "You will need to be with him. We would scan and know when conception is most likely to occur, so likely it wouldn't be more than a few months of trying."

Beth's mouth dropped open and Kahtar squeezed her hand, but she pulled from his grasp. "People in the clan *do* that? Welcome would do that? You'd *want* him to?"

"Infertile couples do, sure. I don't think Welcome has ever done it, but I think he would for us." Always scanning, he sensed Beth's blush and open hand swing for his head. He reacted without thinking, catching it in his hand and fighting his warrior instincts to permanently disable that hand. He let it go after a warning squeeze.

"Ow," she said. "That hurt!"

"Sorry. Never take a swing at a warrior, Beth. You don't want to get into trouble for hitting one. It's no small thing. I'm on duty."

"Isn't there a special dispensation for when your stupid husband tells you to sleep with another man? If another man even touched my heart like you do, I think, Kahtar, I think I'd half die."

Jealousy surged through Kahtar and he growled, "If another man touched your heart like I do I'd kill him with my bare hands! Welcome Palmer wouldn't do any such thing. It would just be sex."

"Oh!" Beth drew out the word and it took Kahtar a few beats to recognize sarcasm in it. "Just sex."

Kahtar chuckled.

"I really want to smack you again."

"Don't. It's almost a bigger crime than if I were to hit you. The penalty is brutal."

"The clan rules make no sense at all."

Kahtar chuckled again. "I really love you, Beth." She'd forever make him see the world through fresh eyes.

"I love you too. I really don't get it though. If it's *just sex*, how does that create a child born in love? And what would you do with your heart if you're having sex without it? Is that even possible?"

"Your heart would be with mine the whole time. I'd be there too. The child would be conceived in our love, but also by using another man's body."

Beth said the f-word quite loudly. "Are you kidding me? You're talking about having a threesome? I do not think so, Kahtar Constantine. I mean, hypothetically that's kind of hot, but in reality there is no way I'd do that. It's invasive! You would *want* to do that?"

The truth. She spotted a lie before it left a man's lips. "Of course not, but I would for you."

She shook her head. "Wow. This is so not how I pictured having this conversation. Now instead of talking about babies I want to ask questions about your sexual predilections."

Kahtar fought an urge to burst out laughing, not wanting to wake Beth's parents. "You don't know them?"

She grinned. "I know. You just sounded really kinky there for a second."

Kahtar chuckled low. "Welcome is beautiful. Most of the Palmers are. I'm sure you've noticed that. But that's not what I'm interested in. He has good genes and a stellar heart, Beth. I've long appreciated that heart of his. I cannot imagine a better father for our children."

"I can."

"Surely not Honor Monroe? Beth, there's no way I'd be comfortable with that. He was practically your lover for a time."

"Ew. He was not. You're just dying for me to smack you tonight. I was talking about you, you numbskull."

The comment made Kahtar's eyes well with tears. Sweet ilu, the woman could touch his heart in uncharted places.

"Are you okay?" she said.

He sniffed. Not once in his existence had Kahtar regretted his inability to father children, not being who he was. Yet here he sat with his Orphan of the Inquisition wife, in her seeker father's house, nearly immediately after their wedding, wishing they could have a child together. "That's the most loving thing anyone has ever said to me. I'm sorry to have to disappoint you." Loss for what they could never have touched him and tears spilled out of his eyes, warming his cheeks.

"Oh, Kahtar!" Beth scooted closer to wipe away his tears. "And here I was so afraid to tell you!"

"Afraid to tell me what?"

"Okay, don't freak. I've had a few hours to think about this, and here's the thing—sometimes in life we just have to accept. It's better to accept and move forward than to have a fit about something we can't change anyway. Can you agree with that?"

"Yes, but what exactly are you trying to say?"

She took a deep breath. "I'm pregnant."

For a moment Kahtar's mind skidded to a complete stop, as though all the gears had been churning forward in high speed and needed to divert down an unknown path he hadn't even known existed. It took him awhile to find it.

But he did find it, and panicked. "Old Guard!" he shouted.

"Kahtar, no! Don't panic," said Beth, but their light had already filled the room as three of them lit into being. Two were shimmering knee deep inside the bed, only half materialized.

A gruff voice sounded down the hallway. "Who's that? Bethy! What's going on?"

Kahtar sensed Ted White scrambling out of bed. He jumped to his feet and grabbed his gear and Beth's phone off the nightstand. "Take us to wherever Welcome Palmer is," he ordered. "Quickly."

Two Old Guard reached for Beth, who pressed against the headboard in a futile attempt at escape. A twinge of pity struck Kahtar. Sometimes he forgot how terrifying Old Guard could be. The third man touched Kahtar's shoulder as Ted White turned the door handle and they all vanished.

THE OLD GUARD let go of Kahtar's shoulder before his feet hit the floor. He landed roughly, almost dropping his duty belt and Beth's phone.

He couldn't think straight. The simple fact that two Old Guard had transported Beth confirmed her assertion of pregnancy. One for each heart. Kahtar had believed her from the moment the words left her lips, but somehow the Old Guard's knowledge made his hands and feet ice cold with fear.

She's having my baby.

Beth wrapped her arms around herself, shivering, and sank to the carpeted floor.

"Palmer!" Kahtar shouted for the clan doctor and bent over Beth. "Shake it off. You'll get used to the Old Guard's touch."

Without raising her head Beth made a vulgar hand gesture.

He straightened. "Palmer! Get up!"

"I'm up!" Welcome Palmer appeared in the doorway of his bedroom rubbing his eyes, clad only in pajama bottoms. "What's going on?"

Beth's teeth chattered as she answered, "My husband just ruined what should have been the most beautiful moment of our lives, that's what's wrong! Is there a cure for that?"

"Beth's pregnant!" Kahtar linked his hands behind his head and began pacing.

Welcome hurried to Beth and crouched at her side. "She is, but barely—it's very early. Beth, I'm surprised you even noticed." He chuckled, pulled Beth to her feet and wrapped an arm around her. "It doesn't matter when or how you tell the father though. I don't know why but it always seems to come as a surprise to us men. Come sit down." He led her to the sofa as a light lit the room, brightening in gentle increments as their eyes adjusted.

Welcome motioned for Kahtar to sit too, but Kahtar knew sitting still would take his fear to madness.

"Now why is this pregnancy an emergency worthy of Old Guard transport in the middle of the night? There's absolutely nothing wrong that I can sense."

"I'm sterile," said Kahtar. "Does that make it a bit more noteworthy?"

Welcome looked from Kahtar to Beth, his dark brows raised over green eyes. He yanked a throw off the back of the couch to wrap around her. "What exactly are you saying, Kahtar?" He pressed his hand against Beth's pelvis and scanned; an act which Kahtar would be perfectly capable of doing if his hands weren't shaking so badly. He stopped pacing and waited.

Welcome looked at him. "She's further along than I first thought. It's a perfectly healthy division of cells—Beth's and yours."

"Mine?" Kahtar snapped.

Welcome's green eyes took on an angry light, but he kept his voice light. "Yes, Warrior Chief, yours. Constantine DNA mixed perfectly with Beth's." He turned his focus to Beth. "Are you nauseous? You're going to want to eat a bit more often."

Beth turned her glare from Kahtar and nodded. "A bit queasy, but I will."

"Palmer!" Kahtar said, interrupting Welcome as he launched into an explanation of the right food for a queasy stomach. There were more important questions to answer.

"Kahtar," Welcome said through clenched teeth, "obviously you're not sterile. What made you think you were?"

Thousands of years of sterility!

Kahtar took a deep breath and swallowed. After examining his own body over the centuries, he knew that had always been the case. He had long ago given up the idea or possibility of children. If Beth had conceived, he needed to know if something had changed.

Or if this is something worse.

He had to ask now. It would be unbearable to wait until the baby came to be certain. "You once told me you can scan light inside DNA, and everyone has colored lights inside them. Are those lights a genetic phenomenon or more individual? Do children have the same color lights parents do?"

Welcome blinked at him, his anger gone. "It has a basis in genetics; certain color combinations of parents can produce differing results. But like I told you then, you're the only—regular person—

I've ever known to have white light. Beth's is blue and yellow, very distinct and separate. It never mixes together and turns green." He turned his attention to scanning Beth, frowned, and looked back at Kahtar questioningly.

"What color is the baby's light?" Kahtar's voice came out so hoarse he cleared his throat.

Palmer's eyes widened and something like understanding lit in them, but he didn't press for details. He never did, another reason why Kahtar always sought him out when he needed help.

"You're being a jerk," Beth interrupted. "I don't know what I expected, but it wasn't to be hauled around the state by Old Guard. This is happening, Kahtar. None of your carrying on will change what's already happened. Is the idea that this baby will be like you really the worst thing that could happen? Because that's how you're acting." Her sky blue eyes were on him, unwavering. Kahtar ignored the fact Welcome was watching them and gave Beth one curt nod, wondering if she really had no understanding of what immortality had done to him.

She lifted her chin. "What could be better than a baby like you? You're the best man I've ever known."

Kahtar didn't bother responding. She had absolutely no idea. No clue. The woman was a child, a zygote in time.

Welcome held his hand over Beth's belly, looking into her eyes for permission. She nodded and lifted the warm throw to grant access. Welcome surprised them both by slipping his hand underneath Beth's nightshirt and Kahtar knew without scanning he'd put it right inside her silky panties. "Sorry. I've never tried to scan light in a being so early on. Your baby is only a very healthy division of cells and genetic coding right now." He smiled at Beth as he put one hand behind her for support and pressed the other against her. His green eyes looked a bit near-sighted as he focused on his scan. "Your baby will be female. Does your father have red hair?"

"He did. Most of his hair is gone now. Will she?"

"No," Welcome chuckled. "I just sense it in your genes. A lot of Cultuelle Khristos are red heads too. Such traits tend to repeat in clans because we have a smaller gene pool."

Kahtar crossed his arms impatiently, aware Welcome was trying to soothe his angry wife and too impatient to endure blathering.

"People marry outside the clan though?" said Beth.

Kahtar blew out a breath, but Palmer ignored him, smugly sitting with his hand inside his wife's drawers while he chatted.

"Of course! Not all clans do everything the same, mind you. We're as diverse a group of people as any in the outside world. We follow the same ten laws, but interpretation differences can be vast. Still, even clans with strict beliefs understand small gene pools can be a bad thing."

Beth blanched and her mouth fell open.

"What's wrong?" both men demanded.

She bit her lip, trying not to answer, but as always the words tumbled out against her will. "I just realized no one in the clan will love my child because you're all so caught up in genetics, everyone will think only that I've given her my seeker blood!"

"Of course they'll love her!" said Welcome.

Beth shook her head at him. "You're all horribly prejudiced!"

"I know," Welcome sighed. "But babies have a delicious defense against even prejudice. You've sensed babies' hearts in the Arc, right? Few—whether Covenant Keepers or seekers—can resist a baby's heart."

"But no matter how sweet it is, she won't always be a baby!" said Beth, her eyes tearing up. "I want the clan to really love her!"

At that moment Beth's worries seemed a small thing to Kahtar. Welcome finally removed his hand.

"What color?" asked Kahtar, tense from head to toe.

"Red," said Welcome.

None of the tension in Kahtar's body drained. "How does my white and Beth's blue and yellow make red?"

"Almost all of your family—the Constantine's—have red light in their DNA, and I'd bet Beth's mother does too. Maybe even her Seeker father. All that red overrode the rest."

"No sign of white?" Kahtar dared hope.

"None, not even pink edges. Good luck when this one is two years old. Maybe this is my prejudice, but people with red light tend to be quite hot-headed."

The thought of a temperamental two-year-old daughter—his biological daughter, made of Constantine DNA and Beth's DNA—with none of the danger of immortality—made Kahtar laugh out loud as relief flooded his heart.

Sensing it Beth smiled, tears shining in her eyes. "Finally catching up?" she teased. "We're having a baby and I've been swinging between scared and wow, too."

Laughing, Kahtar grabbed Beth's shoulders and hauled her up for a proper hug. "Sweet ilu! Imagine this! And the clan will love her, you watch." Joy danced into his heart and wiped the fear away. He buried his face in Beth's smooth hair, allowing himself to feel it.

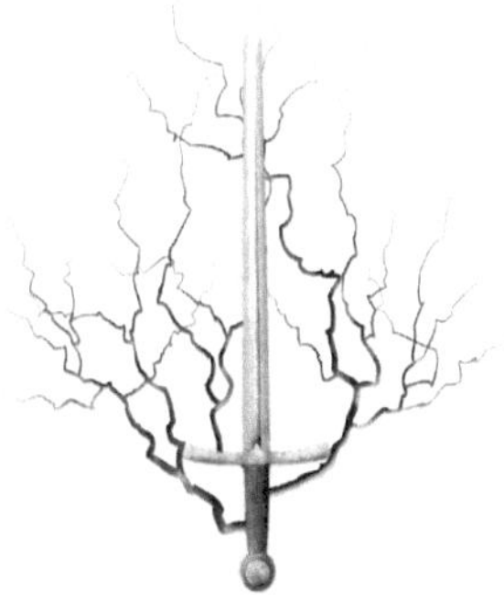

CHAPTER

THREE

Bloody Details—Thanksgiving Eve

AS SHE WALKED down the porch steps, Beth went over the picky Covenant Keeper checklist.

> *Nothing from this world in the Arc.*
> *Natural fabrics.*
> *No nail polish.*
> *No watch. Not even the wind-up one.*
> *No hairspray or perfume.*
> *All white clothing, including my underwear, for a funeral.*

It might or might not be a problem that her skirt had a zipper and she'd worn a nude bra. Beth's head felt foggy and she wanted to take a nap, not go to a funeral for someone she'd never met. Kahtar had said she couldn't worm her way out of any funeral, because clans supported every member.

"Pfft," she scoffed to herself. "Unless your dad is a seeker and you've spent the past month barfing your way through every clan function." Beth doubted any member of the clan would mind if she tossed her breakfast at home this morning rather than in the cave again. *Holy smokes does sound amplify in that cave!*

Trudging to the tesseract she patted her clothing to make sure she hadn't tucked her cell phone into her bra strap or waistband. In addition to public vomiting, she'd also recently exposed the clan to ringtones. Forgetting the device in her pocket, the explicit version of Eminem's *No Love* had sounded a five minute warning, completely ruining the fact that for once she'd been early. Her punishment had been to stand outside the cave and apologize to every single member as they left the Glory service. The Mother had suspended the sentence halfway through when Beth had fainted—something pregnancy had done to her four times now. It might have been the most embarrassing moment of her life, but today was young.

Beth double checked the shallow pockets of her skirt before stepping into a wavering spot of darkness next to a bush. In a flash of veined light the tesseract transported her to the Arc. Avoiding direct eye contact with any of the Old Guard standing watch, Beth hurried through the windy doorway. The blast of air blew her skirt up, obscuring her vision and wedging her panties somewhere no cloth had gone before. She wondered if that's why so few women left the Arc, and realized with the eyes of Old Guard on her she couldn't fix it.

Beth ran the entire path to the cave without knocking the offending fabric loose. Despite the cold November day, the exertion left her panting. The sound echoed as she descended the switchbacks into the limestone cavern. Several Covenant Keepers turned to look at her and quickly looked away. Instead of being embarrassed, Beth fought the urge to fix her undies right then and there.

In the cavern thousands of the clan were assembled, holding candles and chanting a quiet prayer. Beth couldn't see where they were getting the thick white candles. Maybe she had been supposed to bring one, or maybe there was a place in the cavern no one had mentioned before. The words to the prayer weren't familiar either. Beth took an empty seat among a group of kids and remained silent.

At the lowest point in the main cavern, the man who had passed on, Gamper Foid, lay on a stone slab in the flickering light, surrounded by his family and hundreds of Warriors of ilu. From Beth's vantage point, Gamper looked every day of his age. Kahtar had said he'd died in his sleep at one hundred and fifty-seven years old. It seemed like a nice long life to Beth, but a woman who appeared to be his wife sobbed heartbrokenly beside his body. The empty ache in her heart where Gamper belonged drifted over the crowd and Beth felt the shadow of it. Her heart ached in response, and tears filled her eyes.

Someday I'll leave Kahtar feeling like that and he'll have to feel it forever. That thought made her heart really ache. The only comfort Kahtar would have when she died would have to come from his clans as he repeated through time, dying and being born again and again, but never again being with the only one who ever knew his secret.

Beth suddenly wanted to be part of the clan bringing comfort to Gamper's widow. It's what clans did. She listened closely to the chant of the children around her, and at last was able to join in with the familiar chorus as they knelt. The sound of so many changing position echoed in the vast limestone cavern. Old Guard shimmered brightly, their inner light illuminating the cave, reflecting across stalactites and stalagmites. A particularly brilliant blast shimmered like a drapery of diamonds above Gamper's body.

The glittering lights in the cave felt like a song in Beth's heart. Comforted and relaxed at last, she fearlessly shifted position and dislodged her wedgie, watching the lights change. They glittered red and blue like a disco ball, sparkling over Gamper's family. It really didn't seem to fit the somber ceremony. The children beside Beth fidgeted, and others began to look around. Beth avoided eye contact, certain the children had noticed her wedgie action. It shocked her they'd misbehave at a funeral; Covenant Keeper children seemed to know the rules as well as the adults. Over the last few months she had often been amazed at how easily the children fell into the routine of cave gatherings.

Near the light show and Gamper's body Beth at last spotted Kahtar, head and shoulders above the other warriors in his funeral white. Her heart skipped a beat. Kahtar was the reason she endured the rules and strangeness of Cultuelle Khristos. That man owned her heart, and for all his warrior chief bossiness and serious demeanor while with the clan, she knew inside he was kind, loving, and had the driest sense of humor she'd ever known. In the crowd of young warriors he stood apart somehow, a bit weathered, but looking capable enough to lift the marble table Gamper lay on.

The pain of the widow's grief assaulted her again, and Beth turned her eyes away from admiring her husband and closed them to focus on the hearts around her. She sensed the kids on either side poking at each other and whispering and wondered at their overreaction. It was as if they'd never seen a wedgie maneuver before. Maybe Cultuelle Khristos didn't get them. Maybe their underwear was magic.

Someone grabbed Beth's arm and her eyes popped open, encountering a glaring young woman. Beth recognized her as a relative of Gamper's who had been standing by his body moments before. The murmur of shocked voices around them grew. Beth immediately thought of the last time she'd gotten in trouble and patted her pockets again. Definitely no phone.

The woman shook her arm and hissed, "Why did you do this? What did my grandfather do to deserve your disrespect?"

She couldn't believe this was happening because of one subtle tug, but Beth still had to answer direct questions. Having been born with the inability to lie was a nuisance, especially at moments when all she wanted was the ability to disappear. "I'm sorry! It was really uncomfortable. I didn't think anyone would notice and I didn't mean any disrespect to your grandfather!"

Kahtar appeared, his bulk parting the assembling crowd. He took one look at Beth and hauled her to her feet. The colorful lights sparkling around the cavern vanished.

Beth's heart sank in sudden understanding as her husband muttered, "The soles of your shoes are colored!"

They were worse than colored. They were prisms. It was the designer's trademark. There was sympathy in Kahtar's steely eyes as he bent toward her ear, ignoring the growing speculation about the disruption and the hissing comments about orphans.

"It'd be best if you go and I'll sort this out," Kahtar whispered. "Old Guard? Or walk of shame?"

Beth kept her eyes on his, unable to bear looking at the condemnation of the clan around her. The Old Guard could take her arm and transport her to the cabin under the veil in a split second. She could hide her red face in private there. But the thought of the giant Old Guard touching her again, moving her like light, was more than she could bear. The Old Guard terrified Beth more than any walk of shame.

Besides, this wouldn't be her first walk of shame.

After a lifetime of blurting the truth, they were familiar.

"I'll walk," she whispered.

Kahtar's heart brushed hers with reassurance and admiration. That touch kept her from crying the whole way out.

KAHTAR WALKED INTO his cabin and spotted a long, lean bump under his cloak. It had been removed from its hook and tossed over the couch like a blanket. He moved to the opposite sofa and sat down. "Beth."

She yanked the top of the cloak up further over her head. Wolves' furry, multi-colored head popped out from the edge of the cloak. Kahtar crossed his arms. Dogs did not belong inside, especially not on the sofa or under his cloak. Beth knew exactly how he felt about allowing the dog inside. He snapped his fingers and Wolves bolted, taking the cloak halfway across the room with him. He ran into the door headfirst, clawed at it until it swung open and ran across the porch.

Beth sat up, dark circles under her eyes. Kahtar bit off any condemnation. Pregnancy didn't agree with her and that had him worried. But The Mother's decree was law and Beth knew there would be a punishment for her mistake. "You're to make restitution to Gamper's family. The Mother wants you barefoot at every Glory until the new moon."

Her eyes widened. "Through the winter solstice? It's already freezing outside!"

"It's a punishment. You can wear shoes to the cave entrance and take them off there. It's sixty-eight degrees inside the cavern. Wear a sweater and you'll be in no danger whatsoever."

Beth squared her shoulders. "Fine. You do realize I didn't do it on purpose?"

He took a deep breath. "You know that's irrelevant."

"Fine."

Three months of marriage had been plenty of time for Kahtar to understand *fine* meant anything but fine. "Weeks ago I told you to have funeral clothing made, but you didn't take the time. If you had this wouldn't have happened."

Beth opened her mouth, closed it, and nodded. "You did say that."

The rough skin on Kahtar's palms caught on the threads of his white leggings as he ran his hands over his thighs, avoiding Beth's gaze he continued to unveil her punishment. "You're to gather all but three pair of the most functional of your shoes and give them away in the outside world."

"You cannot be serious."

Kahtar met her eyes and after the briefest moment Beth narrowed hers at him.

"Fine. I'm going to head over to see my parents now." She scooted to the edge of the sofa.

"No."

"I'll get rid of the shoes first. Besides I have some there too I'll need to pick up."

"You can't go see your parents."

"What do you mean? We agreed I could go for Thanksgiving!"

"The rest of your punishment is to spend the remainder of this week fasting like the Gamper's are. It's a sign of mourning for the immediate family of the deceased. You're to participate. It will show solidary and remorse to the Gampers. Death fasts aren't dangerous for pregnant Covenant Keepers. You shouldn't have any problems with it."

"I can fast at my parents' house!"

"During their Thanksgiving?" Kahtar asked, holding her gaze. "They'll ask questions, and you're only allowed bread and water until after Glory on Sunday."

It was four days away. Kahtar tried not to show how much the thought of Beth fasting during pregnancy bothered him. Normally it didn't bother pregnant Covenant Keepers, but Beth had already lost weight. He tried to reassure himself the plain fare might stop her vomiting. *I should have told The Mother she's lost weight. Surely I could have said that much.*

Beth lifted her chin stubbornly. "I promised my parents I'd come."

"The Mother would prefer you fast here, where we can be certain you don't suffer any ill effects."

"If she was worried about it bothering me she wouldn't be doing it. When you say The Mother *prefers*, what exactly does that mean?"

"You have no choice."

Beth widened her eyes, and Kahtar knew she was trying to hide her tears. He looked away.

"I thought so. Fine," she whispered, and stood. The white blouse and skirt hung on her thin frame almost like it did the hanger in the closet. "I'm going to my room."

Kahtar knew that meant she'd be holed up in there or her shop over the next several days, angry and avoiding him. "Don't shut me out, Beth. I'm only doing my duty. I'd be doing this to anyone in the clan who did what you did today. The fact that The Mother is allowing you to keep three pair of your shoes is a huge concession. Anyone else would likely spend the winter barefoot. She's also allowing you six daily servings of bread and as much water as you like—instead of the two meals and limited water the Gampers will have."

"I'm tired, Kahtar. And don't kid yourself. No one else in the clan would ever make the mistake I made today. The Mother thinks I was being vain, but I was simply rushing to comply with rules I'm still learning. She's not allowing me extra food because I'm pregnant. Any warrior in this clan could use his healing gift to take me and this baby to the brink of death and back twice a day if they chose to. She's allowing me extra food because she knows she's punishing me for being part seeker."

"Please don't," Kahtar pleaded, trying to keep desperation out of his voice. "Don't criticize The Mother of Cultuelle Khristos. You force me to choose between my loyalty to the clan and you! Nobody else would dare talk to a Warrior Chief like this. If anyone else talked back, I'd institute punishments of my own. If you think The Mother is harsh, it's because you haven't been punished by me."

"Punished by you?" Beth's brows rose in a threat of their own. "Why do you talk to me like that? If you ever even laid a finger on me, Kahtar Constantine, I would beat you to within an inch of your life." She didn't raise her voice, her words even and low, and for the first time ever Kahtar saw Beth hold a posture like her shieldmaiden mother. Although he tried not to, he felt his eye twitch and his lips turned up in a smile. There was no hiding the sudden amusement in his heart.

Instead of getting angry, Beth smiled too. "I'm glad you're taking it so well, but you know I don't lie. I meant every word."

"I know. I think that's what makes it so funny. Blazes, Beth. This is difficult. I can't think when I've been so conflicted. I love you so much. Don't be angry with me for doing my duty. Bear in mind I'm the proverbial messenger here."

"I love you too, and that's the only reason I'm here and trying every day."

Running a hand over the top of his head, Kahtar sighed, his amusement fading. "You shouldn't threaten to hit, love. Anyone else would get double the punishment for talking like that, especially threatening to hit me. I shouldn't have laughed. Hitting a warrior is borderline law—and it is rule—breaking."

"But when you talk like that, it sounds like you're threatening to hit me!"

"Oh, for the love of—Beth, husbands do not beat their wives in our world. You know that! I would *never* lay a hand on you!"

"I know! But when you talk about punishing me, it sounds violent! The clan rules seem so arbitrary and the punishments barbaric. You're always threatening to beat the plebes!" She pressed her hand against her belly and rubbed.

"You don't know what barbaric is."

"I'm pregnant, and even if I weren't, the barefoot thing is savage, Kahtar. You know it is!"

"If I agreed with you I wouldn't be free to express it. Not in this situation. No matter how much I might want to. Don't put me in the middle. Try to fit in."

The sky blue eyes studied him for a moment. At last Beth shook her head and turned for the stairs.

Kahtar watched her take a few steps and shot to his feet. "Beth! Do you have cramps?"

Still rubbing her stomach she turned back to look at him. "A little. I'm mostly just really tired."

In three strides he was across the floor and scooping her into his arms. She rested her head on his shoulder. "I'm not even going to complain. Carry me if you want to. Arguing with you makes me that tired."

"Beth," Kahtar said, cradling her tightly against his chest, and trying to keep the fear out of his voice. He headed for the front door, "don't panic and take slow, deep breaths. I can sense the baby and she feels fine to me, but there's blood on the back of your dress."

WELCOME PALMER SHUT the door of the surgery, his striking eyes on Kahtar. "Don't go in there just yet. She's exhausted and resting."

"Why's she bleeding?" Kahtar demanded.

Welcome touched the back of his hand to his nose, shaking his head. "This pregnancy is really hard on her body. It's not unusual for women to have some breakthrough bleeding early on, but the amount of stress this is putting on her has me worried. Didn't you notice her blood pressure is sky high?"

Kahtar scanned through the door toward Beth, sensing soft snores. "I do now."

"There's no way I'll agree to restricting her food. Kahtar, she's lost ten pounds in the past month!"

Kahtar paled. Why hadn't he noticed it had been so much? "She's having trouble keeping food down. I thought maybe bread would at least stay."

"She needs protein too. I wish the Old Guard would provide her with pemmican. Could you get them to do it?"

Kahtar huffed. "You know they won't. Old Guard won't cook for us. I'll ask them, but I'm certain they won't."

"I'll try my hand at it while she's here, but I have a feeling she'll throw it up. Whatever they put in theirs doesn't come back."

"But what's going on? Pregnancy is a perfectly natural state. Why is it causing so much trouble for her?"

Welcome waited until several people passed them and got further down the corridor to respond. "Can I be candid?" he asked, his voice low.

"I expect it!"

Welcome raised his dark brows. "It's not uncommon among seeker women. They're just not as strong."

Kahtar clenched his jaw. This was one comment he hadn't expected. "Beth isn't a seeker woman."

"But she was born and raised in that world—with their food and toxins, and through her father her body carries centuries of dishonor. It does weaken the body."

Kahtar glared.

"Warrior Chief, I'm not criticizing her. Beth is as much Covenant Keeper as we are. At heart and with her gifting of truth, I would say she's more so. That doesn't change the fact that physically she's weaker."

Kahtar crossed his arms. The belief that Covenant Keepers were genetically superior had become deeply woven among his kind, particularly since the Industrial Revolution as seekers polluted their world and themselves more with each generation.

"I've never wanted to believe it either, and I never saw it until this pregnancy put so much strain on Beth, but it's right in front of my eyes now," Welcome said. "I'm a man of science. There's no other reason for her to have these problems, not when we can heal any deficit along the way. But it's not a few weaknesses. It's a cascading problem and her entire physiology is weak."

"That makes no sense with a heart like hers. I don't believe you."

Welcome held up his hands in a gesture of defeat. "As Beth would say, it's the truth."

"I don't think she would." Kahtar glanced away and bellowed, "Old Guard!"

One of the brightly lit men shimmered half-formed in front of him. "Warrior Chief?"

"Would you provide pemmican for my wife? She can't hold food down. She's wasting."

The man turned black eyes on Kahtar. Kahtar held the solid black gaze, though everything in him made him want to turn away from it. He knew they wouldn't, knew it was wrong to ask and fully expected the man to stare and vanish without a reply. A dark twist of anger snaked through Kahtar's heart. Clan law would prevent feeding Beth through tubes like seekers would, and Old Guard wouldn't do a thing to help her. It struck him as wrong and sudden fear nibbled at the edges of his soul. She could starve to death over the next eight months and their laws would prevent him from doing anything to help her.

Something flickered in the depths of the Old Guard's eyes, and Kahtar knew the man had sensed his anger. Suddenly a clay bowl appeared in the Old Guard's hands. He shoved it into Kahtar's, and vanished. Stunned, Kahtar gazed down at the sticky gelatinous mixture of seeds, insects, and sap.

"You have some serious pull," remarked Welcome.

"That's a first," said Kahtar, extending the bowl toward Welcome.

He took it. "This overrides The Mother's decree for bread and water?"

"It does," said Kahtar, still stunned. "With food she'll stop wasting?"

"And with rest." Welcome turned toward the door and paused. He glanced up and down the hall, then added quietly, "Intercourse probably isn't a good idea, either."

It took a moment for Kahtar to realize his mouth was open.

Welcome looked away from him and stared at his hand on the doorknob. "Because of the bleeding. I'm sorry, Kahtar."

THE SOUND OF a vehicle right outside Sweet Earth caught Beth's attention. Sometimes seekers stumbled onto her shop, but most people in town had discovered her by now and knew she didn't open early. Depositing a forbidden cup of coffee—a habit that Kahtar knew nothing about—onto a marble topped table, she shoved aside a sheer curtain to peek out and decide whether or not to unlock the front door.

Down by the curb, the passenger door of her dad's non-descript blue sedan swung open and her mother stepped out. Beth dropped the curtain and flattened herself against the wall.

Shit! My parents!

For a brief moment Beth determined that she would not unlock the door. What if someone from the clan came by while Ted and Carole were there? What if an Old Guard shimmered into being right in front of them? What if Kahtar used a tesseract and popped out of thin air?

A knock on the window told her that her panic had taken too long. "Open the door, Bethy!" Ted called, as if he knew exactly where she was.

Shit!

Beth unlocked the door.

Joy flooded her heart at the sight of her father's smiling face, erasing her anxiety.

"Surprise! The baby clothes we ordered on Amazon came! Wow, this place is really something. I don't know what I expected, sweetheart, but this is a mansion. Smells good in here too. Is that coffee? You're drinking coffee?"

"Yes, Daddy! Want some?" said Beth, ignoring her mother's condemning glance. Coffee helped disguise the godawful taste of the pemmican she ate twice a day. She might not vomit that stuff, but burping was another matter. Beth rushed to nab two cups from the shelf behind the cash register. "It's clean, Mom. I order it special for the shop. I can hardly keep it in stock."

"I'd love a cup, unless you have some of that tea you used to have. I crave that stuff." Her father dropped a pile of Amazon boxes onto the hardwood floor.

"Sorry, that tea I can't keep stocked. Everyone in the cl—I mean, town, likes it. Well, mostly the guys, but still." Beth poured the coffee and steam curled in the morning light. She offered the cups to her father and mother.

Carole shook her head, her shorn blonde hair messy and uncooperative looking.

"Mom, it's clean, even for a pregnant woman."

"It's coffee. I don't drink it. I'm fine." She leaned against a far wall and crossed her arms. Carole White wasn't the kind of mother to accept a cup of coffee she didn't want, or the kind to make small talk, or ask curious questions about her daughter's business. Beth wondered how on earth her dad had managed to get her there.

Sighing, Beth plopped her mother's mug next to her own on the little marble topped stand. "Were you in the area?"

"Pfft," said Carole.

"Nothing is in this area," Ted joked. "My GPS couldn't even find the place. If your mother wasn't a human GPS, I don't think I'd have ever found it. You never did give me directions." He shot her an accusing glance, but Beth turned her attention to her mother again. Carole must have wanted to come or she wouldn't have helped find it."

Carole glanced at Beth's stomach and Beth smoothed her hand over the small bump and smiled. *At least she worries about this like a normal mother.*

"I'm fine, Mom," Beth said with complete sincerity. She'd felt better all morning, and hoped it would continue to if she drank black coffee and didn't think too much about whatever was inside the pemmican the Old Guard kept bringing her.

"You're tired," said Carole. "You have dark circles under your eyes and you've lost weight. What's wrong?"

"Nothing! Pregnant women get tired," said Beth. "And they throw up a lot."

"Pfft," said Carole again. "Not us."

"Us?" said Beth, instantly on alert. It was the same comment Kahtar and Welcome Palmer had made to Beth several times lately. Covenant Keeper women had easier pregnancies than seeker women, likely due to healthier lifestyles.

"Your mom thinks because she could skydive pregnant and eat buckets of kelp that you should too. When you didn't even call the last couple weeks, she got worried."

Beth couldn't keep the surprise off her face. *Mom got worried?*

Ted grinned. "I figured Kent was just being overprotective. Is he upstairs?"

Beth blanched. Why did her dad think Kahtar was in her shop? She blinked, her mind scrambling for the cover story. Did they think that she and Kahtar lived at the shop? Had he told them that? It didn't really matter though, because she couldn't lie.

"No. He's at work," she said, relieved to be able to tell the truth, even if she couldn't tell them that he was actually being warrior chief inside an Arc at the moment. Still, her mother's direct gaze was making her nervous, and they needed to leave. Beth's eyes lit on her mother's shorn, messy hair. "Mom, I got a new conditioner in that could do something with your hair."

Carole's hand flew to her head and she smoothed the mess self-consciously. "Like what?"

"Make it look more like hair and less like a dandelion gone to seed."

Ted grinned but Carole scowled. Beth scurried across the creaking floorboards and pulled bottles off a shelf, glancing back at her mom. The distraction appeared to have worked. Carole's eyes were already glazing over in boredom and her gaze wandered toward a sunny window. Beth's heart skipped a beat as an unnatural formation of light shimmered outside that exact window. *Old Guard! Shit!* Purposefully she dropped the heavy glass bottles to the floor. Several shattered, drawing her parents' attention back to her.

"Don't move!" Carole crossed the room in an instant, somehow already holding a wastebasket. "That'll cut right through your shoes!"

Ted crouched beside Carole and lifted Beth's foot out of the goo as though she were two and unable to manage it on her own. For once it didn't bother Beth, and she glanced out the window to see the sparkle had gone.

"I'm hungry!" said Beth, realizing with surprise it was true. This was the first time she'd felt hungry since she'd gotten pregnant.

"You're hungry?" said Ted, his eyes darting around with the intensity of a hunter providing for his starving family. "You have food here, don't you?"

"Yes, but all I really have is crackers, because I've been avoiding stocking much food. Even the sight of it usually makes me sick. You know what I'd like right now though? There's a place over in Coventry that Kah—Kent and I found right after the wedding. It has Greek salads, the real kind with good tomatoes and cucumbers and slabs of feta. Mom, what do you think? I could murder a salad and a plate of hummus. They make their own pita bread, too."

Carole's brows lifted in interest and Beth had a feeling her mom hadn't even made breakfast before they'd come hunting her. Beth should have been texting and calling them like she usually did, but the last couple of weeks she'd done little besides lie around and wish she could vomit pemmican. Until today. Today she'd woken early, made love to Kahtar twice despite whatever bull Welcome Palmer had said about no sex, eaten all her pemmican and half his breakfast eggs, and not wanted to vomit even once. She'd headed for her shop as soon as he'd left for the Arc.

Ted immediately lost interest in showing Beth all the pink clothing he'd brought, instead peppering her for directions to the restaurant while Carole busied herself cleaning busted bottles. Beth shoved more shampoo into a box, relieved when her dad took the box and headed outside. Anxious to leave before anything weird happened, she followed Ted and Carole.

The cold sent her scampering back in for a jacket. "I'll be one minute! Turn on the heater!" she called, letting the door slam shut on her mother and heading for the cluttered pile of coats on a bench a few feet away. A big hand grabbed her arm and pulled her deeper inside the shop. Beth turned and met Kahtar's angry gaze.

"You didn't call them, did you? I told you to make sure you called them! You said you would!"

"Kahtar, I forgot! You know how sick I've been!"

"Blazes, Beth! No excuses! There is no room for mistakes! If your mother senses the hearts of the clan and finds us, she'll be susceptible to our rules. You know what happens to Covenant Keepers who blend with seekers! Get them out of here and make sure they *never* come back! Do you have any idea—Beth, the Elders are already gathering in the Arc to discuss this!"

"How am I supposed to make sure my parents never come here?" Beth demanded.

He leaned closer, his steely eyes fierce. Beth tried to pull away but he wouldn't let go. "They will die if they discover us. Do you understand me?"

Tears filled her eyes. It wasn't fair. She nodded.

"Fix it, Beth. When you come back you're going to have to give your word to the Elders this will never happen again!"

Kahtar let go of her, almost pushing her toward the doorway. Beth raced out, forgetting about her coat. Her parents were already at the car. Carole took one look at her and met her halfway, her watchful eyes scanning Beth's face.

"What's wrong?"

Beth blinked back tears. "Mom, you guys can't come here. Not ever. No matter what. Please?" she whispered. "I-I need space. It was Dad's idea to live close to me, but this was my dream. You know I love you both, but I really have to have some space with m-my shop and m-my stuff." The explanation sounded lame and ridiculous, like that of an abused wife. Or a daughter who'd joined a cult that was a threat to her parents' lives.

Carole glanced from Ted in the car to the little house next door hiding an abstract inside. Beth wondered if she'd chosen the wrong words, if she'd already said too much and condemned her parents to the mists.

Carole held her gaze intensely. "Are you okay?"

"Yes, Mom. I am, but I'd be better if you'd just—not come here. Please?"

A faint sound of humor escaped Carole. She looked again at Ted, who was now fiddling with the heater and gesturing impatiently at them, before looking again at the abstract house. Beth's mom shivered and she turned toward the car. "Let's go, then."

Beth wondered if she should say something more, secure a promise from her mother—or heaven forbid, say something to her dad. But as she climbed into the front seat at her mother's insistence, she noticed her dad too eyeing not her pretty Victorian house, but the little one next door. His hands tightened on the steering wheel and the red hair on them seemed to be standing straight up. Ted shivered.

Good lord, they sense it. Beth looked toward the innocuous looking house, knowing it had to be full of Warriors of ilu this morning. Could they see out? She shivered too and met her dad's eyes for a brief moment. For the briefest space of time there was a question in them, but it faded as he stepped on the gas pedal.

"Going to call that husband of yours and invite him to join us for breakfast? I could swing by the station and pick him up." His voice sounded shaky.

"He's not working there this morning, and he already ate breakfast with me about an hour ago."

Ted laughed, but it sounded forced. "So you're hungry for second breakfast, Beth? You're awfully tall for Hobbit habits."

Beth put her hand on his shoulder and squeezed it. Ted ran the stop sign at the end of the street.

He won't come back. Ever.

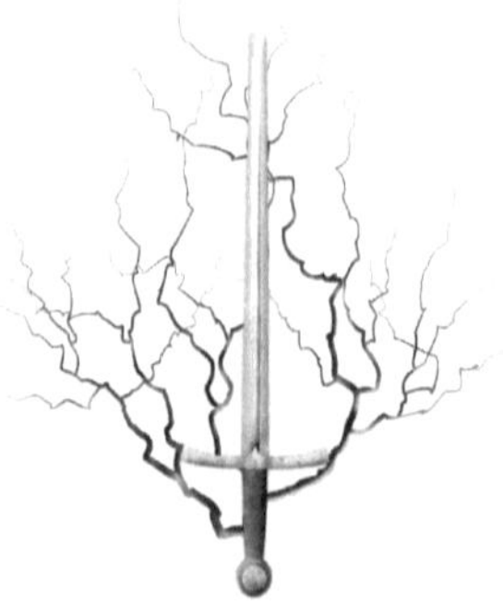

CHAPTER
FOUR

Blood Moon—Before the Easter Holiday

DESPITE MILLENNIA OF war and battle experience, Kahtar couldn't defend himself against his wife. She cheated with far more skill than any desperate man on a battlefield. Beth held the blankets up, bare skin beckoning in the moonlight.

"Take your clothes off and come teach me a lesson," she purred, ignoring the threatening glare he was trying to maintain. A wicked smile flickered across her lips.

She always sees through it! Who would have thought lying to your mate was so important? He'd yell, but had a bad feeling she'd laugh.

After months of nausea and holding down little but pemmican, Beth had spent her sixth month of pregnancy eating—and holding down—enough food to feed four good-sized warriors a day. The hollows in her cheeks had filled in and dark circles vanished. Her complexion glowed, and her breasts looked fuller. Kahtar forced his gaze away from them and swallowed.

Beth waggled the blanket open, revealing more. "I have been very bad today. I think I broke nearly all your OCD rules. Whatever are you going to do with me?"

"Beth," he warned, tugging his shirt off, "don't joke about it." *She wins, she always wins.*

"Okay. You can stand there and lecture me about how dogs in the house are a precursor to the fall of civilization while I lay here and get colder, all by myself. Oh, look! I'm getting goose bumps!"

"It's not about the stupid dog," he said, although he could sense Wolves slinking around the kitchen downstairs in search of crumbs on the floor. He had noticed a correlation between the ridiculous pampering of canines in Rome, Alexandria, and even Atlantis, and the fall of those great civilizations. Unbuckling his belt, Kahtar dropped his trousers to the floor and hurried under the covers. Arguing would increase Beth's stress level. He mentally excused his submission as cooperating with the doctor's orders rather than the enticing things goose bumps did to the female body. "It's never been about the dog," he couldn't help pointing out. "It's about obeying rules. There were complaints today for both excessive use of your car and for causing trouble at Cerulean Blue."

Beth snuggled against his body, her long form fitting against his like corner pieces in a puzzle. Everything in the pit of Kahtar's stomach and below seemed to liquefy. He really didn't care whether she drove her car to the clinic or took a tesseract. He did both. It helped them blend into the town better to be seen driving. As far as the eatery in town next to Beth's shop, the proprietors of Cerulean Blue probably resented the fact she brought a couple more seekers to town. As long as they weren't her parents, they really had nothing justifiable to complain about. They had never welcomed her like members of a clan should.

Beth's teeth grazed down his throat and he slid his hand to her bottom, pulling her closer. The swell of her pregnant belly poked against him, reminding him of the doctor's orders, and he let go. "We need to be careful."

"Huh-uh," Beth mumbled, her hand trailing down and into outright cheating territory. "Neither of us is frail. We're normal and healthy and I haven't had any problems in the past *six* weeks. I have way more energy now too! I'm down to three naps a day. You can scan inside me as well as any Covenant Keeper doctor can. Is there any danger, anything abnormal? I know there's not. I feel great! Better than before I got pregnant."

Kahtar closed his eyes and tried to will his body under control. Since the clan doctor had restricted lovemaking, their relationship had become a bit like Sampson and Delilah. Although Kahtar enjoyed being the captive of a seductive temptress, he wanted her more than his next breath of air, and his body and heart responded to her touch despite the orders of his mind.

The months of abstinence hadn't been about sex. As a warrior chief constantly meting out punishment against his own wife, it felt like far too long since they had joined heart and body to strengthen their bond. Despite the times of bending Welcome Palmer's rules a bit, they hadn't been together in the way they needed. Without a way to reset their relationship physically, Kahtar didn't know what would happen between them, and he feared distance more than he feared hurting their unborn child.

Beth spoke the truth. He could scan inside her and know there was no medical reason for lovemaking to cause harm. Not now. Still, habit made him resist breaking orders, even those of the clan doctor. Rubbing his thumb over her lips, he whispered, "As you've pointed out nearly every night lately, there are other ways to get to where we're going."

Beth slid one long, smooth leg over him. "I'm up for hitting them all tonight, but I need you. No more games." She sounded desperate.

"You have me. It's only three more months." Even as he said it, it sounded like eternity, and his heart and brain rejected the words as though they'd come from someone else entirely. Giving in without ever really intending to, Kahtar slid her pillow from beneath her head and tossed it, gently rolling her onto her back. "We'll go slow. If you feel anything uncomfortable, or if I sense anything at all, we're stopping."

BETH SMILED AS Kahtar dropped onto the mattress at her side, sweating and breathing hard. With her heartbeat thundering in her ears, she floated in that disjointed, jelly-bones feeling lovemaking left behind. *Thank Heavens. If he'd said no again tonight, I think I would have cried.*

Kahtar's large hand found hers and he threaded their fingers and held tightly. Beth sighed into the night, secure in the feeling of their hearts once again entwined securely.

It's been every bit as hard for him. He's just ridiculously obedient to even the most inane suggestions at this point. For once being able to sense the truth that it would be okay had been reassuring, even though Kahtar hadn't seemed to believe her.

Still flat on his back, Kahtar began to snore.

That's ridiculous! The sound made her smile, and she hoped he'd sleep peacefully, untroubled by night terrors. Burrowing comfortably into the mattress, she pulled the blankets higher with the hand not held captive by Kahtar's and shivered with delight. Everything felt so good and she shivered again.

Suddenly Beth bolted straight up in bed and doubled over, her heart rate accelerating with fear.

I just have to pee, she reassured herself.

Kahtar shot up as though he hadn't been sound asleep a split second earlier. In one fluid motion he was kneeling in front of her, his attention on her bulging stomach. He slid their linked hands over the mound of belly, and Beth fought another shiver.

"What's going on? What do you feel?" he said.

"It's nothing," Beth said between clenched teeth, certain nothing was wrong. "I think I just have to go to the bathroom."

"Are you sure?" said Kahtar. "Old Guard!"

"No, don't!" Beth protested, already too late. The blinding, shimmering light of one of the giant men filled the room, and she leaned forward even farther, fighting the feeling of needing to empty her bowels right in front of them.

"Get Welcome Palmer here!" Kahtar ordered. "Is my wife in labor? I can't tell!"

Beth felt the Old Guard's scan cut through her. Kahtar often insisted only warriors felt scans, but she was quite aware of the warmth of it *down there.* It made the need-to-go feeling worse and she kicked at the blankets to free herself, tugging her hand out of Kahtar's.

"Lay back down," Kahtar ordered.

Beth swung both her feet to the floor and half stood, covering what she could with her hands under the black gaze of the man she was certain was some type of angel. She walked half-hunched over toward the bathroom.

Kahtar followed. "Beth, listen to me and lay back down. Welcome can do something to stop labor if it doesn't go too far. Walking hastens it!"

"I'm not pooping in the bed in front of an Old Guard!" Beth hissed. The light in the room brightened and suddenly several more of the big men were there. "Oh! This just gets better!"

Trying her best to preserve some sense of dignity, Beth shuffled out the door. The Old Guard seemed to be following with her husband, but blessedly didn't attempt to enter the bathroom. Beth shoved Kahtar away and slammed the door in his face. "Give me a minute!"

"Don't lock it!" he warned, but Beth dropped the old fashioned latch into the metal hook anyway. Privacy was important to her, and she'd bought the hook and latch at Lowes, sneaked it through the veil and nailed it up herself. Kahtar had had a fit. Apparently nails were as wicked as dogs in the house.

The flame from a single lamp flickered by the sink—a necessity approved only because pregnancy involved a nightly trip or two to pee and she couldn't scan in the dark like her husband. She shuffled to the toilet.

"What are you doing?" Kahtar shouted through the door as Beth sat down. She knew he was scanning and could tell exactly what she was doing.

"Really?" she shouted back. "I'm going to the bathroom like I said! Stop it, Kahtar. Some things should remain a mystery between us!"

Kahtar didn't respond, and she could hear the grumbly sound Old Guards made when they spoke low. Beth hurried, grateful when everything proceeded as normally as she'd suspected it would. She made it to the sink and washed her hands, planning to give Kahtar a piece of her mind.

The shivery feeling hit again and something warm spurted from inside her, dripping a wet trail down both legs. Now afraid, Beth touched the dampness. The dim light from the candle showed faint streaks of blood on her trembling fingers. "Kahtar!" she wailed.

He kicked the door open, sending it slamming against the wall. Crossing the floor he lifted her into his arms as easily as he had before she'd gained twenty-five pounds in six weeks, and carried her out.

In the hall right outside the bathroom, an Old Guard took hold of Beth's wrist. "Set her down," he demanded.

Kahtar obeyed, laying her on the hardwood floor facing the railing. In the oddly reddish glow of the moon outside Beth could see the great room below. She could see Wolves through the windows, his wet nose leaving streaks of snot over the glass as he tried to see the commotion. The coward was more afraid of Old Guard than she was.

A blanket appeared to drape over her midsection, protecting Beth's nakedness. Another urge to empty herself hit and she leaned forward, unable to resist it.

"Don't push!" Kahtar warned.

"It's too late," said an Old Guard. "It comes."

"Where's Welcome?" Kahtar shouted. "I want him right now!"

Beth turned her head to try to read him. Fear showed plainly on his broad face and in his steely eyes. Her heart sank. This early they'd lose the baby. At six months it wouldn't be able to breathe. It would be too small. Covenant Keepers didn't have Neonatal ICU.

What have I done?! Why didn't I listen? She'd been so certain it would be safe. Kahtar's fear seemed far away and wrong, and a sense of normalcy and reassurance warmed the edges of her frightened heart. *Why does it feel right when it can't be? Why did I think it was okay when it wasn't? Why didn't I know the truth? My baby will die!*

Kahtar dropped a big arm across her shoulders, supporting her, half-holding her up as he pressed his head against hers. "If you can, don't push!" he pleaded.

Beth watched him move his head to growl at an Old Guard busy examining Beth far more intimately than even Kahtar had ever done. "Did you not hear me? I said I want Welcome Palmer. This is not a request!"

Beth tried to not push, but the reflex felt almost like vomiting, and her muscles contracted in a downward heave. Instinct made her pant and she struggled to suck oxygen in and fight her own body, refusing to allow it to expel her baby. A second downward heave hit hard and Beth dug her fingernails into Kahtar's hand, holding his gaze.

No! No! No! Not yet!

A third contraction hit and Beth knew there was no fighting it; her body wasn't listening. With a flash of pain like fire scorching her inside to out, something lava hot slid from inside her and a pained sob escaped her lips. Somehow Kahtar shoved the Old Guard's hands aside and caught the thing in one hand.

Beth's heart sunk so far it seemed to have left her body. Her face crumpled.

This is my fault.

Long heartbeats later Kahtar whispered, "Merciful, ilu!" Balancing what appeared to be some sort of slimy creature in the palm of his hand, he shook his head, tears streaming down his face. "She's beautiful!"

The comment brushed against Beth like a lie.

"What is that?" Beth gasped, horrified. The thing he held in his hand didn't look human, and it certainly didn't look beautiful.

"It's our daughter!" Kahtar said with reverence. "This is our daughter, love!"

Another sob tore out of Beth's chest. It looked lifeless and grotesque, a reddish ball of flesh and what looked like wet feathers on top, with a horrible cord hanging from the belly. An Old Guard now held the pulsing thing. Not only was she dead, but something had to be horribly wrong with her.

A dry sob wracked Beth's entire body. "She's dead and there's something wrong." But the words didn't ring true.

"No, love! She's alive! Not a single thing is wrong! Thank you, ilu! Thank you, Beth!" Kahtar reached for the little creature and cradled it in his hand, poking it gently. It moved, unfolding itself from an oval ball to reveal a large head, with tiny arms and legs punching and kicking the air as if in slow motion. It made a sound, like a weak version of when Wolves got his tail stepped on.

"She's breathing!" Kahtar said wonderingly. "She's breathing all by herself! Beth! Do you see this?"

Nodding, Beth stared, trying to understand what he wasn't telling her.

Welcome Palmer materialized from thin air at the side of an Old Guard, a bag valve mask in hand. He dropped to his knees beside Beth and allowed the forbidden bit of plastic to fall to the floor. Beth watched her alleged daughter between her knees, hopeful as Welcome bent his dark head over it, examining it even as he fingered the twisting umbilical cord still attached to Beth's insides.

"Of all things miraculous, what do we have here?" he breathed. The cord turned black in places and dropped from his pinching fingers.

"Apparently it's a daughter," said Beth. "Kahtar said it's a normal one."

Welcome's green eyes shone in the shimmering light of so many Old Guard. He smiled. "And so she is."

"She doesn't look right," whispered Beth, needing to tell the truth.

Welcome tugged the yellow blanket lower, hiding the fact that his hand snaked beneath it to touch her as invasively as the Old Guard had done. His eyes slid out of focus briefly, and Beth felt things inside of her shift slightly as he rubbed none too gently on her parts.

"Please. What's wrong with my baby, Welcome? Tell me the truth."

"Nothing is wrong with your baby. She's just very tiny. I suppose the truth is at birth no babies are very pretty in the traditional sense. Some are less pretty than others, but babies are always wet and wrinkly like that when they're born. I've never seen one so small breathing, though! She does look rather like a bald bird, doesn't she?" Welcome smiled at her. "But the truth is she's amazing and a miracle. Wait a couple of weeks. I promise you'll see what we do. Kahtar? Give her to Beth."

Beth tried to lean away when Kahtar brought it closer, but his other arm was still firmly around her shoulders. She looked down at her daughter. The baby's face looked like a shriveled apple, the features a series of wrinkles.

Kahtar moved the blanket covering her and placed the thing against Beth's bare skin, whispering in the ancient tongue, his dialect old. Beth's shades didn't go back far enough to understand much of it, but the words, "Filia mea Dianta" translated clearly.

"You want to call her Diana?" Beth eyed the little thing critically, trying to determine which wrinkles might be hiding eyes.

"Dian*ta*," Kahtar corrected. "Diana is a virginal name; I wouldn't inflict that legacy on our offspring." He looked hopefully at her, as though awaiting her consent.

She'd had a list of girl names picked out, but in this moment couldn't think of any that would suit what had come out of her. *This is my baby.* Beth tried to make herself believe it. *She doesn't look like an Elspeth or a Lelia.*

Kahtar ran a big finger over the furrowed body. "I like the name Mars too, and as she was born under a blood moon, it would suit."

Beth shook her head, unwilling to inflict that name on a girl. Her father would never forgive her.

Kahtar smiled. "Dianta, then?"

Somehow it suited. Beth nodded.

"It's the name of a prolific huntress. And Mars for a middle name, as our daughter is strong with life. Do you feel it?" He kissed Beth's sweaty cheek, his lips lingering.

Beth felt nothing beyond a hazy dream-like shock. She bit back the words on the tip of her tongue and settled for shaking her head slightly and muttering, "Huh-uh. Are you absolutely sure she's okay, Welcome? She doesn't look like I thought she would!"

Kahtar chuckled, whispering into her ear, "Remember the Constantine's? You met my grandparents and cousins. They're all ruddy and dark and small." He glanced at Welcome Palmer as though just remembering the doctor was there. "I'm the fluke in the gene pool."

Welcome eyed Kahtar through narrowed eyes for a moment, and returned his attention to moving Beth and the baby into the bedroom.

Within a few more hazy moments all the Old Guard flickered away and Kahtar stood at the foot of the bed with the baby balanced in both hands, seemingly unable to stop admiring her. Welcome tugged and shifted Beth, adjusting a nightgown over her, thick towels under her, and blankets around her the way she suspected her father would if he were there. Suddenly she wished he could be, and her heart burned with loneliness as tears stung her eyes. Her dad would probably never know his granddaughter's middle name. More than anything Beth wanted to be home. But this was supposed to be her home now.

"Kahtar, you're interfering in their bonding. Bring the baby back over to Beth."

Kahtar tore his gaze from the baby, his steely eyes wide, and hurried back to the bed, holding the baby under Beth's face. "Smell her."

Beth wrinkled her nose. "Why?"

"Please, humor me."

The creature writhed in Kahtar's hands, as though burrowing. There was something horrifyingly small about it. Beth cooperated and leaned forward slightly to sniff it. "It smells like—what is that?" Beth sniffed again. "Oh! She smells good!"

Tears warmed Beth's eyes, and she touched her daughter tentatively, running a finger over the naked torso. The skin felt incredibly soft, just a wrinkly doll of a baby. Her baby. Doll-sized. The tears pooled out of her eyes and Beth carefully took one of the grasping hands between her fingers. The impossibly wee hands were perfectly formed. "That's adorable! Do you see that, Kahtar? Look at her hands, look at her thumbs! Oh, heavens! Look at her toes! She doesn't have any nails!"

"She will," Welcome promised from the sidelines. "They often don't at first, especially when they're early."

"Can I hold her? Please? She's so small that I'm afraid of her, but I want to—I need to!"

Kahtar tugged at the gaping opening of Beth's nightgown, fully exposing one breast, and turned the baby onto its stomach as he laid her down. She looked like a hairless squirrel clinging to the side of

Beth's breast with her face planted on top the nipple. "She can't possibly fit her little mouth on that," Beth said, fairly certain which wrinkle was the mouth part.

Welcome frowned as he wedged himself fearlessly in front of Kahtar to position Beth's hand properly against Dianta. Beth's entire hand, fingertips to palm, was the exact same length as the baby.

"Support her head. Their necks aren't strong enough to support—"

Just as he spoke, Dianta lifted her head up despite Beth's hand gently cupping it, opened her mouth like a python and did a face plant back on the breast, sucking the entire nipple into her mouth.

"Ow!" Beth protested. "Ow! Welcome, get her off!"

Welcome laughed as though delighted. "I can't believe what I just saw!"

Kahtar laughed his deep, genuine belly laugh. Beth was not amused.

"Holy ow! Seriously, guys! I think she has teeth."

"Beth, let her feed anytime she manages to latch on." Welcome had one hand on the top of Beth's head as he caressed her hair. Behind him Kahtar mirrored his movement with a finger on Dianta's dark hair.

Beth still thought it looked like drying feathers.

Trying not to complain, she hunched her shoulders forward, hoping the baby would let go.

Welcome leaned closer. "Try to relax…" he paused, his attention back on the mouse-sized creature latched onto Beth's breast. The feet were moving fast, toes digging into the crease beneath her breast.

Kahtar pushed his finger between Beth's nipple and the baby's face, and it stopped struggling. "Keep your finger here when you nurse her. Her nose is so small your flesh blocks her airway."

"Is there even any milk? I don't want to endure this for nothing."

"There's a precursor to it, but there's something more crucial than milk." Welcome turned his attention to Beth, his dark brows pulled together in a frown. "Close your eyes and really feel your daughter."

Frowning, Beth obeyed. Tonight when she'd gone to bed with the blood moon shining through the window, she hadn't expected to meet the little acrobat who bounced on her bladder and left her craving red meat and anything with malt in it. Yet here she was, months early, safe and sound.

This amazing little wonder is my daughter.

Beth smiled, really feeling the life against her skin, the body breathing fast beneath her right hand. It hit then, the touch of Dianta's heart against hers, grabbing hers in a freefall and burrowing inside it with haughty fierceness.

You will never be the same, it told her. *You're mine. I own you.* The truth of that hit Beth hard, like she'd opened her eyes for the first moment to discover she was a mother—which she had.

"Oh! Feel that! It's a marvelous heart! She's so strong!" said Beth.

"Yes, she is," said Welcome Palmer. "What a heart!"

Kahtar laughed again. The joy shining on his face made it every bit as handsome as Welcome Palmer's. "That heart reminds me of your mother's!"

"I don't know how to be a mother," said Beth, feeling inadequate with this little life pressed to her breast, gnawing.

"Nor does she know how to be your daughter." Welcome smiled sagely. "You will learn together."

Beth winced as Dianta savaged her breast, biting brutal and sharp against her nipple.

"Oh, hold on," said Welcome, impertinently jamming his index finger against Beth's nipple and forcing Dianta to detach. The flickering lamplight showed pin pricks of blood on his finger. Welcome shoved another finger into Dianta's mouth. "Yipes. She does have a tooth, sharp as a needle."

Beside him Kahtar grinned from ear to ear, as though this was somehow a good thing.

Beth shifted in the bed, leaning against the pillows and bringing her knees up she angled Dianta's head onto her other breast, trying to avoid the tooth. "Come on, wild thing. I won't keep track of your mistakes if you don't keep track of mine."

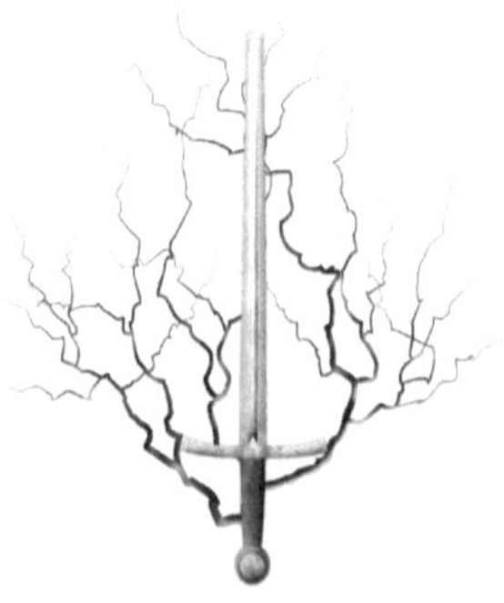

CHAPTER

FIVE

Blood and Bone—Beltane

STANDING IN THE bathhouse, Kahtar flicked soapy foam into a bowl of water from his straight-razor. Tipping his head back, he scraped the blade up the length of his throat. A deep gash ran from his elbow to his armpit, only half-healed by the Old Guard who'd inflicted it. It burned every time he lifted his arm.

The wooden door to the shed slammed inward, startling him. He nicked his throat.

"Kahtar!" Beth practically flew at him. "There you are! Hey, are there Macaws inside the veil?"

A ribbon of blood ran down Kahtar's throat. He grabbed a washcloth and held it to the wound. "You slam in here to ask me that? Where's Dianta?" He scanned toward the cabin.

"No, I came because I want to show you something. The plebes are watching her until I get you. Come on! Hey, you're really bleeding there! Did you nick yourself shaving?"

Kahtar scowled at her. "Why did you leave her with plebes? I told you they're inept."

"Because you also told me you don't want her outside and I needed you. I think we should take her outside though. She's bigger now and I think the rain has finally stopped. It's gorgeous out. Do you realize this is the first sunny day since Dianta was born?" Standing in the doorway, Beth motioned for him impatiently. "Come on, you have to see this!"

Kahtar grabbed a towel, wiped the rest of the soap off his face and tugged his shirt over his head. Holding the washcloth to his still bleeding throat, he followed Beth out the door.

"You look nice." He nodded toward the summery dress she wore, noticing her clogs were still the ugly felt ones she'd worn every day since Dianta was born.

"Thanks, I'm celebrating—and this is the only dress that fits, because I've been eating everything. You know the cookies you made last night? Gone. The problem with getting rid of all my shoes is that not one of the three I kept will fit now. These things are one of the plebes."

All that eating had left Beth with a softness Kahtar found appealing. The last time he had seen that dress Beth hadn't filled it out quite so expertly. Swallowing, he forced himself to stop staring. "Are you celebrating Beltane?"

Beth didn't answer for a moment as they sloshed across the expanse of somewhat marshy backyard. It had been raining for nearly a month. Kahtar glanced at her to find Beth turning nearly as pink as her dress, chewing her lips like she did when she tried not to answer a question. He knew instantly what she was celebrating and it wasn't dancing around a Maypole, per se.

A month. It's been a month today!

Kahtar smiled and took a good look at Beth this time. Palmer had been adamant that they give Beth's body a month to heal. Despite the fact that Welcome had used his skills to quicken the healing process, he'd instructed the only demands placed on Beth would be Dianta's, and he'd followed the command with a meaningful look at Kahtar. It left Kahtar fully aware the good doctor had known they hadn't followed his pregnancy instructions to the letter. Welcome had taken him aside to reiterate his demands the night of Dianta's birth.

Make Beth rest. I won't go so far as to say I know why she delivered so early, because this has been the strangest pregnancy I've ever seen, but I mean it this time. Let her rest.

Beth couldn't resist answering for long. "Of course I'm not celebrating Beltane. I don't even know what it is." She pouted a little. "I can't believe you forgot our month of waiting is up." Self-consciously she tugged at her dress to pull it up higher on top, while simultaneously attempting to tug it down over shapely thighs. There simply wasn't enough fabric.

"I never count days when I'm fasting. It makes it seem longer. But I'd be happy to enlighten you about some old Beltane rituals tonight." Kahtar held her gaze until she flushed, and they both looked away, grinning as they gave up keeping their feet dry and sloshed through the yard.

"You never answered me about the Macaws," she said.

Kahtar managed not to roll his eyes. "This veil is a few hundred years older than everything outside, but it's the same otherwise. When you're on the other side of it do you see many Macaws flying around Ohio?"

"Of course not. I realize they're not native, but I saw one fly over your bath shed a few minutes ago."

"You probably saw a barn owl, there's one hanging around," said Kahtar as they stomped up the porch steps and left their muddy footwear outside the front door.

"I think I know the difference between owls and tropical birds. You should have seen Wolves; he practically took flight after it. He knew it was something new." Beth held the door open.

"Once I watched Wolves chase his own tail for forty-five minutes. I timed him. You might not want to use him as a witness." Kahtar sneaked a kiss against Beth's soft cheek, and crossed the great room to where half a dozen plebes bent over Dianta's cradle. Relieved they weren't holding her, per his orders, Kahtar bit back a smile when he heard one of the thirteen-year-old boys comment, "She's a wee mouse, isn't she? Oh, yes, she is!"

The boys noticed him then and backed away, looking fearful—although for once they were doing exactly what they should be doing. Kahtar didn't mind if they basked in the delightful touch of her baby heart while they watched over her. He leaned over the cradle to bask some himself.

The touch of Dianta's heart felt nothing like Beth's or his. It reminded him of cliff diving, or gorge scrambling. "What new wonder did she perform today? Did she turn her head by herself?" he asked Beth.

Dianta lay on her back, pumping her fists and legs within a nest of soft blankets. The babe had grown a bit, and now stretched longer than the length of Kahtar's hand, but still smaller than a newborn should be. Kahtar reached into the cradle and lifted her out as Beth joined him.

"Well, of course she did that too, but that's not why I came and got you." Beth ran her fingers over Dianta's ruddy cheek, and the babe turned her head in that direction, opening her mouth wide. "Always hungry, aren't you?" Beth teased her fingers over Dianta's wrinkly face. "Have you noticed how unique she is? I've been trying to find something about her that's familiar to you or me—like my toes, or your fortitude—which she definitely doesn't have! She wants everything now. But then today—"

Kahtar stopped smiling as he remembered something else Welcome had said. *Maybe someday you'll trust me enough to explain why your baby is as strong and developed as a full term baby, at only twenty-six weeks gestation—or even why you're genetically a Constantine but physically not.* Kahtar had made it a point to avoid Welcome since that night, though he stopped by twice a week to check on Beth.

"—this is so you," Beth said, sliding a little spoon into Dianta's tiny hands and making certain one clutched the mouth-piece and the other the end of the stem.

Kahtar glanced toward the plebes, uncertain if Beth had brought him into the equation as a cover. It didn't seem like her. Dianta would never look or act like him because she carried the DNA of a Constantine. The Constantine family looked and acted nothing like the immortal repeating being Kahtar was. Although Kahtar and Beth were tall and blonde and Nordic in appearance, genetically Dianta had inherited the swarthy Mediterranean genes he carried. She may as well have been conceived by another father entirely for all the similarities they'd ever share.

Beth continued to wobble the spoon between Dianta's clenched fists. The little angel opened and closed her mouth. Kahtar tried to determine if her mouth looked like Beth's.

"Just wait until you see this!" Beth enthused.

Dianta screwed up her face and shivered with the effort of holding onto that spoon. Her mouth opened wide and she bellowed something in her deep voice that sounded very much like, "Nom, nom, nom, nom, nom!"

Beth and the plebes burst out laughing.

Kahtar smiled into his wife's joyful eyes. "Are you saying I do that when I'm hungry?"

"You do!" she said.

"You just said I had fortitude. That didn't look like patience at all."

"All bets are off when you're hungry!" Beth leaned closer and tugged the spoon off Dianta. She brushed her lips across the skin of Kahtar's bicep, right where the sleeve of his t-shirt ended. He resisted sliding his fingers through her shining hair to hold her and really kiss her back. He'd have to excuse the plebes first.

Later. Tonight I'll show her what all bets are off looks like.

Sunshine shone through tall windows and lit the room. Kahtar hoped the grass would dry on the higher slopes today so he could really show Beth an old Beltane ritual. He'd spent centuries observing customs he couldn't participate in. That had changed with Beth.

She smiled up at him. "Kahtar, look how pretty Dianta's hair is with the sun shining on it. Look at her lashes! Aren't they deadly? I knew they were long, but it's really ridiculous!"

They both looked at their daughter, smiling. Dianta chose that moment to open her eyes wide for the first time, with full-on sunshine instead of rain-dampened light spilling through the windows, making each detail crystal clear. The lashes looked like pitch black butterflies.

For one split second Kahtar beamed at the wide-eyed wonder in his arms. And then his world ended.

Very familiar steely gray eyes glared up at him.

Dianta did have something of Kahtar's.

She had his eyes.

NO! HOW COULD Dianta have his eyes?

Dear Sweet ilu, no!

The entire universe seemed to shift, spinning to Kahtar's left. If it weren't for Beth standing beside him, Kahtar might have dropped the baby, having lost the ability to control his limbs properly. He stumbled in that direction, but caught himself.

"Easy, Kahtar, you have to support her head!" Beth caught Dianta out of his arms, seeming not to notice the entire cabin had slanted east.

Kahtar staggered to keep his balance as a roaring sound filled his ears. From somewhere far off he heard the young laughter of a plebe and swung his head in that direction.

"Go!" he shouted, but his voice sounded far away. "GO!" he bellowed, louder this time. Six plebes' mouths hung open, as though they didn't understand him. "GO, NOW!"

Quickly the boys obeyed. The entire room appeared to shift again as Kahtar watched them running for the door, two falling over each other as they tried to exit en masse. They scrambled to their feet again and were gone. The baby was screaming.

"Kahtar, you scared her!" Beth said from far away. "What're you yelling about?"

No Constantine had those eyes.

Neither had Beth's family.

Welcome had been wrong about the light inside her.

Dianta shared something of Kahtar's.

Doom.

The entire world dropped out beneath Kahtar.

A baby's screaming echoed in his ears and he turned his eyes to focus on the blurry pink of a woman's dress.

Oh, sweet ilu, she has my eyes rumbled through his mind.

A woman held a baby against her shoulder, jiggling her up and down—or maybe the entire world was jiggling up and down. The crying made such a big noise for someone so small; it was a roar—or maybe that was just in his head, too.

She has my eyes, dear ilu, she has my eyes.

Despair raced through him, and the image of the woman in pink seemed to race away, shrinking into a dot on the horizon until the only one left in the universe was Kahtar, alone as always. Kahtar threw his head back and cursed at the heavens, fury lighting through his entire being. "ilu, dammit, NO! But that's what you've done, haven't you? Damned me! Damned her!"

From another world a woman's voice spoke, but Kahtar couldn't understand what she said. He spun on the spot, trying to find her, and bumped into an empty cradle. His focus latched onto it. He knew this cradle. He'd spent three months carving it for his child, his child who had his eyes. It seemed to touch him, like a soft hand patting his shoulder, mocking him. He pushed the touch away.

Suddenly he changed his mind and charged it, tripping over the cradle. Regaining his balance and snatching it up, he threw it against the stone fireplace. It shattered as though made of glass, and the pieces seemed to scream. Kahtar bellowed at them to shut up. A shield shining in the morning sunshine crashed to the floor and knocked a rack of pokers into Kahtar. Nabbing them up he dashed them against the floor and walls repeatedly, until long gouges were torn out of the wood he'd spent years cutting, hauling, sanding, laying, finishing.

Kahtar shouted the entire time, in a litany of languages, throwing things, kicking furniture, cursing his creator, his life, and the universe. Shades flickered—all those he'd failed, those he'd killed, they all filled the room, centuries of wrongs—and the screaming of women, one in particular, but he couldn't think who it was or why it tore through his heart deeper than others. The shade of Golgotha intruded before he could puzzle it out—always Golgotha! The same shade that had haunted him for the past two thousand years dropped over him, though this time he was wide awake. There ilu was—Jesus, as some called Him—bound to a tree, bleeding—dead or dying, Kahtar could never tell, hadn't even been able to tell the day it happened, when the shade had been real and he had been known as Longinus.

Without a lance in his hand this time, Kahtar took Longinus's place and marched up a stairway to get to the tree. Instead of plunging a spear into Him as he had in his shades for thousands of years, Kahtar shouted at Him. "I want to know! I want to know! Why?" he bellowed at the man hanging there, although with every beat of his heart the man seemed to waver and vanish.

Between heartbeats Kahtar tried to focus on him. "I took it! I took it all! Everything you gave me because I had no choice, but I took it all! But not—" Kahtar's voice broke, "—not, this! I can't take this!" He sobbed, peering at the man through his tears. "I can take anything but this!" But it wasn't a man, and it wasn't the God from his Shade. Beth cowered on the stairs, her back to him, splotches of blood on her dress like flowers. Dianta's little head rested on her mother's shoulder, peeping through the silky curtain of Beth's hair, steely gray eyes wide open, oddly fierce in the face of such a tiny baby as she wailed. *She has my eyes.* Standing on the stairs towering over them, Kahtar collapsed.

BETH'S SOBBING PENETRATED the fog.

Kahtar came to lying at the bottom of the staircase. He tried to move, but his head was too heavy to lift. The baby wasn't crying anymore and Kahtar struggled to angle his head so he could see her, just to make sure she wasn't hurt. That thought made him laugh without humor. The sound echoed in the big room.

It's not like I need to worry. Nothing can really kill her, even if she begs for it. And she will. Many times.

The pain in his heart seemed to go supernova, and despite the fact that he couldn't move, he started to cry. Part of his brain automatically assessed his injuries: a broken leg and collar bone, and a wicked concussion. There was blood spreading across the floor from the impact his head had made against the hardwood.

This kind of concussion could be fatal. Stay conscious. As if he ever really needed to fear fatal. Kahtar's sudden sobs morphed again into laughter.

Behind him the screen door creaked open, and the sound of dog toenails click-clacked across the floor—a sound that meant scratches in the wood, something that used to anger Kahtar. Wolves paused above him, his shaggy fur glossy and combed thanks to Beth's dedication. He didn't smell as bad as usual. Wolves gazed down at him with one brown eye and one half blue. His lolling tongue came for Kahtar slowly, right across the mouth. Kahtar's laughter died in his throat and once more sobs took its place. Wolves stepped over him and went up the stairs toward Beth, and Kahtar closed his eyes.

GREEN EYES SWAM into view. Pain greeted Kahtar this time. His head could feel the very particles floating in the air. They felt like torture. Light seared through his eyeballs into his brain like lightning strikes. The house wasn't spinning anymore, but he was still in the cursed place, lying flat in his own bed. *How'd I get up here? Did Beth call Old Guard? She'd never call Old Guard.* Welcome Palmer sat on a chair beside him, waiting patiently, his hands pressed against Kahtar's head as his lips moved in a silent, healing prayer. If Kahtar had the strength he'd have pushed him away.

Kahtar wet his lips. "Go," he muttered. "Shesh go."

"Beth told me you've always had night terrors."

The traitor. Kahtar closed his eyes. *Why the blazes would she tell Welcome that?*

"You could have killed her," said Welcome, and Kahtar opened his eyes. Welcome's eyes held both sympathy and censure. "I won't judge you, Kahtar. You can tell me anything. I might be able to help you."

"Can't," Kahtar said, wetting his lips again. "Go."

"Are you too proud to ask for help or too stupid?"

"Too bloody tired, Palmer. Go."

"So it doesn't matter to you that you could have killed your wife? Or your daughter?"

Kahtar's heart iced over. He tried to remember, but it was all a blur—madness. It had happened before, in other repeats, usually on a battlefield.

"So it does matter?" Welcome said.

"Dianta hurt?" Kahtar whispered.

"No, but only because Beth shielded her with her own body. Beth, however, is hurt."

"Where? Where's Beth?"

"Not here. She's shattered, Kahtar. I sent her home to her mother."

"Shit," Kahtar whimpered. "No."

"What happened? I don't think I've ever even heard you swear before."

Kahtar ignored him.

"Beth needs love right now, not the censure of the clan. After what you've done she'll only get that at her parents."

Kahtar tried to sit up, his torso could be coerced but his head wouldn't come with it. He fell back against the mattress. White light exploded inside his head. Time seemed to pass, and he thought Palmer had gone. Through his eyelids the room had gone dark, but a wet rag came to his mouth now and then, and water trickled down his throat. Tears slid from the corners of his eyes and ran into his ears. After a time, weak sobs escaped via pathetic gasps, shooting fierce pain through his entire body. Something told Kahtar it was late, but his head couldn't even scan to know, and opening his eyelids only showed darkness.

TURNING ON THE light seemed like a bad idea. Welcome had said not to, that it would aggravate Kahtar's head injury. Mostly Beth worried if she saw Kahtar's face she'd start crying and never stop.

Kahtar sprawled on his bed, moaning in his sleep. The bed he threw her out of whenever his night terrors were bad. Beth had her own room, one that was more of a giant closet, because even when Kahtar's night terrors were bad she sneaked back in here. This is where she belonged. With Kahtar.

What am I going to do now?

Where do I belong now?

Wolves nosed the bedroom door open wider. Beth sensed him standing there watching for a while. Eventually the dog left, his nails clicking on the wood floor.

In his sleep Kahtar whimpered. The touch of his heart circled hers. *Lost. Broken. Afraid.* Exactly the same feelings in her heart.

Beth leaned forward and brushed her lips against his forehead.

"Too far," he protested, his voice too hoarse. The words were barely recognizable.

He thinks I'm Welcome.

Beth took the bowl of cool water Welcome had left and lifted the linen cloth from it. She held it to Kahtar's lips and squeezed so water ran over his parched tongue to soothe his throat.

"It's not like I'll ever stop loving you, Kahtar."

He tried to turn his head toward her but stopped. Beth sensed the pain of it in her heart.

"Where's Dianta?" he asked.

"She's with my parents."

For a moment he didn't respond.

"She hurt?" he whispered, as though afraid of the answer.

"No," she said. *But you might have, Kahtar. If not for me you might have hurt her! What then?*

"You?"

"Yes," she said honestly, battling back tears. "Welcome fixed everything, except my heart."

Even in the dark Beth felt Kahtar reach for her. For a moment he struggled with the sheet covering his large body, but eventually got his hand out. The ache of his heart reaching made her place her hand in his.

"Has that ever happened before?" she asked. *Please say no.*

"Yes," he said.

Beth waited.

"Long ago. Thousand years since last time."

"Why, Kahtar? What am I supposed to do now? I can't let you around our baby! I don't understand! You were smiling, you were laughing, and then…" Beth couldn't stop the tears this time. "You went crazy. I was so afraid."

A dry sob escaped Kahtar, but he swallowed and responded through tears, "She has my eyes."

Beth waited for more, unable to understand. She recalled Kahtar smiling into Dianta's face as their daughter batted her black butterfly lashes. *He was so happy!* "What? What does that even mean? Is there an emotional trigger that makes you go crazy?"

"Beth, listen. You met my grandparents in the Arc. They're dark, my father was dark—my mother, my biological mother in this repeat, she was black. But I look like this. I always look like this."

For a moment that information threw Beth. *He always looks the same? No matter what his parents look like?* It seemed unfathomable. Beth couldn't imagine how some clans must have reacted to that. "Oh. I hadn't thought—always?"

"Every single time."

"Oh. But—what do people say when—?"

"Listen to me," Kahtar interrupted. "Genetically I am dark, like Dianta. This time around my DNA is Mediterranean and African."

Beth knew that much. "I'm confused. I mean, I get it, that's why Dianta's dark, but why are you going over this right now? What does it have to do with you going insane?"

"She has *my* eyes," Kahtar growled. "Mine, my immortal eyes." His voice broke and the next words were a sob. "She's immortal, Beth."

For several minutes Beth held onto his hand. The words washed over her and made the hair on the back of her neck stand up like lies did.

What does that mean?

Beth had noticed Dianta's steely eyes right off. It hadn't even startled her. They were strangely pretty, so unique and unexpected with her dark lashes and cocoa skin. They were so Dianta that Beth hadn't for one moment thought of them as Kahtar's.

But he's right. They are his eyes.

Does that make her immortal?

The hair on the back of Beth's neck continued to stand up.

She let go of Kahtar's hand. The thought of immortality was simply too much after everything else that had happened. She got up and walked out of the room. Just outside the doorway she stopped and looked back into the room. "What if she's not?"

Kahtar didn't respond to that. For a moment she thought maybe he'd passed out or fallen asleep again, but then he whispered, "Goodbye, my Beth."

Goose bumps rose over her flesh and something in her heart emptied.

Beth shuffled back into the room, afraid to get too close, but afraid to leave. "Why did you say it like that?"

"You know why. We can't be. We can't risk another child, and I could never be your brother. Go back to your parents, Beth. I'll think what to tell the clan in time."

Unable to take in this abrupt dismissal after all that had happened, Beth turned and walked away.

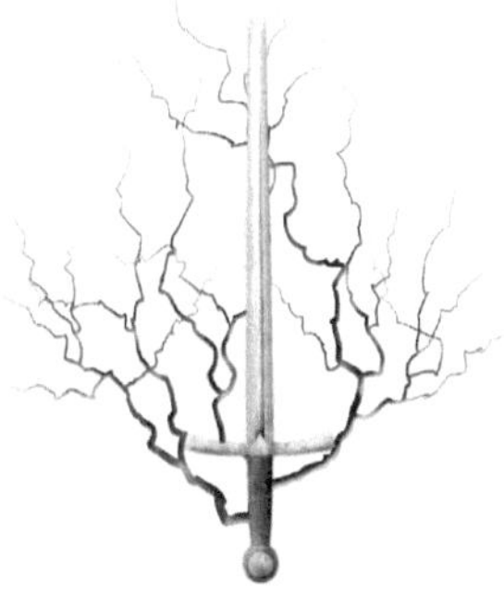

CHAPTER
SIX

Bloody Facts—Mother's Day

BETH SAT IN the kitchen of her parents' home, a mug of tea between her hands, trying to not think. It wasn't working. After sitting silently on the stairs in Kahtar's house listening to her husband's hoarse crying, she'd left him without a word.

What is there to say?

After what had happened part of her didn't want to ever take Dianta back to that cabin. She thought she'd never been more terrified in her life than to see Kahtar bearing down on her with a poker in each hand, but the finality with which he had whispered, "Goodbye, my Beth" frightened her far more than his madness had.

Remembering to breathe, Beth took a loud gulp of air and noticed her mother's watchful eyes from the other side of the breakfast counter. *How long have I been sitting here? Did I talk when I came in?* Beth couldn't remember. She couldn't recall the long drive to her parents' house. Mentally she shook herself and forced her attention to the reality around her.

In the twenty-four hours since her parents had learned of Dianta's birth, Beth's dad had apparently purchased every baby gadget sold in a first world country. Dianta sat strapped inside a purple baby carrier, perched on the cluttered granite countertop in Ted and Carole's kitchen. She looked like a bald squirrel in a frilly doll dress. Slumped in the very bottom of the seat, she snored with a gusto equal to a man with at least fifty years on her. Piles of unopened boxes and bags crammed the normally immaculate room.

"Hot refill?" Carole asked, pushing a steaming teapot past an assortment of pacifiers, rattles, stuffed animals, and glass bottles. She motioned to the sandwiches she was preparing. "Do you want avocado on your sandwich?"

Beth nodded, but made no move for the teapot. Yesterday when she had arrived, Carole had hardly said a word about her new grand-daughter, taking in Dianta's existence with the same stoic silence she'd given her nearly seven foot son-in-law the previous year. Still, Carole seemed taken with Dianta, and alternated between touching her granddaughter and taking the baby seat with her when she moved around the kitchen. Not once in the months since Beth had married Kahtar had her mother asked why they hadn't seen him since the wedding, or why they were never invited to Beth's new home, or even why only six months into her pregnancy Beth had shown up with a perfectly healthy, impossibly small baby.

Carole returned to the counter with both the baby and sand-wiches and pushed a sandwich in front of Beth. She moved around the island and took the stool next to Beth, tugging the baby seat like a snowplow through all the baby paraphernalia until it rested against her elbow.

"Eat," Carole ordered, ignoring her own sandwich as she ran her fingers over Dianta's miniscule ears.

Beth pulled her sandwich closer and tried to rouse herself. No matter what happened, she had to play the part. Cultuelle Khristos could take her away from her family forever if she didn't, or worse.

"Where's Dad?" she managed.

"He drove all the way out to Erie this morning to try to get some sort of heated crib for preemies. I told him you wouldn't use it, but you know your father. I think he's just trying to wrap his head around all this."

Beth took a deep breath. *All this* was dangerous territory. "She's healthy. She doesn't need it."

"I know. He'll probably just come home with all the junk to make halo-halo ice-cream for you two." Carole moved one hand to pick up her sandwich and took a bite. Across the kitchen Beth could see the two of them reflected in the spotless chrome of the refrigerator, two oddly similar blonde blurs: Carole with her short cropped hair wearing her usual plain t-shirt and olive pants, and Beth with longer hair, dressed in—she had to look down to confirm what she was wearing—the same pink dress she had been wearing when Kahtar went berserk yesterday. It occurred to her that despite Welcome's healing there were probably bloodstains on it, and even if there weren't, she was covered in bruises. Outside the kitchen window on the sunny patio Beth spotted a shimmer of light. *Old Guard. Crap.*

"Do you need more shampoo from my shop, Mom? It's doing nice things to your hair." It was the best Beth could do—not having the ability to lie could be a telethon worthy handicap in her opinion.

"Sure. Your dad's still out of that tea you gave him, too. Do you need a napkin?" Carole asked, uncharacteristically participating in small talk. She stopped toying with Dianta long enough to grab two napkins and push one under Beth's elbow.

Beth's mind raced, searching for another safe topic. "That tea is popular. I should be able to get some more soon," she said at last, hoping the Old Guard heard her. Brack tea was an Old Guard favorite, and apparently hard to come by. Maybe they were outside just to make sure she was safe in the seeker world, or maybe they were out there making certain she kept the unspoken vow of secrecy required of all Covenant Keepers. There was no way to know for sure, unless she got it wrong.

Her mother pushed the napkin closer to Beth's sandwich plate. *Since when does Mom use paper napkins?* Beth reached for it but paused before picking it up. Something was written on it in pencil.

Do you need to disappear?

Her mother had gone back to playing with Dianta's ears, but Beth saw her watching out the corner of her eye. *Shit.*

Beth's hand trembled, and she moved it away from the napkin to nab her sandwich instead. Shoving a bite into her dry mouth, she chewed. *What does Mom know? How does she know?* Beside her Carole took a deep, calming breath, and both Beth and the sleeping baby automatically followed suit.

She knows I showed up battered and lost with Dianta. She knows I spent hours in my room crying yesterday. She knows I left the baby with her in the middle of the night and returned this morning like a zombie. What am I going to do? Beth glanced at Dianta; her mother's petting was waking her. Turning her focus back to her sandwich Beth gave a subtle shake of her head. Even if it were possible to disappear from Cultuelle Khristos, she'd given her word—and her heart.

Carole put her hand flat on the counter and made a slight circular motion with her finger. It took Beth several beats to figure out to flip the napkin over.

Did he hit you?

Beth turned her eyes toward her mother, fighting tears. She couldn't imagine a world where Kahtar would hit her. Not even a day ago it would have been inappropriately laughable. Beth thought of the way he'd thrown the cradle against the fireplace, the way he'd blindly charged after her, swearing. She wished she'd left with the plebes instead of staying and trying to talk to him. But it was Kahtar's behavior at fault, not hers. The memory of the look in his eye as he demolished the living room made gooseflesh break out over her body. Almost since she'd known him she'd understood what he was capable of, but not until then had she really understood what Kahtar could be if he wanted to. *But Kahtar doesn't want to. He isn't a bad man.* Beth glanced at her mother and suddenly knew if he were, she could leave and be safe.

But he's not bad. He's terrified. Not once had he hit her, but if she hadn't run, if she hadn't shielded Dianta from flying shrapnel, something equally as bad might have happened in his madness. Thankfully her mother's question was easily answered.

"No," she whispered, and jammed her sandwich into her mouth. He hadn't hit her, and she was betting her life on the fact that he never would.

Carole palmed the napkin from beneath Beth's elbow, tucked it inside her sandwich between the tomato and homemade bread, and ate it in four enormous bites. Chewing around a mouthful she said, "It looks like Dianta's waking up."

Beth somehow managed an acerbic answer. "Don't pretend you didn't wake her on purpose, Mom."

Carole laughed and stood, unbuckling the carrier straps. She lifted Dianta and held the fussy baby against her torso.

"She has your husband's eyes," Carole said, examining the steady, fierce gaze of her tiny granddaughter.

Beth's heart sank, leaving her unable to nod, smile, or pretend. *What does it mean that Dianta has his eyes?* She tried to sense the truth in her daughter's gaze.

Carole frowned as she passed Dianta from her arms to Beth's. "Is he a good man?"

Tears warmed Beth's eyes, and she fought and failed to keep the telltale wobble out of her chin. All she could manage was a brief nod, but Carole didn't move away, still touching the now squalling Dianta in Beth's arms. Beth finally raised her eyes to look into the somewhat fierce gaze of her own mother.

"If you've given him your heart," said Carole, "you need to make it right."

ONE WEEK LATER Beth's convertible shot through the veil, a blast of wind rocketing it roughly. Beth's grip on the steering wheel tightened, and from the backseat Dianta grumbled.

Towering trees rose on either side of the driveway. Thick patches of purple and white spring flowers greeted her. Returning to the veil for the first time in over a week made Beth's eyes water, partly because of what had happened last time she'd been with Kahtar, and partly because of pain and fear.

The pain in her pelvis reminded her Kahtar would have a reason to go justifiably ballistic this time. Tears prickled in her eyes.

I'm making it right. Kahtar will have to forgive me this time.

In her car seat Dianta whimpered, and Beth could feel her own fear and pain reflected in the touch of her baby's heart. She glanced into the rearview mirror at her teeny baby curled up in the car seat like a little pill bug, her Kahtar-like eyes shiny with tears. For the first time in a week Beth's emotions took control, and she lost it. She stopped the car halfway down the driveway, climbed out, slid her seat forward and leaned painfully into the backseat. Unbuckling Dianta, Beth held her baby close and kneeled on the dusty driveway, sobbing.

Maybe because this morning her dad had made a big deal about it being her first Mother's Day, today the loss of other children seemed huge. There would only ever be Dianta. Beth couldn't accept Kahtar's hypothesis about immortality as truth—no matter how logical it seemed. She understood Dianta shouldn't have Kahtar's immortal eyes, but the eyes from the genes he carried. But Kahtar didn't know anything about himself for certain, and when he had declared Dianta immortal like him, it had brushed roughly against Beth's heart like an untruth.

Still, the memory of the look in Kahtar's eyes during his madness couldn't be denied. Beth knew truth when she saw it and Kahtar *believed* it. He would never risk inflicting his existence on another. She took a deep breath. *Dianta is enough.*

That reassuring thought cut through Beth's tears, and Dianta followed suit, sniffling savagely and heaving a shaky sigh as she stopped crying the same moment Beth did. Beth kissed her, and tucked her into the backseat again. Bending over and straining with buckles and belts, Beth felt a vibration beneath the thin soles of her borrowed sneakers.

Beth straightened to spot Wolves racing through the weeds alongside the driveway, moving so fast the heads of purple and white flowers were weed-whacked right off their stems. A trail of them fell in Wolves' wake. He looked worse than usual, his hair sticking up oddly. Beth quickly slid the driver's seat back into place and hopped inside, closing the door. It was bad enough moving around and lifting Dianta; the dog hurtling against her might tear her stitches and reopen her new incision.

"No!" Beth snapped at him through the closed window.

He ignored her, slamming right into the car door. Rearing up on his hind legs, Wolves scratched frantically at the door. It wasn't his usual enthusiastic greeting; the dog seemed terrified. Looking down the driveway at the path he'd ripped through the weeds, Beth saw high weeds moving. Something was chasing him, and judging by the movement, it was more than one something. Goose bumps prickled up Beth's back and she swore under her breath as she opened the door and braced for impact.

Wolves crashed over her, clawing her legs with his toenails as he bolted into the far door in his rush to escape. Crumpling to the passenger floor, the dog attempted to dig a hole to hide in. The sound of Wolves' pursuers made the hair on the back of Beth's neck stand up. She'd heard that sound before, but only in Malaysia and India. For a split second she sat there, certain she had to be wrong, but it didn't matter; she had Dianta in the backseat and Kahtar's terrified dog next to her to protect.

Beth slammed the car door shut, laid her hand on the horn and held it there. Judging by the movement of the tall grass, whatever things were pursuing the dog took off into the woods.

Beth put the car in gear and accelerated. The sudden whip of the car hurt her abdomen. "Whatever you've stirred up, Wolves, I do not have time for it! I'm locking you in the house with me today!"

Wolves looked over at her, his half-blue eye looking crazed while the dark one appeared to be in agreement, as if he understood and was all for it. Holding one hand out to keep him in the passenger seat, Beth drove the last mile to the house. Kahtar's police cruiser sat parked by the front steps, and she realized part of her had been hoping he'd be away.

For a minute she sat there, delaying the inevitable.

At last she opened her door. Wolves blasted across her lap, stepping on her abdomen. She gasped and blinked back tears. Climbing out and bending to get Dianta hurt even more. Beth tried to keep her movements normal in case Kahtar was scanning. If he was, she couldn't feel it. Leaving the piles of baby gifts from her dad inside the car, she climbed the porch steps, crossed it and opened the screen door.

Wolves shoved in front of her and went straight to his belly, marine crawling across the floor like he did when Kahtar was around. And Kahtar was around. He sat sprawled on the sofa, legs wide, staring toward the kitchen without even a glance in her direction. *Maybe he knows. The Old Guard might have told him. I know they were at the clinic with me.*

"We're home," she said as normally as she could manage. "Did you get the message I left for you at the police station?"

"Yes." Kahtar's voice sounded hoarser than usual and he cleared it. He said nothing more about the message she'd left with the officer called Francis Snickerbacher.

K—I'll be home next week. If I decide to stay there, I'll explain about condoms. Love, Beth

Beth had sensed Francis' embarrassment as he'd taken the message, but at the time she hadn't cared.

"How are you?" Beth asked, and Kahtar looked in her direction, still avoiding direct eye contact.

"Are you kidding? How are you?"

"Oh, I'm just—" Beth stumbled on the next word, unable to force even a polite lie like *fine* out of her mouth, so she went with the truth. "I'm just wondering if the Old Guard remember who your first parents were."

Kahtar's mouth dropped open.

"Did you ever ask them?" she said.

He blinked but recovered quickly. "Do you honestly think you're going to come up with an approach to uncover answers about me I haven't considered or tried over the millennia?" He sounded annoyed.

"Yeah, I do," said Beth.

Kahtar snorted and turned his head to face the kitchen again. Beth made her way slowly to the opposite couch. An area rug now covered most of the floor that Kahtar had torn up. The coffee table was gone, smashed to smithereens like the cradle. The rocking chair, end tables, shelves, armoire, and all the other wooden structures from the great room were gone too. The sofa Kahtar sat on looked battered, with stuffing showing through huge tears and flat stones where the wooden legs once were. Beth sat down on the opposite one, realizing the reason it looked intact was because it was new, and the glowing glass globe feet told her it had likely come from Cobbson Compound.

Kahtar watched her examination of the room. "For what it's worth, Beth, I am sorry. It won't happen again. I can promise you that much—for what that's worth. My apology isn't nearly enough, because it shouldn't have happened at all."

Beth held his gaze for a moment. "I don't expect you to be perfect, Kahtar, and I think I would forgive you anything, unless that were to happen again."

Dianta fussed, rooting for a breast and Beth turned her eyes from Kahtar's. Feeling oddly shy after all that had passed between them, Beth slid the baby underneath her shirt to nurse her. His eyes went to the bump beneath her shirt, and she felt the warmth of a scan cut through her.

And here we go.

"What the—did you have to have some kind of surgery? Did I hurt you that much, Beth?" Kahtar looked thunderstruck.

"I had to have surgery, but it had nothing to do with your— episode. And no—you didn't actually hit me. I didn't get out of the way fast enough when you started throwing stuff around and—"

Kahtar looked pale. "You had your—you had that surgery seekers do so they don't have children! Didn't you?"

"Yes. And the good news is that means I've come home to stay— provided you go to counseling with Welcome."

Kahtar put both his hands on his head and laughed.

"Is that funny?" Beth snapped.

"Not even in the least. For the past week I've been mentally begging for your forgiveness, planning what I could say to make it better and how I could convince you it won't happen again, but knowing there is nothing adequate. I've been trying to wrap my mind around Dianta's fate, knowing I'll never again be able to honorably integrate into a new clan in the future—not when I'll be forever searching the world, looking for my repeating daughter. But once again you've managed to take my thoughts away from my own worries, Beth. You shouldn't have done it this time. Eventually the clan will know you did it and they will judge you harshly."

The clan already judged her harshly. Beth wanted to say she didn't care what the clan thought, but that lie wouldn't come. "But you're not angry I did it?"

"I'm angry you didn't discuss it with me first."

"You wouldn't have let me," she said.

"That's true," Kahtar said. "I especially wouldn't have allowed you to go to a clinic where they'd cut you open! You could get an infection! Come over here so I can heal your incision. Don't be afraid to sit beside me, Beth. You know I would never hurt you on purpose."

"You come over here," Beth scowled. "I'm kind of busy, and it hurts to move."

Kahtar made a faint sound of amusement again.

"Why is any of this amusing you? I faced the bloody facts and I did what needed to be done, Kahtar. I didn't dare come home without having the surgery first. It's not like Welcome Palmer would do it for me! I know it's against the clan's rules, against the ways of our people— but they don't know our situation, do they? They don't know you're immortal! We belong together—none of what has happened changes that! What I'm trying to do is make it right between us." Dianta fussed as Beth pried her off a breast and moved her to the other side. "And I know you wouldn't risk another child."

"No, I wouldn't," said Kahtar with no trace of amusement in his steely eyes. "Would you?"

Beth eyed him candidly. "Not if I knew for certain your children would be like you. I'm not convinced that because Dianta has your eyes she'll repeat. I think you're wrong about her."

"You're fooling yourself."

Beth shook her head. "I don't do that, remember? I can't even lie to myself. Kahtar, I think you're wrong. I'm not saying something isn't different about her, but the idea of her being a repeating immortal doesn't sit right with me. It's like when I first met you and you told me you didn't like me. I knew it wasn't true."

"Likely centuries will pass before I have any proof even for myself, so I'm not going to waste time arguing with you. But it's the only logical reason for her to have my eyes. Beth, I know I'm right."

"You can't. You don't even have all the facts about yourself, so there are bound to be holes in your logic!" But Beth knew he meant it, and that he was done talking about it. He was putting this subject into that place he stuffed all the things he didn't want to look at. No wonder he'd exploded. He stuffed pain away and sat on it. The fact he didn't blow more often suddenly seemed impressive.

Kahtar scooted to the edge of the couch and slowly rose to stand, holding a small pillow against his crotch. Frowning, but with a gleam in his eye alerting Beth to the fact that this was the official subject change, he lifted it off to show her an ice pack. "My logic is not the only place with a hole. This hurts like the time I was eunuched. Now that is a memory time cannot erase."

"You had a vasectomy?" Beth shouted and winced as Dianta clamped harder.

"Welcome Palmer did it the old-fashioned seeker way, said he wouldn't use his giftings for it, but that he was pretty good with a scalpel. He wouldn't even heal it with his giftings afterward—said if I was going to break the rules I could suffer my own consequences. Yep, my logic might have holes in it, but it appears we both faced the same bloody facts. At least we'll be doubly covered. Although I sincerely doubt I'll ever want to use this appendage again."

"Hmph," said Beth. "You do remember I can always tell when someone is lying, right? I give you twenty-four hours."

Kahtar grinned. "Ah, Beth. I do love you. Thank you for doing what needed to be done."

"You're welcome, and you too."

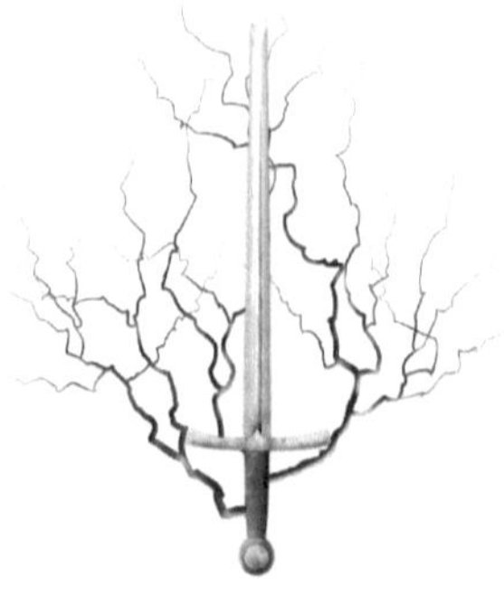

CHAPTER
SEVEN

Bloody Crazy—Summer Solstice

WHERE IS HE? *I'm not going to panic. I'm going to find him and we'll figure this out.*

Beth shaded her eyes against the setting sun of the Arc, searching for Kahtar. Afraid to shout she kept an eye on a mastodon grazing near the shoreline of the great lake. The sun silhouetted the elephantine shape as it lifted dripping grasses with a weaving trunk, depositing them into its chomping mouth. The impossible image both thrilled and frightened her.

What if the thing stampedes? How fast can they run? Surely faster than I can.

Shifting her wriggling baby, Beth kissed the squished red face. She couldn't blame her inability to run fast on her teeny mouse of a daughter. Beth ran long fingers through Dianta's black curls, already thick as a blanket against her baby head, and continued searching the horizon for her husband.

Where the heck is he? There's nothing down here!

Kahtar had instructed her not to be late to some summer solstice thing at The Mother's, but instead of going straight there Beth was looking for her husband. She absolutely had to find him. They needed to talk privately. Now.

A familiar warm wetness trickled down her arm, dripping off her elbow. *Stupid cloth diapers! There has to be a better way than these things.* Digging in her baby bag with one hand, Beth crouched in the grass. She spread a soft blanket and sat her sopping baby on it, cooing over tiny baby feet while she worked. At first glance Dianta still seemed delicate and frail, but at two month's old her development was advanced. She had a fierce grip, ate like a hog, and had a deep man voice she was employing at the moment.

"If that's your singing voice, you're not going to fit in around here any better than I do," Beth teased, smoothing Dianta's feathery eyebrows and studying her steely gray eyes.

She'd been holding onto the belief Kahtar had been wrong, that his immortality wasn't genetic or contagious, but today that hope felt very much like the wishful thinking Kahtar said it was. Unless she was very much mistaken, something that seemed like an immortal impossibility had happened to her—and she didn't know whether to be terrified or thrilled, so she'd settled for both at the same time.

"Oh, Kahtar, where the heck are you, and what are we going to do now?" she whispered, tying a fresh cloth diaper on Dianta while the low grasses of the Arc rippled around her in the summer breeze.

Goose bumps prickled up Beth's spine as she thought about her husband. Kahtar had repeatedly refused to ask Old Guard about his first parents, claiming he'd asked them what he was long ago, and many times over the ages, and they'd never answered. He'd also refused to talk to Welcome Palmer, calling him a pretty pup. Kahtar believed nothing good could come of making yourself conspicuous in a world that survived on being unobtrusive.

Beth's emotions swung toward the terrified end of the spectrum, and she stood, wiping ready tears with her thumbs. *Why did I accept any of that? Why didn't I argue with him? I was so stupid, and now...*

She put a hand on her belly.

Now what will happen to us? What will Kahtar do?

Along the shore a familiar figure emerging from behind a pile of boulders caught her eye. Smoothing her gown, Beth took several steps in that direction and squinted against the sun; the silhouette looked like Kahtar.

"Kahtar?" she shouted. Her voice didn't rise above the sound of the waves lapping the shoreline or the squawking of circling gulls, and the mastodon in the distance kept right on eating. The Great Lake seemed as big as the sea, and here inside the Arc it stretched in primordial glory, neither tainted nor tamed by man like the lake outside the Arc. Still, a few rotting fish along the reeds stunk every bit as badly as the lake in the outside world. Beth's soft shoes skittered over mounds of tiny river rocks as she moved closer.

"Hey, Kahtar! We're here! I need to talk to you!" He didn't answer, and she tossed a cautious look back at Dianta flailing in the grass, before jogging a few steps closer.

"Kahtar!" she bellowed again, halting in surprise when he backed into full view. A woman stood on a rock beside him, gripping the collar of his cape as he bent low to kiss her. For the briefest moment Beth faltered at the sight of Kahtar brushing aside a dark waterfall of hair and holding the kiss long, longer, too long.

Her mouth dropped open and something propelled her numbly forward. *No. Kahtar wouldn't!* As she neared Beth realized some of the dark hair was the man's own. Honor Monroe.

Exhaling a breath she hadn't realized she'd been holding, Beth stopped walking, relieved but embarrassed. Honor looked in her direction then, as did the pretty little brunette. She held a finger to her lips, shaking her head at Beth. Beth shivered.

"Beth?" Honor said, his voice sounding funny.

Beth flushed. "Never mind." If there was one person on earth she'd rather not see right now, it was Honor Monroe, her once best friend who'd turned on her fiercely when the clan discovered her father was a seeker. "I thought you were Kahtar. Sorry to interrupt you two."

Honor frowned at her, resting a hand on the hilt of his blade. "Interrupt who?"

Beth pointed to the brunette at his side, who frantically shook her head at Beth.

Honor's blue eyes widened as he said, "There's no one here but me."

"Oh, come on!" Beth stared at the woman who now waved her hands back and forth in front of her face. Why was Honor lying with the woman standing right there in full view? Beth shivered again. Honor's response didn't sound like a lie—but it wasn't the truth, either. The brunette stopped her frantic gesturing and a sad look crossed her pretty face.

"Beth?" Honor sounded fearful. "Where's your baby?"

Eyes still on the brunette, Beth motioned behind her where Dianta lay grumbling in the grass. Without warning Honor moved, faster than Beth would have thought a human being could. His sword hissed as he pulled it from the scabbard and he ran right at her. She froze and her heart plummeted, but he shoved past, knocking her over and scattering mounds of tiny pebbles with each footfall.

Beth landed hard. "What are you doing?" she shouted.

Honor growled a wordless snarl as he ran. Beth scrambled across the pebbly beach on hands and knees after him, craning her neck to see Dianta.

Her heart dropped.

A circle of big dogs surrounded Dianta, with only Honor blocking them from her baby. Beth screamed and jumped to her feet. *God, please, no!* Each step seemed to take forever as she moved over the tiny stones, her feet sinking deep into them.

Honor waved his blade, and the dogs sidled away into the tall grass as Beth reached them. The warrior dropped his blade and scooped Dianta out of the grass, examining her.

"Is she okay?" Beth cried, heart thundering in her chest.

Honor turned on her, cold fury in eyes that had once shone with only kindness for her. "You stupid idiot! What kind of mother are you?"

"The new kind! Give her to me! Is she okay?"

Honor elbowed Beth away, jostling the baby, and Beth heard her daughter's familiar throaty chuckle. Relief shot through her. "Oh, thank God, thank you. She's okay!"

"Why would you leave your baby in the grass?" Honor shouted, blue eyes blazing.

Beth took a step backward. They weren't friends anymore, but she'd never expected to feel afraid of him. Her eyes went worriedly to Dianta. Honor held her with both hands high above his head, as though he expected Beth to jump for her. She was thinking about it.

"Give her to me, Honor," she warned. "I sat her in the grass to change her diaper. I thought you were Kahtar until I saw you kissing that girl!"

"Have you completely lost your mind?" Honor said. "What are you talking about?"

"No, I have not lost my mind! I'm talking about you kissing that brunette who wanted me to pretend like I didn't see her!" Beth glanced back, but didn't see the woman anywhere. "I didn't do anything wrong! Look, I turned my back for one minute. I didn't know those dogs were here."

"You've lost your mind! And those weren't dogs! They were wolves!"

"Wolves?" she repeated. It didn't sound like a lie, but Beth knew the difference between dogs and wolves.

"This isn't a park or a playground! It's an Arc! You don't belong down here yourself, let alone with a baby. If those wolves had been hungry, she'd have been torn apart!"

The words hit Beth's heart like slaps, and Dianta began to cry.

"You're hurting her!" Beth's long arms reached desperately. "You're not holding her right and you're scaring her! Give me my daughter!"

"I will not! I'm speaking to The Mother about this! You are not fit to—"

Beth brought a knee up, but Honor sensed it coming and moved. A hard elbow hit her right in the face and her nose exploded with pain. He caught her with his shoulder and shoved. Beth shot backward, landing so hard on her backside her tailbone jammed against the rocky ground.

Then she heard Kahtar. At least she thought it was Kahtar, although she'd never heard him roar like this. The sound shot cold terror right through her.

"CEASE!"

Ignoring the well-worn path, her husband came through the long grass at a run. Dressed in chainmail, he looked like something out of a shade. Combined with the horror of the dogs by her baby—surely they had only been dogs—and Honor dangling Dianta in the air, it was too much. Unable to breathe through her broken nose, Beth managed a painful breath through her mouth. Dianta still dangled from Honor's hands, turning purple.

"Get her under control, Chief!" Honor shouted. "Something is very much wrong with your wife—I think she's hallucinating, and she attacked me!"

Beth shot to her feet and headed right for Honor. *Why is he lying?* The fact that his words didn't feel like a lie didn't stop Beth from going after him again, determined to get her baby.

Kahtar intercepted her. One big hand—a hand that always touched her so gently, especially the last weeks—a hand that cradled Dianta as though she were priceless glass—planted itself in her chest and shoved her.

"Don't you dare attack him again!" he said.

"What!" Beth bellowed, staggering backward.

Kahtar planted himself protectively in front of Honor Monroe, both hands on the hilts of his swords as he shouted, "You heard me. Back off!"

Defiance rose in her heart so strongly that she knew Kahtar felt it. That didn't stop her from launching herself in the direction of Honor Monroe, determined that if she had to claw her way through Kahtar, so be it.

Beth didn't make it two steps before Kahtar elbowed her to the ground harder than Honor had.

Sharp rocks tore her dress and scraped her hands and legs as she skidded to a stop. Kahtar stormed after her, the ground vibrating with his footfalls. In a flash of fear, Beth remembered the night he'd lost it.

But when he bent to look into her face, there was no insanity in his eyes this time, only anger.

"NEVER. EVER. HIT. A. WARRIOR! You know the rules!"

This time it was Beth who snapped. She swung a fist right for his head, making contact with every bit of strength she had as she bellowed out two words no lady should ever say—especially not to her husband. Instantly she started to cry. Blood gushed from inside her nose, down her throat and into her mouth. Kahtar reached for her nose, certainly to heal it, but angrily Beth punched him in the other side of his head. Hard. It felt like she might have broken her hand.

Silence descended as Kahtar looked at his wife. After a moment he turned to Honor, who relinquished Dianta. Beth watched Kahtar blow gently into Dianta's face. The baby blinked and began to bellow. Kahtar moved to Beth and placed Dianta in her arms.

Honor was there in an instant. "Beth left her lying in the grass unattended! A pack of wolves nearly took your daughter! When I asked what happened, she didn't even make sense, Chief. She went on about interrupting and kissing—I don't know, it sounded mad! There's something wrong with her. She shouldn't be down here, and she certainly shouldn't be taking care of a baby in her condition! She's unbalanced and unfit!"

Kahtar watched as Beth tried to get their hysterical daughter to nurse, tugging at the soft material of the Arc-appropriate dress—a gift from The Mother. Blood dripped onto her daughter's dark head from her gushing nose and Dianta thrashed, at last latching on as though determined to teach that breast a lesson.

Kahtar's words were measured as though feigning calm when he asked Honor, "Do you think Beth was trying to feed my child to the wolves?"

"I think she doesn't belong in this Arc!"

"In such a situation, Monroe, what is the danger in handing a baby to its mother?" Kahtar bent over Beth and yanked her to her feet. She scrambled to cover her exposed breast from Honor's eyes, failing miserably when Dianta refused to let go. It was not a flattering Madonna moment.

"Apologize," Kahtar said to her.

Beth almost choked on the blood dripping down the back of her throat. "What?"

"Apologize to Honor for making him hit you."

Beth spewed the same two words again, this time for both their benefit, adding, "He took my daughter and pushed me down! Why the hell should I apologize to him?"

"Because you do not hit a warrior! That is the bottom line! Everything else is irrelevant. You don't break rules like that!"

"Do you have any idea how absurd that is? Do you have any clue how ridiculous you're being? You storm around this stupid Arc, enforcing inane rules, for what purpose, Kahtar? Who the bloody hell do you think you're protecting? Not me! You're protecting warrior stupidity!"

"Watch your mouth, Beth! Don't say things you can't take back!"

Beth repeated the same two words.

Kahtar took one threatening step toward her and stopped. "Stop. Talking. That is not a request. I'm your warrior chief and I'm ordering you to shut your mouth now."

Fury made her tremble, and attached to her breast Dianta sensed it and growled. Pain scorched the inside of Beth's nose as blood continued to gag her, and she couldn't stop her angry tears.

"What will you do? Hit me again? You told me husbands don't hit their wives! I am so sick of clan bullshit, and I've had it with you! You all pretend like you want to make the world a better place! But what do any of you *ever* really do? You're supposed to be some great Christ-like clan, but your love is all for yourselves! I've known far more honor among seekers than I have with this clan! I don't know what I was thinking getting involved with any of you! Especially you, Kahtar! Most especially you!"

The hot blood in her throat forced her to stop shouting and concentrate on drawing another breath. Neither Kahtar nor Honor spoke for long seconds, frozen in place as they stared at her. The only sounds were of Dianta's growling and Beth's gagging.

"Old Guard!" Kahtar shouted his voice much hoarser than usual. Several of them flickered into being, like shimmering gladiators, taller and broader than Kahtar's ample mass. "Take my wife and daughter home. Do not heal my wife." His steely eyes flickered to hers. "When I give an order, even you are expected to obey it. Because of your tantrum I'm now duty bound to report this incident! And then we will talk, and despite what you say or think, you will apologize to Honor and to me."

Beth wished she had the fortitude to once more shout those two words, right in front of Old Guard. Instead she was forced to tug Dianta loose from the breast she was mauling, and surrender her into the giant arms of a black-eyed shimmering Old Guard for transportation.

The Arc vanished, and in an instant both Beth and Dianta were transported back home to the cabin in the woods, still safely hidden from the world inside a veil. One of the Old Guard returned Dianta to her without a word, and all three flickered away in a shimmer of light. Dianta snarled, rooting blindly for a breast. Beth stomped across the dusty driveway and opened the door to her old Monte Carlo yellow, Saab 9-3 convertible. She strapped the protesting baby in, slid into the front seat and turned the key.

Beth produced her own roar going up the driveway at a forbidden speed. She hoped Kahtar could still smell the fumes when he got home. He could take his rules, his Arc, his orders, his duty bound bullshit, and suck it.

COVENANT KEEPERS COULD be bleeding hearts at times, and at others they could be completely without pity. Beth decided as she stalked the corridors of Cobbson Clinic, bruised and bloodied, that this was one of those pitiless times. Not a single warrior offered to help her, but averted their eyes. Crossing the atrium she spotted a tall, vaguely familiar young Warrior of ilu, Francis Snickerbacher. He worked at the police station with Kahtar, and she remembered she'd left her note about condoms with him.

Beth cleared her throat of the blood still dripping down it and drew a deep breath through her mouth since her nose was no longer functioning. "Excuse me, Francis, right?" She sounded like she had a horrible cold and paused to draw another breath. Her nose might as well have been crushed flat for all the good it was at the moment. "Would you scan for Welcome for me?" In the labyrinthine buildings and rooms of the compound she could think of no other way to find the doctor.

Pale and freckled, Francis always struck Beth as shy, but he drew himself up and looked at her down a long and perfectly functional nose. "You should ask nothing of someone you have so little respect for. If you truly speak the truth and believe the clan warriors do nothing, you should expect exactly that from us."

Beth's jaw, already open out of necessity, dropped lower as the warrior turned on his booted heel and marched away, still dressed in the lightweight tunic and leggings the men wore in the Arc on Sundays.

"Are you unaware how quickly news travels among the clan, or are you just that heartless?" Standing at the edge of a park-like area of autumn trees near the glacier, a small black woman glared at Beth.

"Memma Rosa," Beth greeted Kahtar's grandmother through her plugged up nose. "I'm not aware of much that goes on in the clan, and I may be too bold, but I'm not heartless."

The petite woman held out impatient arms. "Give me my granddaughter. You're bleeding on her."

Beth complied and felt a brief flash of jealous annoyance when Rosa gave Dianta a welcoming smile. *She's never once smiled at me.* Some ugly part of Beth took consolation in the fact that Dianta fussed at being passed to the interloper, although Beth knew all her daughter really wanted was to maul her breasts a bit longer.

"I'm bleeding," said Beth, rather unnecessarily. She suspected the one dress she was permitted to wear inside the Arc was ruined.

Rosa's smile vanished. "Perhaps you shouldn't force warriors to hit you, and that wouldn't be a problem."

"Force them to hit me? Are you crazy?"

"Did you or did you not strike two Warriors of ilu today?"

Beth considered the events and nodded, her eyes tearing up. "Yes, but I didn't attack them. Honor took Dianta! He wouldn't give her back!"

Frowning at her, Rosa adjusted the struggling baby in her arms. Dianta didn't seem quite so small in her petite grandmother's arms. "I suppose I've seen other women go off kilter after having a baby."

"I'm not off kilter!"

Motioning with her head, Rosa said, "Welcome's having a bite to eat in the first room outside the abstract. I'll keep Dianta with me in the Arc until you get better."

"There's nothing wrong with me, and I don't want her in the Arc!"

Looking at Beth as though she'd committed murder and blasphemed ilu all in the same day, Rosa clutched Dianta closer.

"Honor said there are wolves in there!" Beth added.

Responding with a tone surely reserved for the dim-witted or insane, Rosa said, "Yes, some, but I won't leave Dianta with them. She'll be safe and sound. Don't you worry about my granddaughter."

Beth's heart leapt in her chest as Rosa took a step away. "No, Rosa! Don't take my daughter, I have to feed her!"

"There are plenty of nursing mothers in the village. She'll be fed and fine."

"No! I don't want anyone else to nurse her!"

"Why don't you want anyone else to feed your baby?"

"It's gross!"

Rosa shook her head. "You have strange thoughts. What is grotesque about feeding a baby? Send for her whenever you want her and I promise I'll bring her back myself."

Beth could tell Rosa meant it, and didn't protest when the tiny woman turned her back and took shuffling steps away.

"Wait! How do I send for her?"

Rosa turned around. "You just tell someone you want her, Beth, anyone. They'll spread the word. I daresay it's faster than those walkie-talkie phone things you seekers use." She placed Dianta against her shoulder and headed for the oval shaped tesseract that went to the Arc.

"I'm not a seeker. I'm a Covenant Keeper," Beth whispered. But the truth echoed in her heart. *Not to them.*

BETH IGNORED THE critical glances shot in her direction, knowing her conversation with Rosa had been overheard. She wondered if the looks were for her disparaging remark about Arcs or if everyone already knew and judged her for being hit by Honor Monroe. Fighting a shiver, she hurried across the edge of the abstract, her feet moving over fresh spring grass with a few colorful autumn leaves scattered in. A snowball someone had thrown sat half-melted near the edge of the dream-like park area.

Stepping from grass onto the odd porous floor of Cobbson Clinic, Beth hurried up the hallway, her felt clogs making a faint clomping sound. Spotting the door to the room the healers used as a dining area, she shoved through and froze.

Welcome Palmer stood near the counter with a sandwich in one hand and a brunette in the other. He appeared to have mixed them up, because it looked like he was eating her face. His sandwich-free arm supported her waist as he leaned over her, bending the woman so far backward her dark hair hung nearly the length of her short red dress. Using his lips as leverage he bent the woman back even farther, and Beth feared for the safety of her spine. The only sounds in the room were their unattractive sucking noises, until the slow door swung shut behind her and caught Beth in the shoulder. Already bruised and sore, she whimpered. Welcome didn't notice, but the brunette twisted her head Beth's way, her lips attached to Welcome's with the tenacity of a sucker fish. She opened one bright blue eye at Beth.

Beth blinked. It was the same brunette that Honor Monroe had been kissing earlier. Blindly Beth reached behind for the door. The woman pulled her mouth free with a loud, wet sound, but Welcome stayed bent over her. The brunette eyed Beth's bloodied appearance dispassionately, and ordered, "Be quiet!" before returning to Welcome's lips.

A shiver rippled over Beth like an adrenaline rush. "Not even!" she said. "Welcome, can you help me and get back to that later?"

The blue eye widened, and to Beth's astonishment the woman appeared to fall into the floor and vanish. Fear shot through her, and she barely noticed when Welcome Palmer straightened. He looked in her direction, blinked and put his sandwich on the counter. It took a moment for his eyes to focus.

"Beth! You poor thing!" He crossed the floor and took her arm, peering into her eyes. "Your hands are shaking! What happened?"

"I just saw a woman disappear into the floor!"

"Breathe, through your mouth. Here, let me fix your nose! And then you can tell me what's going on with you."

TWENTY MINUTES LATER Beth sat on the exam table, her long legs dangling. She still hadn't mentioned the fact that Welcome had been kissing the same woman Honor Monroe obviously liked to kiss. For starters who they kissed really wasn't her business, and for another, Welcome acted like it had never happened—the same way Honor had. Having her broken nose repaired hurt so much that for several moments Beth felt like she could see through time and she really didn't care.

"Surely you're not still worrying about the disappearing woman— in a place full of tesseracts I would have thought you'd be used to it. Maybe it would be a good idea for you to stay here at Cobbson for a while," said Welcome, holding up a mirror so Beth could see her nose. She only glanced, knowing she looked like a mad woman with dried blood all over her face and in her hair.

Welcome sat on a little rolling chair like any doctor in the seeker world, except for here, the soft porous floor absorbed blood, the time needed to heal wounds was moments, and the doctor apparently had no idea he'd been strangling a woman with his tongue a few minutes ago. Still, sometimes Welcome seemed reassuringly close to the outside world and Beth's comfort zone.

When she thought of comfort she thought of her dad, and sneaking out to get ice cream that Mom forbade. All of a sudden Beth felt homesick. Staying with her parents wasn't much more normal than women disappearing into the floor, but at least it would be a familiar weird. They might have secrets no one talked about, but at least Beth knew their rules.

"I think I'd rather go stay with my parents for a while," she said.

Welcome stood, brushing her bloody blonde hair gently over her shoulders. He took his time and didn't pull a single hair, and while it might have been strangely awkward if the doctor who'd given her the tubal ligation had done it, with Welcome Palmer and the caring touch of his heart heralding his honest intentions, it felt perfectly natural.

"Do me a favor and take a minute to think that through. Even your bruises have bruises. I can't fix that. How are you going to explain your condition to your parents?"

"The truth!" she snapped.

Welcome smiled and slid up to sit beside her on the exam table. "It can't be easy to always have to tell the truth. It's a beautiful gifting, but I can see where it would be a burden. Most of us depend on the luxury of little white lies, especially with our parents. In fact, I think they appreciate it."

A faint laugh escaped Beth. "I think my parents would love it. Instead we just don't talk about anything important. We don't dare."

"I imagine they know many things you're forbidden from telling them, but this shouldn't be one of the things they secretly know, Beth. Not implied, and certainly not spoken, because they're sure to misunderstand it. Fact is, from what you've told me, your friend broke your nose, and your husband pushed you down. That doesn't sit well in either world. Not in the world they live in, the world you grew up in, and certainly not in your new world of Covenant Keepers. But our ways are not their ways, and your parents don't know the laws we're bound to follow here. That said, I need to ask you if you're afraid, or have you ever been afraid of your husband?"

Glancing down at her lap Beth tried not to cry. She shook her head no and it was the truth. It surprised her to realize that not even on the day he went crazy had she truly been afraid of Kahtar. What had really frightened her was she couldn't make him listen, because she knew if she could reach him, that she'd never have anything to be afraid of.

Even now, after Honor had broken her nose and Kahtar shoved her to the ground, bellowing machismo madness at her, she wasn't afraid. She was pissed.

From the corner of her eye Welcome's face looked doubtful, but he accepted her words for the truth they were. Beth wished she could tell her husband how much she hated him right now, but it wasn't true. The inability to lie was a curse in both worlds. Besides, Kahtar hadn't come after her, so she couldn't tell him anything. She'd thought he would, was glad he hadn't, but the fact that he hadn't made her that much angrier.

"I have to admit you're the only one who's ever been able to say they're not afraid of our Warrior Chief. I couldn't say it. I'm still going to ask you to please stay here for a time. You're upset, I can feel it." Welcome tapped his chest. He had a strong, caring heart, and Beth knew right now he could feel every honest angry emotion in hers.

"You just had a baby after a rough pregnancy, and I know she's been running you ragged—all babies do that, especially preemies. Although the only thing preemie about Dianta is her size..." Welcome stopped and put a hand over her stomach, frowning. Beth felt the warmth of his scan heat through her, different than the sharp scans of warriors and Old Guard, but still a shadow passing right through her body.

Suddenly everything that had happened that day was swept away in the memory of what had happened that morning. Morning sickness had returned.

Oh, please no, please no. Please let it be something else. Something he can fix.

"You're pregnant again." Welcome sounded disbelieving and Beth jerked her head up to stare into his stunned green eyes. "Which is, of course, not possible in either world." His eyes widened as he moved his hand over her belly. "Because you had some surgery of your own too, in the outside world. I'm surprised I didn't sense your tubal ligation sooner. That was reckless, and you're right if you were thinking I wouldn't have done it. It was that important to prevent this?" He frowned at her for a moment. "Does Kahtar know both your efforts have failed?"

Beth shook her head. "I think I'm going to throw up."

Welcome slid off the table and brought her a metal bowl. "Is there any chance of an explanation? That you've conceived is medically impossible. Mathematically speaking you're not but two weeks along, but the life inside you is strong and advancing too quickly—I don't know how I missed it with Dianta."

Clutching the bowl to her chest, Beth tried not to puke. She'd felt it that morning, that full and familiar nauseating sensation, and the draining sensation in her bones and muscles. She tried to recall how many times she'd been with Kahtar since the surgery—images of Kahtar's big bed, the bath house, the sofa, the stairs, the porch, the police car, flitted through her mind. He'd told the plebes he'd let them know when he needed them, and anytime Dianta took a nap had presented an opportunity.

"It never occurred to us that my surgery wouldn't work," she whispered. "We didn't wait to be sure about Kahtar's because we thought mine was a sure thing."

Welcome took a seat on the little rolling chair. As he moved closer, Beth noticed it didn't have wheels, but hovered about an inch off the ground. *No wonder it doesn't make noise.*

Welcome put a hand over hers, gently massaging it until her death grip on the bowl lightened. "Both surgeries worked. Your cycle hasn't even resumed since Dianta was born. I suspect Kahtar's sperm can move by—"

Beth interrupted by spectacularly barfing her double oatcake and banana breakfast into the bowl. Welcome jerked his hand away too late, but stood and wiped her mouth before moving the bowl to a far table and cleaning his hand off.

"Don't talk to me about Kahtar's sperm," she said, wiping sweat off her forehead. "I hate Kahtar's sperm right now." She meant it.

"Sorry."

Beth slid off the table. "I think I would like a hot bath. If I'm not allowed to go to my parents' house, I'll go down to my shop. I haven't been since Dianta was born. That's over two months it has been sitting there."

"I think going to your shop is a good idea—but I'll need to ask The Mother first," said Welcome. "Why don't you just take your old apartment down the hall for tonight? It's empty, and there's a nice sized tub. Just don't make the water too hot." He pointed toward her stomach. "Pregnancy no-no."

"Of course." She headed for the door, but turned around. "You won't say anything to anyone, will you? About our surgeries or Kahtar's sperm?"

Welcome crossed the floor and stood beside her, his gaze intense. "No, and I won't tell Kahtar about this pregnancy. That is a conversation you need to have with him. Soon."

"No," said Beth. "I don't want to talk to Kahtar. I don't want to see Kahtar. He expects me to apologize to him and Honor, because I *made* them hit me! I'm not even sure I could accept *their* apologies!" To Beth's surprise the words rolled out angrily and easily. They were the truth. She put her hand on the doorknob, and turned back to Welcome. "Do the women in the clan actually do that? Do they apologize to a warrior for making him hit her?"

Welcome rubbed his lips together as he considered her, his green eyes troubled. "It's never happened before that I've ever heard of, not in our clan. Nobody would attack a friendly warrior in any situation, not if they wanted to walk away from it."

"Honor took my baby and wouldn't give her back. She couldn't breathe."

"I'm not saying warriors don't make mistakes. They make plenty of them. And I'm not saying nobody gets angry with them, because you can believe they certainly do. I know I sure do. But if you have a discrepancy when they're on duty, you summon an Old Guard."

"I didn't think of that." Although she wouldn't have done it if she had. It was bad enough when Kahtar summoned Old Guard for transportation.

"It's why they're here. Warriors of ilu take a blood oath to protect us. They've also sworn to annihilate aggression. The fact that you turned aggressive against a warrior means that not only did he not protect you, he hurt you, and even worse—he didn't annihilate you as a threat, as he was duty bound to do. Technically he chose dishonor over his vow. For you."

Beth knew Honor well enough to know how much he valued his honor, but the convoluted thought process struck her as ludicrous. "I was no threat to him! I just wanted my child!"

"I understand that. But you're concerned with intention. You forget our laws are black and white. Call it a cultural difference if you will."

Beth yanked the door open. "I call it ridiculous!"

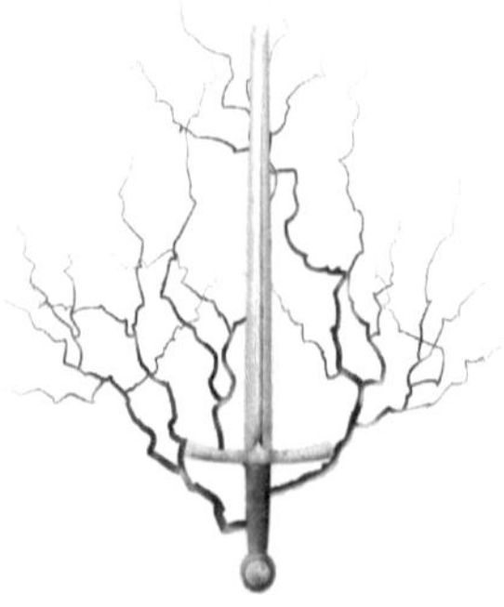

CHAPTER
EIGHT

Bleeding Hearts—Hunting Season

EVERY DAY MOVED like a lifetime, yet summer had evaporated in a moment and October trees were already at peak color. Kahtar kept his mind on daily minutiae or how many minutes until he saw Dianta again, but never allowed it to stray to the fact that he hadn't seen Beth in months or how that time was irretrievable and wasted.

Sitting in his creaky chair in his police chief office, Kahtar signed forms without bothering to read them. Twice he had to get up and cross the office to the paper shredder to shred documents he'd forgotten to sign as *Kent Costas*, his alias. The third time he didn't bother to stand, wheeling his chair across the floor and jamming paper into the machine as he memorized the information on it. He'd need to fill out new forms, or give the new seeker cop that responsibility. Maybe paperwork overload would be his Achilles heel. The guy needed to transfer out soon.

Wheeling his way back to his desk Kahtar nabbed a pencil off the computer table, picturing the case numbers in his mind as he reached for his notepad. He pressed the pencil to paper before noticing Elder Abagail Adit now sat in the chair across from him. Startled, he pressed too hard and the pencil cracked in half. The woman knew how to make one of her tesseracts nearly undetectable to a scan and always managed to creep him out.

"Blazes," he swore. "You could at least make some noise. There's a seeker here so tessering around the police station isn't a good idea."

"Hmph," said Abigail smoothing her standard ugly green dress. "Seekers are half blind to the comings and goings of old ladies. Kind of like Covenant Keepers, eh? If you made things right with your wife and slept nights, maybe you wouldn't be as nervous as that dog of yours."

"Mind your own business."

"It's been four months, Kahtar. She's not going to apologize. You do realize her gifting of truth prevents insincere apologies from passing her lips, unlike the rest of us."

"You do realize I said to mind your own business."

"You do realize I'm an elder of this clan and like your wife I'm not above slapping your smart mouth," hissed the chubby woman.

Kahtar laughed at the ludicrous threat. It sounded rusty and the muscles in his jaw almost seized from the unexpected upturn. "What do you want?" he asked.

Abigail put an elbow near his *Police Chief Kent Costas* business cards, leaning forward conspiratorially. "Look, this separation is almost against the laws of being."

She was not going to let it go. Kahtar put his arms on the desk and leaned toward her. "This is my personal business and I'd thank you to keep out of it. Again I ask you, what do you want?"

"Is this separation Beth's idea or yours?"

Kahtar focused on his hands. The entire clan knew Beth had left him and now spent almost all of her time holed up at her shop. Few knew she'd called him at the station several times, calls he hadn't returned. Even fewer knew she'd taken to trying to deliver Dianta to him personally in the evenings. He made it a point to dodge her. None of it was anything he wanted to discuss with anyone.

"You have no right to ask me that," he finally said.

Abigail sighed, a deep and weary sound, as though it came from the very earth beneath them. "Look," she said, rubbing her forehead.

"The clan is turning on Beth. We all see how miserable you are, and they blame her."

"I'm not miserable," Kahtar lied, ignoring Abigail's eye roll to the heavens. "Beth is ensconced in her shop minding her own business. The clan barely sees her. I think she's safe from their pitchforks—and tongues."

Beth hadn't been in the Arc since the incident four months ago. Most days they traded Dianta back and forth via warriors disguised as police officers. Despite the fact that Beth had started showing up in person, Kahtar, like most of the clan, hadn't laid eyes on her in four months.

"This separation doesn't just affect you and Beth!" Abigail jammed her glasses onto her nose. "It creates animosity in the clan! Instead of you setting an example and showing how an Orphan is as much Covenant Keeper as the rest of us, you're showing them that you think Beth's as big of a mistake as they do!"

"Don't put that on me," Kahtar growled. "Can you sit there and pretend you don't think the same thing? The Mother herself told me it had been a mistake allowing Beth into the clan."

Abigail sat back. "Anwyn said that?"

"Are you surprised someone said it to my face? It doesn't matter. The Mother said that too. She said it doesn't matter that it was all a mistake—Beth is in the clan for life like all of us, but she just wondered if I regretted joining with her."

Abigail sucked in a breath. "Do you?" she whispered.

Anger made Kahtar snap. "No! I should, but I'm not that good of a man. None of this is your business, Abigail. And it doesn't matter what the clan thinks or says about Beth. Unless she decides to apologize, it isn't likely they'll see her again."

Abigail shot to her feet and leaned toward him. At less than five feet tall she stood barely taller than Kahtar did sitting down. She poked a finger onto the desk near his hands. "I'm sorry if your wife isn't as perfect as you would have liked. Did you really think her gifting of truth wouldn't be a burden for you too? I thought you loved her!"

Kahtar rose to his feet slowly, and the chair rolled across the room behind him. He looked down at Abigail from his nearly seven foot height, steely eyes flashing. "Love doesn't make Beth belong with the clan. Can you stand here and tell me after all that has happened, my wife belongs with Cultuelle Khristos?"

"If you do, she does," Abigail shot back.

And therein lies the truth of it. We, neither of us, belong.

The fight went out of Kahtar. "Do you not realize the gravity of what happened in the Arc? It could eventually cost Beth her life! There is no room for error in our world. Do you think the clan should make exceptions to our most basic rules and just hope for the best?"

"Yes, to both questions. Do you think tossing Beth aside and ignoring her will fix anything?"

"I think I'm doing what I have to do."

Shrewd green eyes widened. "It's not your idea. I knew it. The separation isn't your idea! What's going on? It can't be The Mother's decree!"

Kahtar didn't answer, but neither could he hold Abigail's knowing gaze.

"It was Anwyn? The Mother of Cultuelle Khristos told you to stay away until Beth apologizes? She has no right to separate a husband and wife!"

Kahtar sagged. After four months he almost needed to tell someone. "It wasn't like that. That day in the Arc Beth disobeyed me. Twice."

"Oh, come on, Kahtar. She's your wife."

"I was speaking as her warrior chief at the time."

"You're her husband first."

"It doesn't work like that. Because of her disobedience to me and what she said that day, the warriors voted to shun Beth until she makes it right."

"They won't protect her?"

"As Warriors of ilu they'll shun her until she apologizes, and that includes not offering her protection, but since Beth isn't in the Arc it hardly matters. They will protect her as police officers in this world because that's a different oath. Besides, she has the Old Guard."

"You. Are. Shunning. Your. Wife."

The look she gave him made Kahtar feel two years old with a dirty nappy. "Don't look at me like that, Abigail. The warriors voted. I have to stand with them. It's a democracy."

"Oh, please! Since when? It's a dictatorship and as both the police and warrior chief you're the dictator!"

A faint smile ghosted briefly over Kahtar's lips. "A good dictator knows when his people are right."

"Apparently not."

"I can't remain warrior chief if I don't stand by my men in this. It's my duty."

"Are you insane? Your duty is to Beth."

Kahtar rubbed his hand over his face. "And who would be the warrior chief if I did that? I'm needed. I can't turn my back on the clan."

"So you turn it on Beth?"

"The things she said to me, she meant them."

"She was angry, Kahtar. We all mean ugly things at times."

"All she has to do is apologize and the shunning will end. The only way that's going to happen is if she comes to that conclusion on her own. Can you deny that?"

"No, but you're wrong to choose the clan over your wife and they're wrong to demand it of you."

"I didn't say they demanded it of me. It was my choice."

"Bollocks."

"Besides, I know Beth well enough to know even if I could approach her seeking an apology, it would do no good."

"You're wrong."

"You don't know her. Beth's apology needs to come from her heart. She needs to make this right with the clan, not with me."

"I've never accused you of being a smart man, but I never really thought you were this stupid. You are Beth's heart and her clan. When you make that right, everything else will follow." Abigail stepped backward, and with the faint sparkle of a tesseract light she disappeared.

"Mammoth plop! Spare me your fairytale wisdom!" Kahtar said to the empty room, despite wanting it to be true.

With a heavy sigh he settled into his seat and began to recount the information from the shredded forms, refusing to acknowledge that Beth was only three streets away and he might possibly never see her again.

THE URGE TO change the structure of the old Victorian had faded since Beth first opened her shop. The rambling rooms and odd staircases remained. Now she barely remembered why she'd even wanted the place. Her shop, Sweet Earth, sprawled on a side street in the village of Willowyth, seemingly light years away from the veil that hid Kahtar's cabin. Beth had no real plans to return to that place, although she dreamed of it at night—and in her dreams it was closed to her now. Part of her feared that might be true.

Surrounded by rooms of organic and natural goods she'd spent years gathering, Beth would have gladly traded it all for the cabin full of Kahtar's mucky boots, weapons, and militant-style order.

On the floor at her feet, Dianta teethed on a wad of cheesecloth, seemingly content. At only six months old she had grown sturdy, though still a tiny wisp. Now able to sit unassisted, Dianta wobbled slightly on the floor with her short legs spread wide, her steely eyes focused with the concentration of an Olympic gymnast as she practiced her newfound skill. Beth knew one good sneeze could send her daughter tumbling feet over head, like an armadillo. She quietly set her laptop on the floor so it wouldn't startle her.

"Mem, mmm," Dianta growled through a mouthful of soggy fabric. Beth's jeans strained as she squatted to the floor beside her daughter, resisting the urge to bother her by kissing the top of her curly head, or touching the tiny nose, or tugging those itty blue jeans up over the little bum where they sagged too low.

"You are the best sitter I've ever seen," Beth said with complete sincerity, sliding her long legs past Dianta and plopping the laptop onto her lap. Adjusting her bulky sweater, Beth hid the fact that her pants weren't buttoned over the bulge of her belly. Like with her first pregnancy, no one had noticed her baby bump—but then it had bothered her. Now it meant Kahtar had no idea either, which was good. Despite everything, she wanted to be the one to tell him, privately. Sometime over the past four months she'd gone from too angry to speak to Kahtar to the realization that they were at an impasse, to growing dismay that he planned to leave their relationship in limbo like this.

Beth missed Kahtar so much she could barely speak his name out loud. Some small part of her even missed the Arc; she starved for the clean clear air and waving grasses and the simple life Dianta could have there. Beth briefly pressed a hand against her chest and took a deep breath. She missed the veil far more than the Arc. She worried about Wolves and wondered if Kahtar had thrown him out of the house. Most of all, she missed Kahtar every second of the day and night, because she hadn't seen or spoken to him in four months.

Beth pressed her hand against her chest again. Even if she'd wanted to she couldn't apologize for what had happened. She couldn't lie, and that included insincere apologies. Not for the first time she mentally cursed her gifting of truth. If she had one lie in her, she'd gladly give it to Kahtar.

Beth opened her laptop, distracting her heart with the boring repetition of inventory.

DEEP INTO COLUMNS of numbers while attempting to track a shipment that had gone astray somewhere between Ohio and Bombay, Beth nearly jumped out of her skin when a young woman suddenly plopped down onto the hardwood floor beside her. The laptop slid neatly from Beth's lap toward her daughter. Both Beth and her uninvited guest reached for it to prevent Dianta from being beaned. They managed to grab it, but the near miss broke Dianta's concentration and she rolled feet over head before Beth caught her. A furious Dianta spat the wad of cheesecloth out of her mouth and bawled.

Plopping her baby onto her knees, Beth studied her intruder, wondering why the bell on the door hadn't jingled an entrance. The brunette looked familiar, and after several moments of fruitless jiggling attempts to calm Dianta, Beth realized why. This was the woman she'd seen kissing both Honor Monroe and Welcome Palmer that day back in June.

"Sorry," the woman said over Dianta's angry shouts, but she didn't look the least bit apologetic, though her words didn't have the ring of a lie to them. She looked young, with creamy skin and dimples. Beth wondered if she was more girl than woman, then remembered how she'd kissed Honor and Welcome. *Definitely a woman.* The deceptively sweet face tilted at an innocent angle as curious blue eyes examined Beth with equal interest. "I'm Delphine Green. I'm the clan storyteller."

Beth narrowed her eyes. She'd never heard the name or known the clan had a storyteller. "That sounds interesting. I'm Beth Constantine," she half-shouted.

"Do you want to see what I can do?" Delphine yelled back.

"Not if you're going to kiss me," Beth bellowed.

Delphine arched her brows over a pair of very blue eyes, as though surprised Beth had recognized her. She turned her attention to the baby. "Dianta." Delphine's voice sounded sing-songy. "Listen, baby girl, looky puppies, looky!"

Right there on the floor, crawling around Beth's lap, puppies appeared as if by magic. Beth blinked in astonishment. Half a dozen fat little golden retriever puppies waddled around her, yipping, scratching at the floor and rolling onto their backs as though trying to get Dianta's attention. Dianta's screeching morphed into squeals of approval, and she leaned off Beth's lap, grabbed one by the ear and yanked. Beth tried to rescue the creature, but her hand passed right through it and she jerked away shocked. Dianta somehow held firmly to the puppy ear, pulling as she tried to get it into her mouth.

"She can touch the puppy," Delphine explained. "You can't, but she can even smell them. They have that clean, sweet puppy scent."

"She's hurting it," Beth said, again reaching for it only to be disconcerted once more by the lack of substance. The ear in Dianta's hand looked as real as Dianta's fingers.

"The puppy is fine. This is just a story I'm showing Dianta. Some would say that it's not real, but some don't understand story. My story isn't solid to you because fiction doesn't work on you. You can tell when things aren't true, so you can see through it because of your gifting. That's a little sad. Before you joined the clan, did you like to watch movies?"

Beth looked into the young woman's eyes. "I liked documentaries mostly."

"Maybe if I told you a true story you'd be able to touch it."

Beth gazed at the puppies as they crawled over her legs. She couldn't feel them, but she could see their paws and nails making slight indentations across her jeans as they moved. A creepy, uncomfortable sensation crawled up her back and she looked away from the odd phenomenon. "But you were really kissing Honor and Welcome when I saw you. That wasn't just a story."

Delphine waved a hand dismissively. "I'd like you to forget about that."

Beth shivered. The words seemed to push against her like a lie, but that didn't make any sense.

Delphine's red lips pulled into a childish pout and she crossed her legs akimbo so that every inch of her patterned leggings were visible beneath a short red dress. Blue eyes fringed with black lashes locked onto Beth's. "Forget. About. The. Kissing," she demanded.

Beth tried not to roll her eyes. "You know the entire clan thinks I'm weird because my father is a seeker, and here you are with your holo-grammy puppies acting like you're trying to wipe my memory or something."

Widening her eyes in surprise, Delphine laughed, a loud ringing sound that Dianta mimicked in spite of a mouthful of puppy ear, which the dog seemed to be enjoying. "Well, at least I don't have seeker cooties," said the little brunette with a sniff.

"Is that supposed to be funny?"

Delphine shrugged, bouncing waves of dark hair on her shoulders. "Only because I have real—not holographic—seeker cootie protection." Displaying crossed fingers Delphine waved them as though performing some mystical incantation, her eyes shining with amusement. Beth wanted to say it wasn't funny, but it was. She grinned despite herself.

Delphine learned forward, her hands on her knees as she asked, "Does Kahtar come here a lot?"

The answer slid out as they always did. "No, not anymore."

"How old are you, Beth?"

"Twenty-six next month."

"How tall are you?"

"Five eleven and three quarters."

"Lucky! You're very beautiful in a fashion model way. Do you ever eat?"

"Of course I eat!"

"Have you ever eaten at Cerulean Blue next door?"

"No."

"Why not?"

"They wouldn't let me in."

"What! Why not?" Delphine sounded shocked.

"They said I didn't have on Covenant Keeper clothes."

"Wow! Did you tell Kahtar?"

"No."

"Why not?"

"I fight my own battles. Besides, Kahtar isn't speaking to me. Apparently he's shunning me along with all of the Warriors of ilu."

"Is the clan always rude to you?"

"Mostly. You could say I'm not very popular in the Covenant Keeper world." Beth frowned at her.

"Are you popular in the outside world?"

"No."

"Why not?" Delphine's dark brows drew together.

Annoyed at the barrage of rude questions, Beth spat the answer. "Pretty much the same reason in both worlds. Nobody wants to hear the truth."

"Yeah, I heard you have a problem with that. I'm surprised Kahtar lets you live here by yourself, though." Delphine sounded envious. "Why does he? Don't you have some kind of protection? They never let clan women in town alone—like every seeker is going to go ga-ga over the touch of our hearts. Which is so not true."

"We're separated and I have to live somewhere they can keep an eye on me. The cops drive by about every fifteen or twenty minutes. And I think that restaurant next door is always open, and Old Guard are always there. I think they keep an eye out or something, because I see them shimmering sometimes. Now would you please stop interrogating me? It's rude." No one from the clan had ever used her gifting of truth against her before.

"I'm sorry. I need to ask you a big favor, and I'm trying to figure out the best way to do it."

"Not like this," said Beth. "You could try just asking me. Do you manipulate everybody?"

"Yes," Delphine answered, and Beth knew it was the truth.

"It must be exhausting."

"It is, but I have a lot of energy."

"Are you finished with the nosey questions now?"

Grinning, Delphine said, "For now."

"You're not going to ask why I'm separated from Kahtar?"

The grin vanished. "Of course not, but I know why. Everybody knows why."

Beth's heart sank, and anger bobbed to the surface. "So, are you going to try to talk me into apologizing for being hit? Or is the clan secretly delighted Kahtar and I are apart? Surely they're glad they don't have to pretend to like me during Glory every Sunday?"

"Um," said Delphine, "you do realize that I don't have to tell the truth, right?"

Beth's anger vanished and she smiled. "Yes, but it would be fair."

Shifting on the floor, Delphine wrapped an arm around one knee and scratched a puppy with the other. "Well, since you were so accommodating—even though you really had no choice—I'll answer you. It's tough enough keeping to the laws of being. We don't tend to harp on each other about following them, but you really should apologize since you were unspeakably wrong. The clan's pretty much openly delighted you're not around. It justifies their prejudices against seekers—another reason you should apologize.

"And during Glory they actually feel terribly guilty because they see how miserable Kahtar is without you. If you'd seen him lately you probably would apologize because the man is in serious pain." She frowned at Beth and commanded, "Apologize to Kahtar!"

Beth shivered as the words seemed to fall around her like boulders. "Obviously it doesn't work on me! Geez! Stop it!" She glared at Delphine, wondering if the power of her gifting had caused a mental problem.

"Just checking. It would come in really handy for the favor I need."

She's nuts. "So you use your gifting to conjure puppies and kiss guys. I understand the puppies, but—"

"Really? You don't get the kissing? Have you *seen* Honor and Welcome?" Delphine's eyes gleamed with humor.

"Okay, yes, I have. I'll give you that too. So your gifting can make people see stuff that isn't there, *and* make people kiss you?"

Delphine shifted into a kneeling position. "Look, the kissing is no big deal. There is nothing dishonorable about it. You should see what goes on behind the stalactites after Glory on Sundays!"

"I'm willing to bet most people remember what they do behind those stalactites, unlike your victims. How many guys do you go through on an average Sunday?"

"Are you judging me? I'll bet Kahtar is not the only guy you've ever kissed!"

"That's not the point. You're like kiss-raping guys and using your gifting to roofie them."

Delphine looked angry. "I've spent enough time with seekers to know what a roofie is."

"Good. I wasn't trying to be cryptic!"

Flushing, Delphine turned her blue eyes away. "Look, I'm not going to talk to you about *who* I've kissed."

The way she said *who* made Beth flush with intuition. "Have you kissed Kahtar like that?"

Delphine shrugged, suddenly studying Dianta's Wonder Woman diaper bag sitting on the countertop above them as though fascinated with it.

"You'd better answer me or I'm—telling someone!" Beth threatened.

Delphine's face turned as scarlet as her dress and her eyes flashed like blue lightning as they returned to Beth's. "Have you ever poked a snake? Kissing Kahtar is like that—dangerous. The first time I did it I was just a kid goofing around to see if I could make him do it. By the time I was fourteen I thought Kahtar might kiss me back someday, of his own free will. I've been gone a very long time—eight years—and I came back to find that's never going to happen, because he joined with a seeker chick. But now I figure, what with this separation, you're not using him, so someone ought to! I like the way he tastes."

Scalding jealousy torched Beth's heart before she realized Delphine's words rang with the falseness of a blatant lie, and her hand snaked out. She slapped Delphine so hard the sound echoed across the room, and the puppies scattered, yelping.

The blow knocked the smaller woman to her side, where she clutched her face. Dianta's face crumpled as the puppies ran toward the corners of the room and vanished. Beth's hostility quickly faded, although not quite to forgiveness. *What is wrong with me?* She hadn't ever gotten into fist fights as a kid.

Long, dark waves of hair hid Delphine's face, but she wiped at her mouth and blood smeared her hand. Beth's stomach dropped. What was the punishment for drawing blood against another member of her clan? Even a lying one! She shifted Dianta, who was now sobbing over the vanished puppies. Beth moved to Delphine's side, nabbed a clean square of cheesecloth off the counter above her and offered it guiltily to the brunette.

Delphine accepted it and sat neatly onto her backside, dabbing her bloody mouth and eyeing Beth speculatively. "This solves the problem of how to ask you for that favor. I'm sorry to say I'm not above extortion."

She picked a fight on purpose! Dumbfounded, Beth glared at her. All the questions had been a manipulator looking for a chink in her armor. Delphine couldn't use her devious gifting against her, so she had gone with blackmail.

Beth fought the urge to hit her again.

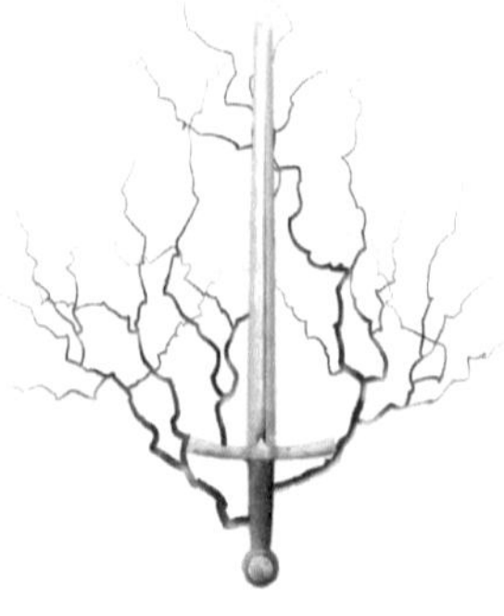

CHAPTER
NINE

Blood Lust—Harvest Moon

BY TWO O'CLOCK in the afternoon the temperature had dropped twenty-five degrees since midday. A cold wind had kicked up, ripping autumn leaves off the trees, and lake effect snow joined the unseasonably cold weather. Kahtar hurried up the porch steps to his cabin and found a shaking Wolves leaning against the wall. Pity stirred his heart and he crouched beside the mangy-looking dog. Wolves looked worse than usual, with nasty bite marks and bald patches of fur.

"What happened, buddy? Did the barn cats get you?" Gently Kahtar ran his fingers over him, parting fur, but didn't spot a single flea. Standing, he held the screen door open for the animal.

"Come on," he said, but Wolves remained still, pathetically shifting his eyeballs upward without moving his head, as though not daring to hope. "Save the theatrics. I know you've been sneaking inside every night." He held the door open wider and Wolves darted in.

The wind blew inside through the open windows, and Kahtar stomped to the kitchen to shut them, cursing the plebes beneath his breath. A mess greeted him. Of the forty-seven quarts of tomatoes the boys had canned that day, twenty-nine of them lay broken across the countertop and floor, mixed with the remains of his dinner. It looked like the boys had thrown the jars. Stewed tomatoes decorated the walls, cupboards, and an impressive amount of the floorboards, and broken glass lay everywhere.

"What were they doing? Go, Wolves!" Kahtar shouted as the dog opened his mouth to taste the mess on the floor. Wolves bolted back into the great room.

Glass crunched beneath Kahtar's size seventeen black military boots as he shut windows. "Old Guard!" he bellowed. The shout must have sounded worse than the usual summons because three of the men appeared. Kahtar turned to the shimmering men with their merciless, pupil-less black eyes. "I want every plebe that was involved in this—and I do not care what happened here—to be brought back here so they can see this mess. I want them to clean it and I want each and every one of them caned." Two of the men shimmered brightly and vanished. Kahtar turned his attention to the last one, not quite meeting his eyes. "And I'd like a livestock farmer to come check my dog." He almost expected the man to continue shimmering in place and ignore the request, but after a long, uncomfortable moment, the man vanished. Kahtar exited the kitchen and shut the door behind him.

Wolves sat obediently by the front door, staring hopefully at Kahtar's hands like he did when dinnertime was late. Kahtar held his empty hands out in explanation, and Wolves flattened his ears in disappointed understanding.

"I'll bring you leftovers," Kahtar promised, and the ears went up with interest. A few years ago he'd brought home a container of leftovers from Cerulean Blue and thoughtlessly left it sitting on the front porch while he ran to the bathhouse around back. Wolves had eaten every bite of a beefsteak, mashed potatoes, and the paper container that held it. The dog watched hopefully as Kahtar headed for the front door and risked an impatient whine as he opened it.

"I won't forget," Kahtar assured him as he walked out.

"NO." STANDING IN the entryway with Dianta in her arms, Beth changed her mind. "Just turn me in for hitting you. Tell The Mother or the Old Guard or whoever. I'm not going to do this."

Pretty and petite Delphine waited beside her, somehow making sparkly butterflies flutter around Dianta, who watched through sleepy eyes with her head on Beth's shoulder. "Look, I need a distraction," Delphine said, "It's a matter of life and death! This will take you one minute, maybe two."

They were truthful words, but Beth demanded more information. "Whose life and death?"

Delphine half-breathed a humorless laugh. "Several people, but it includes yours and Kahtar's eventually. Believe me, this is crucial. Besides, you do not want me to tell on you." A bruise horribly shaped like a handprint already told plenty, and Delphine's split bottom lip had swollen into a permanent pout.

Beth shook her head; Kahtar would never forgive her for this. He might honestly rather they died. "Couldn't we just set the porch on fire? There's gasoline in the shed out back."

"That we could get in trouble for, besides the Old Guard wouldn't even flinch if you set the entire block on fire. There are four of them inside Cerulean Blue right now. If you do this my way, one will go straight to The Mother and another will come out to make sure Dianta's not hurt. Bet he'll take her to Cobbson just to be sure. If you refuse to go inside, it will take the other two of them to move you and that will give me plenty of time to do what I have to do. Please, Beth. I need your help."

Blowing out a breath Beth glanced through the window of the front door. It was snowing outside, hard for October. She wondered idly how Delphine could know how many Old Guard were inside the abstract next door, but knew the woman was telling the truth. She didn't dare ask how many other people were inside, but suspected Delphine knew that, too. "How much trouble will I get into for this?"

"That's the beauty of it," Delphine enthused. She talked with her hands. "Technically, none. There are no rules or laws against it!"

"Kahtar will bust something," Beth muttered, "and the clan will hate me even more."

"You're wrong there. First off, the clan doesn't hate you at all; they're afraid of you, but this won't make any difference one way or another," said Delphine.

"Okay, fine," said Beth, tugging Dianta's little hat securely to keep her now snoozing daughter warm. "I'll do this—but not because you're blackmailing me. I'm doing it for my own reasons—"

"They'll have to quit ignoring you now, eh? Shun this! You should have thought of it yourself. It's a beautiful plan for both of us."

Beth shot her an acerbic look. "You're not very likeable."

"I know, right?" Delphine agreed. "We have so much in common. I think you and I are going to be great friends."

"Oh, great," groaned Beth, opening the front door. She thought so too, and she didn't like the idea, or the way Delphine treated her friends.

CROSSING THE PORCH, Beth held the bundled Dianta tightly and hurried down the steps to the sidewalk.

Shoot it is cold! Bet the roads are going to freeze.

Beth's new pink Timberland boots—size eleven thanks to pregnancy—left a pattern in the light snow. "I guess I'll never get to eat inside Cerulean Blue now," Beth said to Dianta, wondering how often the Old Guard checked on her. She couldn't feel the warmth of a scan, and saw no shimmer of Old Guard in the falling snow. Beth adjusted her hat with mittened hands, her booted feet moving across the limestone sidewalk toward the walkway and the house next door.

To her absolute horror a police car turned onto Pearl Street. Beth moved faster. *Oh my, no! Did Delphine know this was going to happen? Did she orchestrate it? Surely not!*

It crossed to the wrong side of the road, approaching her, and slowed as she moved up the sidewalk.

No! Please, God! Not Kahtar!

An automatic window whirred down as it approached.

"Excuse me, Miss. May I ask what you're doing?"

Relief went through her. It wasn't Kahtar. Forcing herself to look, it hardly surprised her that the cop wasn't clan. One of the warriors would probably have continued to shun her as he drove by. This man was a seeker and she'd never seen him before. Dark, almond-shaped eyes swept her up and down with keen interest.

"You're Beth Costas, aren't you? The Chief's ex-wife?"

"We're not divorced," she said, shifting Dianta onto her far shoulder, and continuing on her way. The car shifted into reverse and followed slowly. Beth knew he was staring, and she might have blushed if she weren't freezing to death.

"Are you planning to walk onto Main Street like that? Because I'll have to arrest you if you are. How about you turn around and get back to your house, and we'll pretend this never happened."

"I'm just going next door. It's almost time for my husband to get our daughter. I'm delivering her." Technically the words were all true.

The cop considered this for a moment. "The things we do in a custody battle. I'm divorced too, so I get it, but this is going a little far—especially in this weather."

"I'm not divorced or in a custody battle!"

With raised brows the cop looked her up and down again. "If you say so, Mrs. Costas. I'm going to give you two minutes to get inside a house or I'm afraid I'm going to have to put you in the car. Neither one of us want that."

Beth stopped moving to glare at the man and he braked.

The Old Guard wouldn't come outside with him there. Delphine's plan would be for nothing. Not that Beth wanted to help her after the way she'd acted, but Delphine had said it was a matter of life and death and Beth had heard the truth in those words. She glanced toward the quiet house that hid Cerulean Blue. It housed an abstract and the food she'd always wanted to try, but it looked like any other well-kept house in the village. Nothing about its appearance would draw attention from a seeker, except the naked pregnant woman standing in front of it.

Kahtar will kill me.

Turning without shame, she faced the cop full-on.

He has got to leave. If I don't freeze to death first I might have to kill Delphine for this.

"How about you and I make a deal? I'm sure I have something you'd be interested in." Unable to even fake a smile she didn't mean, Beth forced her lips apart and revealed her teeth in a gesture she hoped wasn't too feral.

The cop's eyebrows rose in disbelief and his eyes flickered to her pregnant belly. He slid the gear into park. "Ma'am, I'm afraid you're going to have to come with me."

"No!" Beth implored, leaning toward the window. "I meant toothpaste that will whiten your teeth and not leave them sensitive, or deodorant you only need to use once a week! I didn't mean anything weird!"

The officer shook his head and unbuckled his seatbelt. "So you only meant a retail bribe?"

"No! This is coming across all wrong! It's just that you're wrecking my plans! You know my husband, right? Chief Costas? Kent?" Beth forced the alias out of her mouth, talking quickly. "We've been having some problems. And I'm just trying to get his—attention, you know? He can't ignore this, can he?" Straightening, Beth motioned with her free hand at her nudity. "He used to love when I didn't wear clothes. Sometimes we'd go the whole weekend without wearing any. Well, we did before we started having problems!"

I'm talking really loud and saying way too much to a total stranger.
Even if it was all true.

Clutching Dianta to her chest, Beth added, "If you could just drive on by just this once, you'd be a life-saver. Let this be between Kah—um, my husband and me. Please?"

For what seemed forever the cop stared into her eyes. It reminded Beth of the way she looked for truth. Shaking his head, he put the car into gear, motioning at her with his left hand. "Look, if I ever see anything like this again, I'm going to arrest you and report your husband, too. Just get inside before you freeze."

Thank heavens, because she could barely feel her legs as she moved woodenly toward the little house. Her woolen hat, scarf, mittens, and socks, coupled with warm boots, did nothing with the rest of her completely bare.

As soon as the police car turned the corner an Old Guard took full form. Beth handed over her sleeping baby and watched the man vanish, as Delphine had predicted. Beth reached the front door of Cerulean Blue, which had been flung wide open, and stood shivering until two more Old Guard appeared. She wondered if the rest of Delphine's plot was going according to plan, and if she'd save lives. For a split second she wondered if she should have asked more about Delphine's plan and motives, but something told her that she didn't really want to know.

The last of the Old Guard shimmered as they moved her and her unborn baby. The transportation felt instantaneous and she wondered how Delphine could possibly do anything in that nanosecond, especially when Beth reappeared right inside the entrance to Cerulean Blue. *Was that enough time? It doesn't seem like it could be!*

Her concerns vanished at the sight of Kahtar standing in the entryway awaiting her, his steely eyes wide with disbelief. At that moment Beth knew that the only life she should worry about was hers.

SOME SMALL PART of Kahtar's brain managed to function as usual as he slid out of his police jacket and draped it over Beth's nakedness. Gripping a handful of the fabric, he hauled her across the glass floor of the abstract where a cerulean blue sky encircled the room overhead, around, and beneath them. Wispy clouds drifted from both above and below. His heart hammered in his chest so hard Kahtar could see his pulse flickering in his eyes.

Sitting inside the abstract, with a clear view of Pearl Street and Beth's shop, the bustling eatery had gone completely silent as Beth traipsed out her front door wearing nothing but a pair of pink boots, mittens, scarf, and a fuzzy hat. Yet watching his long-legged wife strolling naked along the sidewalk, clutching a bundled Dianta, and chatting about divorce and his penchant for nudity to a seeker hadn't been what nearly took him to his knees.

The swell of her belly announced a second pregnancy.

The fact that it was impossible had turned Kahtar's world upside down and shook it a few times.

Unable to issue a single order, he'd watched the madness unfold along with everyone else inside the eatery.

It took all the concentration he had to move and vertigo caused him to stagger into a table. Beth took his elbow with an icy mitten, steadying him surreptitiously, surely wondering if he could keep it together. Unable to bear her touch, he pushed her into a chair and took a seat safely across the table from her, trying to focus.

Snowflakes melted in Beth's hair as she stared at the table, avoiding his eyes. People were ogling her, but Beth didn't seem to notice as she shivered, her arms wrapped over the pregnant bulge beneath the coat. Kahtar's mind shifted backward, trying to make sense of it. They'd both permanently destroyed any chance of conception. *Another immortal child* reverberated in his brain as though it were bouncing off canyon walls. *How is this possible?* Covenant Keepers reproduced the exact same way all mammals did. *Except me.* The warrior part of Kahtar's brain noticed everyone in Cerulean Blue gawking, and he forced his attention onto what he could control at that moment.

Motioning to a blonde he said, "Bring her something hot."

The woman looked startled by the request, and exchanged looks with several other servers, all recognizable in bright yellow.

"Quickly, she's—" unable to say pregnant, Kahtar managed, "too cold."

The woman moved slowly toward the kitchen. Kahtar sat still for another long moment, the words *another immortal child* bouncing through his brain.

Within moments the server returned and slid a mug of something piping hot toward him, not Beth. "You're refusing to serve my wife?" he said, stunned. "The shunning is only for warriors."

"It's my right to participate," she said, not looking at him. After an uncomfortable silence she added, "I brought it for the sake of the unborn babe, and have no objection if *she* wishes to take it from you."

Abigail's words from that morning returned to Kahtar. *"The clan is turning on Beth. We all see how miserable you are, and they blame her."* Glaring, he fumed at the woman, "My wife is clan and in need of warmth as much as my unborn baby! Old Guard!"

The appearance of three of the large men caused a commotion in the room as people tried to get out of the way. "Take Beth…" Kahtar paused, wondering where his wife belonged. Where could they take her? "Take her to Cobbson, to her apartment there. Make sure she sees Welcome Palmer first." He had no idea if the rooms were even available.

Two of the big men hauled Beth from her seat, and though Kahtar had been avoiding her gaze he saw the fear in her eyes. Sorrow lit through him, and then she was gone.

THANKS TO WELCOME Palmer, Beth was able to feel her limbs again as she pushed open the door to her old apartment in Cobbson Compound. *They're not going to let me go back to Sweet Earth. Ever.* It hadn't occurred to her when she made her deal with Delphine what the repercussions might be. Delphine had said there was no crime against the diversion, but that didn't mean there weren't consequences.

The door shut behind her with a silent whir Beth more felt than heard. She shoved a chair in front of it. The only person she wanted to see was Dianta, and Welcome had denied her that until morning.

If then. Apparently the Elders were discussing it.

Rubbing her arms still clad in Kahtar's police jacket, she shivered. Welcome Palmer had said she suffered only windburn and stress and needed a hot drink and quiet. *Like I haven't had enough quiet.* A humorless chuckle escaped. She crossed to the sink, filled a kettle, and heated it on the ice-blue square that made water boil instantly. Quickly dumping loose tea and hot water into a cup, she lifted the barely seeped beverage to her lips and blew.

"Was that really the best way you could think of for me to find out?"

Beth knocked the teacup against a front tooth and scorched her tongue. The liquid sloshed onto her boots as she spun to look at Kahtar. At nearly seven feet tall, the man was formidable on a good day. *How did he get in here? Oh, man, he's furious!* She pressed her tongue against the tooth to make sure it was still there, and pressed her heart toward his so he'd know that, despite everything, she was glad he'd come, glad to be with him after four months without the touch of his heart.

Kahtar's heart was non-receptive and on lockdown, but the touch of it still filled the room the same way the smells of good cooking drifted from Cerulean Blue to Sweet Earth—tantalizingly close, but nothing Beth could have.

"Hi," she said, but moved so the curvy kitchen island stood between them. The look in his eyes demanded the precaution. Still wearing his police uniform, he stood watching her with no readable expression on his face. She'd forgotten how imposing he could be, but recognized signs of tiredness behind the mask. He probably wasn't sleeping well either. Her heart skipped. "You didn't return my messages, Kahtar. You ignored me even when I sat in the police station waiting for you. The tesseract from Sweet Earth to the cabin disappeared. You wouldn't talk to me."

"You could have simply sent a message," he said, his eyes focused on a spot somewhere above her head. Tears burned behind Beth's eyes. This is what shunning was, and it was the meanest thing she could imagine.

"That's what I was trying to do in person. This seemed big enough to warrant a face to face conversation with my husband." She put a hand on the buttoned up jacket he'd loaned her, resting it against her belly. The plan to walk from Sweet Earth to Cerulean Blue in nothing but boots and accessories hadn't been to announce her pregnancy—that had simply been a passive aggressive bonus. Of course her deal with Delphine kept her from expounding upon that.

"You realize the entire clan now thinks you're a lunatic?" The question was directed at her even if his eyes weren't.

"What do you think?" Voice hoarse, Beth drank in his presence, the dusting of beard across his face, the blond hair on the back of fisted hands, every inch of him in his ugly polyester police uniform. She'd missed it all. She pushed her heart toward him, and he cruelly repelled her touch like water on wax.

"I think there are reasons for the rules in this clan, and that is the only reason why I'm here," said Kahtar, his voice pitched low and cold, all warrior chief, nothing in him the husband she missed. "We don't draw attention." He held up one big finger. "A seeker saw you." A second finger popped up. "Young people don't flaunt nudity in front of the opposite sex." A third finger rose. "You endangered the health of a baby, and I'm not talking about Dianta! It's twenty degrees out there, plus wind chill! Maybe since it's my child you think it can't die? I assure you it can and it will, many times—and it will feel each one." For the briefest moment he paused, and the pain of that perceived reality did transfer from his heart to Beth's.

A fourth finger shot up and Kahtar closed his heart against hers so firmly she felt nothing from it. "You refused to go inside when the Old Guard told you to. After what happened in the Arc, you are digging your own grave by disobeying an Old Guard. *It is not done!*" The thumb. "Old Guard had to move you. Likely they would have allowed you to freeze to death if not for our children, who apparently couldn't count on their mother's good sense to protect them! With Dianta and the unborn child it required three Old Guard to move you all. That means that part of the perimeter of the Arc went completely unguarded while you wasted their time.

"You disrespected Old Guard today by refusing to obey them, and they have every right to punish you for it. Have you forgotten what it was like to be put on trial by them? Because you chose to ignore them, they will now do the same to you. They've joined in the shunning." For a moment Kahtar met her eyes, and while anger still burned in them, so did fear.

Kahtar held up his five fingers for a moment, then brought up his second hand and another finger. "Covenant Keepers do not get divorced, despite rumors you've ignited in the form of your naked encounter with Sergeant Chen. Your little scene, in addition to setting tongues wagging at warp speed in two worlds, has given naysayers within the clan fuel against Welcome Palmer.

"Your actions have consequences for other people too." A seventh finger went up. "Palmer's recommendation that you could be trusted on your own stood between you and the more conservative of the Elders. You've damaged his reputation by showing that his good faith in you was misplaced, and nothing he or I say can sway them now!" Two more fingers popped up, but Beth had stopped counting. "You've exposed the clan to the attention of seekers, and you did all this damage, Beth, unleashed this madness in a childish attempt to gain my attention!" The last accusation was hurled at her with full eye contact, and his heart might as well have been a seeker for all she felt from it.

Beth slammed her cup onto the countertop, anger shooting through her so hot it seemed to sizzle in her ears. "Don't flatter yourself! I didn't do it for your attention! And since I don't want it, feel free to take it elsewhere. I don't need the protection of Old Guard, warriors, or you! I can take care of myself! I've done it all my life! Don't feel obligated to protect me from the Elders' great decree either! What are they going to do, take my daughter and tell me when I can see her?" Beth made an invisible check mark in the air. "Done! Or not allow me to run my shop?" She made a second check. "Ditto, and it's a place I've spent almost my entire life planning and working for! Or how about this? How about they let my husband hit me and tell me it's my fault?"

Kahtar flinched as though she'd backhanded him. Beth wished she could take the last words back, and dropped her hands onto the countertop instead of making the check a third time.

"No, Beth." Kahtar appeared to shrink in size, his anger vanishing. "They are going to shut off all your contact with the outside world, including your parents."

It was a good thing Beth had both hands on the counter to steady herself. Angry tears filled her eyes. They couldn't do this to her. "I'll still see them! I'll find a way. Are they trying to make me run? Because I could! My mother would help me disappear—" The bravado was useless because she started to cry mid-threat.

Kahtar's eyes looked ancient in their sadness. "I know." He took a deep breath as one tear slid from the corner of his eye and moved south along his jaw. "I know you can, and no one will even try to stop you now, not until your list of crimes includes breaking a Law of Being. And then…" Kahtar's voice trailed off, and he wiped his eyes. "It was a mistake bringing you into the clan. But I can't regret it, Beth. No matter what happens now, I will never regret you."

For a moment they stared at each other. Kahtar put a hand on the counter, moving it close to hers. He tapped the countertop and turned away. "Goodbye, Beth," he said, without looking at her.

"Kahtar, wait!" Beth followed him. "Is that everything you came here to say? To tell me my latest crimes against the clan and leave? We need to talk! What about us? What about this baby?" Beth rubbed her hand over the rise beneath the big jacket.

At the door Kahtar turned to her. "There is nothing to say. That baby—and Dianta—are mistakes I do regret."

"Kahtar! You don't mean that!" But Beth knew he did; the words flowed through her as absolute truth.

He reached for the door handle as Beth shouted, "Don't go, please. This has gone on long enough and too far! I'm sorry. I'm sorry for what happened in the Arc. I truly am. I'm sorry I made you push me. Come back to me, please. This doesn't have to end badly, Kahtar."

Turning toward her again with a half-smile on his lips, he said, "Why, Beth. I do believe you just told your first lie." He pulled the chair out from under the door handle and left.

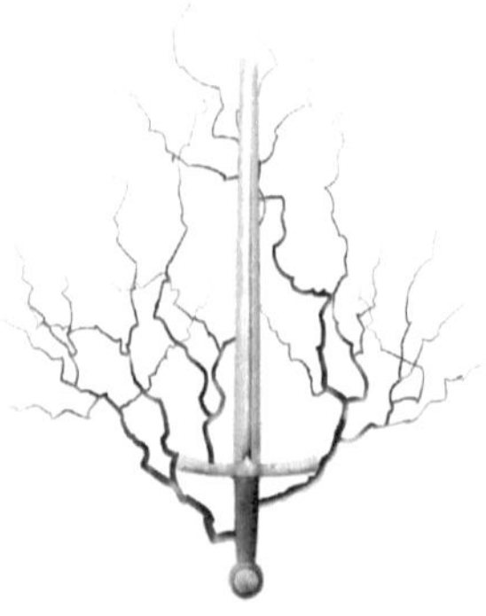

CHAPTER
TEN

Bloody Complications—Samhain

INSIDE THE ARC no snow had fallen yet. Colorful leaves rained from autumn trees like red and gold glitter. At the edge of Cultuelle Khristos' settlement, a group of small children raked leaves into heaps and bigger kids rode hover boards through them, scattering the piles.

Kahtar scanned for danger as he walked. There was really nothing dangerous inside the Arc. Old Guard watched it to protect those exiting. Inside it was the same as a veil, impossible to enter uninvited. The only dangers were accidents or animal attacks, but the latter were few. The pack of wolves spotted near Dianta that summer hadn't been seen again. The Arc was clean, and safe, and Kahtar knew he should want Dianta to grow up there, and wondered why the idea didn't appeal to him.

The Mother's large house stood next to an old-fashioned thatched cottage, rising three stories high with a tiny tower at one end and a large glass domed library that looked like an observatory in the middle. The dwelling reminded Kahtar of a wedding cake.

Entering through a small mud room, Kahtar jogged up three steps to the kitchen, where the smell of roast chicken beckoned. Despite his reluctance in coming, Kahtar's stomach growled at the promise of good food. He'd lost weight and muscle mass since the fiasco with Beth in the Arc, and like his heart, his body craved sustenance. At least here he could satisfy his body.

A small Spanish woman stood at the stove top stirring spinach into a soup with a wooden fork. She glanced in his direction before turning away without meeting his eyes. "There you are. I'm making my meatball soup for you." Even in childhood she'd never once called him by name.

"Thank you, Memma Rosa." His voice sounded hoarse.

The Mother glided into the room with a young clanswoman. Like Rosa, the young woman avoided greeting him with the customary kiss, opting for rearranging hot pies on the countertop and burning her hand. The Mother kissed him while Kahtar wondered why she tortured her company with his presence. The massive kitchen table was set for ten, and Kahtar scanned the rooms to see who else he'd need to endure in exchange for a good meal. All the elders were there, including his grandfather, Nehemiah Constantine.

This will be about Beth, then. A set up. They forced their spouses to come so they could pretend to themselves that it isn't official.

"Your scanning will spoil my appetite." Nehemiah entered the kitchen, graying and fit. "Where's my granddaughter?" Nehemiah hurried across the expanse of hardwood as though expecting Kahtar to turn out his pockets and produce Dianta.

"With her mother."

Nehemiah shot The Mother a reproachful look. "I still say babies should be living in the Arc. Dianta can stay with me until you sort your wife out. I told The Mother I can add rooms onto my house before winter."

Kahtar frowned. "Babies belong with their mother."

Nehemiah flinched. "There's no quick fix for your problems and we don't want your children growing up in that world learning El knows what. Think about it." Nehemiah sidled away to nip crusts off a pie, leaving Kahtar dumbfounded.

They want me to take the children off of Beth!

Not because she'd broken any laws. The clans' dislike of Beth had never been so blatant. Kahtar saw Abigail watching him from across the room, and he turned away, heading for the table.

Despite anger growing in Kahtar's heart, the meal tasted delicious. Cooking was Rosa's gifting, and a delight to the senses, somehow soothing and nourishing too. Seated at the foot of the table opposite The Mother, Kahtar thought only of Beth.

She didn't belong and the clan let her know it, but she never said a word against them. What they don't know is that neither do I belong— with the possible exception of Memma Rosa. She knows.

Kahtar shoveled food into his mouth as the conversation moved from the Samhain celebration at the cave that morning, to offering a priestly position to The Mother's daughter in hopes that she'd return to the Arc now that Delphine Green had returned, and whether or not bubble tea would taste good when made with brack tea.

Some twisted part of Kahtar, a relation to that part that always went first into battle, or refused to talk under torture, brought up the landmine topic, interrupting Silas Jacobson's pontificating about the dangers of a female priest and Nehemiah's soliloquy on what exactly brack tea smelled like. "—like earth in a feminine way, or have you ever been to the Fortunate Isles? There's a still pool there, above the waterfall by the—"

"I promised Honor I'd pull a few hours at the station for him tonight, so if there's something you wanted to say to me, we best get to it."

All conversation stopped as they waited for The Mother to weigh in. She finished chewing a mouthful of chicken, and her eyes went quickly from one Elder to another before she responded. "If you needed to relinquish your role as chief of police, who would you recommend for the position?"

This he hadn't expected, and as his mind flittered over his choices frustration won out. "Maybe I've just gotten too used to Beth's candor, but how about you tell me why you'd want to replace me as police chief? What are you really asking?"

Elderly quester Orange Stoddard exchanged stunned glances with Father Wixen while The Mother glared. "I've asked you exactly what I really needed to know, and I'd thank you to be polite. This is not a game of intrigue, Kahtar Constantine. This is something I've considered since I found out Beth's father was a seeker last year. Your closeness to the world of seekers could compromise your mission there, especially now that we've cut off communication between Beth and her parents. If they come looking for her it's best if you're not involved at all."

Putting his elbows on the table, Kahtar leaned toward The Mother. "If Beth's parents were to come looking for her and I'd vanished like Beth and Dianta, the publicity could be irrecoverable."

Every head in the room swiveled toward The Mother.

"You make it sound like the safety of this entire clan could be compromised by Beth's parents."

"The safety of this entire clan could be compromised by any seeker in the village of Willowyth, especially if we took away their families, forcing them to examine us! We say we participate in the world of seekers to help them, but unless we seclude ourselves and retreat to the Arc there is always risk. You know that, we all do."

"I am referring to immediate threat."

"Permanently keeping Beth from her parents makes Ted and Carole White the highest exposure threat to the clan."

Abigail Adit's second voice sounded inside Kahtar's head. *"Are you actually trying to get sent into the mists, accompanied by Beth and her parents?"*

Kahtar held The Mother's gaze. "There's no point in replacing me as chief of police at this time. Right now Beth's parents think she's on a buying trip to Mongolia for brack tea, with Dianta. There is no risk."

"Thank you, Kahtar. I'm perfectly aware of that. My concern is for when they stop believing that."

"I don't foresee that as being an issue. The problem is going to resolve itself."

"Oh? Please enlighten me. What has changed?"

"Beth apologized to me over a week ago. I expect Honor's apology will follow. The shunning will end. In time there's no reason she couldn't resume some sort of relationship with her parents, even if it's just a ruse for the sake of security."

"Well played, you bastard." Abigail's second voice sounded amused. *"But try to remember that I'm an old woman. If you ever scare me like that again, I'll escort you into the mists myself."*

Nehemiah fingered his beard. "Do you think she meant it? My gut makes me question her sincerity."

"Me too," said Silas Jacobson.

"You would have to wonder," said Orange Stoddard's very young wife, easily a century younger than her quester husband, "what took her so long? She's very uncooperative. It reminds me of Delphine, which is ironic isn't it? I mean, she liked our Warrior Chief too."

"Elnova, don't perpetuate girlhood rumors," said The Mother, shaking her head at the slight woman, with an apologetic glance at Kahtar.

"Oh, I do apologize! Delphine was just a girl back then. She's Tener Mulier now, I'm sure she's much more cooperative—"

Abigail interrupted. "Do you have a point, child?"

Elnova straightened, missing the glare Kahtar shot at her. "Yes, I do. Beth came to me asking to have funeral clothes made a full week after the Glory announcement that I was donating our supply of white fabric to Clan Uragh. They lost fifty warriors to the Middle East. Beth knew that but still asked me to set aside yards of material for what she needed instead of just borrowing clothing until next season. She thinks of herself, not the clan. Notice her apology came only after she was cut off from her parents, not when it would have soothed discord among the warriors. She let it go all the way to a shunning!"

A chorus of agreement rose, with several loudly questioning Beth's motives.

"You're probably right," Abigail piped up, stirring the pot. "Beth's lying has got to stop."

The absurdity of Beth lying silenced the mob mentality for a moment. "Abigail," The Mother chimed in, "I hardly think Elnova meant to imply that Beth lied, I think she meant Beth's timing is suspect."

"Oh, is that it? As far as the funeral clothing goes, Anwyn, didn't you punish Beth for not having the right clothes? I assume that's why she was running around the cave barefoot last winter. It sounds to me as though she asked and was refused. Elnova, did you suggest Beth borrow something instead? She doesn't know our ways! She asked for what she needed and you refused her, expecting her to know what to do next."

"If she spent time with us, she'd learn our ways."

"Excuse me. I'm still speaking. You're all accusing Beth—who doesn't lie because she literally can't—of apologizing without meaning it? You might have to explain that one to me, Anwyn," said Abigail.

"Well," The Mother argued, "what exactly did she regret? And how much time will Honor wait for his apology?"

Abigail slammed a wrinkled hand onto the table. "Look, none of you are giving her an inch! Elnova, if you had to leave the Arc where would you get seeker clothes at? You have no idea! And how would you feel if Nehemiah punched you in the face and broke your nose, and Orange shoved you across the floor for bleeding, and The Mother told you to apologize to them for making them hit you?"

Elnova eyed her gray-haired husband while fingering her little upturned nose. "That's not the same thing."

"It is to Beth!" Abigail argued. "That is exactly how she sees it. The fact that she tries to see that situation from our point of view is huge. The least we can do is see it from hers and give her time!"

"We have given her time," said Silas Jacobson. "And I for one want to know what kind of apology she gave to Kahtar. On top of that I want to reiterate to our warrior chief that he is not to coach Beth on this subject at all. He agreed to stand with the warriors in this shunning. Any apology has to come from her heart, out of regret for the shame she brought on Honor, on the warrior chief of this clan, and on all the warriors of Cultuelle Khristos!"

The Mother looked at Kahtar. "I stand by that, Kahtar. We are not telling you to stay away from your wife, but we are telling you that if you interfere in any way, you have relinquished your role as warrior chief."

On that note Kahtar dropped his napkin on the table and stood. The conversation made the food churn in his stomach. He'd been as wrong as they were. Only centuries of experience kept his voice polite.

"Thank you, Anwyn, for reminding me of my duty, and Memma Rosa, for a delicious meal. And of course I appreciate all of you questioning the sincerity of my wife's apology—ilu forbid I trust my own heart about it. In turn I would encourage you all to look into your hearts for your motivation in how you treat my wife, because your criticisms would be considered bad form even among seekers." Kahtar fisted his hands against his sides but kept his voice even. "We as a people take great pride in judging based entirely on heart and nothing more, but, though Beth's heart is as much Covenant Keeper as any of yours, you don't trust it. The truth is you see her and treat her as less than and she *knows* that. Do you? Be honest. If nothing else we owe her our honesty. That is all I will ask, since it is now apparent that civility is beyond your capability."

Allowing himself a moment to make brief eye contact with each person at the table, Kahtar turned and left without another word, the equivalent of storming out after a temper tantrum in the eyes of the clan. Maybe they'd see that despite everything, he and Beth had at least their tempers in common.

IF THEY THINK, Beth tugged Dianta's tiny cap over her curly head, *they can keep me in this compound without answering my questions they do not know me.* It had been over a week since Kahtar's farewell. Her car had been taken away, and access to computers and telephones cut off. The clan was shunning her openly, and even Welcome Palmer had barely spoken to her.

After a week of despair, followed by mounting anger, Beth had set her mind to a solution.

"Mommy can think outside the box." Beth kissed Dianta's dark cheek. "And someday I'm going to teach Daddy how."

"Gah! Mum. Mum. Mum!" Dianta chanted, gazing with worshipful eyes, Kahtar's eyes. Beth was certain she saw black sparkling in their depths, very much like Memma Rosa's.

Bundled for outdoors Beth lamented the fashion and practicality of her too short dress coupled with a warm corduroy jacket and boots. There was nothing to be done for it. Even if she left her jeans completely unbuttoned, they were too uncomfortable to wear over her protruding pregnancy and there was nowhere to score another pair of jeans while trapped in Cobbson Compound. She pushed out of the apartment door into the dimly lit hallway.

Nobody paid Beth much heed while she trotted up the corridor. In honor of Halloween Dianta sported a sparkly unicorn horn on the top of her hat, made in a pinch from a pointy paper cone and sequins off a belt. It bobbed as they walked to the atrium.

"Yous makes the bestest unicorn ever!" Beth told her. Drool dripped down Dianta's chin, which only made the unicorn cuter.

"Gah, Mum!" she said, somewhat demurely in Beth's opinion. They passed dozens of clan in the halls, all somehow resisting Dianta's obvious charms in favor of shunning Beth.

Evenings in the atrium were usually busy, but there had been a special Glory service earlier in the day and the Samhain celebration now spilled over to the popular abstract. Little kids slid down the glacier and young couples and teens played in the waterfall. Beth saw no sign of costumes or any of the trappings that made Halloween popular in the outside world.

Walking through the crowd Beth searched until she spotted Honor Monroe at the top of the waterfall in his swim trunks. Several of the warriors who worked at the police station now wore swim trunks from the outside world instead of the standard clan kind. Beth thought it was a good call, since the cream colored diaper-looking ones revealed a very detailed outline of one's junk. Every one of them had gotten the seeker trunks from her shop. She wondered if they were prepared to go back to the weenie wraps when these wore out.

Honor leapt off the top of the falls, plunging twenty feet to the water and executing a spectacular cannonball that sprayed water over young women on the sidelines. Beth smiled. *That's the Honor I know.* She made her way to the edge of the water as Honor climbed out. Pushing his dripping but still perfectly cut hair out of his blue eyes, he glanced at her and quickly looked away.

"Hi, Honor," she said, and cheated. "Deenty, this is Honor Monroe. Say hi." She picked up Dianta's arm and waved it in an adorable hello.

Honor hesitated, but turned his back on them and got back in line to climb the waterfall. Beth followed, tromping over sandy beach and grass in her pink Timberlands. "I need to talk to you."

Honor didn't turn around. Several of the young women cast their eyes in Beth's direction. Beth wondered how Kahtar could have gone on about flaunting nudity in the clan with women's swimsuits being what they were. Most wore tiny swim dresses that revealed more than enough when wet.

"Look, I get the shunning thing. You all hate me because I won't play by the rules, but how am I supposed to make it right if you won't talk to me?"

Honor turned to her, chewing his lip. A couple pretty girls were whispering in each other's ears as they watched. Beth wasn't certain what the clan term for cock block was, but she was pretty sure she was doing it.

"Nobody hates you."

Beth breathed out a whispery laugh. "Don't forget my gifting." She glanced pointedly at the two young women. One had a finger aimed at Dianta's unicorn horn as she shook her head. Beth raised her voice. "I remember when you were enamored with me. Aren't you glad now that you never asked me to join with you? Imagine if I'd said yes!"

That was enough for Honor. Furiously he took her elbow and moved out of line, away from the beach area to stand near the glacier. The happy screams of children provided some privacy there.

"Fine. Apologize. Those are the only words I want to hear from you. And maybe add what has taken you so long."

"I can't lie, that's what's taken me so long. But this has gone on long enough. I want to make it right with my husband. That means I need to make it right with you too."

"So I'm just a means to an end? That doesn't sound very sincere."

"Yes, you are! But that's all I've got, and I am sincere." Beth took a deep breath. "Honor, I'm sincerely sorry you punched me in the nose and felt like you had to because of the way I was acting."

"Are you kidding?"

"No."

"That's not good enough."

"What were you expecting?"

"I was expecting not to be attacked in the Arc by someone who doesn't belong there or in this clan in the first place."

It hurt. Beth knew it was true, had known it was true even when she first came, but it still hurt. "But I am in the clan, Honor. Even if I don't belong, I'm here now. Since I'm not going away, can you forgive me for not belonging, and give me some credit for trying? Please come with me tonight and tell Kahtar you understand and forgive me?"

Honor laughed, but there was no humor in the sound. There was nothing left in him of the friend she once had. "But I don't understand, Beth. All a Covenant Keeper has is their honor, and you took mine and Kahtar's. The things you said to us—do you think we can forget them? And your only regret lies in the pain it caused you. Spare Kahtar your sham apology. You have no idea how much pain you've caused him. You would let it go if you did."

"Please, Honor? Come with me anyway. Let's the three of us talk. I want to make it right. Help me to see your side."

"The fact is that you can't make it right and neither can we, but it would be nice if you genuinely tried, and until you do, don't talk to me again." He stalked away.

"Well." Beth took a deep breath and swapped Dianta into her other arm. "That doesn't bode well for how it'll go with Daddy."

Beth made her way past the iceberg to the far side of the abstract where geometrically shaped tesseracts hung in the air as if by magic. It felt weird not to be stopped before she got to the one that went to

Kahtar's cabin. She could feel Honor watching her, but had no doubt that at this point she could walk out the front doors without someone stopping her. "They're giving me all the rope I need to hang myself, just waiting for me to mess up worse!" Beth shivered. "But there's no law being broken going to the cabin."

Standing at the narrow tesseract that would take her to her husband, Beth eyed it suspiciously. It didn't have a distinctive shape and looked almost like a curtain, nearly hidden. Kahtar didn't like company. Tucked into the crook of her arm, Dianta chewed her fingers and bounced in place, content for the moment. Beth kissed her nose. "At least Daddy likes your company."

She stepped into the tesseract.

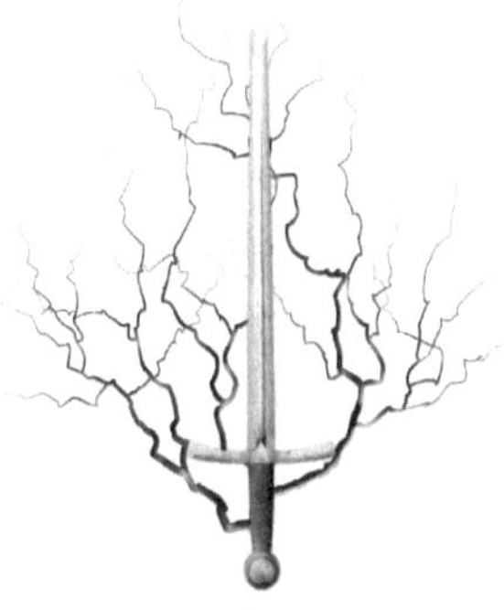

CHAPTER

ELEVEN

Bloody Dark—Autumn Night

AFTER THE BRIGHT daylight of the abstract, it took Beth a moment to adjust to the lack of light on the other end of the tesseract. She could barely make out the outline of the wraparound porch, and there were no lights shining through the cabin windows. Dianta bounced in her arms, the sparkly horn bobbing as she chanted with enthusiasm, "Dah! Da, da, da."

"But where is Dah? He's usually home on Friday night." Beth's eyes adjusted to the light of the young moon and she could make out the pond and tree line at the far end of the yard.

Maybe he's in the bathhouse. He doesn't need light to see.

Wishing she could scan too, Beth stepped onto the gravel driveway. A familiar chirping sound reached her ears and she froze, eyes straining toward the porch. Sitting on the railing were several strangely familiar shapes. Beth blinked several times, certain they couldn't be real, but the distinctive shapes remained. She'd only seen them once on a family trip over the Shira Plateau when her dad had been stationed in Africa. Blue monkeys.

"Shit," Beth said, and guiltily covered one of Dianta's listening ears, pressing the other against her chest.

Why are there monkeys inside the veil? Where's Kahtar?

Movement between the gaps in the railing caught her attention. At least a dozen more of the big furry creatures loped into sight to wait on the porch steps. Beth whispered the rudest word she knew, keeping Dianta's ears safely covered. There had to be at least thirty monkeys on that porch, and she had enough experience with monkeys to know how a gang of them treated a lone intruder.

What if Kahtar is still at the station? It's Halloween! He might still be working!

One of the furry beasts dropped off the bottom step.

Do. Not. Run.

Backing away, she tried to shush Dianta while backing as calmly as possible toward the exit tesseract located across the lawn and about impossible to see in the dim light. She would have sworn every monkey head had turned to focus on her slow progress over the slope of yard and out of their line of vision. Beth shivered. Would they follow? She wondered if Wolves was okay.

Feeling with the hand behind her back Beth located the tesseract, a smooth force in the dark, like touching an over-filled water balloon but as easily penetrated as the surface of the pond. With her heels pressed against the big rocks encircling it and her hand safely on the tesseract she felt braver. The more she thought about those monkeys, the more she worried about Wolves. Dianta's happy bobbing in her arms gave her determination.

"Wolves? Here, puppy!" she shouted, determined to take him with her. It would at least guarantee Kahtar followed. Almost immediately she heard the familiar bark from deep in the woods. She gave Dianta a happy squeeze. "There he is!"

The sharp crack of a branch sounded close by and Dianta twisted in her arms to growl. "Da!"

"Kahtar?" Beth shouted, her heart lifting hopefully at the sound of big feet tramping through brush. "Kahtar? I need you! There are monkeys on the front porch!" Her voice echoed across the pond and she couldn't help but remember Kahtar's comments the day she'd seen the Macaw in the yard. *He's going to think I'm nuts now!* "I'm not kidding, Kahtar, there really are!"

A shiver rippled up her back and she rubbed her fingers against the surface of the tesseract, glancing toward the watchful creatures in case any of them headed in her direction. The sound of footsteps in the woods got closer and Wolves' barking sounded again, this time from farther off.

"What do you want to bet Wolves is running the wrong way?" Beth muttered.

Dianta giggled, making a sound that seemed impressively like, "Woofs, woofs," in her deep man-voice.

Beth breathed a sigh of relief as the footsteps neared. All of a sudden the monkeys were funny, not threatening. Amazing what a difference Kahtar's presence made. Spotting his shadowy bulk shoving through evergreen trees, she headed across the slope to meet him.

"I brought Dianta!" Beth shifted Dianta in her arms, nervous and excited. *Why didn't I do this sooner?* She'd make him listen to facts. She hadn't told Kahtar her first lie. She was sorry she'd hit him, and especially sorry for the things she'd said. She'd never meant to insult every warrior in the clan or hurt Kahtar so deeply! Nothing was worth being separated from him like this. She loved him, and she wasn't afraid of him or his over-developed sense of duty, or even of trying to follow or failing to follow the clan's rules. As long as they were together they'd figure it out. Together they'd figure everything out, including this pregnancy and what to do next.

The footsteps came closer and Beth's heart lifted in anticipation, reaching for his heart with everything she had. *He's going to listen! I'm going to make him!*

"Here comes Daddy," she mumbled into Dianta's dark curls. She was rewarded with a slobbery kiss on her chin.

Kahtar kept the path around the pond smooth and clear. Beth knew it well. Confident the monkeys weren't following, she took a few more steps to meet him. "I'm on the path now," she said in a normal voice, although she could feel his scan on her.

Kahtar stopped in the brush watching her from the deep shadows of the tree line.

"Oh, don't be like that, please! I'm so willing to make this right for everybody, but I need you to show me how!"

In her arms Dianta bounced happily. "Da! Da, da, da!"

Without a word Kahtar bent his head and moved past the bald lower branches of a tall pine. The moon illuminated just enough for Beth to see he wore a thin hood. A skeletal twig brushed it and Beth realized she was wrong. It wasn't a hood. Long strands of dark blond hair scraped over branches and fell against his broad shoulders.

He stepped onto the path in front of her.

It wasn't Kahtar.

It was his doppelganger. The touch of his heart hit Beth's open one like a blast of greasy filth from a dirty smokestack. She took a step backward, every muscle in her body tensing to run. The man in front of her lifted his head up, tilting it to study her with Kahtar's steely eyes. Beth knew she wouldn't make it two steps. Dianta reached for him, but Beth grabbed her hand and held it against her chest, attempting to fill her daughter's heart with reassurance, attempting to lie.

"Who are you?" she whispered, her voice trembling.

His head tipped the other direction. To look at him anyone else might have thought he was Kahtar but for the long hair. Their faces were identical, down to the faint bristle on his chin. He licked his lips in a gesture painfully familiar to Beth, and shifted his weight. Lightweight cotton robes covered his big frame and the hilt of a single foreign blade gleamed at one hip. Large feet were only half protected by lightweight sandals and even in the dim light Beth saw deep scratches from walking in the woods. Almost as soon as she saw the wounds, light shimmered along the edges and they vanished. Beth took several hasty steps backward until the trunk of a large maple stopped her.

He followed.

In her arms Dianta struggled, grunting in a determined attempt to reach for him. Beth held her hood, pressing Dianta inside her own coat in an effort to hide her. She didn't want her daughter to look at him, or worse, for him to look at Dianta.

Stopping in front of Beth again, he shifted from foot to foot as he watched her, his head still tilted curiously. Bending forward he brought his face so close that Beth could smell him. He smelled of warm sand, clean sweat, and sage. Wonderful. Like Kahtar might. Beth's body betrayed her and her mouth watered. She swallowed, turning her eyes from his, clutching Dianta tighter as she tried to keep the touch of her own heart filling Dianta's so she wouldn't feel his polluted one.

He leaned so close she felt his briny breath on her face, and he sniffed. Like something out of a horror movie he inhaled deeply and held it. Unable to resist, Beth looked into his face.

He laughed then. Straightening, he threw back his head and laughed a deep belly laugh, clearly amused. Resting one hand on the hilt of his blade he studied her, a huge smile on his face as he kept right on chuckling. Despite the laughter there was nothing welcoming or kind in that face. Something unspeakably dark lived there. His delight showed clearly, and Beth had never felt more threatened in her entire life.

Smiling a horrible reproduction of Kahtar's smile, he shook his head back and forth and took a single step backward. A tunnel of jet black light hissed to life behind him, shining and whirling, something Beth had never seen before, like a tesseract made of liquid coal. It sucked him inside and he vanished. The tunnel closed on him with a whoosh that pressed painfully against Beth's ears like a vacuum, but the liquid coal kept whirling. It pulled on her, tugging the edges of her jacket and sucking the ends of her hair into the same black void he'd vanished into. Beth tightened her arms around Dianta.

THE STRENGTH OF the vacuum increased and Beth's knitted cap slipped off her head and vanished into the hole. The back of Dianta's coat lifted outward, tugged toward the whirring tunnel. Fighting the pull, Beth turned her face away, clasping Dianta tight as she put her weight against the tree and dug her boots into leafy ground, attempting to find the edges of the pull to escape it. Leaves whirled into the air around her and disappeared into the hole, but to the left and right of her the thick ground cover barely shifted. She tried to determine if falling over would free her of the suction, or if she would be pulled inside the moment she lost her balance.

The sucking sound tugged painfully at the ear facing it, as though it would tear the eardrum from her head. The unicorn horn on the top of Dianta's hood twisted in the force, pulling sequins loose and sucking them one by one into the void that seemed to be reaching for them. Beth sensed a dark cloud spiraling from the hole toward them. Dianta's mouth opened wide, her long lashes fluttering against the wind as the muscles in Beth's arms strained to hold onto her.

It's taking her shot through Beth's mind at the same moment she jumped. No sooner had her feet left the ground than the suction changed. It reversed and instead of pulling, a hurricane force wind shoved through the hole, lifting Beth off her feet and blowing her deeper into the trees, blasting her against brutally cracking branches and tearing Dianta from her arms.

Trees creaked and bent in the gale force wind. Leaves scattered and dirt scooped off the earth created whirling dervishes of blinding darkness and debris. Flat on the ground Beth felt for her baby with her heart, certain the horse-like cries she heard weren't Dianta's. She sensed the touch of Dianta's heart nearby, bellowing against Beth's with a familiar fury that she thanked God for. This was the fury of a baby who wanted the breast *now* or out of the crib *now*, or hold me, Mom, *now*! That meant she was okay, well-padded by thick undergrowth and her heavy coat.

Beth's heart responded with genuine comfort. *I'm coming!*

As she marine crawled in the direction of that blessedly demanding heart, the cold wind stopped like a door had been slammed on it, sudden and done. Beth's ears popped.

"Devil damn!" a man's gravelly voice shouted. "What the blazes was that?"

Beth froze. Through brush and bramble she saw two men and the outline of what appeared to be a swayback old horse. Strangers. Inside the veil. Although too far away to feel their hearts, Beth already knew. They weren't Covenant Keepers.

HOW CAN THEY *not be Covenant Keepers?*

The impossibility of that frightened Beth almost more than Kahtar's double had. *This is not possible.* Nobody could enter a veil uninvited, and Kahtar said without the heart of a Covenant Keeper no veil would open even invited. It was why they couldn't invite her dad over.

Yet these men were very real and they were inside the veil. *They came through the hole the doppelganger left!*

In the faint moonlight a tall, rail thin boy ran his hands over a horse. "Dunno what it was, Pap, but it took the harness off Hector, and pulled out some o' his hair!"

The shorter, broader man said, "It sucked Grane out from under me, bent him clean in half poor beast. Do you have your rifle, William? Mine's gone with my horse."

Beth tried to sink further into the earth, praying for Dianta to be quiet. Whoever they were, they didn't belong.

"Old Guard," Beth breathed, her heart thundering against the ground. Would they come? Surely for this they would! To Beth's left Dianta growled with frustration.

"Did you hear that?" said William, and Beth heard the metallic clack of a rifle.

"Old Guard?" Beth whispered a bit louder, trying to reassure Dianta with touches of her heart.

"Who's there?" shouted Pap into the trees.

Beth shoved her face directly into the earth, fighting not to answer. The urge to do so whipped out of her mouth like vomit, but she controlled it by answering a low, "Beth Constantine" against closed lips with her face shoved into mucky leaves. Dianta grunted again.

"I can hear ya!" said Pap. Beth heard the rifle cock.

"Don't shoot!" She lifted her head. "I'm pregnant!"

"What in tarnation," said Pap under his breath. "Stand up where I can see you!"

"Old Guard!" Beth whispered again, trying to push a mental summons in second voice at the same time. *Help me! If not me, help Dianta! Help my unborn babe! Old Guard! Please!*

Not even the faintest sparkle of light responded. She pushed to her hands and knees. In the dim moonlight filtering through the trees she could see the shorter square-shaped man named Pap. On the path beside him William, tall and gangly, stood next to a long-eared mule, with the shotgun in his hands pointed directly at her. "I'm getting up," said Beth, trying to exaggerate the size of her belly by pushing it forward. In her corduroy coat she barely looked pregnant. "Please, don't shoot me!"

Pap pushed the barrel of William's gun to the ground. "Who are you and why are you out here?" He sounded incredulous.

Mentally Beth cursed her gifting while her mouth answered. "My name is Beth—Costas." As if the alias mattered to anyone showing up under the veil, but these men weren't Covenant Keepers and that clan rule had become second nature. "I was looking for my husband."

Spinning in a quick circle, William pointed his rifle into the trees as though he'd shoot a husband. Beth brushed debris from her clothes, wondering if they'd shoot her if she screamed for Old Guard.

"Costas? Your man with the railroad?" asked Pap.

What? "No." Beth took a few tentative steps toward them. William drew up and rested his weapon against his shoulder, gaping at her as though he'd never seen a woman before.

"Huh," William said, in an aside to Pap. "She's a big one!"

Pap looked her up and down, seemingly confused by a tall woman too. "Ma'am, are you out here alone?" His eyes flickered to her bare legs sticking out beneath the bottom of her short coat. William's eyes seemed to be glued to them.

"No," she said. If it weren't for the gun, Beth might have thought the men were Amish. Their clothing looked homemade and old-fashioned. They didn't smell like they'd ever bathed in their lives, or used deodorant.

"Where's her skirts?" asked William, and Pap smacked a hand against his shoulder.

"Are you all right?" asked Pap, his eyes returning only briefly to her legs as his bushy brows drew together in a frown. "Did somebody hurt you, Ma'am? Harm you in some way?"

"No, I'm okay," said Beth, trying to tug her jacket down a bit. She could hear Dianta's whispery grunting, a sound she made when eating, and had a bad feeling she was happily stuffing something she'd found on the ground into her mouth. "That wind knocked me down."

"Your knees are bleeding," said Pap. "Why don't you take a seat and we'll see to you until your man returns. I'm Thomas Waterhouse and this is my son, William. We're from up Sandusky way, down here to see about work with the Kalamazoo Railway, but that tornadey took most of our supplies." His voice trailed off and he paused as though expecting her own lengthy introduction. Since he didn't ask, Beth withheld it and after a brief silence he glanced at his boy. "Start a fire and make some bandages."

"Oh no," said Beth. "You don't need to bother. I'm fine. You can go." She hoped they wouldn't head toward the cabin because she had a feeling it would shock them more than she apparently had. "Kah-Kent will be back soon." At the man's steady gaze she flushed slightly and added, "Kent Costas. My husband is Kent Costas and I'm Beth Costas. Kent's the Chief of Police in Willowyth." She hoped that would be enough to make them leave, but knew in her heart it wasn't.

The two men glanced at each other and the boy said, "Thought one of the Maloney's was Sheriff."

Thomas shook his head slightly. "Mrs. Costas—ma'am—we can't just go off and leave you out here alone. My boy and I were gonna make camp about here any—"

Behind her, Dianta bellowed a scream of fury in her deep-man, sick-of-waiting-for-mom voice. The barrel of Will's rifle moved to point in that direction and Beth spun toward Dianta, thinking only of protecting her daughter as she plowed through brush and bramble.

"It's a baby! Pull your fool gun up!" Thomas shouted at William.

Beth crashed toward Dianta half-buried inside autumn dried berry bushes. Before she could reach her, Thomas was there and scooped the baby up.

"Give her to me!" Beth said and to her relief the man tucked Dianta into her outstretched arms. He stomped on brambles to help Beth extricate herself from the chest deep bushes. Relieved to finally clutch her furious baby to her breast, she didn't mind the scratch and sting against her legs as they fought their way back toward the path. Thomas stopped and pushed her down to sit on a stump, then dropped to a knee to try and see her screaming baby.

"Is he hurt?" Thomas shouted over Dianta's anger.

"She," Beth corrected. "No. The wind blew her into those bushes. I don't think she has a scratch on her." She held Dianta tightly. "You're not going to hurt her?"

Thomas' lined dirty face reflected horror, reassuring her. "Mrs. Costas, I assure you my son and I do not harm women and children."

From his place over by his mule, William's voice quavered as he called, "Pap."

Thomas ignored him, gently feeling along Dianta's tiny limbs for injury and even sliding his big fingers under her hood to dig through her springy hair and examine her scalp.

"I see you've got yerself a nigra baby, but you can't possibly think you're safe hiding out here in the woods what with winter coming."

"Pap," said William again, a bit louder.

Thomas moved his gaze from Dianta to the bump of Beth's belly. "Is that one a nigra baby too?"

Beth fought the urge to bust his nose apart, but of course she had to answer him. "My children have the same father. My husband. If you say that word again I'll shove your teeth down your throat."

Thomas blinked. "What word?"

"Pap," said William, his voice taking on an urgent tone.

"Nigger," said Beth and she clenched her teeth together, hating her gifting.

"Begging your pardon, ma'am. If she's not, she's mighty dark like one. What is she?"

"Pap!" hissed William.

"A baby," hissed Beth in turn, but her anger changed to fear as a now familiar dark heart touched hers and she knew why William sounded afraid.

Kahtar's doppelganger had returned.

Maybe Thomas sensed something because he rose slowly from his knee and turned. The horrible Kahtar-looking man stood on the far side of the path, his robe and hood a white outline in the dim light. Thomas moved slightly as though to block the man from seeing her and Dianta.

Further down the path William's voice shook. "Don't you move a step, Mister."

Beth knew without looking that the rifle was now pointed at the doppelganger. She clutched her wailing daughter closer, mentally willing William to shoot *now*.

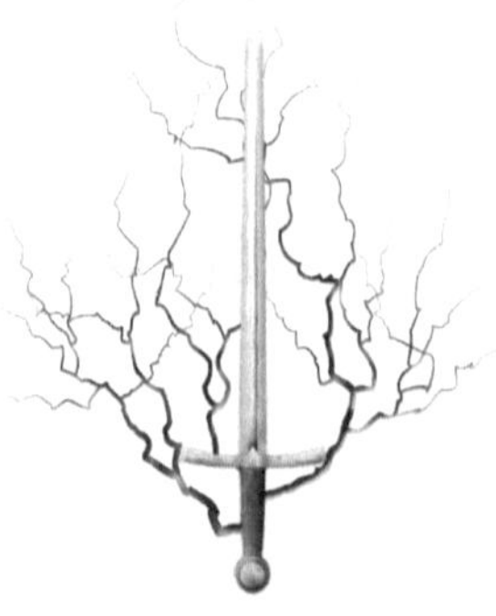

CHAPTER
TWELVE

Bloody End—Hallowmas

A STREAK OF white shot across the path toward William, like a silent deadly missile. Beth opened her mouth to warn the boy, to tell him to shoot while he still could, but Kahtar's doppelganger appeared beside him that fast, already reaching for the weapon. A gunshot sounded, ricocheting through the woods. Beth heard it the same time something knocked her off the stump and punched her to the ground.

She couldn't breathe.

I've been shot.

Flat on her back with bare legs still hooked over the stump she struggled to take a breath and wondered why it didn't hurt.

"Dear Lord!" Thomas knelt beside her, somehow now holding Dianta in his arms. "Mrs. Costas!"

Air seeped slowly into Beth's lungs and brutal pain shot through her body. Her eyes watered and she blinked them, trying to focus. "Thomas! Help Will!" It took all of her air and she struggled to take another breath.

Thomas pressed a hand against her shoulder and it felt like gravity had nailed her to the earth.

From the path a voice came, familiar, yet nothing like Kahtar's. "I need her."

Thomas jumped to his feet and whirled around. Kahtar's doppelganger moved closer, towering over Thomas, his summery robes covered in Will's blood. Beth's heart shrank in fear for him. Thomas, who moments ago had made disparaging remarks about Dianta, now held her protectively. Dianta reached a grasping hand toward what she thought was her father.

"Dah."

"No," Beth gasped.

Thomas grabbed the little hand and held her against his chest, pressing the hood of her coat over Dianta's face like Beth had done.

He senses it. The darkness of that heart oozed over them. Beth fought to keep his touch out of their hearts, brushing Dianta's with her own.

"Will?" Thomas said, looking in his son's direction. Whatever he saw or sensed filled his heart with a wave of despair so crippling that Beth felt it in his seeker heart, a pain so large it crowded out even the darkness of the doppelganger's. With Dianta still in his arms, Thomas rushed toward William, his boots leaving a wake of dead leaves and brush.

Not sparing Thomas even a glance, Kahtar's lookalike bent over Beth and with one massive hand hauled her to stand. Pain slammed through her, but as she found her footing her breathing became easier and her head cleared.

"I need her," he said again, steely eyes glaring into hers. Still holding tightly to her arm he yanked Beth closer. Something in his cruel eyes looked desperate. Behind him Beth saw the dark outline of Thomas with Dianta against his shoulder and Will's shotgun in his hands. She quickly returned her eyes to the steely ones before her, hoping this being of darkness hadn't felt the sudden hope flair in her heart.

"Who?" she said, hoping the sound of her voice would cover the faint clack of the rifle. "Who do you need? What do you want?"

Whatever old type of rifle Thomas fired sparked in the dark trees. Beth kept her eyes on the steely ones during that nanosecond, waiting, bracing herself, knowing the bullet entering his back would slam the giant man against her and take them both to the ground. Something flickered in the depths of his familiar eyes that reminded her of Kahtar's when disappointed, and she remembered that warriors could scan to sense both a gun and approaching bullet. He never even flinched. The same healing light Beth had seen erase scratches from his feet glowed beneath his lightweight robe.

Something lifted Beth off her feet and threw her into the trees. Alone.

BETH WOKE CERTAIN that she lay at the bottom of Lake Erie. All that dark water seemed to be pressing her deeper into the mucky bottom while suffocating liquid filled her lungs. She knew the baby in her belly was gone now. It had to have been ruined. This bullet had hit below her breasts and taken the baby and all feeling with it. The only thing left was pressure.

Kahtar's rough hand slapped Beth's cheek and she realized she still lay on the ground in the woods behind the cabin with only gravity weighing her down, drowning in her own blood.

With effort she sucked in a deep, bloody breath of air.

"Rouse." The hand slapped again. Not Kahtar's. Beth tried to move her head away from that hand. It surprised her when her neck obeyed and turned for her. She opened her eyes. A filthy heart pressed against hers as Kahtar's doppelganger again slapped her cheek, hard. "I need my anchor," he said.

"I need my daughter." Beth's words came out with a hissing gurgle that slipped from a puncture in her chest. The bright slice of moon hung above the trees now and she looked away from the nightmare kneeling over her to find another right beside her. The remains of Thomas lay almost against her arm, his body facing one way but his head twisted wrong so that he stared at her with dead, empty eyes. He had beautiful, trustworthy eyes. In the dim light she could see the soft brown of them. Pain slid through her heart.

"Where's my daughter?" Beth pleaded. She couldn't sense Dianta's heart through the dirty touch surrounding her own, huffing against her heart like airborne puffs of grease, and fear seemed to weigh her deeper into the ground.

"Where is my anchor?" asked the Doppelganger with another slap.

"I don't know!" Beth had no idea what he wanted and she didn't care. "Where's my baby?"

Kahtar's eyes came closer, staring into her own. The dark heart pressed against hers, attempting to surround it.

"Stop it!" Beth screamed. "Kahtar! Old Guard!"

The face moved away for a moment, to raise up and look at the surrounding trees before returning. He smiled. "You anchor him, don't you?" Something in his eyes shifted, taking on a familiar look. A look she welcomed when in Kahtar's eyes now caused bile to back-wash from her gut into her throat. The face above hers tilted curiously, the mouth smiling. "Anchor me like you do him." He shoved a giant knee between Beth's thighs, his body weight crushing them, stapling them to the ground with pain, and his heart approached intimately, smoking hers.

Fear entered Beth's heart, ugly and mean, and darkness from shadows she'd been protected from all her life slithered toward her, reaching long fingers into places that should never be touched, not like this. Beth's mind shut down and instinct made her try to scream. She tasted blood in her mouth as the sound spewed from her throat in a burst of wet blood, sprinkling her face.

The scream didn't affect the monster bearing down on her, but something familiar and good thundered through the woods to her left. Hope wove its way among strands of fear as a familiar galloping sound echoed through the ground under Beth. From out of the trees Wolves shot out, snarling and hairy, and landed on Kahtar's looka-like. Fierce growls ripped from his throat as he bit down, his massive mouth covering half the man's head. The force of impact toppled the doppelganger over and onto Thomas' body.

Wolves' presence gave Beth the strength to shoot to her feet. She had to find Dianta and get away. Her legs seemed to weigh hundreds of pounds, and every step took effort. She searched the path for Dianta, her heart begging and desperate for the touch of her baby. A sparkle caught her eye; the horn on Dianta's hood, reflecting in moonlight. She thumped on wooden legs and grabbed Dianta by the back of her coat. The slight bodyweight yanked on muscles around the hole in Beth's chest and she nearly fell. She knew if she fell that she'd never be able to get up again.

Stumbling down the path, bent half over, she ignored the canine growling and pained yelps behind her, ignored the fact that the crunching sounds were Wolves' bones shattering beneath fists and that he would lose the battle with the cruel giant and wouldn't walk away from it. Beth never hesitated or turned to help him, but moved faster, stumping forward on numb legs. Dianta hung limp from her arms, her bottom half bent wrong.

Holding Dianta close to her face Beth tried to feel her breath, tried to sense her heartbeat or the touch of her bubbly baby heart. There was nothing to feel. Beth stopped moving at the same time Wolves screamed a canine gurgle of pain. The sound tore through the forest to echo across the pond Beth now stood beside, so close to the tesseract and safety.

But too late.

Beth spun, already sensing that somehow the giant had moved that fast. "You did this!" The words tore from Beth's throat like agony, and she beat back fear and pain to shout her fury. "You killed my baby! You killed her!" The words scorched her throat and whispered in bloody puffs of air out the hole in her chest like an echo. "She did nothing to you! You monster!"

The giant wretched Dianta from Beth's grasp as though to toss her aside.

"No!" Beth screamed, grabbing hold of Dianta's coat with a death grip, attempting to pull her back. "Don't you dare! Dishonor breeds death! You can't do this and keep your giftings! You can't!"

"I can," he growled into her face, daring to be amused. But he allowed Beth to take her daughter.

"You heal her! Dammit, you fix her, or I will rip your head off your neck and eat it!" Beth spat the words at him and saw her bloody spittle spatter his face.

He grinned down at her. "You are a worthy anchor, despite your dirty blood."

"To hell with you and your filthy heart! I will kill you for this!"

"Anchor me and I will make her live."

Beth looked into the face, certain she was making a deal with the devil and not even caring what he meant. "Okay. Anything. You fix her!"

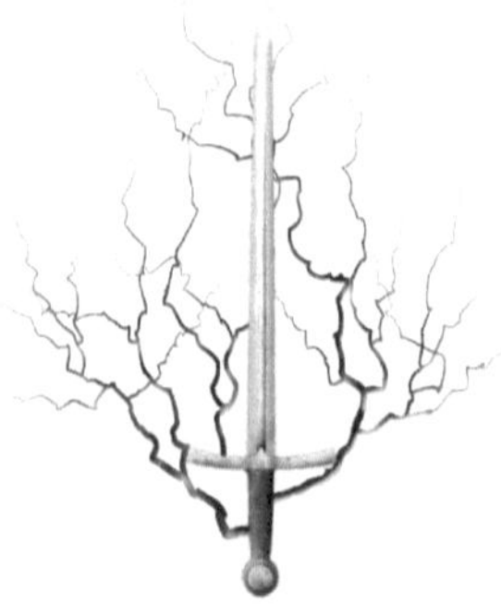

CHAPTER

THIRTEEN

Bloody Hell—Day of the Dead

"WHY DID *YOU* bring Dianta? Francis was supposed to," Kahtar growled as he exited the tesseract near his cabin, too annoyed to be polite. Honor Monroe couldn't stay far enough away to suit him. After a long day, the last thing Kahtar wanted to see was this man who'd both wooed and hurt his wife. He couldn't believe Honor had the nerve to show up any day. "And why are you standing in the middle of the driveway with my daughter? Get her inside! It's cold out here!"

A loud sob echoed across the driveway and Kahtar froze. The warrior stood unnaturally still in the wet grass where the driveway turned into path, holding Dianta, his head bent over her. Kahtar moved to his side in a flash and reached for her.

Honor turned away. "Don't! Don't! She's hurt badly! I've never healed a baby. I don't know—I don't know if I'm hurting her worse."

Scanning his baby, Kahtar bellowed hoarsely, "Old Guard!"

They appeared, their light revealing a sight that froze his heart. Dianta looked broken like a doll, her legs bent wrong, her eyes wide and glazed. He couldn't tell if she was breathing. In a flash of light she vanished from Honor's arms, and a second flash took Kahtar with her.

NOT BOTHERING TO look up and take in his surroundings, Kahtar bent low to blow breath onto Dianta's face. Welcome Palmer's familiar hand gripped his shoulder, and the surgery at Cobbson Clinic swam into his peripheral vision.

"That's it, she's breathing. I can fix this, Kahtar. I can fix it. I promise you. It's the same as with anyone else, only smaller, but it's what I'm good at and it's just going to take a while."

Behind him, Kahtar heard Honor's sobs of anguished relief. "You did right, Honor," Welcome said, "reducing the swelling in her brain came first. You did very well. You saved her life. Now, where's Beth? She should be here."

For a moment Kahtar ignored him, watching his unmoving daughter's miniscule body sprawled on the marble operating table while Nurse Hippolite cut her tiny jeans off.

Welcome's green eyes turned toward him. "Pray, Kahtar, and you too Honor, but I'm going to ask you two to help Dianta by leaving the room. Kahtar, you won't help her by watching this. You can be certain she senses your heart. Your fear could hurt her more."

Leaving that room was the hardest thing Kahtar had ever done.

THE DOOR SWUNG shut behind them, and the bustle of the surgery shut off, making the hallway suddenly quiet.

"What happened to my daughter?" Kahtar grabbed a handful of Honor's shirt and shoved him against the stone wall, only then noticing the man wore a robe over wet swim trunks.

Shivering in his sopping clothing, Honor shook his head. "I didn't fix her."

"I asked you what happened to my daughter."

"I don't know! But somebody else healed her! Not just healed her! I think she was dead, Kahtar. Before I found her someone else had restarted her heart and left her there. Who on ilu's sweet earth would have breathed life into a baby and left her with those monkeys? What kind of monster would do such a thing?"

"Monkeys?"

"I don't understand! I don't even understand how monkeys got inside your veil, let alone who would leave a helpless baby with them?" Tears soaked Honor's face.

Kahtar scanned directly and mercilessly into Honor's head to see if he'd had a stroke.

"Stop!" Honor clutched his forehead. "Listen to me! I was heading home for the night when I passed your tesseract and I *knew* something was wrong!" A sob tore from his trembling lips. "I felt Beth's heart screaming for help! Chief, Beth had Dianta! She was in that veil too! If somebody did that to Dianta, what did they do to Beth? I can still feel her pain, but I couldn't sense her in there."

Kahtar let go of Honor, who slid down the wall and dropped his head onto his knees, shaking.

Not caring who sensed or saw him do it, Kahtar vanished.

SEVEN MINUTES. IT had been at least seven minutes since they'd taken Dianta from the veil when Kahtar reappeared inside it. As soon as his feet touched the ground he scanned, pushing it far and wide. *No one is here.* Taking a deep breath, he blew it out. Beth wasn't there. *But she wouldn't have left Dianta.* Fear pressed against his heart, but he proceeded as he'd always done, logically.

"Old Guard!" he bellowed. One flickered into being beside him. "Are there monkeys inside this veil?"

It occurred to him as he asked that the increase in foxes he'd sensed lately could well have been something else. And there was the unexplained vandalism. The Old Guard shimmered brightly, and put his hand on Kahtar's shoulder. In a burst of light several more Old Guard lit into being, their expressionless black eyes on him.

"Monkeys and bodies."

No.

Light from Old Guard lit the yard and across the slope of grass not twenty yards away Kahtar's gaze fell on the body of a dead boy. His chest had been torn open. Duty required Kahtar study it. *Seeker?* In disbelief he looked at an Old Guard for confirmation. "He's a seeker?"

The Old Guard nodded.

The bloodied clothes stirred a distant memory. *Homespun, denim, silver buttons, early manufactured boots—1830's or 40's.* His scan produced similar results; this man's tissues held none of the toxins of the more modern world outside the veil, but those from the mid-nineteenth century—mercury, lead, and arsenic. A second body laid close by, its chest also caved in, but the neck broken and the head turned to face its back. Kahtar sensed the same poisons, with traces of tobacco and alcohol. A second seeker.

Still scanning, Kahtar watched the Old Guard, wondering if they could make sense of the injuries. Each man had died from a single blow through the chest. The bodies had been mangled, but after death, as though in anger. *Who would have the strength to kill like that?* Kahtar doubted anyone but an Old Guard could have the strength to do it, but never in all his time had he seen an Old Guard kill with such merciless drama.

A few feet away from the pond, several Old Guard knelt in the grass with their backs to him. Kahtar refused to look away from the seekers and see what they were looking at. He knew. Felt it. Recognized the composition, even lifeless. The heavens above seemed to fall toward the earth, landing on his shoulders with their weight. A shield dropped over his heart.

Kahtar refused to stagger. It was his duty to bear and endure, and duty always came first. Long ago he'd created armor for his heart, strengthened and refined it over millennia. He would die later, and this pain would destroy him.

Merciless, an Old Guard took his arm and moved him closer in a flash of light, forcing him to see the lifeless body of a woman, lying at an angle, almost face down.

A heap of filthy fur lay over her legs, covered in blood, and Kahtar focused his attention on that as the weight of the universe bore against him. His feet seemed to be sinking into the grass with it. The fur whimpered. *Wolves.* Kahtar hadn't recognized his own dog soaked in blood.

"Buddy," Kahtar whispered, the weight moving into his throat. Sprawled over the body, Wolves didn't raise his head. From a trail into the woods a blood trail coated the vegetation for yards, stretching from the woods to the woman. The dog had crawled to lie in a pool of her blood.

"The dog is broken," said an Old Guard. "Shattered and left to suffer."

"I'll end him," said Kahtar, reaching to put him to rest, but Wolves growled, a fierce but fearful threat low in his throat, rippling the skin over his snout to bare bloody teeth he snapped at Kahtar's fingers. Withdrawing quickly, Kahtar gaped at the animal. In the years he'd had this dog he'd never heard it growl.

An Old Guard reached for Wolves and in a shimmer of brilliant light the dog vanished. Kahtar knew he'd surely never see him again, but focused on the body and refused to feel anything, not even the tortured weight scorching his throat. This ruined woman sprawled flat on her back wasn't Beth, it was a dead body he reminded himself. Still, something hit the shield around his heart like a battering ram and the universe above seemed to echo with the sound.

Kahtar knelt to ascertain cause of death, landing heavily. He'd done this many times. An Old Guard ran his shimmering hand over the body. The head was turned to the side and the man brushed blonde hair off it, but Kahtar still didn't look at the face. A gunshot wound in the right shoulder wasn't visible as more than a faint hole through the thin material of a dress, but Kahtar knew the exit wound in the back would be significant. A second gunshot had entered from the front, just below the breast line, grazing the spine. It had blown open a lung and littered both with rib fragments, tearing a hole so big that she'd surely died from blood loss.

An Old Guard's large, glowing hand moved downward, past the dress bunched over a protruding belly to touch a naked hip. It smeared blood as it moved. Kahtar struggled to take a deep breath to continue his mental assessment—this woman had been used as she died. A torn pair of blue underwear lay in the grass nearby.

"She bled to death," the Old Guard said, running a large glowing finger down the bridge of the woman's perfect nose.

"Can you heal her?" Kahtar's voice sounded dead.

"She's gone," the Old Guard said. The shimmering hand touched the pelvis. "These bones are shattered. She was used roughly." Heartlessly the Old Guard pressed his hand between her legs and jammed the other against the swollen belly.

All three of the Old Guard shimmered in tandem, and six pair of black eyes flickered in Kahtar's direction. Had he ever seen surprise on an Old Guard's face before? "The babe inside still lives," they said in unison, a chorus of gravely voices.

"That's impossible," Kahtar said, though he sensed it too then, the small life inside the dead woman's body. Not Beth's dead body—that would be unbearable—but the woman's.

Impossible.

The universe paused in its assault.

THE CLEARING LIT like day. The bright light of so many Old Guard barely shimmered as they glowed solidly into form. Silas Jacobson, Elder and Arc physician, appeared at the side of one. A look of horrified disbelief crossed his thin face when an Old Guard pointed at the dead woman, indicating his reason for being summoned.

Soaked in blood, she lay on her back with her corduroy jacket so saturated with blood the color was impossible to know. An Old Guard bent and pushed the woman's dress higher to better reveal her pregnant torso slick with blood. Another respectfully draped the underpants over her shattered pelvis, underlining the belly. Although Kahtar still refused to look at the face, he saw from the corner of his eye that the woman's expression wasn't peaceful. It had not been an easy death. A furrow trenched between her brows, her jaw tense. Kahtar recognized the expression; she'd gone with regret. He'd worn it greeting death many times.

Jacobson's countenance mirrored it. Surely the man had never been to the scene of a murder in his existence. Life inside the Arc was so much different, and Kahtar doubted Jacobson had ever been outside the Arc before today.

"The babe is still alive," said Kahtar, struggling to push the words past the gravity bearing down on him.

Frowning, Jacobson bent forward as he scanned. He looked curiously at them, knelt and touched the woman's stomach. He shook his balding head and looked at them again.

"No, it isn't alive. I'm sorry, Kahtar. You know that's not possible. There's no oxygen and no heartbeat, and the blood is congealing. Every cell doesn't die at the moment of death. The fetus is better protected than the mother. You're simply sensing residual of a very strong being." He removed his hand and cleaned his bloodstained fingers on fallen leaves.

Gravity resumed its assault full-force. Kahtar tried to press against it and remain erect.

"I've never sensed it so strongly in all my time. It will fade though. It is a sorrow. That being would have been a very strong Covenant Keeper had it lived." He shoved his hands into his pants pockets, shivering in the cold night air in nothing but his trousers and blouse, his focus now returned to Beth's lifeless form. His eyes darted away and he stepped from Beth's side to gaze curiously down at one of the dead men. Silas poked at him with his booted foot. "Merciful torment! Is that a seeker? I've never seen one before."

"May you never see one again." Kahtar growled. Words of hatred came easily and filled his heart for what these seekers had done to the woman.

"Well, yes. I hope not," said Silas. "But they didn't do that to Beth."

The name blasted against the shield around Kahtar's heart like a bomb. It felt like the force of it could take him off his feet and bury him with the potency of a tidal wave. He wanted to hit Silas for daring to speak it, but then the rest of Silas's comment penetrated. He had to be wrong. Of course the seekers had raped the woman, shot her, and Honor had found them and killed them both. It was the only thing that made sense. Seekers in his veil didn't make sense, but the evidence lay in front of him. Honor Monroe's life would be forfeit for killing the men without permission and Kahtar lifted his head to tell an Old Guard to find him and take it. He wished he could thank the man first.

"She wasn't raped," said Silas. "Not in the traditional sense, and those men are fully clothed. I sense nothing of them on her."

Kahtar glanced at the seekers, duty forcing awareness into his brain. How had he missed that obvious fact? *Because your world is collapsing. You are done.*

Silas knelt next to the woman's head and briefly laid his hand on her chest, drawing back instantly as though it were hot. "ilu save us from such darkness. You poor, dear woman. Kahtar, no one could blame you for shunning her, but you had no right. Old Guard, take him. Kahtar did this to Beth."

Kahtar shifted his gaze to the Old Guard, but they didn't move, staring at him with their solid black eyes. Kahtar turned his scan to the woman, razing it over her, trying to sense DNA on her that didn't belong to her, Dianta, or Wolves.

"It's not DNA I sense," said Silas. "But the light beneath his DNA is all over her. It's white, pure white. I've not known anyone with white light but Kahtar. He did this. Who else could it have been?"

IN THE COOL humidity of the cave Kahtar sat on the cold ground forever, his back against the stone plinth holding the woman's body.

Jacobson had been right about one thing; the life light inside her had faded away so that Kahtar could barely sense it anymore. Brushing his hand over his bristly head he watched a swirl of white gowns brush past him. Legs rushed past, busy doing whatever women did before a funeral. Above his head a clan woman directed the others with hushed words, and after a time she squatted beside him.

"We're finished, except perhaps for the gown. White is tradition."

"Not for this woman," he said.

"This woman is Beth, Kahtar," she said firmly, and Kahtar focused his eyes on The Mother's blue gaze.

"You're not alone," she said, and leaned to kiss his blessed spot, her lips cool as they lingered on his forehead. "I'm sorry for Silas's accusations. Welcome has disputed them and the Old Guard back him up. That is all the proof we need. You must know that, Kahtar. I know if you had done something like this, you'd have the honor to admit to it."

Kahtar wondered if she really thought he cared what any of them thought or did to him now.

"I'm allowing Honor to attend the funeral. After that, if you want to speak to him, do so soon. Today will be his last."

His words came out too slow to his own ears. "Honor doesn't have the strength to kill like that. I thought at first, but no, he couldn't have."

"Honor admitted to it, Kahtar." She pressed her cold hand against his cheek. "Remember, you're not alone." The Mother stood and hurried away, herding the others all clutching rags and bowls of bloodied water.

The Mother was wrong. In many ways he'd always been alone until Beth. Now he was alone again.

It was nearly time to be finished.

Kahtar rose to face the truth.

The woman on the limestone altar now looked exactly like Beth. Her hair, still damp from washing, had been combed neatly into place. An inappropriately short flowered sundress clothed her, far too tight over her swollen belly and he knew the buttons behind her were completely undone. Yellow heels, her favorite, were strapped to her feet and her toes were already turning dark. Kahtar quickly moved his gaze to her hands, folded neatly over the bump of her belly. He reached to touch it and drew his hand back, certain that his world would end this second if he did. Duty required he finish the ceremony.

A plump arm reached around his waist and a head leaned into his torso. *Not as alone as I'd prefer.* Tiny Elder Abigail Adit offered a one-armed hug. The familiar gesture surprised him. This was family time, time for those closest. He'd thought to be alone. Abigail had spoken to Beth maybe once in the past year, refused to take her on buying trips. Now she hung onto him, her old face wrinkled up with sorrow and tears. Out of obligation Kahtar awkwardly patted the top of her bun, wishing she would go.

Honor Monroe appeared beside the marble plinth, his face buried in his hands. "I did this! This is my fault. My sin!"

No wonder they think he killed the seekers, Kahtar thought as Honor threw himself across Beth's body and begged her forgiveness. *That should be me. Why can't I feel this?*

"It's too big of a loss," said Abigail, as though she'd heard him. "Grieve as you will. I am sorry, warrior, sorry for everything. I thought you'd be good for each other. But it just hurt you more, didn't it? I made it worse and I failed and now we'll all suffer for it."

Kahtar had no idea what she was talking about, but he didn't care enough to ask. He wanted them to go, and didn't speak in the hopes of hurrying their departure.

IN THE BACK of his mind Kahtar eventually sensed that the entire clan now filled the cavern. He hadn't heard them come in, and wondered how thousands could enter a cave so silently. Gazing down at the woman on the altar, he now knew it was Beth, and the shield around his heart disintegrated until all he knew was loss. As the chemistry of death changed her body, he felt it claiming her, pulling her away, going where everyone eventually went, except him.

I knew this day would come. I selfishly hoped to move on before it did.

Kahtar moved closer, and his sword glanced loudly off the stone plinth. He looked down, wondering when he had changed into the familiar quilted tunic and tight pants, the silver balteus and his swords. He should have worn color for Beth.

Finally he touched her, resting his left hand on her chest. She was cold and stiff, and agony writhed deep inside him. This he would not recover from.

The sound of Dianta's cry drew his eyes away, and he looked to where Nehemiah held his daughter. His arms ached to hold her. Welcome Palmer had healed her as well as anyone could have. She'd have a limp, he'd said, whispering it as though it were his fault. Kahtar wondered if his grandparents had already begun to build the extra room on their cottage, if they felt anything but the vaguest remorse that Beth was gone. Surely for the entire clan it was more relief.

Kahtar's gaze flitted over the crowd. It was different than usual, an awkward funeral. Even in death Beth didn't belong.

He turned his eyes from them, moving his hand over Beth's chest, desperately needing one last touch of that heart. "My Sweet Beth," he whispered, voice breaking. "Don't."

Tears slipped down his face and dotted her dress. Even in cold death she looked beautiful, whole. With the blood washed away, the worst of the damage was hidden from sight beneath the flowery little dress.

Movement in front of him caught his attention. The girls from Avalon were gathering to sing. Kahtar held their gaze, forbidding it. Sliding his hand from Beth's chest and bulging stomach, hard with rigor mortis, he slid his hand under her, to hold her one last time. Something shifted beneath her, something that didn't belong inside the Arc.

Kahtar tugged Beth's iPod from beneath her, his gaze searching the crowd for Honor Monroe. Honor stood with arms crossed, shamelessly sobbing, and Kahtar nodded his thanks. Beth would have appreciated the gesture from her one-time friend, even if the motivation was only guilt. Tears stung Kahtar's eyes and he pressed the button on the side of the device. The screen sprang to life. The electronic tapping echoed in the cavern until Kahtar hit the play button and the Ramone's *I Wanna Be Sedated* blasted into the cavern.

Bending to Beth's left ear, Kahtar whispered, "The truth is you were such a bad influence on me." Shifting, he bent to the right ear. "Thank you." He kissed her forehead, his lips lingering on the cool blessed spot. "You've given the clan their perfect ending this way." Kahtar straightened, sliding his hand back to her heart. "That's not like you, Beth." He ran his hand down her torso to her belly. Their belly.

He stepped away as the song ended. There would be time later when he put her in the ground, to speak to their unborn babe. Surely it would repeat like he always had, though he would never know or be able to find it. Kahtar shoved that knowledge away. He'd have forever to know it.

The girls in gray moved out of the crowd, falling in line and approaching. Kahtar watched impassively as their serene features turned in his direction. Almost as one their expressions changed. Mouths opened and eyes widened, but instead of their heartfelt song, a very familiar voice echoed through the cavern behind him in a scream.

"Dianta!"

Kahtar whirled as gravity receded to its proper weight. Beth lay upon the stone, her head and shoulders raised as she gazed toward her daughter. Her eyes landed on Kahtar for a brief moment, and her expression reflected sheer terror. "Ahhh!" she croaked, and dropped back onto the marble.

Inside the cavern, panic erupted.

"Be still!" Kahtar roared, but it was useless. Cultuelle Khristos was used to miraculous happenings, but someone rising from the dead— the very cold and dead since yesterday dead—wasn't one of them.

How?

Kahtar knew dead. It was a permanent condition, for most people. He'd never stayed that way for long, but it hadn't worked like this. He took several fast steps to Beth's side, afraid to believe it. Old Guard shimmered to her side, lighting her corpse—her body—as they flickered in what looked like their own state of panic. Blood from the bullet wound now stained the front of Beth's dress where moments ago no blood had flowed.

Kahtar touched her cold cheek, sensing blood moving through her body as it did through someone submerged too long in icy water. He leaned closer and felt air blow from her nostrils.

Beth opened her eyes, and for a split second the entire cavern whirled around Kahtar. Beth wasn't the same; the eyes weren't the sky blue they'd always been, but a very recognizable steely gray. They were his eyes, shining from Beth's face. All feeling vanished from his arms.

"Shades of Misery. What have I done to you, Beth?"

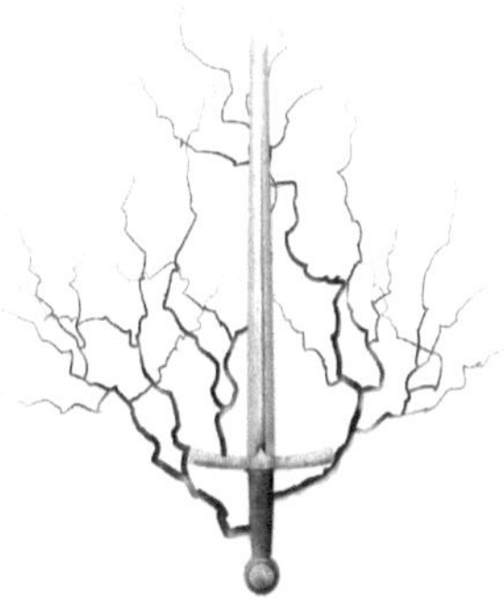

CHAPTER

FOURTEEN

Gory Bloody Surprise—All Souls' Day

BETH'S THOUGHTS CAME slow, disjointed, nightmarish, and strange.

Rotten filth grinding into her heart.

A sequined unicorn horn.

Cruel, steely eyes laughing.

She kept her eyes shut, afraid to open them. Memories stirred, until the mental image of thousands of wide-eyed Covenant Keepers clutching candles swam to the forefront. *I'm not in the veil anymore.*

An image of Wolves interrupted, and she could almost feel his fur brushing past her as he leapt over her, snarling. *Wolves! Oh, Wolves!* The remembered sound of a gunshot reverberated in her head, followed by Wolves' cry and the memory of being pounded into the ground with hot horse breath on her neck.

Cruel, steely eyes watching.

Despair gaped open in every direction.

Dianta, broken.

Cruel, steely eyes laughing.

Darkness beckoned to Beth from all sides, and she wanted it. *Emptiness. Nothing. Escape.* All she had to do was step toward it.

Another image cut through the horrible memories—Nehemiah holding Dianta, a dusky hand patting a reassuring rhythm against the back of a lacy white dress. Dianta's steely eyes, wide and scared—*alive! Dianta is alive! That matters, nothing else matters.*

Beth opened her eyes. Shadows clouded her field of vision like in the candlelit memory of the cave. The gentle ceiling tiles of Cobbson Clinic came into view. They looked like blurry pink scallop shells.

Safe.

Blinking, Beth swung her gaze, searching, and steely eyes appeared above her.

No!

She tried to escape but her body wouldn't obey. She opened her mouth to scream and nothing came out. Terror iced her heart. *My filthy, ruined heart.*

"Beth, you're safe, my love. Dianta's safe. You're at Cobbson. Can you hear me?" Kahtar's voice, her favorite voice on earth, soothed with its calmness. These steely eyes were his. Kahtar's eyes, so like Dianta's.

The good kind.

Beth wished she could claw them out of his head.

"Do you hear me, Beth?"

Beth opened her mouth and again nothing came out. She tried again, and realized she couldn't feel her mouth. She felt nothing.

It doesn't matter.

Kahtar leaned nose to nose. By the angle she thought he had his arm under her shoulders, but couldn't feel it.

It doesn't matter.

She couldn't feel the touch of his heart either.

It doesn't matter.

Kahtar shifted so she could see that he held Dianta in the crook of his other arm.

That is all that matters.

Beth took a quick breath of air. It sounded dry, like wind rushing into the opening of the cave. Dianta blinked at her, her little chin quivering.

She is alive!

"You died," Kahtar whispered, like it was a secret.

Beth heard truth in the words, and tried to remember what dead had been like. What had happened in the woods inside the veil wasn't something she wanted to ever remember, but it wouldn't go away. Terror waited impatiently for attention, a cloud of filth floating around her numb heart.

"I think—in some strange way—I'm contagious," said Kahtar, his hoarse voice cracking. "Because you came back. Thank ilu in heaven, you came back."

Beth tore her eyes away from Dianta to look at him. His broad shoulders were hunched, and for once he looked his age. Ancient. She saw grief and fear in his eyes. Had he been afraid he'd lost her? Why? He'd abandoned her. Hadn't come when she needed him most. His doppelganger had used her. Ruined her. Destroyed her.

Unable to move, Beth stared at him. He wasn't contagious, he was insidious, and he'd walked away, abandoning her. He'd shunned her and left her alone in the veil with that monster!

Under her stare Kahtar flinched. He dropped her gaze but didn't move away.

Where were you? Where were any of you? She wanted to scream, wanted to rage, wanted to get up and scratch his eyes out. Returning her gaze to Dianta's trembling face, Beth tried to shove all other thoughts away. *All that matters is she's alive.*

Again Kahtar's face moved into view and her head shifted as his arm slid her closer. "You're safe now. It would be better if you allowed yourself to remember. You don't need to be afraid here."

No.

Kahtar, who so often knew what she was thinking, whispered, "Yes. We are nothing without our hearts. You have to feel, to remember, to heal. Your heart can heal from this."

No! You don't know!

"I do know," Kahtar spoke as though she'd said it in second voice, but she hadn't. There was nothing she wanted to say to him.

Old Guard and Welcome Palmer circled the bed, their hands touching her, but she couldn't feel them. She startled when Kahtar continued,

"Do you think in all my years that I haven't been violated? My heart destroyed? In more ways, Beth, than most minds could comprehend."

Allowing her eyes to focus on his, Beth saw tears in them. Somewhere deep inside her heart she felt his tears and it made her angry. *Where were you? Nobody came! I called! I screamed!* A sob tore through her. She couldn't feel it with her body, but she heard it, and in her heart she felt it; pain, a ragged burning pain, consuming her heart—fear, loss, fury, filth.

Old Guard and Welcome were at the foot of her bed, holding her legs in their hands and rubbing them, silent prayers moving their lips, but Beth felt none of it. She focused her anger at Kahtar. *He didn't come! No one came!*

Tears slipped out of Kahtar's eyes, and his lips trembled not unlike Dianta's. "Welcome has already tended to Dianta. She'll be fine, and so will you—eventually. I'll help you."

Beth felt his warm breath touch her face, and it made her angrier. She tried to shout at him, to rage against his abandonment, to curse the Old Guard for theirs. All that came out was a grunt.

Kahtar swallowed and his Adam's apple bobbed. "I failed you. There is no justification for it. The veil should have been safe. I don't know what happened. None of us do, not even the Old Guard. In all my time I've never seen this. It should have been impossible and yet it happened. I am so sorry I failed you."

Beth managed a dry scream, low in her chest. Welcome Palmer's face replaced Kahtar's.

"Don't upset her right now. This can wait."

"No, it can't," Kahtar argued.

"Send Dianta out at least," said Welcome and Beth realized her tiny daughter lay on her chest—but she couldn't feel it, not the body or the heart. Another dry sob ripped through her.

"Beth needs to be with our daughter right now! She needs to be with me!" Kahtar tilted Beth so she could see nothing but him. Closing his eyes, he leaned forward and kissed her. At least Beth thought he did. She couldn't feel it, but his head bent at that position and he stayed there too long, blocking her vision. She growled, and he backed away.

"I'm sorry. I thought you were gone forever." His entire face crumpled. "Oh, Beth, I'm sorry!" Tears ran from his eyes and Beth heard Dianta sniff in sympathy and hiccup a small sob.

Somewhere in her heart a vein of heat lighted, feeling their fear and relief. Beth shied away from it, not wanting to feel anything because of the filth that now slimed her heart. Nothing could purify what Kahtar's doppelganger had done to her, what she'd allowed him to do. She glared at Kahtar for making Dianta cry.

He seemed to understand and kissed their daughter, glancing at an Old Guard who had come to stand by his side. The man gave him a meaningful look.

Kahtar frowned, returning his full attention almost rudely from the Old Guard to Beth. He shifted his arm beneath her and said, "Can you tell me what happened, love?"

Beth dared him with her eyes. He continued, not meeting them, "What we've gleaned makes no sense. I think the men who attacked you were from another era. They scanned like seekers from the 1840s. Time travel doesn't exist, although we've long known it's technically possible. Even if they somehow came from the past, we still don't understand how they got into the veil. What I've always told you about veils has always been true, is true. No one can enter uninvited. They open only to a heart that belongs there. This makes no sense."

Beth stared at him in silence.

The Old Guard waited beside Kahtar, as though listening for her answer. Beth didn't care. Where were they when she needed them?

"I'm sorry, but I have to ask if you saw who killed those men?"

Kahtar's sorry did nothing to assuage the cold fury building inside Beth, or the despair clawing at her.

"There are many veils in the village. Beth, it's my duty to keep this clan safe. Help me to keep from failing anyone else. Your answer could save someone from the same fate—or worse." At the sound Beth made, he said, "Yes, there's worse. There is always worse. You can believe me about that. Dianta is alive, you are alive, and I thank ilu for that. You have every right to be angry, but it is my duty to find out what happened—as the Old Guard have reminded me. Whoever killed those men saved our daughter. Her injuries were fatal. I need to know if someone from the clan was involved in this. It had to be a Covenant Keeper to heal her, someone who cared about Dianta, if not you."

No! He didn't care about anybody! He laughed! Beth couldn't get the words out.

"Only Honor entered the veil after you, and he was seen arguing with you before this happened."

Beth tried to speak, but it came out as dry gasps.

"Honor doesn't have the strength to kill like those men were killed, and despite the shunning my heart says he'd have protected you with his life. But he was the only one there who could heal. Somebody healed Dianta, tore those seekers apart, and left you to die. That is an unpardonable crime. Honor's so guilt ridden he won't defend himself! He will only say that it's all his fault."

"Oopid!" Beth managed, and Kahtar made a sound somewhere between a laugh and a sob.

"Yes, Monroe's stupidity is the one thing you and I could always agree on. But this could cost his life. If you saw anyone else—even if you only caught a glimpse, I need to know what he looked like."

Beth's voice came out dry and primal, like an animal trying to speak. "Oo!"

Kahtar ran his left hand over his head. "Me? Do you mean my coloring or that he was big?"

"No," Beth grunted, at last getting her dry tongue to obey. "You brother."

"I don't understand what you mean. I don't have a brother."

The way he said it didn't feel like the truth.

"You do. Must. Hear me. You do. You must have forgot."

Kahtar's face went white, and the room went silent. The Old Guard stopped working on Beth's legs and shimmered brightly. In a blinding flash of light many more appeared, crowding the room. The one standing close to Kahtar grabbed onto his shoulder and jerked, and they vanished.

Without his arm supporting her shoulders, Beth's head dropped onto the table, but she couldn't feel it. Colorful lights danced in her eyes as though from a camera flash. Welcome Palmer moved swiftly to catch Dianta before she slid all the way off Beth's chest, his green eyes wide and wondering. Beth closed her eyes so she wouldn't have to see them.

BEING YANKED AWAY from Beth's side, felt like claws being scraped over Kahtar's already bloodied and wounded heart. If she never forgave him he couldn't criticize her for it. He'd promised her much, and none of it had proved true. He'd sworn the veil was safe. He'd promised her his heart, then withheld it and shunned her. Abigail had been right. The truth of his betrayal hit like a spike into his heart. *I betrayed the only heart ilu has ever joined to mine.*

"Take me back to her," said Kahtar, but the Old Guard ignored him, moving across dry leaves inside the veil to congregate with others of their kind. For a brief moment Kahtar considered flickering back under his own power. Surely they knew he could, though he had never flaunted the ability.

One of them turned to look at him, his black gaze expectant. Kahtar stomped across the grass to join them. The bodies of the seekers had been taken away. The Old Guard solidified as they moved across the sloping cabin yard, looking like glowing giants from a seeker movie.

Turning his scan on the grass, Kahtar couldn't sense any information. Facing the cabin he swept his scan across the ground in the other direction, but it too produced no evidence. It looked as if someone had used their gifting to scorch the vegetation, burning away every clue it might hold. Come tomorrow morning it would show. This grass would shrivel and die. In the spring it wouldn't return. It had all been killed and even the soil beneath it emptied of life. Nothing would ever grow in it.

"Is it like this everywhere?" asked Kahtar, but none of the Old Guard responded. Solidly they continued to search with their black eyes focused on the ground. *Who would do such a thing?*

Someone had wanted to cover their tracks. Despite the giftings of both warriors and Old Guard, there was now no way to know who else had been in the veil.

"ARE YOU GOING to explain?" The Mother sat across her kitchen table from Kahtar, her hands wrapped tightly around a mug of tea and Kahtar had no doubt it was to still their shaking. For the first time she looked truly afraid of him, and it made him sad.

"How can you expect me to explain the unexplainable?"

"So you have no idea how your wife came back from the dead?" Anwyn let go of her cup to press fingers against her forehead, closing her eyes.

If she thinks it's tough to say those words, I wonder if she can imagine trying to answer them.

"I don't know what to think. Nothing makes sense." Anwyn pressed both hands against her head. "The entire clan is going berserk. People are terrified."

"Don't you wonder why that is?" said Kahtar.

The Mother dropped her hands to glare at him.

There you are! I was worried for a minute.

"What are you saying?" she said.

"That we witnessed a miracle. That we should be rejoicing, but I seem to be the only one feeling that way. That maybe the clan is terrified because they'd rather Beth stayed dead."

The Mother swallowed, her ivory column of neck moving.

You too?

"People don't come back from the dead."

"Well, it happened at least once before," said Kahtar, and waited.

"Are you seriously comparing Beth to the Christ?"

For once Kahtar couldn't hold her gaze. "Of course not, but it has happened to us now, so apparently it is possible. I can't assuage the clan's guilt over the way they've treated Beth—nor would I if I could."

The sigh coming out of Anwyn sounded ancient. "Stick to the facts, Kahtar. Beth died, murdered by seekers inside your veil. Honor is facing a death sentence for killing them. Now Beth is, somehow, alive. Should I send someone to check the seekers' bodies? Should I consider that they've somehow come back to life, too? If so, has Honor committed no crime? No. Of course he has. Despite the outcome now, he did what he did." She put a trembling hand over her eyes.

"Honor is no friend of mine or Beth's, but he didn't kill those seekers. Nor did those seekers kill Beth. Honor wandered in after the fact and he'd assert his innocence if he wasn't finally aware of how awful he's treated Beth."

With a wave of her hand The Mother dismissed the subject of Honor Monroe. "You know it's impossible for seekers to even get inside a veil. I won't get into the fact they somehow moved through time! And there are monkeys in your veil? It all fits together only in its madness. I'm having trouble wrapping my head around all this, but it did happen, and one thought keeps whirling to the surface of my mind." She waited, and eons of obedience at last forced Kahtar's eyes to hers. "If no one had saved Dianta—would she have come back to life like Beth did?"

"I don't know," Kahtar responded honestly. "It doesn't make any more sense to me than it does to the Old Guard."

"Welcome sent word that the unborn babe is now viable, or she will be in time."

Joy sparked in Kahtar's heart. "How much time?" He wanted more than anything to return to Beth's side.

"Does it matter? Kahtar, I'm going to ask you a question you will not like. Keep in mind who I am. I have to ask this."

Kahtar steeled himself.

Anwyn hesitated, then plowed forward. "I don't think anyone in this clan has ever asked you why you're physically different than every member of your family. Since your parents died so long ago, I think most of the clan has never given it much thought—until now. Most of us assumed you were a love child, but Jacobson assures me that genetically you are Constantine. I'm going to ask you, Kahtar, for your honesty. Do you have any idea why you look different than your family?"

"I wish I knew. None of any of this makes sense to me!" Kahtar said truthfully.

"Doesn't it, Kahtar? You have no clue why your wife, like Dianta, and I'm going to assume the unborn babe too, now has your eyes? Did you think we wouldn't notice?"

Kahtar put both his hands on the table. *I owe her an honest answer to this.* "I really don't know why. When Beth opened her eyes it was the strangest moment of my life. Obviously whatever is going on somehow comes from me, but I don't understand what it is. I wish I did. At least, I think I do."

"Is there a reason you think you wouldn't want to know?"

"What if it's something terrible? What if there's something dark and twisted that I carry like a disease, and I've given it to my family?"

Anwyn looked paler than normal, almost whiter than the woolen Grecian gown she wore. Before she could reply, the door from the mudroom swung open and Abigail Adit huffed in, somehow privy to Kahtar's last comment. "You mean like a genetic sexually transmitted witches' curse, Kahtar? Sometimes I think you're special needs."

Kahtar looked at the little redhead and fought back the inappropriate urge to laugh. Abigail's eyes twinkled, and she looked at The Mother and winked. Anwyn's perfectly sculpted lips twitched faintly.

"If you carried a disease," Abigail added, "I think that Welcome Palmer or Silas Jacobson would have rooted it out by now. Evil is always a choice, not a genome. You know that."

Sitting back in his chair, Kahtar relaxed. *That is true.* All of a sudden exhaustion weighed on him as though gravity had increased tenfold. *When was the last time I slept?*

"When was the last time you slept?" Abigail mirrored his thinking, and Kahtar had a feeling that it wasn't a coincidence. "Where will you even sleep now?"

"You're right, Abigail, and you do look like you could drop, Kahtar," The Mother agreed. "Of course returning to your veil isn't an option. It's obviously not safe. Unless you're accompanied by several Old Guard and investigating, I don't want even you to go back there. It sounds like there is no evidence to find anyway."

"Looks like you'll be living in the Arc now," said Abigail, and Kahtar's heart sank. *Why don't I ever want to live in the Arc?* He fought to keep the frown off his face, but one glance at The Mother and he realized she didn't want him living in the Arc either, and she wasn't as successful at hiding it.

"But first Beth is going to need you," Abigail said. "So I guess you'll be living at Cobbson for a while, and then you'll both have to move into the Arc. Maybe you could stay here with The Mother for a while. Anwyn, you've got the space, don't you?"

"No," said The Mother. "When Beth recovers you can live at her shop. It's safe enough for her there, especially if you stay with her. I'll address what to do about her parents when my head stops pounding."

Relief shot through Kahtar. That would work. He glanced at Abigail and she winked at him surreptitiously. *She orchestrated this!*

Abigail winked a second time.

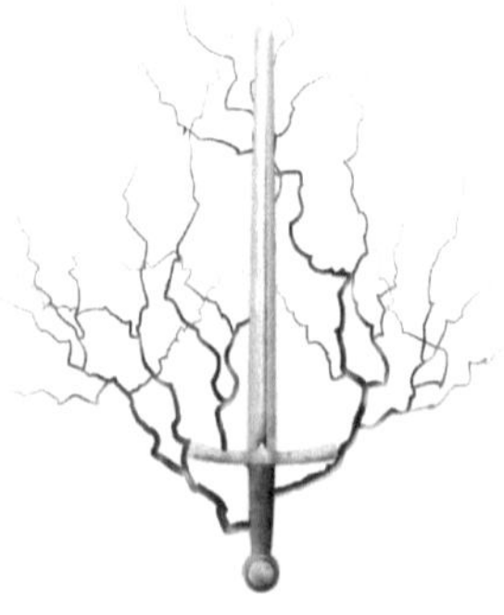

CHAPTER
FIFTEEN

Bloody Details—Remember November

"I'M NOT IMMORTAL," said Beth with conviction. Thanks to whatever drug Welcome had injected into her veins that fact floated to the forefront of her consciousness. It took her far away from what had happened inside the veil, far away from anger at Kahtar and worries about immortality or mortality. Beth's head swam freely, her thoughts sliding pleasantly, dark and filthy memories forgotten. "I'm definitely not immortal!"

Kahtar, sitting next to the hospital bed with his head resting near hers, stirred.

"It's the truth, Kahtar. I'm not immortal. Just because I regenerated from being dead and now have your eyes too, doesn't mean I'm immortal." She paused, but Kahtar didn't look up. "Wake up! Did you hear me?"

"I hear you." The comment, muffled against a pillow, sounded sad. He lifted his head and tried to smile at her, avoiding her gaze.

"How come you never believe me? Look, my eyes aren't even really all that much like yours." Beth managed to heft a hand mirror with her left hand. Unable to really control her muscles, she ended up smacking herself in the face with it. "Glad I couldn't feel that," she said from beneath it.

Kahtar took her hand and positioned the utensil so she could see her eyes. Widening them for study, Beth could see flecks of her normal blue in there. "Seriously, look at my eyes. I'm still in there."

"So you are," Kahtar agreed, stretching.

Beth succeeded in turning her head a bit in his direction. "And if you look close at Dianta's, they're not completely yours either. They're black some. Yours are gun-metal gray, but sometimes when you're outside they reflect light beautifully."

"Do they," he said without interest.

"You know I can't lie! Why aren't you relieved?"

Kahtar stopped stretching. "Do me a favor? Say out loud that I'm not immortal."

"You're not immortal," Beth replied without missing a beat, and her heart sank.

Kahtar settled back in his chair and crossed his arms. "And that's why I'm not excited about it. You can say I'm not, but I am. I remember the twelve tribes of Egypt forming—blazes, I remember the flood! If that's not immortality, what is? You can't shout out facts and tell me what is real. Your gifting has never worked like that. It's more of a Rorschach test for truth."

"No it's not," said Beth, certain he was wrong. Her heart lifted. "Holy cow, Kahtar! I know why I could say it! You're not immortal *anymore!*"

"Beth, stop. You're killing me." He sounded like he meant it. "Do you honestly think you can shout out random facts and know if they're true or not? You could answer all of the world's questions."

"Maybe I can."

"Welcome gave you that seeker medication I told him not to, didn't he?"

"Maybe he did," she hedged, but nodded her head in confirmation.

"I understand why he did it, but you need to face what happened in the veil sooner rather than later."

"Now isn't the time to worry about what happened in the veil! *Everything* is so clear right now. The laws of being! Old Guard! The

Bible's flood—hey, it wasn't water! That's a metaphor! Did you know that? You were there, weren't you?"

"Just because you think something makes sense doesn't necessarily mean you're right."

"The Big Bang Theory is—pretty much spot on."

"Beth."

"Global warming is—actually I have no clue about that. The universe is saying something about an old-fashioned whipping instead of answering. Do you think Mother Nature is into corporal punishment?"

"You're not making any sense. Rest, love."

"I don't think she'll be satisfied with having us put our heads on our desks. Hey! Aliens are—real. Holy shit, Kahtar! Did you know that?" Beth managed to turn her head and gape at him.

"No, they're not, Beth. Please don't swear. I'm going to get Welcome. I think you've got some head thawing going on."

"You're right! Not about aliens. That's true. But I shouldn't swear, swearing can create—bad karma or something, I think. You're right about the head thawing too. It doesn't feel very good. I think a pipe in my brain might have burst. Don't! I can feel when you scan into my head. It hurts."

"Only warriors can feel scans."

"Why do you always argue with me about that? My mother's a shieldmaiden. I think I have the gene. Oh my heart, did you know my mother's a shieldmaiden? I never knew that. I mean, I knew something was weird but…" Beth's mind drifted to her mother. It would explain a lot.

"If you feel like talking, why don't you tell me more about what happened in the veil? I'm going back over there in a bit—"

"No. Don't go in there. That brother-clone is connected to you, but he's—he's evil, Kahtar. Don't trust him. Don't go near him."

"I don't have a brother, evil or otherwise, and I certainly don't have a clone."

Beth snorted. "Why do you think that the Old Guard grabbed you and disappeared when I first said you did? They know it's true. Where'd they take you anyway?"

"To the veil. They wanted to scan for signs of another Covenant Keeper, but they didn't find anything."

"Oh, yes, they did."

"No, they didn't. Whoever killed those seekers scorched everything with his scan. There's no evidence, but the Old Guard want to look again."

"Your brother didn't do any such thing. He doesn't care what any of us know about him. He doesn't care about anything."

"Who scorched the evidence then?"

"Isn't it obvious? The Old Guard did it. They don't want you to know about your brother."

"Hellfire and blazes, Beth! You can't say things like that."

"Why not? It's the truth!"

Welcome pushed the door open and stuck his head in. "You called, Kahtar? I thought I heard your second voice."

"You need to check Beth."

"I'm fine," she said, holding both hands up to demonstrate. Almost instantly her muscles gave and they dropped.

Kahtar's hand shot out, protecting her face from the blow. "No, you're not."

Welcome moved to stand beside her, and Beth felt his scan brush through her. She grinned at him. Everything that had happened in the veil had receded, replaced by a floating laughter in her heart. She was glad he had given her the medicine Kahtar didn't like.

Welcome's cool hands brushed her hair off her face. "I had to give her something to take the edge off. Ever have a migraine? To the nth power. Besides, I don't want her upset right now."

"I don't like it."

"You haven't tried it," said Beth, smiling as the universe whispered its secrets to her. The scalloped ceiling tiles appeared to be opening and closing like clams. It looked beautiful and she stared silently for several minutes while Welcome poked and prodded and Kahtar spoke to him in second voice. The universe told Beth everything he said, but she didn't mind if she was going to have a stroke, post-traumatic stress, or even permanent brain damage. Not if it felt this good. Her mind drifted to more important things.

"Honor Monroe is bisexual. Did you guys know that? I wonder if he knows that. I don't really get that. I mean, pick one. Everybody only ever gets one person and I'd want to be their favorite sex, wouldn't you? Surely he has a preference. I thought he was going to declare to me once, but apparently he liked Kahtar a wee bit better."

Beth smiled at Kahtar, but he was glaring at Welcome. "It's your muscles. He likes muscles. Me too. You've got nice ones, but I also love—" Soundlessly Beth mouthed her favorite male body part at the clan doctor. Welcome's eyes sparkled with humor and the brush of his heart caught her attention. It felt like laughter. "Why's that so funny?"

"You're going through a hallucinogenic phase. It won't last very long."

Beth beamed at him. "I don't mind. Suddenly everything seems so obvious! So simple! It's expanding my mind so much!" She used her arms to show how much, pleased when they responded. Her hand caught Welcome in the jaw. "Oh, no!" she giggled. "Dang, now Welcome and all the healers will be shunning me."

In an instant all of the lightness and humor evaporated.

Fear lit through her heart as the universe retreated, dropping her back into her own life.

On the ceiling the friendly tiles turned to rotten teeth, and a tongue licked them, coming closer and closer. The taste of earth touched Beth's tongue, or maybe it was the tongue and the teeth. Vomit filled her mouth.

"*Giddy up.*"

Someone with horse breath shoved her to the ground and rode her, crushing her, grinding her into the forest floor, breaking her bones.

"*You'll do.*"

Hate and despair filled her.

"*You agreed.*"

He was using her like a portal to the dark side.

"It feels good, doesn't it?"

The remembered taste of that dark heart filled her nose and mouth with muck and filth.

"Say you like it."

Beth screamed, trying to escape. Arms wrapped around and pinned her in place, nailing her down forever.

"Be still or I won't help her."

Mushrooms bloomed from the ground around her, poking right up through the middle of her heart, right through Dianta's dark, staring eyes.

Beneath Beth the earth became a bed of worms.

Cruel, steely eyes laughing.

Beth fought, screaming and screaming until the sound scraped her throat raw and only ragged whispers came. Still he pounded, and his foul heart and breath drifted into her nostrils and mouth, choking her with worms. Something in her heart broke, and she knew nothing would ever be funny or good again.

Beth wanted to die.

And stay there.

"DEAR EL, COR meum! Palmer, do something!" Kahtar forced Beth flat on the table as hoarse screams tore from her throat and she struggled to escape. She flung her head from side to side and vomited again, coating her face, the sheets, him, Palmer.

The worst part was Kahtar could feel her heart, and knew what was happening inside her head. Tears soaked his face and his own bile torched his throat. What kind of Covenant Keeper had done this to her? Why?

"Beth, Beth, love, it's over. *Amica mea cor meum.* It's over. You're safe now."

Somewhere in the back of his mind where he always scanned, Kahtar sensed the door open and in his peripheral vision saw a flash of red. He didn't realize a woman had entered until she had wrapped her arms around Beth's kicking legs. There wasn't much to her size-wise, but it helped keep Beth from hurting herself further.

"Where have you been?" Welcome demanded over the sound of Beth's struggles. "I've been trying to find you for over twenty-four hours!"

Kahtar focused on her then and worked to place her. *Delphine Green.* Vague memories surfaced. *Warfield's daughter. In trouble often as a kid. Sent to Avalon to become Tener Mulier. When exactly did she get back?* The information came clouded, as though he'd known the answer to that question but somehow forgotten it. He refocused on Beth.

Delphine answered Welcome, but Kahtar barely heard her reply. He knew only she'd been busy doing something honorable that he didn't need to worry about. Beth continued to thrash.

"I don't dare knock her out, Kahtar," Welcome said. "Everything inside of her is a mess still. I'm afraid she would have a stroke. A bad one."

The little brunette climbed onto the table with Beth, one knee on either side of her torso and her red skirt hitched up to her thighs. She took Beth's vomit splattered head in her hands. Surprise mingled with admiration for Kahtar until Delphine began to shout into Beth's face.

"Knock it off! It's over, Beth! Shut up and be still! You're safe now! You can survive this. That's the truth! Do you hear me? It's all true. This you can see and feel! This is your non-fiction! You're safe, and you will survive this and be well! It's gone, he's gone. You're clean and whole and safe!"

To Kahtar's astonishment, Beth stopped fighting. Her eyes continued to roll upward, her body jerked, her face twitched and she remained unfocused, but she'd heard and believed the woman.

"Delphine's a storyteller," Welcome explained. "Remember when she was little? She'd tell stories and you could smell it, or feel it? The gifting has grown into something amazing. That's why I've been trying to get hold of her. I thought she could help." The men both looked at the young woman.

Delphine continued to speak, her voice soft now as though she were singing. "Nobody can hurt you here, and that bastard that attacked you—he's nothing to you. He violated himself, not you, damaged his soul, not yours. Meanwhile you're erasing him from your heart, and every moment he recedes further away. You're loved here, Beth. Can you feel my heart? I do love you, girlfriend. So does Welcome. Do you feel that? How about Kahtar? You're one lucky woman to have him. I know he's a challenge, but you can read him like a book."

"Watch it," Kahtar warned, wondering when Beth had met the mouthy little storyteller.

Delphine leaned forward, whispering in Beth's ear. Her hair hid her mouth, but Beth's ramrod stiff body began to relax. Her shoulders dropped to the table, and her legs straightened to lie flat. Delphine continued to whisper until Beth's fists unclenched and her arms relaxed beneath Kahtar's fierce grip. Delphine peeked at Welcome and scooted down to lift a leg over the bulge of pregnant belly. "How's the baby?" she asked, dismounting.

Welcome shot a glance at Kahtar before he answered. "Her growth rate is the same as her sister's."

"But?" prodded Delphine, and when Welcome shook his head ever so slightly at her she insisted in her sing-songy tone, "Kahtar wants to know now."

"I do?" said Kahtar, surprised by the fact that he suddenly did want to know. He'd been avoiding scanning the baby, unable to bear the potential for bad news. "I do," he repeated with certainty, relaxing his grip on Beth's arms and repositioning them to rest at her sides.

"This baby will surely live, probably to be born early like her sister." Welcome ran the back of one hand over the bump of Beth's belly and lowered his voice. "I won't say she'll be as healthy as her sister. The trauma during the reanimation process was severe. It's not all going to fix itself, it's not possible, and no one can heal neurons that have never existed. Likely she'll be developmentally slow and possibly deaf."

Delphine wiped her vomit splattered hands on the silky red fabric of her blouse and shrugged. "So in other words she'll be imperfectly fine like the rest of us. Well, I'm so hungry the smell of that vomit makes my mouth water, and that is pretty damn gross, isn't it?"

Despite her help, she left Kahtar with a definite feeling of dislike as she pranced out of the room.

Welcome leaned to Beth's ear, whispering. Kahtar only caught the last words and his heart sank at the absurdity of the declaration. "Whatever magic your husband has infused into you and your baby will soon make you both well."

Magic, Palmer? It's not magic, it's madness. But today I will gladly take it, though we will all surely pay—forever.

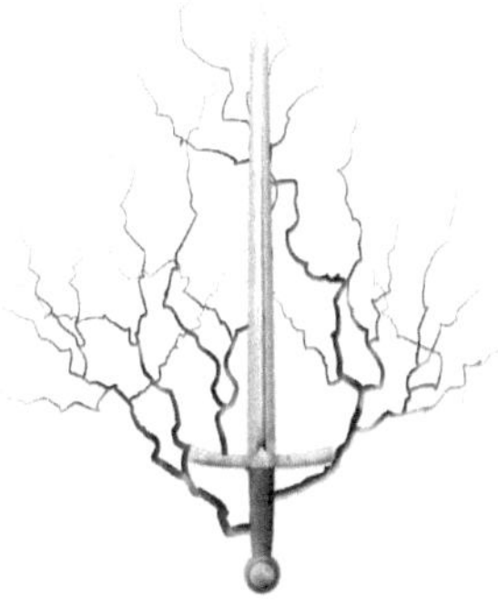

CHAPTER

SIXTEEN

Bloody Truth—Day of Reckoning

BETH WOKE FLAT on her back, buried beneath a ridiculous heap of blankets inside her familiar old apartment at Cobbson. The euphoric floating sensation had evaporated and her body felt heavy. Through cloudy vision she saw Kahtar asleep on top the covers next to her, wearing only his under layer of warrior clothes. Glad to see him at her side, she still wished she had the strength to put her feet against him and shove him to the floor, hard.

With effort Beth turned her head toward the window. Daylight peeked in around the edges of the shade, further blurring her vision. She closed her eyes and the act hurt. Every muscle and bone ached, from the roots of her hair to her nailbeds.

Of course it hurts. I've been beaten not half to death, but all the way.

The thought might have made her shudder, but apparently her body hadn't regained that function. Taking a deep breath came easy, and she moved her hands to touch her belly, finding the numbness had faded from her hands enough to feel it. Beth exhaled the breath with relief. Beneath her hands the belly moved.

Joyful fury lit through her.

Fuck you, Doppelganger. We're going to be fine. At least she hoped so. No matter what, it would surely be miraculous perfection compared to how that bastard in the veil had left her. Beth wiggled her fingers and toes and they responded stiffly, although a beat behind. Her mouth still felt like leather and sand, and licking her lips only smeared them with whatever lemony oil they'd put inside her mouth. Turning her head to look at Kahtar again, she discovered he'd somehow managed to do an about face without her hearing.

There were tears in his eyes. "How do you feel?" he whispered.

Unable to bear the intensity of his gaze, she looked away and rasped, "I am dead tired."

"Not funny."

"Practically killed me." Beth didn't think dead jokes were funny either, but some base part of her wanted to remind Kahtar, to grind his face into what had happened because he had abandoned her.

"Please, don't," he said. "Do you think I'll ever forget this was my fault?"

How does he always know what I'm thinking?

The thought was followed by the realization that his admission wasn't even true, what had happened wasn't Kahtar's fault at all. He didn't even know the magnitude of what had happened. She had to tell him. As warrior chief alone he had to know what was out there, what had found its way into his veil.

Kahtar knelt next to her, looking almost adorable in the maroon one-piece, but Beth still wished she had the strength to shove him to the floor. Even if it hadn't been his fault, he'd still been wrong to treat her like he had. He neatly folded the blankets down, avoiding her gaze.

"Too cold," Beth complained. He seemed too close without the mountain of covers between them.

"I'll warm you," he said.

Beth hadn't been this close to Kahtar without being in trouble in many months—not since the day before the trouble in the Arc. The touch of his heart circled hers, cautious and respectful, but very much receptive as it hadn't been in a long time. *So long!* In one deft movement he slid beside her and shoved a familiar arm under her neck. The other hand reached for her hip to bring her closer and she balked, attempting to scoot away and failing miserably.

Kahtar paused. "What is it?"

"Suddenly it's all right? Suddenly—because I died, you want me? You've forgiven me? Everything is right between us? Just like that? The laws haven't changed, Kahtar. But I'm glad to know what I have to do to earn your forgiveness."

Emotion clouded his steely eyes as he took hold of her far hip and rolled her onto her side, pulling her closer. The belly got in the way of real physical contact, but the intensity of two joined hearts simmered because they were so close. Unable to forgive him so easily, Beth kept her heart on lockdown.

Kahtar sighed. "I deserve that, and no, it's not all right. But I am the one at fault and you get to determine if this breach is insurmountable, and no matter what you decide, we are one heart and you aren't well. Please let me help you. Let me in."

"I'm so angry with you I can't. I don't want to. If I had the strength, I would hit you so much worse than I did back in June. I would take every weapon from that nightmare collection of yours and hit you with it."

Kahtar's brows rose and he pursed his lips, nodding. "That isn't a bad idea, Beth. I think I'd like that too, when you get your strength back."

"You're serious? Do you want the clan to send me into the mists?"

"There would be no crime in parrying with me. I think I would like it very much. There needs to be retribution for what I've done to you. I know I'd feel better for it."

"I will never understand the rules. Not ever."

Although she tried to escape it, he took her chin between his thumb and finger. "Probably not. Now talk to me, tell me anything. What do you need to say?" He formed it as a question, forcing the bald truth from her lips.

"You've acted heartless. You made me feel like that half-seeker, less-than Covenant Keeper person the clan thinks I am."

Kahtar dropped his hand but held her gaze and Beth knew those words hurt him. The truth did that.

"I'm not her. I'm not less-than. You know that, but you treated me like they do! The clan must be so disappointed I survived."

"Many of them are," he admitted.

"I'm tired of being the better person with the clan and I refuse to allow you to treat me like they do. You shunned me, Kahtar. I tried to apologize to you for months! And when I finally did, you refused it just like Honor did!"

"I did not refuse it."

"Don't you spit half-truths at me!" Beth tried to escape the arm wrapped under her neck, but Kahtar held her close. "You said I told my first lie!"

"You said you were sorry you made me push you. What was that?"

"It was the best apology I could offer! It was the truth, and I meant it!"

"Well, you shouldn't have apologized for me pushing you. That's the part I apologize for."

"How can I ever get anything right with you people? I said I was sorry and you wouldn't accept it!"

"Listen. You're right that I didn't accept it right away. I couldn't. I had to wait for Honor's apology and the shunning to officially end. Beth, this will make you even angrier, and I'm going to ask you to be the bigger person with me just once more and hear me out. Please remember that I've always been warrior—as far back as I can remember. My earliest memories aren't of me as a child, but of me as a warrior. I never had a wife before you, but I've had many close relationships with brothers and soulmates in a way that only soldiers can understand. Warriors have stood by me for ages, in life and death. All my heart has ever had has been the love of those men. That is my history and will always be part of me. I can no more change that than you can stop telling the truth."

"So you stood by them instead of me."

"Shunning requires solidarity, especially among warriors. For me to break with them—especially as the only one who wouldn't agree—

would have meant stepping down as warrior chief to the clan. For a brief moment I considered it. But the only one qualified to take my place is Orange Stoddard and he's a hundred and thirty years old. I was angry after what you said and did in the Arc, and when I returned to the veil and found you'd gone I'll admit I was furious. I was coming after you when the decree was being finalized and I was summoned to the cave. In the end I trusted my sense of duty and my experience, and I stood with my men, as I always have."

Fury burned hot through Beth, and she didn't try to hold it back. "No. I will not be the bigger person even once more. Go to your warriors, Kahtar, and give them all of your heart. I'm not going to allow you to hurt me anymore!"

"No. Look, Beth, even on that day in the Arc, as angry as I was, I assumed you'd apologize fairly soon and the shunning wouldn't be as awful an act as it sounds in retrospect. I kept thinking you needed to learn to submit to the clan's rules."

The act of completely closing her heart against Kahtar's took effort, but it was the one act of violence she could manage despite her condition. It felt as though she'd physically slammed a door with her own body trapped inside it, like she'd been clamped in a metal vise across the chest, and her heart crushed. Beth closed her eyes against the pain of it, struggling to hold to her resolve and keep him shut out.

Kahtar's hoarse voice sounded pained. "Perhaps since you've felt me do that to you, you thought it would be effortless? I deserve being shut out, but you don't. I did choose to join the shunning and I deserve your contempt for that, but know I was also ordered to keep away from you until you made it right with the warriors. That made my choice somewhat a given. They didn't say I had to keep apart from you, but only that if I didn't, if I interfered in your choice in any way, your sentence would be decided by the clan's warriors of ilu."

"So what?!"

"What do you think they would have done, Beth? What do you think the clan wants from you?"

Beth considered, and the answer scorched her heart. A dry sob preceded her answer. "They want me to go away."

"Yes."

"They hate me."

Kahtar considered that for a moment. "I want to argue that assessment. None of us are made for hate. I want to say they need to keep apart from the world of seekers, that they hate the thought of mixing those two worlds. But you've spoken it as truth, and I've seen us from your perspective lately, so it would be wrong of me to reword your feelings, wouldn't it?"

"Yes."

"Over the past year I suppose I've excused the clan's actions because their fear of the seeker world is natural, and you've never once complained."

"I'm used to being an outsider, and I knew they needed time. But I'm tired of it, and I just don't like them anymore."

"Does that assessment include me then?"

"Yes. I don't like you at all. So much that I wish I could stop loving you. I want to beat it back and kill it and be free of it."

Kahtar smoothed Beth's hair off her face, tucking it behind an ear. He left his hand there, resting against her neck. She could feel him twirling hair around his fingers as he spoke. "You can't be free of me. That's what joining means. Even though you are angry and disappointed because I failed you, your heart is bound to mine."

"That is something you forgot quite easily! You chose the clan over me!" Beth couldn't hide the pain burning through her.

Kahtar tugged her closer, until the entire length of their bodies lay touching, her stomach pressed against his so hard he surely felt their child moving. Beth's heart clawed at the door she'd closed on him like a tiger in a bamboo cage, shredding the barrier, desperate.

"I was a fool and wrong. I can't undo the wrong I've already done, but in this case I can promise not to ever do it again. Next time even if I know it's wrong to stand with you, I will. How many times have I led a man into the mists because he stood with his heart? Because he blindly followed the first law to love while ignoring the others? But I give you my pledge here and now to be that man. I will follow my heart and my oath to you first, even if we both suffer for it." Kahtar pressed his forehead to hers. "I should give you time to forgive me, to open your heart to mine willingly. But I can't wait anymore, Beth. What you're feeling right now? Having shut yourself off to me? It seems I've felt that forever, and then you were gone. *Dead.* And I couldn't find you or fix it. There was no escape from the pain. So I'm sorry for this too, but I'm claiming what is mine here and now and nothing is going to separate us again."

Kahtar's heart moved through the barrier as effortlessly as he moved through water. Suddenly it was if he stood bare beside Beth. She could feel him with every inch of her skin, though physically he hadn't moved. "Your move," he whispered, his heart open like a pool of clean water in a dusty desert. *Come to me,* it pleaded.

"You're not being fair," Beth said, her voice quavering.

"I know." He smiled, his fingers twisting her hair as he waited.

"I don't like cheaters!"

"I know. I also know if I'd seen you any of those days you waited for me at the police station, that you'd have done this to me."

"That's beside the point!"

Beth didn't know which of them moved first, but in an instant they were one again, complete and whole. Kahtar's heart claimed her heart like a sinking ship, swallowing it. She burrowed into him, plowing into the mattress and awkwardly wrapping her arms and legs around his body as she roughly shoved her heart inside his, claiming it again.

Home at last.

"I love you, Kahtar, because I can't stop, but I still might never like you again," Beth said, closing her eyes in exhaustion.

OPENING HIS EYES, Kahtar realized darkness had come while they slept. Beth had not eaten per the doctor's instructions, but neither had she moved yet. It was dangerous in her condition. Gathering her in his arms, he carried his snoring wife out of the little bedroom. She opened one eye as he moved down the narrow hall.

"I still don't like you."

"Can't say I blame you," he said, propping her up to sit in a chair in the austere kitchenette. Within minutes he'd prepared a strong tea and held it to her lips. In his second voice he called for someone to bring food.

Beth leaned against him, and Kahtar wasn't certain if she needed the support to sit or if she wanted to be as close to him as he did to her. She rested one arm across his shoulders, fingers clutching his garment as he helped her drink. Between every sip she rested her head on his shoulder and he kissed it. If she held the position for any length of time he found his body responding like a teenage boy copping a feel behind the stalactites during Glory.

"Kahtar, I have to tell you something I don't want to."

The teenage feeling evaporated. "Tell me."

"He raped my heart."

Kahtar's mouth went dry, understanding instantly. "What do you mean?"

"As if we were married. He forced me into his heart."

Hearts were given, not taken. Kahtar tried to keep accusation out of his voice, but even as he spoke he heard it. "How does one do that?"

Beth took a shaky breath. "I let him. I went into his heart willingly. He wouldn't heal Dianta unless I did."

Setting the mug down, Kahtar extricated himself and stood to his feet, running a hand over his head. "That makes no sense, Beth. Forcing a heart—there is no pleasure derived in it."

"It gets worse."

"All right." He waited, still standing, unable to look into her eyes.

"When I said he was your brother or your clone, I meant it. Physically he was every inch you, every movement, every expression. Dianta wanted to go to him, thinking it was you. His face, his body, it was yours."

"His heart?" Kahtar forced the question out of his mouth, jealously throbbing through every inch of his body.

Beth laughed, but she didn't sound amused. "No. His heart was filth. When you touch my heart now, can't you feel where he was? What he did to me? Can you feel I'm dirty?" Her voice ended with a dry sob.

Immediately contrite, Kahtar sat next to Beth again, wrapping his arms around her. They were joined. She could no more have wanted another heart than he could. "No, Beth. His touch is completely gone now. Can you still feel it?"

She nodded and he thought if she had any spare liquid in her body that her eyes would be full of tears. He covered her hands with his and brought them to his lips. "I'm sorry if I sounded jealous or accusing. The thought of someone else touching your heart like mine—it makes me crazy. I've never heard of anyone deriving pleasure from doing such a thing. There have been times I've known of a Covenant Keeper to rape a body. But the heart—even the most base and dark clans hold the heart sacred."

"There was nothing sacred about it. It was the filthiest thing imaginable. It is what killed me in the end. I went willingly to escape it."

"Beth!"

"He ground against me, both his heart and his body, pulled my underpants off to be closer, but he didn't—"

"I know he didn't, but I hadn't realized how sick—"

"I don't know why he didn't do that too. All of it, I mean. I thought he would. It didn't even matter by then, but he didn't. Maybe because he kept saying I was dirty. I guess he knew I was part seeker. I've never hated anyone before, Kahtar, but I hate him."

Kahtar was in complete agreement.

"Sometimes I didn't know what hurt more, my body or my heart, but in the end I knew it was my heart. And nobody came; nobody came at all, Kahtar. I called Old Guard, but they didn't come either."

He knew she'd called for him too, knew she didn't want to say it, knew she had to be furious that he hadn't come. He would never forgive himself. His entire existence was about protecting his people, and he'd failed the one who mattered most to him. Worse still, it was his fault that she'd gone unprotected. As warrior chief he'd known the

Old Guard had joined the shunning and stopped listening for her voice. He'd left her unguarded.

The apartment door swung open, startling him and interrupting their conversation. Kahtar forced his attention to Delphine as she stormed in, dressed like a seeker in a short red dress with leggings. Against clan rules her fingernails were painted as red as the dress. After what she'd done for Beth, he tried to force down his immediate dislike, especially since she carried a tray of food.

"I've been marching up and down the hall carrying this tray for hours waiting for you to wake up and want to eat," she said to Beth.

"My wife needs hot food, not something you've been carrying around the hallway for hours."

"Oh, it's hot then, piping hot. You'll need to blow on every bite so she doesn't burn her mouth."

Kahtar glanced at the tray as Beth sighed. Swirls of steam rose off the soup and out of the teapot. He nodded and Delphine slid it across the table.

"You can go," he said.

"You mean I need to stay."

"Yes," said Kahtar. "You need to stay." Kahtar glanced at the little brunette again, puzzled. "Why do you need to stay?"

"Because Beth really super-duper needs me here."

Kahtar nodded in agreement, wondering why he hadn't realized how much Beth needed the storyteller there. Although Delphine had helped earlier, he couldn't think what good she'd do right now.

"What exactly do you need to do right now?" Unfolding a napkin he dropped it on Beth's lap and scooted closer, reaching for a spoon.

"I need to super-duper help her," said Delphine, plopping into a chair across from them. "'Cause she super-duper needs me."

"Knock it off, Delphine," said Beth. "I don't think it's funny."

Kahtar scooped steaming soup onto a spoon and blew on it, wondering what Beth didn't think was funny.

She eyed him acerbically. "Seriously, Kahtar, you can't see that soup is so cold it's congealed?"

Despite his cooling breath the soup on the spoon still steamed. Beth's steely gray eyes had that candid gleam he knew so well, and she was looking at the soup with distaste. *Why does she think the soup is cold?* He frowned, blowing again as he scanned into Beth's head.

Beth lifted both hands to cover her head, smacking the spoon out of his hand. *She really can sense a scan!*

"Stop it! There's nothing wrong with me! Delphine is telling you a story about the soup! It's cold!"

"What are you talking about?" Kahtar stuck his fingertip into the soup and yanked it out of the scalding liquid, immediately putting it in his mouth. A blister swelled against his tongue.

Beth grabbed his hand and inspected the finger. She glared at Delphine. "Do you have any idea how dangerous your gifting is?"

"Only when you interfere!" Delphine said. "Kahtar knows better than to stick his finger into boiling liquid until you start putting doubts in his head!"

What are they going on about? Kahtar's scalp prickled.

"His skin actually blistered! Look what you did!"

Delphine leveled a gaze at Beth that Kahtar didn't like at all.

"That's your fault," Delphine said.

"Why would it be anyone's fault but mine?" Kahtar growled. "I think you should leave, Delphine."

Delphine's face flushed nearly as red as her dress.

"What about Beth?" she asked.

Kahtar glanced at his wife. *She needs Delphine!* "You're right. Stay," he said.

Beside him Beth gave an exasperated sigh. "Kahtar! Think about this! Why do you want her to stay?"

"Yes, Kahtar," said Delphine, her voice sounded falsely sweet. "Why should I stay?"

Kahtar wiped the spoon clean with his fingers, dipping it into the steaming soup again. "Because Beth super-duper needs you."

Delphine's dimples deepened on either side of a huge smile. "See! Beth just doesn't like to admit that," she practically sang.

Kahtar relaxed, lifting the spoonful of soup to Beth's lips. She slapped it away.

"Knock it off," said Beth to Delphine. "Am I supposed to think any of this is funny?"

"It's just a lark, Beth. I thought you could use a laugh after all you've been through."

"After all I've been through? You know Cultuelle Khristos treats me like a pariah because my father—whom none of them even know—isn't a Covenant Keeper, yet you, a full blooded one, use your giftings to make fun of people and satisfy your lusts on good men!"

"What?" Kahtar sat up straight, looking from Beth's face to Delphine's.

"You have no idea what my motives are!" Delphine's bright eyes sparked with anger. "Don't you dare judge me! You don't know me!" Delphine shoved to her feet, her pretty face crumpling. "You have no clue what I've been through!"

What the blazes is going on here? Kahtar stared at the women. What had Delphine been through? And why was Beth making such outrageous claims?

Beth somehow managed to shove to her feet, clutching the table with both hands for support. "I don't like the way you treat my husband. It's disrespectful, not funny! You have no right to use people just because you can! ilu forbid someone use you someday. Then you'll know how it feels!"

Delphine's mouth dropped open and Kahtar rose beside Beth to gently force her to sit. She tried to resist him, shaking with fury, but didn't have enough strength to hold out. No sooner had Beth taken her seat then Delphine lashed out at her.

"You think I don't know how it feels to be used? I thought you knew the truth!" To Kahtar's surprise tears spilled out of the little brunette's eyes. "You think I'm having fun kissing men who have no interest in me? Let me tell you something, Beth Constantine, I'm just trying to find a reason to live. There's only one man I've ever wanted, and I think you know who that is. But even if he doesn't want me I know that if he can do good in this world, so can I. I might not anchor him, but everything about him anchors me!" Delphine stomped across the floor, somehow making every footstep count despite her small size.

Kahtar let out a breath as Delphine slammed the door behind her. "Whew. What on earth was that about?"

"Don't you know?" said Beth.

"I have no clue. Why is she trying to find a reason to live kissing men who don't like her? And what does anchoring him and anchoring me mean?"

"Kahtar, you don't know what anchoring means? Isn't that a Covenant Keeper term?"

"No. I've never even heard of it."

Beth shot to her feet and Kahtar followed suit.

"Stop her, Kahtar! Hurry!"

"Why?"

"Kahtar, just do it! Hurry! She can make tesseracts! She'll be gone."

Kahtar almost denied it, but Beth couldn't lie. "Old Guard!" he shouted.

One of the giant men shimmered into being. "Warrior Chief?"

"Get Delphine Green and bring her here now."

The man vanished.

Beth collapsed into her chair. "Oh, please! Oh, no!"

"He'll get her. Calm down and tell me what this is about."

Smacking her fingertips rhythmically against her forehead, she shook her head. "No! No! He might not be able to. Not only can she make tesseracts, but I'm pretty sure she can divert Old Guard."

Kahtar moved his chair to go after Delphine himself.

"No, don't go yourself. She can divert you too. She was doing it the whole time she was in here. That stupid soup is so cold it's practically one solid lump of slime, but you actually burned your finger on it because she told you it was hot! She lied and you believed it that much!"

Peering at the steaming soup, Kahtar glanced doubtfully at Beth. "Are you certain you're not imagining these things?"

"Good lord, Kahtar! Anchor, she said anchor! He wanted me in his heart so I could anchor him! She's your duplicate's anchor. He was looking for her! Why didn't I see who he meant? She's kissing everyone trying to find a way to break his hold on her! How did I not see that? It's probably why she's such a pain in the ass too!" Beth started to cry, horrible, dry sobs. "Oh, my heart, what if he finds her, Kahtar? Sooner or later he will, won't he? He's following her! She's probably drawn to him too whether she likes it or not! That poor woman!"

"Are you drawn to go to him?" Jealousy scorched Kahtar's heart at the thought that not only had Beth touched another man's heart like his, but she wanted to do it again.

"No, never! But he just used me like his anchor, she's his actual anchor! I'm—" Beth stopped speaking and her mouth dropped open.

"What?"

"I'm your anchor. He said I'm your anchor. He said he'd heal Dianta if I let him use me like I let you—as an anchor. Kahtar! That's why you're not immortal anymore. Maybe you are contagious. I mean look at me, look at Dianta, and I'm sure our unborn baby is the same way. We have your eyes, and we all died, but none of us repeated. We came right back here. To each other. Kahtar, you're not going to repeat anymore, not like you used to! If you do die, you'll do what the rest of us did. Don't you see? We're anchoring each other, *right here*."

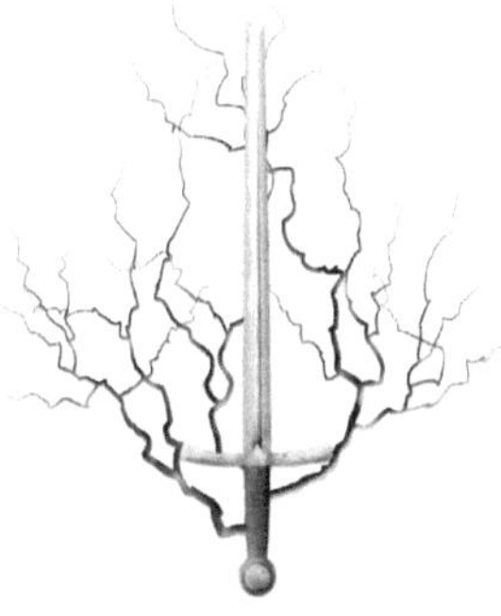

CHAPTER
SEVENTEEN

Ugly Truth—Mid-November

"OF COURSE RETURNING *to your veil isn't an option. It's obviously not safe. Unless you're accompanied by several Old Guard and investigating, I don't want you to go back there again.*"

Kahtar replayed The Mother's orders in his mind as he stood inside his veil, unaccompanied by a single Old Guard.

"But she said I don't *want* you to go back there again. She didn't order me not to, or say *I forbid*," he said to himself.

Really? You've sunk to searching for loopholes like a lawyer? Where is the honor in this?

Kahtar threaded his hands behind his head and paced beneath the pine trees. Yesterday at this time, Old Guard had come to him and reported that a giraffe had to be transported out of his veil. That meant the man who'd left Beth for dead had been inside the veil not twenty-four hours ago. That also meant Delphine—who'd been missing two weeks now—was still being pursued by the same man. Kahtar had no doubt that the young woman was also still tessering from inside his veil. Heaven knew what she was up to.

Apparently both of them can slip under the Old Guard's radar. "And apparently Delphine Green has an even bigger penchant for trouble than I ever suspected," he whispered into the darkening forest. Clad in his warm hunting tunic and heavy leggings, Kahtar had his bow slung over his back and his police pistol jammed into his belt. He wasn't taking any chances.

A gust of wind from the north stirred leaves over the forest floor, but a distinct line down the middle of them moved in the wrong direction. Kahtar froze and scanned, sensing her. Delphine Green—five foot one inch, one-hundred eleven pounds, appeared out of nowhere and moved along the path.

Kahtar backed against a bare maple tree and waited. She moved fast, wearing a bright red cloak like a naughty Red Riding Hood. Kahtar was tempted to follow her unawares, but had a bad feeling she'd vanish into a tesseract and leave him behind.

"Doing recon?" he said.

She screamed and he stepped into her path. Clutching her chest with both hands she gasped, "God, Kahtar! I nearly pissed myself! I thought you were—I thought you were—*someone else!*"

"If you hang around long enough, he might show up too."

"I don't know who you mean."

Living with Beth had certainly sensitized Kahtar to lies, but this one of Delphine's had as much finesse as a child with their hand in the cookie jar.

"He, or as you call him *someone else*, came through here last night right after you did."

Delphine's eyes were huge in her pale face. "You saw him?"

"No, but the Old Guard saw the giraffe he left behind."

"He's mad," she whispered. "He doesn't know how to tesser right and he's going to end up killing someone."

"Hate to bring this up, Delphine. But he already has killed people. Remember? A couple of innocent seekers, a father and son, according to my wife. Not to mention that technically he killed my daughter and my wife, too. So, if you could fit it into your busy schedule, I'd like to meet him. We have some things to go over."

"Oh, Kahtar! I didn't forget, and I was going to explain it all to you, I just had to do some… stuff…first."

"Hey! I assumed you're a busy woman. Is that seeker perfume you're wearing? Smells expensive."

She crossed her arms over her chest. "My reasons aren't trivial."

"I'm sure they're more important than protecting your clan from a heartless killer."

Delphine shot him a dirty look. "I assumed you could take care of the clan for a few days!"

"I assumed you would follow the laws of being your whole life."

"I have never broken a single law of being!"

Narrowing his eyes at her, Kahtar said, "Is that because the truth is you've broken more than a single one? It seems to me you have a way with words and the ability to do whatever pops into your head, without ever getting caught."

"I have never broken *any* laws of being! If I had the ability to avoid being caught we wouldn't be having this conversation, and I wouldn't have a stalker attaching garbage tesseracts to mine and making a mess in my wake."

"Beth says you're his anchor."

Delphine gasped, not in surprise, but as though struggling to take air into her lungs. In the dim light of the forest he couldn't see tears in her eyes, but sensed they were there. It surprised him when she pulled herself up to full height and said, "When do you want to go after him?"

"Now's good."

"Now?" Her voice sounded hollow.

"Yes, now. Beth's at her parents, so she'll be safe. She's had a couple weeks to recover, but if she has any trouble the Old Guard are watching her. I want to go now. Before that monster hurts someone else, or you use your gifting to divert me and slip away again."

A tremble rippled through Delphine from head to foot, but she nodded. "All right. Now. I'm ready, but it'd probably be a good idea if you changed into seeker clothes first."

TED WHITE HAD transformed a storage room into a baby girl wonderland with fairy lights and giant flowers painted on the walls. Dianta slept sprawled in a white iron crib on her stomach, her feet in casts Welcome had insisted would help lessen the limp she'd surely have. They stretched her legs into an uncomfortable Y-shape and forced her full lips into a permanent frown. Carole White stood beside Beth, fingering Dianta's miniscule brown toes.

"Car wreck?" she asked.

Beth nodded. Kahtar and Honor Monroe had staged the accident to ensure she could tell the lie. They'd rear ended Beth's Saab with a Hummer, with Beth and Dianta buckled into the vehicle full of padding, and demanded she make sure it rolled forward from the gentle tap and into the side of a brand new Challenger. All she'd done was dent a door and leave a yellow scratch in the black paint, yet it allowed her to explain her and Dianta's condition to her parents. *A huge black Hummer rear ended my car and I rolled right into a brand new Challenger!*

Ted had a fit, and Carole had wrapped Dianta into her arms and held her for the past three hours. Moving from the baby's toes, Carole smoothed her blanket of dark hair and turned to look into her daughter's eyes, putting her hand on Beth's protruding stomach. "What really happened, Beth?"

Oh no! Eyes darting to the window, Beth searched for the sparkle of Old Guard in the darkness outside but saw none. It didn't matter; she had to answer the question and struggled to find a safe way to word it.

"I-I was attacked and Dianta got hurt. Don't tell Dad! He'll have a heart attack."

"I thought your husband could keep you safe," said Carole, her green eyes searching Beth's face. "Do we need to worry you'll be attacked again? Or someone else?"

In that moment Beth wanted more than ever to ask how much her mother knew. She had the distinct impression her mom was asking if someone might hurt her dad. She shook her head, sticking to the bare minimum. "No. You don't need to worry that they'll hurt anyone again."

"Good," Carole growled, dropping her hand from Beth's stomach. Suddenly she straightened, grabbed the crib railing and squeezed, her eyes focused on a wall of pink decorations. Abruptly she turned and left the room.

No sooner did Beth hear Carole's footsteps on the stairs than Kahtar entered the room in his police uniform.

"I didn't hear your car!"

"I didn't bring it." Kahtar bent over Dianta, running his fingers gently over her. "I think I startled your mother. I'm sure she heard me appear in the back hallway."

"Well, she knows stuff she shouldn't. I can tell."

Kahtar looked down at her, fighting a smile. "You showed up with new eyes, she could hardly miss that."

"My father noticed too."

"Of course he did."

"He cried."

Kahtar stopped smiling. "I'm sorry, Beth. I never knew any of this could happen."

"I know you didn't, but I'd have gone with you anyway. I have no regrets about you, Kahtar, and Dad was great. He just kept asking if I was okay and I talked about contact lenses like you said to and he pretended to buy it, but I know he knows I don't have contact lenses."

"Of course he does. Beth, they both know just enough to know not to push for more information. This is as good as your relationship can be with them. I'm sorry for that."

"I think my mom can scan."

"She can," said Kahtar. "That's why I didn't bother trying to hide dropping out of thin air. I figured she wouldn't say a word. Your mother's a champ. She really loves you."

"Wait. Why are you here? I thought you said you weren't going to come."

"I finally caught up with Delphine, and we're going after him."

"No, Kahtar!"

"Shhh. Your dad won't take my appearing from thin air nearly as well as your mom."

"You did this on purpose! You got me here where I can't argue! You planned it right down to Dianta sleeping in the crib!"

"I'm sorry."

"You say that a lot. How about being up front with me instead of manipulating and having to apologize so much?"

"I have to know that monster isn't going to come back, and I need to know what I am. How many times have you told me to ask Old Guard? For what he's worth, apparently I have a brother I can ask. Maybe he'll answer."

"You haven't felt his heart. I don't want you near him. Please."

"We need to know if you and Dianta and this one," he said as he placed a hand on her belly, "are immortal like me."

"You're not immortal anymore. I told you," Beth insisted as he drew her close.

"I'd like to know what you'd call it then, Beth. You came back from the dead—rigor mortis, decomposing dead. I don't know what that means if it's not immortal. I'd like to know what we're going to face and if we're going to stay like this for the next century or two, or forever, because if I get killed in the line of duty and come back at my funeral, Cultuelle Khristos is going to have questions we'd better be able to answer. We need to know what we're up against so we can make long-term plans."

Beth couldn't argue. She had no insight into the details of what had happened to her and her daughters, both born and unborn.

"No good can come of you seeking him. You can't trust him."

Kahtar kissed her forehead. "It's better I seek him than he continues to seek Delphine here. That's what's been wrong with the veil all along. It explains the monkeys and the bird you saw. Apparently he creates tesseracts that move through space, but pull from where he's leaving. Delphine thinks he can sense hers and piggybacks onto them, but she never realized he'd been tracking her until you were attacked. The Old Guard said a giraffe showed up last night. That means he came back again still seeking Delphine, despite the fact that Old Guard are watching. What if he gets out of the veil and into the village?"

"Do you think you can convince him to leave Delphine alone? Because you can't. He needs her."

"I can be very convincing."

"He'll keep Delphine!" In her crib Dianta whimpered, and Beth lowered her voice to a whisper-shout, "Who knows what he'll do to you! Don't go Kahtar, and don't let Delphine go either!"

"I'm going, and she has to go too. I can't find him otherwise. You already said it; he'll find her eventually. At least I'll be with her."

"Promise me you won't leave her with him!" Beth grabbed the collar of his shirt. "I don't care if she took a blood oath to stay with him. You can't believe she's with him of her own free will!"

"I agree. But the only way she'll be free of him is if he's dead."

"I don't think he can be killed! He'll probably just come back like I did."

Kahtar raised a brow. "That remains to be seen."

"Take me with you."

"Don't be ridiculous. It's bad enough I'll have Delphine to protect. You'll be safe here. There are warriors and Old Guard watching the veil if he goes there. I don't want you anywhere near where he might find you."

Beth clutched at him, stress causing her hands to go numb so her fingers wouldn't obey. Kahtar lifted them to his lips and kissed them.

"I'm afraid," she said.

Kahtar wrapped his arms around her and squeezed. "Don't worry. I've been going into battle for a very long time."

"Not with him," she whispered into his shirt, fear filling her entire being. "Please let me come, I might be able to help you!"

Kahtar looked from her belly to Dianta sleeping in the crib. "You'll help me best by staying safe right here." He kissed her with meaning, his heart twining through hers, and in the crib beside them Dianta sighed happily in her sleep, the frown smoothing out as her baby heart bubbled with contentment at the edges of theirs.

After long moments Beth pulled away. "Nobody can lie to you if I'm there. Please, Kahtar."

Kahtar kissed the tip of her nose and tucked her hair behind an ear. "Nobody can hurt me if you're here. I'll be back, sooner or later." He untangled her hands from his shirt, winked, and left the room.

Beth heard the creak of floorboards and felt the strong touch of Kahtar's heart caressing hers for several seconds, making unspoken promises tinged with the faintest touch of regret. Then it vanished.

Blinking, Beth wondered why she hadn't seen the sparkle of Old Guard. It hit her then that although Kahtar never lied to her, he also didn't tell her everything.

DELPHINE WAITED FOR Kahtar at the edge of the woods near the White's house. "You should bring Beth with us."

"No," said Kahtar. "Start tessering."

Delphine lifted a closed fist and opened it as though to reveal something delicate. A tunnel of light shot out. "Hurry, so no seekers notice."

Kahtar stepped inside and she followed. "I thought creating tesseracts was a rare gifting only older women had. But not only can you do it, so can this man who attacked my wife."

"It's not a gifting I was born with, but I taught myself. I'm good at math—really good," said Delphine.

"A lot of us are good at math."

He sensed Delphine shaking her head before she pushed past him. In the light of the sparkling tesseract a faint frown wrinkled her creamy skin. She looked like a doll, an angel, perfection in miniature. Kahtar did not like or trust her.

Dark lashes ringed bright blue eyes she directed at him. "You don't see me at all. Is it because you didn't like my father? Somehow you got past your seeker prejudices to see Beth, but you hold onto Covenant Keeper ones."

"My impression of you has nothing to do with your father, although he rarely told the truth either."

She put hands on her hips. "No? I don't lie arbitrarily."

"Yet you harbor great giftings and don't even share them with your clan."

The blue eyes were intense. "Why don't you share your secrets with the clan?"

"What do you know of my secrets, Delphine?"

"Possibly more than you do, Kahtar."

"I'm Warrior Chief to you."

"So you've mentioned."

Kahtar narrowed his eyes at her.

"Your secrets are irrelevant to me."

"I'm glad you think so," he said, resting a hand on the hilt of one of his blades and motioning with his head for her to continue walking the tunnel of light. "And you dare to divert Old Guard. That is deception and lying."

Delphine had the grace to avoid his eyes as she turned and walked slowly through the tunnel. "They can sense a tesseract. It's a very temporary harmless thing for me to put their attention elsewhere for a moment."

"They would end you."

"Do you think? Sometimes I think they know."

"Why would Old Guard allow you to divert them?"

"Why indeed." Delphine trailed a petite hand over the veins of light surrounding them. "But that is neither here nor there at the moment. We should speak of him before we get there."

"Please do."

"Do you really not know who he is?" Delphine stopped to turn and search his face again. "You really have no idea?"

"I know that he used and killed my wife and you are his anchor."

Delphine recoiled from his words as though he'd slapped her.

"I'm sorry. Why don't you tell me how that happened?" He couldn't keep the accusation out of his voice. If the woman dared divert Old Guard, it was no wonder she had ended up in this mess.

Delphine turned her back on him and continued her short staccato steps forward. "I was sixteen, at Avalon, with The Mother's daughter. It's a long story. I'll spare you."

"Delphine, maybe it's best I know—the short version."

"I thought he was you at first. I've always had a crush on you, so I went with him. His name is Tartarus."

The name sounded vaguely familiar to Kahtar.

"The first time," Delphine snorted but it sounded more like a cry of pain, "I wanted to be with him. I knew by then he wasn't you. I knew you wouldn't have wanted me like that what with our ages and positions and how you feel about me being like my father. You know I'd almost given you my declaration that summer before I left. Did you really never sense how I felt?"

"No! Please focus!"

"Yeah, and that right there is why I didn't declare."

"What's why you didn't declare?"

"The way you said no, like I'd offered to cut off one of your nipples or something."

Kahtar cleared his throat. "Sorry. You were a little girl."

"Like I said, you've never really seen me. Anyway, his heart was…a hole."

"Sweet El."

"The truth is even then he seemed, well, not really human. But I mean, so do you, sometimes. I was flattered when he singled me out. Oh, what's the point of talking about this anyway? I was stupid. He took me. I escaped. A few years passed. He found me again. It was inevitable."

"You told me his name, Delphine, but who is he really? Who are his clan? Where are they? What do they believe?"

Delphine glanced back, and he caught the glisten of tears. She lifted her hands to wipe them and kept walking, continuing to speak without looking back. "You're asking all the wrong questions, Kahtar. You should ask, what is he? He's a daemonium, same as you."

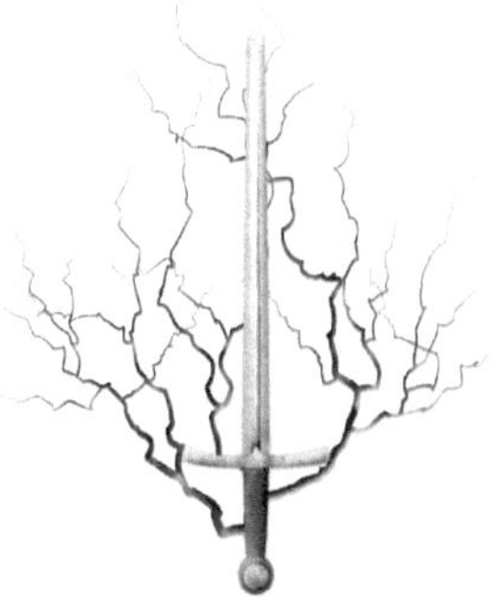

CHAPTER

EIGHTEEN

Bloody History—Gales of November

BETH SAT AT the top of the stairs, her mind racing. The stress of Kahtar's departure had left her limbs weak and numb like they'd been when she first came back. The thought of Kahtar hunting whatever his doppelganger was and trying to kill it terrified her. *Delphine won't be any help! How can he fight this by himself? What if he doesn't come back?*

"Bethy, you okay?" Her dad appeared at the foot of the stairs, peering at her through the bend in the railing. He always seemed to know when she was upset.

"No," she admitted. "I'm not okay, Dad."

Ted stomped up the stairs and studied her for a moment. "Me neither. Come down and help me try my hand at halo-halo ice cream. I found a recipe online."

"That's not going to fix this."

"Bigger than halo-halo? Uh-oh." Ted tugged Beth to stand and tucked her hand under his arm. She allowed him to lead her down the stairs. "You married a big strong guy. You have to trust that he can take care of himself."

Beth managed to keep her mouth from dropping open. *He knows Kahtar was here! How does he know that?*

Ted gave her a sly smile and tapped his chest.

A smile lit Beth's lips and she squeezed his hand. *He sensed Kahtar! Hah! What would Cultuelle Khristos think of my seeker dad now?* "You always make me feel better."

Ted chuckled. The doorbell rang and he tugged Beth to the front door to answer it with him. "If it's the punk rocker Halloween kid again, I'm not giving him any halo-halo. Did I tell you he came back this year?"

"You're kidding. What did Mom do?"

"She opened the front door and handed him the trash to take to the curb. I've got to say, your mother has always had excellent timing."

Beth tried not to remember what she'd been doing this Halloween. "What did he do with it?"

"What do you think he did? He took it to the curb." Ted dropped her hand and yanked the door open.

They both gazed down at the chubby older woman standing on the doorstep. Abigail Adit, Elder of Cultuelle Khristos, looked up at them, her red hair wound into a sharp bun, cat eye glasses jammed onto her nose. Both hands were on her hips and one foot tapped out an impatient staccato on the stoop.

"Took you long enough!" she snapped. "It's freezing out here and did I have time to grab a coat? No, I did not! There's no more time to waste on niceties!" She reached through the doorway, grabbed Beth's wrist and pulled her outside. The woman's strength shocked Beth.

Ted followed. "Hey, lady, what do you think you're doing?"

"Everything!" Abigail said. "Same thing I do every single day, with very little help from the rest of the world, mind you."

Ted followed them. "Beth, do you know this woman?"

Abigail hauled Beth across the driveway. "Back off, Ted White, I don't have time for your nonsense right now!"

What the—Abigail knows my dad?! Beth glanced back at him. "I do know her, Daddy. It's okay—I think!" She held one hand up, signaling Ted to stop following as Abigail hauled Beth away.

They rounded the corner of the house, where Beth's mother blocked their path.

"Oh, ho, just what do you think you're going to do, Miss Carole?" Abigail snapped.

Miss Carole?

All the blood seemed to drain from Carole's face. "Sister Mary Josephine?" she whispered.

"Of course! That too. When I said *everything*, I meant it. Does anybody ever think maybe I'd like a day off? If you have to get in someone's way, young lady, go redirect your husband so Beth and I can get out of here! I have to go catch that stupid warrior your daughter married!"

Beth watched in stunned amazement as her mother obeyed, hurrying around the front of the house. Abigail pulled Beth through the gate into the backyard, stretched out one wrinkled hand, and the light-veined tunnel of a tesseract shot open in front of them. "Well, come on! Do I need to go get a convertible to carry you in? Move it!"

FOR A GIFTING she'd learned and cobbled together, Delphine's tesseract moved them smoothly. Standing inside the tube-like structure veined with light, Kahtar considered that in all his time he'd known few who could tesser and less who could tesser well. Yet Delphine tessered them across the sea almost as effortlessly as Abigail could.

They exited to a grassy landscape dotted with sheep, the sun rising in the distance. A motorway sat on the next hill beside an old ruin on the edge of the cliff, already swarming with tourists. Kahtar felt self-conscious in his American police uniform, with only a single blade strapped to his side. He scanned, recognizing the location.

"This is Wales," Delphine said. "Or Cymru, if you speak the language."

"There are a lot of seekers and eyes here. You said this daemonium hid in Persia."

Delphine's scarlet cloak rippled in the wind as she turned to him, a certain beacon against the green grass. "Tartarus, and he's not in Iran-Persia as we know it; he's in Persia-Persia. You could call it a pocket of the past, kind of like the entrance to the mists is dotted with places that don't really belong anywhere. He lives in a place like that."

Kahtar refused to allow his expression to reflect surprise. *How does this girl, who can't be much more than twenty, know of daemoniums and the mists? I barely know these things after all my time.*

"And how did you find such a place, Delphine?" he asked, unable to keep the threat out of his voice. The girl had been clever enough to find a pocket of the past and young and stupid enough to go there. They would all suffer for her actions, as Beth already had.

"I told you I'm really good at math. I spot patterns," she said, positioning her red shoes on the dry grass of a hillock. "And I told you he found me when I was at a festival just outside Avalon. Can you imagine anything safer? I didn't seek him out."

For the first time Kahtar noticed something in her sparkling, often mischievous blue eyes that reminded him almost of his own, as though she'd seen too much. Her dimple-producing smile gave nothing of her internal state away. "Anyway, what you really need to know is that Tartarus has the same gifting I do, storytelling, but it's not the same at all. He uses it as a weapon to get what he wants."

"You don't?"

Again Delphine stopped to look at him. "No. I do not. I use my gifting to help people no one else will help." She began moving again, motioning for him to follow. "He's dark and evil and although I could theoretically use my storytelling against him, I couldn't ever manage it. His will is much stronger than mine, and when I'm with him I want to be with him, at least I think I do—I can never be completely sure! But you can't trust me once we're there. I only ever escaped him because he didn't know I could make tesseracts, and he thought I'd died."

"Tesseracts seem to be a strong defense to have over someone."

"Not really. He can make his own, also self-taught. It was only useful when he didn't know I could make them. His tesseracts are dangerous. Obviously he doesn't care who or what he damages when he creates them—look what he did to your veil. If he makes one, don't go inside it for anything." Delphine jumped off the edge of a large rock and landed on a flat space of grass. "We're here."

Kahtar looked across the hillside and seascape. They were near the ruin of the old fortress, which appeared to be a popular tourist spot. "We tesser to Persia from here? Right out in the open?"

"Not exactly. This is the part where we sneak inside Clan Aberdyfi's cloak. Cloaks are like a veil, only you can see the outside world from the hood of it. They're thicker than a veil, but have so many openings and pockets they're pretty easy to find and get inside of, one way or another."

"I know what a cloak is," said Kahtar, frowning at her. "You don't just slip into another clan's territory. By all rights they could claim our lives for it!"

Delphine looked delighted by that prospect, blue eyes sparkling, dimples everywhere. She shrugged. "They'd have to catch us first!"

"How many times have you done this? How many times have you sneaked in and out of Clan—what did you call them—Aberdyfi's—cloak?"

"It's pronounced Aber-dovey, the same in English and Welsh. And I've only ever sneaked out once, never in. There's an exit from your look-alike daemonium's lair inside. It's how I escaped. I figure if I could get out this way, I can get back in this way."

"I don't tesser, but even I know that's a big assumption. Tesseract doors don't swing both ways!"

"Let's just say I'm pretty sure I can fiddle with the hinges and force it."

"Pretty sure?"

"Mostly sure."

Kahtar clenched his fists. "Delphine, I don't want to get put to death by some ancient Welsh clan. The clans in this part of the world can be harsh. Worst case scenario they kill us in whatever slow manner they prefer and they get Old Guard involved so both our families go into the mists! You don't fool around with the clans from these lands! They're humorless!"

"That was before Princess Di. They're much more feeling now."

"What?"

"It was a joke, Kahtar. Look, it's the only way to get to him. He's not going to stop looking for me. If he keeps looking for me in your veil he'll eventually figure out where in the world it is. After that he'll know where our Arc is. There's no doubt in my mind he'll know right off that most of Willowyth is our clan. He's not like most Covenant Keepers. He doesn't care if seekers notice him. I'm not here because I think we're going to defeat him and make him go away. I'm here as a sacrifice to protect our clan. I know I won't be coming back with you."

The finality in her voice conflicted with Kahtar's preconceptions of her. There was no immaturity in her action. *Why didn't I realize that was her plan?* "You're not going in with me then. Get me inside and go back to our Arc."

Delphine smiled up at him, her gaze direct. "I wish you had really kissed me just once before you met Beth. I know I was too young back then, or you were too old, but I would have been good for you, and I would have loved you well."

Her words, tinged with depth and regret, slid over Kahtar's heart. He had no idea what to say. Without waiting for a reply Delphine turned her attention to petting the air beside her and Kahtar assumed she had found the edge of the cloak.

"You're a good man," she added.

A faint huff of amusement escaped Kahtar. *Child, I'm not.*

"Now be patient for a few minutes. We need to slip in and slide through this part. They won't even notice we were there until we're gone. The trick is to tesser us inside to Tartarus's lair before anyone in Clan Aberdyfi sees us."

Patiently and stealthily Delphine continued to tuck and wave her hands over nothing. Kahtar saw her fingertips vanish beneath something from time to time, but suddenly she shot to her feet, looking behind them.

"Someone's using the tesseract I made to get us here! I think Abigail's followed us! Come on!" Delphine grabbed the front of his shirt and yanked him through the cloak to the sound of breaking glass. "Run!"

IMMORTALITY WASN'T KAHTAR'S gifting, nor the eons of experience it provided. Kahtar's gifting was gestalt, and at moments like this it saved his life. In the split second Delphine and Kahtar exploded through Clan Aberdyfi's protective cloak and landed in the middle of their village, he saw everything. Light glistened on wind-swept waves below the cliff to his right, boats bobbed in the harbor below. To his left a renovated fortress sat atop a hill, dotted with solar panels and hundreds of tiny windmills whirring in the November breeze. A walled path snaked around it, leading downhill. Everywhere warriors and mariners went about their business. As the sound of breaking glass echoed, announcing the breach of their cloak, they turned almost as one to look at Kahtar and Delphine with various expressions of disbelief.

You and me both, gentlemen!

Delphine hit the ground running, yanking at the ties of her cloak so the heavy scarlet fabric fell free behind her. Shifting his balteus so his sheathed sword wouldn't interfere as they ran, Kahtar moved closer to the seawall, setting the pace beside her. He couldn't cut these men down, and already had deduced the exact spot on the path where they'd be boxed in and captured.

Why did I follow a child?

At his side Delphine kept up admirably, her red slippers flying over flagstone, tiny but fast. Kahtar grabbed the back of her dress and jumped onto the seawall, holding onto her as they dodged half a dozen warriors still trying to figure it all out. The warrior chief in him admonished their slow reactions. He jumped back to the path and steadied Delphine before letting her go.

It took only seconds to reach the scrum of warriors below, but it was enough time for the men to form together to try and block their escape. Four of them spread across the path as a human shield and Kahtar reached for Delphine, intending to hold her and ram through them.

Delphine had other plans. She waved her hand, and the path seemed to drop, sending the men rolling into a ditch. Kahtar and Delphine jumped the dip and ran past. Behind him Kahtar sensed the ground right itself. *Tesseract.*

"You won't call the Old Guard!" she shouted after the people of Clan Aberdyfi in her sing-songy voice, storytelling them into obedience.

Another half dozen warriors with a pack of dogs on their heels rushed forward.

"They're wolves!" Delphine shouted again and again. Kahtar glanced over; like magic, every single dog had become a wolf. Startled by the sight, a couple warriors tripped and fell.

It's not real! It's not real! Shades of the Abyss this woman is dangerous!

"How does that help?" Kahtar shouted. Goose bumps stood up all over his body. Wolves and warriors ran toward them.

"Watch!" The dog-wolves neared, and Delphine nearly sang to them, "Get em! Get em! Good boys!" The dog-wolves turned on their owners. Kahtar wondered if maybe they would clear the entire path, then spotted a big blond warrior stepping into their path, his blade drawn.

Quester.

Internally Kahtar groaned. Battles were won or lost by men who either believed or didn't believe they could win. This one didn't just believe he could win, he knew it.

As Kahtar and Delphine ran right for them, a dozen more warriors joined the quester with their swords drawn, taking position and waiting. The strength of their giftings seemed to form an impenetrable barrier and Kahtar doubted a flick of Delphine's wrist could topple these men.

"Do you trust me?" she shouted, grabbing his hand.

"Hell, no!" Kahtar said, and for the briefest moment he made eye contact with the quester and knew the man had heard.

The quester smiled.

Delphine's left hand flicked, not at the wall of warriors, but at the seawall to their right. Momentum took their feet up an invisible ramp and right over the seawall into thin air, where they dropped straight down.

Bracing himself for a landing that would involve two broken legs, Kahtar fell and sensed Delphine doing the same. Before they crashed onto the rocky beach below they hit a thin filmy bubble. It gave under them and popped, cushioning the blow as they landed on the beach. *Another tesseract.*

Blast. She's good.

Delphine panted, her hands resting on the knees of her stripped leggings. "Did you see that gorgeous quester?"

Kahtar tugged on the back of Delphine's dress to force her upright. "I think you're going to get a chance to meet him!"

Far above them, the man leapt off the seawall after them, sword in hand.

"He'll break his legs!" Delphine twisted her wrist in that direction and a large bubble appeared beneath the man.

Kahtar grabbed her wrist. "Fool girl, let him! It'll slow him down! Where to?"

Delphine took off across the sand, tugging Kahtar in her wake, and despite his grip on her hand she managed to make a creaking and grinding tesseract. It moved them instantly over half a mile of beach to the base of a cliff.

"It's through here." Her voice sounded grim. "And what comes out must go in. I think."

"That quester's crossing the beach, so think fast."

Delphine made a quick gesture. "That should slow him down." She used her right hand to hold her left wrist and moved it in circles, her small body swaying with it. "Just gotta figure a few things out. You don't want to get inside one of these puppies and have it collapse."

Kahtar's stomach dropped, but with the quester still charging across the beach, broadsword in hand, he wasn't certain if he'd rather die slowly crushed cell by cell inside Delphine's makeshift tesseract or hacked to pieces by a man who'd smile the whole time. "Decisions, decisions," he said.

"What?"

"Nothing. Hurry up. You didn't slow that quester down a bit."

"You were making a morbid joke, weren't you? We could have made a great pair."

"I'm two feet taller than you and even my boots are older than you are. We would have made a great joke."

Shimmering lights appeared near the shore. Kahtar swore.

"Old Guard coming?" asked Delphine conversationally as the quester bore down on them not twenty yards away.

"At least we'll have a great death," muttered Kahtar. "Your quester's on us."

Delphine whipped around to face the quester with him. To Kahtar's surprise the man slowed his approach, arms wide, sword lowered and smiling.

"If you wanted to meet me, love, I could have thought of less dramatic ways."

"But how boring," said Delphine. "If you could manage to fit a car chase in with all this I'd follow you anywhere."

Kahtar feigned to his left, but the grinning quester shifted with him. "Don't make me, big fella," the man warned.

"Big Fella's name is Kahtar, and I'm Delphine, and you're not going to do anything but stand right there and cover our backs from the people barreling down on us," said Delphine in her sing-songy, spell-casting voice.

"By all means." The quester laughed. "Anything else?"

"Actually, I would love a kiss."

"Delphine!" Kahtar glared. "No! His Old Guard are coming!"

"Maybe some other time," said the quester.

"I only have now," said Delphine. She rose on tiptoe and kissed the startled man.

Kahtar yanked her back onto her feet. "Can we go?"

"Best ever," she breathed and commanded, "Now stay right there." Light shimmered behind the quester and she said, "Oh, no! Those are our Old Guard, Kahtar, not his!"

Not waiting for his reply, she plunged right through the cliff wall, taking him with her. The stone turned to liquid around them, propelling them forward. Delphine leaned her head back to shout instructions. "Hold onto me tightly, Kahtar! If Tartarus senses me coming he'll close the tesseract off to anyone else."

Kahtar gripped Delphine's slight shoulder. He'd only died from a collapsing tesseract once, and although he'd long forgotten the details of that time, the memory of the pain had remained.

Someone gripped his shoulder, and Kahtar turned to find the smiling quester holding onto him. The man winked as though it were a great joke. The strangely liquid tesseract rumbled around them like an earthquake and shifted beneath their feet, but Kahtar's fear of being crushed cell by cell in a slow and painful death was replaced by a new one. Beth and Abigail were right behind the quester, framed by the sparkle of Old Guard behind them.

Kahtar's heart dropped into the pit of his stomach even as the touch of Beth's neared.

Sweet El, no! If the tesseract collapsed, Beth might die, or be trapped inside for eternity.

"Hold onto each other!" he bellowed, but the sound moved oddly, unable to travel inside the now shaking tesseract. Terror gripped his heart as he watched Beth's pale face and he willed her to understand, shouting with his second voice, *"Hold onto each other! Touch!"*

In the shimmering storm of light he watched her move as if in slow motion, reaching for the quester's shoulder. Her fingers had barely skimmed the man's blouse before the tesseract crackled with the sound of breaking glass. Wind belched through it, and they were ejected out like water escaping the blowhole of a whale.

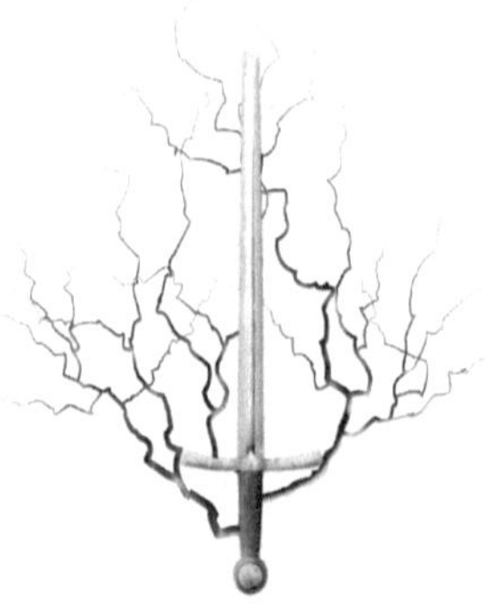

CHAPTER

NINETEEN

Bleeding Relatives—Persian Mists

SKIDDING ACROSS A desert landscape, they landed flat on scalding hot sand. The sound of a collapsing tesseract sounded like the detonation of a megaton nuclear bomb. The flash of an explosion moved through the air causing a split-second sandstorm that buried everyone. The expulsion had saved their lives.

Wiping sand from his eyes, Kahtar looked around the desert landscape. Somehow the quester had remained on his feet, his hair still neatly tied in a sandy bun.

"Kahtar," Beth called, and he scrambled over to uncover her. Gazing at her, both angry she'd followed and thankful she was there, he realized she'd been right. The clear summer eyes he'd come to love were still in there, beyond the steely glint. Lifting her under the arms, he hauled Beth to stand and brushed the gritty dust off her. Kahtar sensed the quester behind him politely assist Abigail and Delphine, his blade clutched in his right hand the entire time.

Spitting sand out of her mouth Delphine asked, "What was that noise?" Her voice sounded dim after the crushing sound of the explosion.

"That's the sound of an Old Guard ending. The tesseract collapsed on him," Kahtar said.

Instinct made them all duck and cover their ears as a second blast blew over them. Kneeling, Kahtar only half-closed his eyes as the force of it moved past them and from a distance he sensed a composition he recognized only too well—his own. It approached from the courtyard of a villa, the only structure on the vast plain of desert.

"And that sound," said a vaguely familiar, deep voice, "is a second Old Guard ending. Very little can kill an Old Guard, but a collapsing tesseract can finish off pretty much anything. It's quite painful I hear. Isn't that a shame?"

Standing, Kahtar forced himself to look at the man, despite the darkness of the approaching heart warning against it. He'd faced evil before, but this was the first time it wore his face. There could be no denying he and Tartarus were related. They were almost identical, yet he felt no real stir of recognition and hoped such a look of wicked delight had never once crossed his own face.

"You!" Beth spat, brushing sand off her arms and taking a brave step toward the man. "How dare you hurt Old Guard and laugh! Your life is forfeit! They will end you!"

Tartarus cocked his head, examining Beth with his brows raised. Dirty hair hung to his shoulders, several shades darker than Kahtar's had ever been. A beard brushed the top of his striped desert robe. As dangerous as his heart felt, the man carried no weapons. His hands hung loose at his sides, his feet encased in sandals. He looked very much a peaceful man of the desert.

Kahtar was not fooled.

If the fierceness of Beth's newfound steely gaze hadn't been enlightening enough for Kahtar to understand why people avoided looking into his eyes, the cold expression in this man's would have.

Tartarus's eyes flickered with amusement over rotund little Abigail still brushing sand off her plain green dress to the big quester, and came to rest on Kahtar as he responded to Beth's threat.

"The Old Guard have no quarrel with me. I didn't invite them, nor any of you, and it was not my tesseract that killed them. You forced your way to my doorstep and the Old Guard paid the price. Since you return what is mine, I will demand no restitution for the trespass. You have my leave to go and bother me no more." His steely eyes carried no threat or curiosity for Kahtar and they moved to Delphine standing partially behind the big quester like a red flower seeking the protection of a tree.

Tartarus licked his lips as he looked at her, and the relief in his eyes reminded Kahtar of his own whenever he saw Beth after an absence. "Come to me, woman."

Like an obedient puppy Delphine skirted around the big quester and darted across the sand to stand in front of Tartarus, eyes lowered, hands clutching the sides of her red dress. Half a dozen plebes jogged through a domed archway in a wall to encircle Tartarus and Delphine. The boys looked old enough to be studying on Atlas, which was too old to be dressed in the broadcloth tunics and tall boots of young plebes. They were the only other people Kahtar could see, but he suspected there were others within the walls of the adobe villa. He resisted the urge to scan.

Tartarus smiled, his eyes shining as he reached for Delphine as though to brush his fingers over her cheek. Instead he made a fist, hitting her so hard she fell to the ground. Kahtar stepped halfway in front of the quester to stop his interference, holding the man's sword arm.

"Wait," he whispered, ignoring Beth's violent protests. Abigail kept her distance and remained quiet.

Crumpled in the sand at Tartarus's feet, Delphine kept her head submissively bowed, but her abuser grabbed a handful of her dark hair, hauling her to her knees. He shot a look of warning at the rest of them.

"She broke her oath to me!" he said, and yanked Delphine's head back to look into her eyes. "And you lied to me, didn't you little one? You will never lie to me again!" he commanded in the same sing-songy voice Delphine used when wrapping someone into one of her stories. "You'll do as I say!" He lifted Delphine by handfuls of hair and dress until her feet dangled above the ground. Tartarus closed his eyes and leaned close, brushing his tongue across her cheek, his expression blissful as he slid his tongue up and over an eye and back down her nose. Reaching her mouth, he sucked in her full bottom lip and bit.

Delphine gave no reaction, expressionless even as he slid one hand to encircle her neck.

"Aw, come on!" growled the quester, pulling his arm from Kahtar's grasp. "You can't allow this!"

Tartarus let Delphine drop to the sand, his lips reddened with faint streaks of blood. He licked them off slowly and said, "My apologies if I've offended your sensibilities, quester. Perhaps you are too young to understand the draw of a woman you can truly feel."

"I sincerely doubt you can feel anyone's heart," said Beth.

Kahtar grabbed her shoulder before she could move toward the man. "She came of her own free will, Beth," he told her, "to fulfil her oath to him. You can't interfere."

"Screw that, Kahtar! I will interfere! I know what he wants to do to her! He did it to me, and he's not doing it to another woman as long as I have breath in my body!"

"No, Beth," said Kahtar. "We will obey the laws."

Still licking his lips, Tartarus nodded. "Yes, and you have no business here. Go, Attar. Take what is yours and be gone."

Attar. The familiar name echoed through Kahtar's mind. *Attar and Artarus.* Perhaps he had heard of this man long ago, but he'd certainly never laid eyes on him or sensed his heart before today. He'd remember that dark heart.

"Are you my brother?" asked Kahtar, unable to keep the doubt out of his voice. "Artarus?"

"Ah!" A look of distaste lit Tartarus's features. "Such a paternal term for an experimentum. A failed one in your case. Our *father*," Tartarus looked highly amused by the term, "is a patient—*man*." Again the look of profound amusement. "He waits for you still, but he hasn't seen her, has he? Your addition." Tartarus gestured with a slight movement of his head toward Beth, his amusement turning to disgust. "I understand needing an anchor. Repeating is a waste of time." He waved toward Delphine, and looked again at Beth. "I use one too! They are rare and attractive, but giving yourself to one of these women—especially that one! You're stuck now and nearly mortal, sharing your energy with her and her spawn. Failed experimentum is an accurate description of you. Go, Attar, you bore me."

"What is our father? Answer me and I will leave."

Beth put her hands on Kahtar's restraining arm and squeezed, her heart swelling around his as though protecting him. Kahtar turned to her in surprise. *She knows the answer!*

"It doesn't even matter," Beth said. "You're mine now, and Dianta's." Placing her hand over the swell of her belly, she added, "And our new daughter's. Let's go, you don't need the answers he can give you."

"Ah, yes!" said Tartarus, "Go, Attar. If I see you again I won't be so lenient to your friends and family." The look he shot at Beth's belly was pure hatred, and Kahtar moved Beth behind him. Destruction was much easier than protection, and he knew what this man was capable of because he knew what he could be capable of, should he ever care to abandon all he believed in. Time had taught him much.

Tartarus lifted his hand and pointed at a spot past the quester. A tesseract blew inward with brute force, like a black hole ripped open in space. "Go. I won't ask you again."

"After you answer my question I will leave, but I will only go in a tesseract Delphine makes."

The hatred in Tartarus's eyes was all for him this time. "If I wanted you dead, *brother*," he drew the word out, every syllable dripping with loathing, "you would be gone."

"It's the truth, Kahtar," Beth whispered. "I don't think he will hurt us."

"There are more than us here, and he left you dead in the veil," Kahtar whispered back.

Tartarus no longer paid them any attention; his eyes were focused on Delphine trembling before him. He seemed to be enjoying it. Something inside Kahtar shifted painfully to see the little spitfire so cowed by any man.

"If you want me to leave her, I need assurance of her well-being."

"I give you my word, Attar." The comment dripped with condescension.

"I can't leave a member of my clan to be abused by you."

Impatience transformed Tartarus's face into something far from Kahtar's as he snarled, "Do not speak foolishness to me!" Slicing his hands sharply through the air, something ghosted from them like a sheet of glass, moving in a semi-circle past Delphine. Like dominos all six of his own plebes dropped to the desert sand, spurting blood. Kahtar shoved Beth roughly to the ground, mentally pleading with her to stay put while he and the quester ran to the plebes' aid.

Kahtar put a hand on two of the boys, not bothering to draw his sword. A blade was no use against this man. The quester determinedly clung to his weapon, somehow managing to heal two boys at the same time despite it. Delphine crawled to their aid as well, shaking, blood dripping from her swollen lips.

"You will not die, none of you. You will be fine. Breathe. Stay conscious!" she ordered in her lilting storyteller voice.

Tartarus circled them, his big sandaled feet scraping through sand. "She's mine, willingly and by her own oath," he snarled. "You have no right to interfere with her choice to stay."

"Give me your oath no harm will come to her and I will go."

"Harm will come to her; she's human. Harm comes to them all." Tartarus's eyes seemed to be drawn unwillingly to Beth, who hadn't stayed in the sand. She now moved from boy to boy to help, though her healing skill did little. "Perhaps not all. Your anchor is more like you than a human now."

"I'm human!" Kahtar defended. Warm anger lit through him as Beth's wide eyes and Tartarus's sarcastic laughter told him that wasn't entirely true.

"What matters is that you have no claim to Delphine!" said Beth. She took Delphine's hand and said loudly to her, "Don't stay with him. Even if you're foresworn and sent into the mists for breaking your oath, you'd be better off."

Delphine didn't respond as she knelt before Tartarus, but her fingers clenched Beth's.

Beth glared at Tartarus. "She didn't give you an oath of her own free will. What right do you have to enforce something you coerced from her?"

The man bent to peer into Beth's face. "She took a blood oath of her own free will."

"Liar."

Kahtar sensed the quester's laughter, but Tartarus moved to strike her. The fist he swung toward her face hit Kahtar's palm instead.

"Don't you dare," he growled. "If you ever touch her again, I will destroy you no matter the consequences."

"You're still here after I asked you to leave," Tartarus growled back. "Your woman is annoying me. You will leave the quester as retribution. He can be of service to me." The way he said *service* made Kahtar look at Tartarus twice, but the quester stood with his hand on his blade, unperturbed. "And the old woman, too. I'm certain I can find some way she can amuse me."

Kahtar half expected Abigail to trounce forward and verbally rip the daemonium to shreds, but she didn't move, her head bowed as she stood close to the tesseract. With the filthy touch of Tartarus's heart polluting theirs he could hardly blame her.

Tartarus ran a long finger back and forth over his bearded chin. "Take too long, brother, and I will not grant you and your anchor safe passage either."

"He's lying, Kahtar," said Beth.

Tartarus narrowed his eyes at her. "Kneel before me, woman," he said, his words dripping with the sing-songy inflection Delphine often used. He grabbed Delphine's hair and jammed her face into his crotch, grinding. Kahtar had to hold tightly to the quester.

Tartarus turned his attention again to Beth. "You will serve me as you did in the veil. My brother will not interfere as I use you again."

Kahtar tried to move, but his body wouldn't obey. Unlike when Delphine wrapped him into her stories for manipulation, he was fully aware of it, and this made it worse.

"How do you keep any giftings with your dishonor?" demanded Beth. "You don't, do you? You steal shadows of other's giftings but have none of your own. Use mine if you dare. Take a good look at what you are and know the truth of it. Your heart is a maw of sickness and you need cruelty to feel anything."

"You will obey me! Now! Kneel!"

"No, I won't!" Beth sneered. "Your words have no power over me, but the truth has power over you. You are an infection! You use people to try to feel, but the truth is if you felt for even a moment what you really were it would destroy you!"

"I know exactly what I am, anchor!"

"So do I," said Beth. "Someone who chose wrong and tries to justify it! You lie to yourself!"

Furious Tartarus pushed a hand against the air in front of him. Something rippled there and the muscles in Kahtar's legs strained as he fought to move, to protect Beth from whatever was coming for her. The air rippled with the approach of something deadly, but the quester swung his huge sword before it touched her. Something exploded like shards of black glass and fell to the sand.

Tartarus moved his hands again, tossing something flat and whirring toward the quester, but the man stopped it with his blade and threw it right back at Tartarus. He made a move as though to sidestep it, but at his feet Delphine grabbed his legs and prevented him, allowing the blast to cut into his torso like a circular saw. Delphine hung on and he shouted, yanking her hair as the thing he'd created dug into his own body, tearing his flesh and staining his robes with blood.

"Die!" he shouted at Delphine in his sing-song voice and she went limp and fell to the ground. "Die!" he bellowed at the quester, but the command seemed to ping off the quester's blade.

"No! He lies, Delphine!" Beth raced for her friend. Tartarus used his hands to dislodge the avenging force digging into his body and he flung it free. Beth dropped into the sand at his feet beside Delphine. "You don't have to listen to him! Fight it, don't you dare die because he tells you to! He's lying! Don't listen to his lies!"

The quester swung his sword at Kahtar, slicing right across the shirt of his police uniform and making a shallow, burning flesh wound. "Feel that?" He grinned. "Thought you might need a wakeup call. How about you draw your blade and we put an end to this?"

The reality of the pain released Kahtar from whatever hold Tartarus held him in. He tugged his sword free and followed the quester, who went after the wobbling circle of darkness and cracked his blade against it like a baseball bat, redirecting it back at Tartarus. "Keep your heads down, ladies!"

Clutching his wound, Tartarus dodged the oncoming whirl. Kahtar pressed the tip of his blade into Tartarus's chest to hold him in place. "Be still or I'll cut you all the way through myself."

"You don't dare!" Tartarus said. "You have no power over me!"

Kahtar suspected it was true, knew if he rammed his blade through the man's heart he'd not die or something equally strange would occur. He did not want to run a man through only to have him regenerate. "Maybe not," he said, "But I think the quester has something for you."

The circle of dark light now whirred on the tip of the quester's sword like a giant pinwheel. "You dropped this," he said conversationally, shoving the undulating bit of darkness into the front of Tartarus's bloodied robes.

Tartarus laughed as it bit into him again, his steely eyes meeting Kahtar's. "You will heal me of this and kill the quester."

Kahtar's heart sank as the words took hold of him like poison, sliding through his veins. Once more the quester's blade poked into him, this time right across his cheek, cleaning the command from his blood like an infection.

"Sorry," the quester said, smiling. "I don't want to have to kill both of you, although I suspect my clan will vote to kill you for trespass after we finish up here anyway."

"My own tesseracts cannot kill me," said Tartarus and his evil grin looked nothing like the quester's easygoing smile. The whirling pinwheel now appeared to be healing the earlier damage. His shredded, bloodstained robes shone with a silvery light. "Delphine! Protect me," he whispered.

The tiny woman moved from beneath Beth's desperately slapping hands, suddenly resurrected. Kahtar kept his sword pointed at Tartarus and one eye on Delphine.

"As you wish," Delphine said, reaching for the quester's blade as though to obey. He tried to yank it from her grasp, but Delphine stretched her fingers to the blade and touched it. Something that looked like a small tesseract stretched from her hand and ran the length of the quester's blade, joining with the whirring tesseract of Tartarus's own making.

Tartarus watched until a bubble of light shot from the blade and right into him. His victorious smile vanished. "Betrayer," he whispered.

"I'm protecting you—or your soul—from yourself," said Delphine. "Goodbye."

That quickly, the man seemed to go supernova like a sun. Something exploded in his middle, scorching Kahtar's vision with the blast of light and knocking everyone off their feet. For a brief moment Tartarus seemed to vanish from the force of the detonation, and then bloody gore and flesh rained down from the skies.

"OH, GROSS! NO!" said Beth as hunks of meat splattered her from above.

Kahtar and the others seemed to think nothing more of it than if it were rain. Even the plebes were grinning from ear to ear. "This is a person! This was a person!" Beth tried to shake it off her hands. Kahtar's huge smile told her he didn't care.

Delphine didn't smile as she knelt beside Beth in the sand. "It's all right. He had to die. I've had plenty of time to come to terms with that. Hold your heart from this part of death. You can do it." Her voice had the familiar sing-song tone, and Beth allowed herself to slip into it and believe Delphine's words. They were the truth.

Kahtar and the quester were patting each other on the back and exchanging introductions like old friends. Delphine tugged her to stand and Beth allowed Kahtar to introduce her to Augustus Vota-dini. She tried not to look at the hunks of gore in his long hair as she pressed her wrists politely to his. Forgoing social niceties, Delphine went straight for the quester's lips. Kahtar bent to Beth's, but his blood-splattered face prevented her from cooperating with him. She apologized with her heart.

"Is he completely dead?" she whispered.

Kahtar shook his head. "It isn't likely, but repeating takes time. Even if he is born in the next nine months or so it will be at least a couple decades before he returns. By then Delphine's heart will belong safely with another and she won't be able to anchor him, as he calls it. She'll be safe from him."

"What of us? I don't think you were allowed to kill each other. Did you sense how much he wanted to hurt you? Something stopped him."

Wrapping his arm around her Kahtar smiled into her face. "ilu lives strongly in my heart, Beth. I think he will forgive me this death. Anyone else's judgment doesn't matter to me."

"It ought to," snapped Abigail Adit from her spot near the ruined tesseract. "You're about to have your memory jogged rather unpleasantly. Try to keep a grip on who you really are, and in case you need that spelled out to you, that would be the man you've chosen to be over the millennia."

Abigail's words got the full attention of Delphine and Augustus, and the quester mumbled, "Millennia?"

"You know about me?" Kahtar's tone conveyed incredulity. Beth wondered why she hadn't suspected all along. She had every reason to believe Abigail had manipulated and arranged her relationship with Kahtar from the beginning.

The ground beneath their feet trembled with an echoing bang as though something from Jurassic Park had taken a step nearby. Beth's heartbeat tripled with fear. Kahtar and the quester raised their blades, both searching the horizon for whatever approached.

"You best sheathe your blade, warrior," said Abigail to Kahtar. "Not you," she said to the quester. "Delphine, Beth, it's probably best if neither of you speak—not that you'll be able to."

A sound echoed across the desert like the roar of a beast, part animal and part monster, and the ground trembled again with another massive footstep.

"What's coming?" asked Kahtar.

"I suppose for all intents and purposes, you could say it's your father," said Abigail.

The quester eyed Kahtar. "Is there something I should know?"

"There's a demon coming," said Abigail, "and he's pissed off."

DESPITE THE HORRORS Kahtar had faced over the ages, real terror seldom infected him before a battle. Pain and suffering were familiar trials to be endured sooner or later; that fact was inescapable. He'd known when he first loved Beth that someday one of them would end. Only weeks ago it had come to pass for him, but ilu had been gracious, had blessed him with more time, even if it had only been days. Now, however, he realized it was likely Beth would lose him this time. The pain that would cause her frightened him and he tried to shove away the reassuring thought that perhaps they'd both die today, together.

Don't find solace in giving up before you've even faced this.

Another echoing footstep sounded. The quester grasped his sword with both hands and Kahtar took a deep breath and sheathed his as Abigail had demanded.

That's my father approaching.

No. My father is ilu. The thought slipped through him, as comforting as rain in a drought. He glanced at Beth, standing wide-eyed and terrified beside him, and smiled with the ease of the quester. She drew a shaky breath and nodded.

"I love you, Kahtar. So much." Her second voice moved through his mind like a kiss.

"And I love you, my sweet Beth."

Another footstep sounded so close it seemed whatever it was would have stepped on them. A man emerged from the courtyard and Kahtar blinked to shield himself from the light. Whatever this man was, he looked nothing like the demon Kahtar had expected. He was as beautiful as light in darkness, his hair golden and his movement like a dancer. Smaller than Kahtar, he moved across the desert as though winged, his fine leather shoes barely leaving footprints in the soft sand. He wore a well-cut black suit fitting each plane and angle to perfection.

Beth had once told Kahtar Old Guard were angels, but at that moment he almost forgot his wife always spoke the truth. This was what angels should look like. The touch of the approaching heart matched the body and it nearly brought tears to Kahtar's eyes. Beautiful. Perfect. A light bringer. Kahtar smiled and looked at his wife.

Beth appeared to be watching something else. She trembled, her eyes wide and terrified. Kahtar wondered how she could fear anyone so right. The sun in the heavens and the planets dancing in the galaxy were a prelude to this glory. This man alone was surely ilu's idea of perfection.

Beth can't lie.

And she can see through lies.

Kahtar blinked again, trying to spot the deception. The cold fear in Beth's heart, always partially encased by his own, told him what she saw.

Nothingness. Hollow emptiness. Hell.

The feelings from Beth's heart made goose bumps prickle over Kahtar's scalp.

That is how she perceives his heart. That is the truth.

The light bringer stopped moving less than ten feet away. Dark eyes swept over them and came to rest on Beth. For a moment the only sound in the desert came from the faintest whisper of wind occasionally stirring a patch of sand. It seemed no one dared breathe, and Kahtar didn't know if it was because of the brilliant being of light standing before them or if the others perceived him as Beth did. The eyes moved to his own face, and golden light glowed in their depths.

"What have you done?" The second voice echoed through Kahtar's very bones and moved through him like late afternoon shadows, blocking the light of this being. The distress of causing even the faintest waning of this brilliant light bringer caused Kahtar's heart to burn.

I've failed him.

"You will atone for diminishing Artarus." Each word dipped Kahtar's heart in shadow, further blocking light. *"You will serve me, yes?"*

Words of acquiescence formed on Kahtar's lips. *I will* was on the tip of his tongue, but the feeling of grief emanating from Beth's heart slowed him from giving his oath to this angel of light.

In the profound quiet, the faintest whisper slipped from Beth. "No."

Flames seemed to flicker in the depths of the glowing eyes as they turned toward Beth.

"Morning Star," Abigail interrupted. She pushed between Beth and Kahtar to stand in front of them, all four feet ten inches of her, a ball of aged little old lady before the universe's golden perfection. "Your lies have no power here." Her words were defiant.

"You," he replied. "What have you done to mine?"

"I've done nothing but allow him real choices. He will not be yours." Strands of hair in the back of Abigail's bun seemed to snap and glow with light.

"You are the one who took Attar from me!" The flames in Morning Star's eyes brightened, their light dancing across his face. His gaze locked on Kahtar's. "She killed you when you were a child. This doorway, this woman she pretends to be, is why you have repeated through time, unable to find purchase. She kept you from me!"

Kahtar didn't need to look at Beth to know the words were true.

Abigail twisted to look at him. Her plump, wrinkled face smoothed and thinned, but the sharp eyes didn't change. "I gave you a choice, Kahtar. I did destroy you in a tesseract long ago. Your eons of suffering are my fault, but it is nothing compared to what you'd suffer if you were his. You have a choice to make, and now you can make it knowing the truth of what he is."

For a moment the memory of that pain crowded out all else. How long had he been trapped inside that tesseract, each cell imploding so slowly? It had seemed forever. His first death. Images of other deaths flitted through his mind. Torture. Hanging. Drowning. Drawn and quartered. There were so many he couldn't remember them all, but the pain of them had stayed in his psyche. Above all, loneliness had taken root inside him like the pain of that crushing tesseract, pressing into each cell of his being. Never belonging, never knowing why.

And now he knew why. Now he knew where he belonged. This creature of light was his legacy. This is what he'd been created to do. To serve this being. He'd been made to live forever, to never suffer death. What would it be to never die?

It would be like Artarus. Hell.

Kahtar looked down at Beth and felt Morning Star's maw of nothing emanating through her heart. The truth was he'd died many times, but it had only been a slight taste of hell.

Death ends. It's finite. Hell isn't. It never ends.

Kahtar took Beth's icy hand in his warm one and threaded his fingers through it. This is where he'd belong now, and when he ended, even if it happened in mere seconds, he'd search for the truth there too. *I belong to ilu now.*

"Thank you, Abigail," he said. "I think I made my choice long ago."

Abigail smiled and turned to face Morning Star. "He's not yours."

Morning Star's glow grew brighter as though the sun rose behind him. "I made him."

"And who made you?" said Abigail. "Kahtar does not belong to you. Go back from where you came from, or I'll send you back to the one who made you."

"Do you think you can?" said Morning Star, appearing to increase in size, the flames in his eyes now bright red.

Abigail shifted, growing wider. "Oh, I think we can leave a mark." With a faint popping sound, hundreds of women appeared in the desert, forming a defensive line between Kahtar and Morning Star.

Kahtar looked left and right. There were young and old women, of all races and ages. Some looked familiar, and a slim redhead quite a way down the line leaned back to wave at him. The nun next to her rammed an elbow into her side and the young woman turned her attention back to Morning Star.

Above them the blue desert sky receded, opening to the brilliance of the heavens above. A galaxy in motion twinkled and twirled far above it.

"I can stop the anchor's heart with a snap of my fingers before you draw your next breath," said Morning Star, almost hidden from view with the crowd in front of him.

"You can." Abigail sounded delighted, and Kahtar drew Beth to his side. "Would that stop him from loving her? Bring him to you? You've lost, Morning Star. Again."

The being of light moved, taking form right in front of Beth and Kahtar. The ground beneath them echoed with his movement. He leaned toward Beth and inhaled, breathing of her. She froze, eyes wide with terror. Kahtar wrapped his arms around her in a useless effort to protect her.

In the blink of an eye Morning Star vanished, and only Abigail stood beside them, patting Beth on the shoulder with a chubby hand.

"He's gone. I always knew you had it in you, young lady."

Beth buried her face in Kahtar's chest, letting loose a stream of garbled profanities.

The line of women vanished with a loud popping sound. Abigail appeared to grow a bit fatter as she smoothed her dress over her hips and glanced over at the quester and Delphine.

"Let's get out of here. This place is giving me hot flashes. Delphine, would you like to do the honors? You're not half bad at tessering, you sneaky little brat."

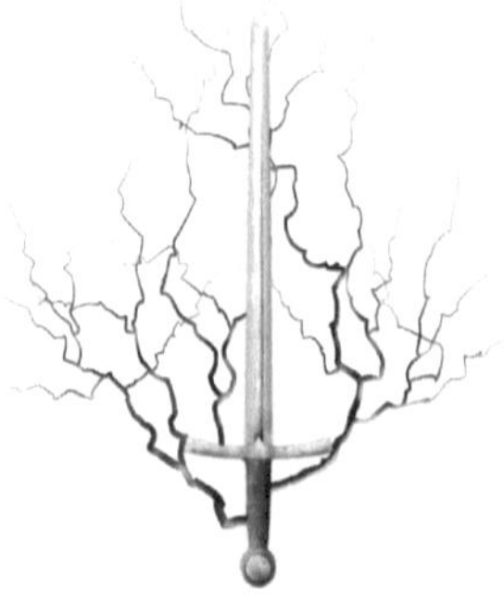

CHAPTER
TWENTY

Bloody Grace—Clan Aberdyfi

DELPHINE WAVED A new tesseract into life and Kahtar led everyone, still dripping with the slime that had been Tartarus, inside it. Instead of exiting into the cloak where surely the warriors and Old Guard of Clan Aberdyfi awaited them, the tunnel vanished, plopping them directly into the sea, deep beneath the waves. From the taste of the icy water filling Kahtar's mouth and the salty sting in his sinuses, they were in the outside world, pollution and all.

By the time Kahtar reached the surface all the bloody muck had been washed away, and he scanned for Beth. She bobbed up beside him, her lips blue and her eyes shining. The steely blue of her eyes was the most beautiful color he'd ever seen, like hot sunlight reflecting against the summer sky.

"I t-thought," she said with chattering teeth, "I r-really thought that was the end of it. I could feel how drawn you were to him, how beautiful you saw him."

"And I could feel the truth in your heart. You saved me." Kahtar wrapped his arms around Beth as waves rocked them. They were a good mile off shore and the weight of his wet clothes and sword tugged him downward, but before he could criticize Delphine, she tessered them from the water to the beach and the warmth of a huge fire.

"It was all Abigail." Beth shivered as Kahtar drew her closer to the flames, their sopping clothing trailing water over sandy pebbles. "She's the reason I came to Willowyth. The first time I met her she was a librarian who told me about the house for sale on Pearl Street."

Pulling her against his body, Kahtar slid warm hands beneath Beth's sweater to warm her pregnant belly. *I thought I've always been alone and the truth is I've never been alone.* Questions filled his mind as he looked for Abigail, but there was only Delphine and the quester. The quester had sheathed his great sword and held his hands to the fire, but Delphine was glaring as if they'd been arguing.

"You forgot Abigail," Kahtar interrupted.

"Nope," said Delphine. "She went home. Left us to the mercy of Clan Aberdyfi's retribution for our trespass." Her voice came out strained; reminding Kahtar they were not home free yet. They'd all invaded Clan Aberdyfi's cloak. By all rights they could be put to death.

The quester turned to look at him, no longer smiling.

Mentally Kahtar swore.

"I'm Clan Aberdyfi's warrior chief," the quester said. "Is there anything you'd like to tell me before I pass judgment?"

"Are you kidding?" said Beth. "Didn't you see what just happened? How much choice do you think we had?"

Squeezing her shoulders in warning, Kahtar said under his breath, "None of that changes the fact we committed a crime against his clan." It took him several seconds to recall the man's name. It seemed long ago that they'd slain Tartarus and exchanged introductions. "Augustus? It's been a long day. Would you trust me to return and face your clan's wrath another day? My wife is pregnant and cold, and I need time to consider what's happened today before I can defend my sins against you."

The quester sized him up with his dark eyes. "What is to defend, Kahtar Constantine? Your guilt is a given."

"After all you've seen today, won't you speak to your clan leaders in our defense?"

"Absolutely not. Would you have me do so? What would you have me say? That you are the immortal offspring of a demon that needed faced today? That you could only access him via our cloak? Do you think that knowledge would somehow make Clan Aberdyfi sympathetic to your cause? Do you think they'd have no concern your demon kin would someday access our cloak trying to reach you? I don't think you'd appreciate the outcome of my intervention."

"What remains of Tartarus is likely being eaten by the fishes now, and the one called Morning Star can find no refuge in the hearts of an honorable clan. What is there to fear?"

"Your argument may be sound to me, but my clan has no reason to trust you and every reason to harbor a grudge against you," Augustus replied.

Kahtar glanced at Delphine. A couple words from her with her storytelling gifting and the quester would be on his way, today likely forgotten. The idea held appeal. *No. It's wrong.*

The quester tilted his head, amusement shining in his eyes. "She's already tried her little talent on me. It doesn't work."

Crossing her arms, Delphine turned her back on the quester. Kahtar raised his eyebrows. "Teach me how to do that and I'll be at your service."

"It's not your service that would atone for the infringement."

"Whose would?" asked Kahtar.

The quester inclined his head toward Beth. "Your child. Pledge your child to my clan and all will be forgiven."

"Hell, no!" said Beth. "You can claim my life before I'll allow you to touch my child!"

"You misunderstand. I meant when she's old enough to mentor. We wouldn't abuse her, Beth Constantine. She would be well loved as part of our clan. We're a seafaring people. The discrepancy between men and women is large and our population continues to get smaller. For years now we've accepted pledges to our clan as penance for even the most serious of infringement."

"How long would she be well loved?" asked Kahtar. "You heard what passed today. My child will be like me. Two or three hundred years from now when my daughter still lives, will Clan Aberdyfi still love her without question? If they were to ever know her true history would they love her at all?"

"Ah," said the quester, taking a seat on a large boulder. "It would seem we are at an impasse. And my clan would consider your refusal to pledge your child an act of hostility, and I'm afraid the sentence for your trespass would be fierce and medieval."

"Fine!" Delphine's eyes flashed. "I volunteer as tribute!"

"Excuse me?"

"I'll join your clan on one condition. Sex. You and me. Tonight."

The quester's face turned red. "What?"

Kahtar shot the woman a condemning glance, and Beth sighed. "Not going to slut shame, but really, Delphine?"

"Don't you two judge me," Delphine said. "Why do you think I've been kissing every warrior in Cultuelle Khristos? I'm trying to get Tartarus out of my heart! After all he's done to me I'm finally free of him and yet I stand here and think only that I've lost him. Don't you dare judge me."

"Sweet ilu," muttered Kahtar. "Look, Delphine, you can't just switch clans anyway. Unless..."

"Unless she joins outside your clan," said the quester, frowning at Delphine.

Spreading his hands out, palms up, Kahtar shook his head. "Delphine. You don't have to do this. As a matter of fact I encourage you not to. You saw what happened today. Love is your best defense in this world. Don't join with someone you don't love. There's no going back."

"It's better than us all being dead, Kahtar! I'm pretty good at puzzling out plots and we have two endings to choose from here."

"How about you, Augustus? Would you even want to join with her?" Kahtar asked. "She's not an easy person to be around."

"Thanks, Kahtar," said Delphine. "Like you are."

The quester laughed. "I have obligations that should forbid my joining and I never thought to thwart them, but I agree with Delphine, there are only two ways this day can end. If she will choose to declare to any of the men in my clan, this day can end well. I can promise we will give her time to know us. There's no reason her heart couldn't find a home with one of our men. And when Delphine joins and becomes part of Clan Aberdyfi, it will reprieve your sentences. In the meantime, you'd be free on her oath to join us. So—" the quester turned his attention to Delphine, "if you're amenable to all this, we have an accord."

"It's not enough," said Beth. "Trying to logic out what your heart might want isn't love, and anything else is not enough."

"Depending on this quester's view of free love, it might be enough for me," Delphine admitted.

Kahtar threw up his hands. "This day cannot possibly get any stranger."

"Sure it can," said Delphine. "I'm a storyteller, so you can trust me on that. I'll now have to join with some man from a clan I don't know, but you're going back to our clan where you'll either have to pretend all is normal—with your wife who can't lie—or you'll have to tell The Mother you used to be immortal but Beth cured you. Only now the two of you and your kids are immortal-lite or something like that, because your biological father was some type of a demon and apparently his mojo is contagious and definitely sexually transmitted. Frankly, I think you might want to consider a new clan yourself."

THE DAY NEEDED to end. Kahtar felt his literal age after all that had happened, and he still had to inform The Mother.

On his way to tell her heaven knew what, he spotted Abigail in the cave, headed in his direction. At the sight of her his energy level increased and he moved quickly down the path. Trotting along in her orthopedic shoes, she appeared to plan on passing him without saying a word.

"Abigail," he said and she stopped, looking impatient.

"What?"

It took him aback. "You rushed off. We never had a chance to talk."

"About what?"

So many questions crowded his mind, but he started with the most relevant. "Why'd you rush back?"

"It's International Games Day at the college library. I didn't want to miss it."

"What?"

She rolled her eyes. "I thought the Old Guard needed to know about Morning Star. He seemed a bit hell bent on vengeance when he left, for lack of a better term."

"He can't penetrate the Arc." Kahtar felt a rush of relief at the thought. It hadn't occurred to him the being would seek retribution against his clan.

"No, but since Tartarus could get into your veil it seemed Morning Star might, but the Old Guard said no. They can watch it if you like, but they aren't concerned it will be a problem. That means you can go back inside if you want. Keep in mind we are two less Old Guard thanks to Tartarus. The rest of the Old Guard sensed their deaths as soon as it happened, but you'll need to explain it to The Mother."

"What should I tell her?"

Abigail snorted. "How should I know?"

"Do I tell her my story? Do I tell her about Tartarus in my veil looking for Delphine?"

"Why are you asking me?"

"I was hoping you had some insight into the right thing to do!"

"You're the warrior chief. Don't you know the right thing to do?"

"So I tell her the truth?"

"Ah. Haven't you noticed how well that works out for your wife?"

"That's my point, Abigail! But I've never willfully lied to The Mother."

"Well, now's not the time to start." She made to pass him on the narrow path and Kahtar stepped to block her.

"Do I need to keep Beth inside the Arc to know she's safe?"

"She'd kill you in your sleep if you tried. Beth's not in any danger from Morning Star. If he hurt her he'd destroy any hope of ever claiming your heart. That's what he's wanted all along."

"He'll never have it."

"Let's hope not after all the work I've put into it! My callouses have callouses."

"Thank you, for everything." It seemed insufficient. How did he thank this woman—this being—for taking care of him since the beginning? Tears filled his eyes.

"Are you going to get out of my way now? It really is International Games Day at the college."

"DELPHINE IS JOINING with a quester she met this morning?" asked The Mother, rubbing her hands up her arms as though cold in the humid cave.

"Yes," said Kahtar.

"After she attempted to copy Abigail's tesseract gifting and it collapsed on and ended two of our Old Guard?"

"Delphine's tesseracts are quite stable. It collapsed because this Tartarus person knew a way to make it. I'm fairly certain he could have killed them in a tesseract of Abigail's too. Apparently he's been stalking Delphine for some time."

"And he got his hooks into her while she was on Avalon?" The Mother's normally calm voice cracked on the last word, producing something akin to a squeak.

"Yes. That shocked me too. The only way I can think to describe his heart is to say it was a hole."

The Mother pressed the palm of her hand against her forehead and slumped onto a bench. Kahtar stepped onto the long stone plinth and took a seat beside her, taking her other hand. It was icy against his warm skin and he squeezed it.

"It pains me to think of her being in a loveless marriage. You couldn't talk her out of it?"

"No, and Beth tried, too."

The Mother blew out her breath. "And this Tartarus person is the reason for what happened in your veil to Beth?"

"Yes."

"Because he could trace Delphine via her tesseracts to your veil?"

"Yes."

The Mother had kept up quite well. Kahtar had often considered her one of the cleverest people he'd ever met. Now he had to add the mental caveat *next to Abigail.*

"None of that explains why Beth came back to life after she'd been dead."

Whoa. You owe her the truth and she's asking for it outright.

"Tartarus was something Delphine called a daemonium."

"Half-demon?" The Mother nearly shouted it.

"Yes."

"So, what, he infected Beth in some way?"

"No. I infected Beth in some way."

The Mother jerked to stand, pulling her hand from Kahtar's. "What are you saying to me, Kahtar? Out with it."

"It would seem I'm a daemonium too."

"What? Since when? Kahtar Constantine, I knew your father before he died! Levi was not a demon! What nonsense are you telling me?"

Still sitting on the stone bench, Kahtar crossed his arms over his chest. "The truth, if you'd like to hear it."

"All right. Proceed."

"There's a reason I don't look like Levi Constantine, apparently. I never knew why until today."

"This daemonium named Tartarus told you this? What did he tell you exactly? That you were his brother? Didn't it occur to you he might be lying?"

"Beth was there and he couldn't lie to her, and he didn't say I was his brother, exactly. He said I was a failed experimentum."

"Like a changeling?"

The term caused actual physical pain in Kahtar's heart. How many times had he been accused of being that in the past? Not all clans accepted that he looked different than he should. Most scanned and knew he belonged to his parents because his DNA always matched theirs. Those clans accepted ilu's will best they could and moved on, like Cultuelle Khristos had. But some clans had called him a changeling and shunned him—or worse.

The Mother sensed his pain and softened her voice even as she continued to press. "Are you telling me you truly believe you are a daemonium, Kahtar?"

"Yes. I know I'm a daemonium, Mother."

After a moment of staring at him, Anwyn plopped onto a bench opposite him. "So for the past fifty odd years Cultuelle Khristos has unwittingly harbored a daemonium-unawares."

Kahtar wished they could quit saying the word, but made himself incorporate it into his mental vocabulary. It was, after all, the truth.

"Yes."

"And this daemonium-unawares has made a fine warrior chief and a fairly good police chief too, with a clan also unaware."

"Yes." Kahtar tried not to make the response sound like a question.

"So the question is—were you biding your time, even unawares, seeking to destroy the hearts of your clan? Some might think taking a half-seeker wife would be evidence of that."

Abigail Adit's nails-on-chalkboard voice interrupted. "For the love of light, life, and love, you just had to open that can of worms and tell her!"

The Mother twisted to watch Abigail stalk into the chamber. "You knew?"

"Yes! I was there today and I had my brains with me." Abigail plopped onto the bench beside Anwyn and leaned forward to rub her chubby legs. "The kid never even knew what he was! So he was not plotting to overthrow the world or Cultuelle Khristos."

Kahtar had to assume he was the kid.

"I cannot conceive of the fact you'd not want me to know this, Abigail," said The Mother. "It's my duty to protect this clan and one of our members is half-demon!"

"And his wife is half-seeker. Anwyn, if you're honest with yourself you've wanted to get rid of Beth since you realized just how thick her seeker blood is."

"Don't you start this with me again, Abigail! I'm talking about Kahtar and demons."

"But you need to be honest with yourself. Kahtar was the only reason you didn't get rid of Beth! How could you send your warrior chief into the mists? That was your problem. Now you have a golden opportunity!"

"I will never want to send Kahtar into the mists!"

"What about Beth?"

"This isn't about Beth!"

"You can't possibly separate these issues in your mind at this point. You can't think straight about Kahtar when you're itching for an excuse to oust Beth! You've allowed yourself to become completely biased against her. You knew when you accepted her into the clan she probably had plenty of seeker blood in her past. Once you knew for certain how thick it was you've regretted her. Admit it, Anwyn Glorianna D'Aval!"

"Would that make you happy, Abigail? Fine. I admit it. Beth was a mistake. I've told Kahtar that! Even Beth knows it! It's the truth. Now may I focus on Kahtar's issue?"

"What's the point? He has to come to terms with this. If you're going to spend the next hundred years shooting sidelong glances at him waiting for him to sprout horns, how's he going to do that? And you!" Abigail turned her hostility on Kahtar. "Must have decided you're sick of being warrior chief because once the entire clan knows about this, they'll all be giving you that look. Do you ever think anything through?"

The Mother clasped her hands together at her chin, fingers skyward, praying. Abigail ignored her and continued, "There's absolutely no choice now, Kahtar. You're going to have to pass the mantle of warrior chief onto someone else in the clan. They'll stink at it, especially our being short two Old Guard now."

The Mother's eyes flew open and she made a sound of protest.

"No, Anwyn! You don't get to question the integrity of a warrior and still benefit from his being your warrior chief! You don't trust Kahtar, then you find somebody else to do that job!"

"I never said I didn't trust Kahtar!"

"You can't get past a seeker father, how on heaven or earth are you going to get past a demon one? Face facts. And, Kahtar, I strongly suggest you shun the Arc too. Otherwise they'll be eyeballing you, expecting to see you making demon tunnels or something so all of your relatives in hell can sneak inside."

"Abigail, stop talking nonsense!"

Kahtar fought the urge to laugh out loud.

"No. I'm angry. We're losing the best warrior chief ilu ever created because you—no, because all Covenant Keepers are prejudiced! We build these beautiful little bubbles to live inside and worry so much somebody is going to wreck them that we don't even notice we're wrecking them! ilu did not create us to hide from the world! He created us to help save it! You're not doing that, Anwyn! Kahtar is!" With a dimpled hand Abigail took Kahtar's arm and hauled him to his feet with ease. "Come on!"

Having seen Abigail stand up to a demon, Kahtar was not surprised by her unnatural strength as she hauled him out of the chamber and through the labyrinthine paths of the cave.

"If she tells all the elders you're a daemonium I will lose all respect for her," Abigail muttered.

"She really doesn't have a choice does she?"

"Of course she does! All she has to do is realize it's your personal business and not relevant to the clan!"

"My father's a demon, how can she think that?"

Abigail stopped tugging him to glare. "You were conceived before this continent was! What are the odds, Kahtar Constantine, that you're going to join the forces of darkness now?"

Exhaling a sharp breath he said, "Nil."

Abigail continued tugging him along. "Exactly. She just has to come to the same conclusion."

"She doesn't know I've lived millennia in the light of ilu."

"Oh, you left something out? I must have interrupted too soon! Did you get to the part where you can impregnate your wife with the light of your heart and will her to conceive?"

"I can?"

"Yes. I'm only mentioning it before you force a dozen babies on Beth in the next six years. You might want to give her a breather. She only has two breasts to nurse with."

"I didn't realize. I guess I wanted children subconsciously."

"You think?"

"Is that a demon thing?"

"How much love and light do you think they have? It's a Kahtar thing. Don't spend your time worrying about what you inherited from Morning Star. Like everyone, he originally came from a place of light. It's our choices that make us—something The Mother of this clan should know."

"The Mother has to protect the clan, Abigail. You can't expect her to understand what I really am."

"The Mother has a brain and a heart and I can so expect her to know what you really are! Your father is ilu and she knows that; your ancient history is irrelevant. I knew what your heart could be when you were a naked little boy in a hut trying to console the woman Morning Star had begotten you on."

"I wish I remembered her."

They reached the cave entrance and walked out into the late afternoon light. Abigail dropped his hand and crossed her arms as they took to the path side by side.

"Well, the pain of a collapsing tesseract can erase everything. That's why I had to do it. Morning Star couldn't find you as you repeated. After a while he made Tartarus. The Old Guard and I have watched you and kept you from their paths, but with every repeat your path neared theirs. It was inevitable they'd find you eventually."

"Will he find me again?"

"No. He knows you now belong to ilu. He'll wait and hope that will change. If he had a heart he'd understand it won't, but his misplaced hope keeps you and yours safe."

"So he won't be able to find Tartarus as he repeats either, will he?"

"No, he won't. Tartarus has never repeated before. It will take him millennia to gain his bearings and it is possible he never will, but that might just be me hoping futilely for evil to die."

"Perhaps we should call our women into the Arc from the outside world? Will Morning Star seek to create another daemonium?"

Abigail snorted. "No. He's only gotten more selfish and greedy with time. He has to give a part of himself to create a life. He'd never be able to bear being so close with a Covenant Keeper again."

Thinking of all the women in Willowyth, Kahtar frowned. "What about seeker women?"

Abigail chuckled and he glanced at her sharply. She shook her head at him. "Never. The process is still the same, if not more difficult. The fact that you're with Beth should reassure The Mother that evil won't find purchase in your heart. The Fallen Ones detest seekers. They'd never use one like that. Couldn't you tell how much Tartarus and Morning Star particularly disliked Beth? ilu has gifted seekers grace the Fallen Ones will never have. They're jealous creatures. They'd have crushed Beth if her heart weren't so entwined with yours. You about gave me convulsions when you took so long to join with her last year. If they had ever stumbled across her they would have obliterated her. Of course her parents dragged her all over the world with her big mouth yapping truth. It was a logistical nightmare keeping her safe."

"You're certain she's safe?"

"Positive." Abigail smiled. "I've followed the women in Beth's family for a long time waiting for her. You were meant to be with her."

"I agree, and again, thank you for making sure I found her, and I assume for protecting her family until I did."

Waddling along the path beside him, Abigail froze.

"What? What's wrong?"

"We need to get to Beth's parents!"

"What? Why? Beth's with them! Old Guard!" Kahtar bellowed.

Abigail's green eyes were wide. "Morning Star! He can't touch Beth because of you, but he can destroy what is hers!"

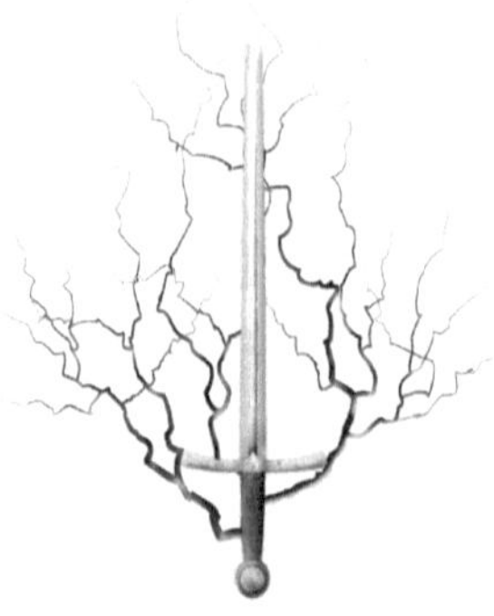

TWENTY-ONE

Bloody Sacrifice—The Devil You Know

CURLED ONTO THE sofa nursing Dianta, Beth thought about Delphine. By now Delphine's requested night with the quester would be over. What then for her? Despite the storyteller's cavalier attitude, she was sacrificing a great deal to protect them. Beth had every intention of going back to Aberdyfi and speaking to that quester sometime soon.

At Beth's breast Dianta dug her fingernails in and grunted, burrowing closer, and from upstairs Beth heard another faint grunt and almost rolled her eyes.

How many people's parents sneak off in the afternoon to be together? Beth grinned, uncomfortably proud that hers did. *But really do I have to hear it? Do I have to know?*

Tipping her head back, she shouted, "Hey, Dad! I'd like some halo-halo ice-cream if you're not busy!"

Dianta growled at her, opening her eyes to slits and Beth felt a tug of remorse. "That was rude and you're going to do that to Daddy and me someday, aren't you?" *Do Covenant Keepers believe in karma? I think it's a thing.*

"I'll be right down!" Ted White called, his voice amused.

Oh, man, he knows I'm messing with him! He is going to embarrass the crap out of me.

Bending to press her lips against Dianta's curls, she whispered, "Mama's inner brat is feeling a bit humiliated." The fact was, seeing Tartarus again had brought back what had happened in the veil, and Beth found she wanted to sit next to her dad for a few hours and forget. Seeing the one Abigail called Morning Star—though she thought Death Star was more fitting—had left her feeling more than a little bit shaky. Nothing and no one could make her forget it.

Beth wondered if somewhere deep in everyone's heart they really knew at a visceral level there were dark and terrifying things in the universe. It was a fact Beth had always been aware of as truth. Yet even as a child she'd known God sat higher, ruling all, and when her schoolmates had shivered over scary games and movies she'd smiled, secure in the knowledge fear was only an emotion and evil merely an illness to be eradicated.

Smiling now, Beth lifted her eyes to the couch opposite and looked directly into the golden gaze of Morning Star.

Sitting opposite her like an invited guest, one leg across a knee and both arms stretched over the back of the sofa, he looked like a beautiful James Bond devil. For a moment they looked at each other and the emptiness of him pressed against Beth's heart as if it could push her and the couch right through the wall and into the front yard.

A door slammed upstairs and Ted White crossed the landing, whistling a Rod Stewart song. *Tonight's the Night. My dad, the joker.* Huge tears blurred Beth's vision. Morning Star lifted a single finger and held it to his lips, demanding her silence. Beth felt as if she were falling, the arms holding Dianta liquefying with her fear. Sensing her heart Dianta whimpered. An invisible hand seemed to wrap around Beth's neck and squeeze off her air, demanding compliance.

No.

Beth shot to her feet and screamed at the top of her lungs, "MOM! DAD! RUN!"

Morning Star rose as though liquid, morphing into a standing position with the back of his head facing Beth, looking up the staircase where her dad stood on the tiny landing.

"Get away from my daughter, you!" Ted shouted, running for the steps.

"No! Go, Dad!"

The bedroom door slammed open and Carole shot across the short space wearing only one of Ted's huge t-shirts. Grabbing the railing, she propelled herself over it and landed on the floor not ten feet from Morning Star before Ted had made it to the bend in the stairwell.

In one smooth move Carole swept a standing lamp from the floor and swung it forward like a weapon. The cord yanked from the wall and the base swung off and shot directly at Morning Star. It passed right through him as though he were a ghost and smashed into the wall, just missing Beth.

Spinning in place Carole flicked the Tiffany lampshade at Morning Star's head, and it also passed right through, hitting the window and crashing through a pane of glass into the front yard.

Morning Star spread his arms like Moses parting the Red Sea and a line of flames lit the carpeting on fire. Carole cut the air with the lamp pole, feigning left and right as she approached Morning Star. He shoved his hands forward and an invisible force lifted Carole into the air and shot her across the room and into the wall. Her body left an imprint in the drywall and she slid limply to the floor. In full charge toward Morning Star, Ted changed direction and raced for his wife.

Morning Star's blond hair shone in the afternoon sun, and his fingers moved, controlling the dancing flames. Dispassionately he watched Ted tend to his wife.

Behind him, Beth could only think of one defense. Clutching Dianta to her breast, she whispered, "I love you."

The demon turned slowly and faced her, locking eyes.

"I mean it. I can't lie. I love you because you brought Kahtar into this world. I can only assume he comes from the part of you that ilu created with love, the good part, the part that loved when your heart worked."

Morning Star cricked his neck in a gesture that Beth had seen the bad Terminator do in the second movie. "I hope this causes you undo pain," he whispered.

Behind him Carole still lay on the floor, her low voice encouraging Ted to protect Beth between groans of pain. Beth knew she wasn't the one who needed protection even as her dad thundered in her direction.

Morning Star changed, half-morphing his body to face Ted and Carole, but before he'd completed the transformation Ted crossed the short distance and jumped, grabbing the now solid demon in a choke hold. "Don't you threaten my daughter! You're not welcome in my house! Get out!"

Morning Star jerked, a move surely meant to dislodge Ted, but Beth's father held on, wrapping his thick legs around the much thinner being and snaking his arms tighter around his neck. "YOU GET OUT!" Ted roared directly into the demon's ear.

Desperate to help, Beth shouted at her father, "I love you, Dad!"

"I love you too, Bethy!" Again Ted shouted for the demon to get out of his house and the tears in Beth's eyes slid down her cheeks.

"I love Mom! I love Dianta! I love Kahtar!"

"Me too, Bethy!" said Ted.

Beneath him Morning Star seemed to shrink and hope lit inside Beth. A burning smell filled her nostrils, something wrong but familiar, something remembered from the darkest of shades. It wasn't carpet.

"Dad! Let go of him!" Clutching Dianta to her side, Beth grabbed her father's shoulder and pulled. Tendrils of smoke drifted from between him and Morning Star.

"Never! I love you, Bethy, and your baby girls, and your mother. God, Carole, how I love you! Always have!"

In Beth's arms Dianta began to scream.

"Ted!" Carole crawled across the room using only one arm. "Let go!"

The smoke emanating from Ted's clothes caught flame. A sound somewhere between a groan of pain and a growl escaped him. Carole reached Morning Star's feet and she wrapped her good arm around them and bit fiercely.

"Mom, don't! It won't help!"

Chuckling, Morning Star kicked Carole and sent her flying across the floor.

"I love—I love—!" Beth tried to say it to Morning Star again but she couldn't. The words wouldn't come out, not with her dad's burning flesh searing her nostrils. "OLD GUARD!"

The room lit with the shimmer of countless Old Guard and Morning Star instantly liquefied into a ball of fire and smoke, shooting upward and vanishing in a split second. Ted White ricocheted backward, consumed in fire, and sailed across the room to land next to Carole.

Suddenly Kahtar was there and his hands were all over Beth, feeling for injury. An Old Guard snatched Dianta from her. Beth shook them off and ran over the burning carpet to her parents. Ted's body arched and shivered. Most of the clothing had been burned off his front and white ribs showed through blackened flesh. His weak screams echoed in the small house. The bile in Beth's throat seemed to clog her heart.

"No!" she shouted, trying to drown out the sound. "Kahtar! Help him!"

Kahtar was there, kneeling beside her mother and pressing his fingers against Carole's back while she heaved herself onto Ted's cooked chest, tears streaming down her face. "Ted? Ted! Please! It won't matter now if I take it all."

Ted's eyes were wide but he turned them in Carole's direction, even as a hoarse scream ripped from his throat.

"Please, Ted? Before you go? Give me all of your heart?" she sobbed.

Kneeling beside her father Beth screamed at Kahtar, "You help him! I don't care what the rules are! You make him better, Kahtar! You fix my daddy!" Kahtar tried to hug her, to gather her against his shoulder and she slapped him away. "I'll go into the mists, Kahtar! I don't care! I'll do anything! Please!"

Tears streaming down his face, Kahtar shook his head, and grief consumed her.

An Old Guard reached for Carole, but she shot to her knees and put her hands over Ted's chest, right into the charred mess as his whispery scream stopped. A hole opened inside Beth where her daddy had always been, and she knew he was gone. Beth collapsed, a silent scream tearing her throat.

Carole's scream picked up where Ted's had ended. It seemed to go on forever.

SHOVING HER FACE against Ted White's neck, Beth inhaled, trying to find his sunscreen, cotton shirt, stolen cookies smell, but burnt flesh filled her nostrils. Carole continued to scream, an anguished howl of agony. Beth couldn't bring herself to look again at her mother's hand sliding around through burned skin, charred clothing and congealed blood.

Kahtar's hoarse voice sounded in her ear. "He's gone, Bethy. Let your mother have time with him alone."

Beth punched him, not caring if it brought another shunning. "Don't call me that!" Kahtar stopped her when she swung for him a second time, grabbing her hand like a catcher's mitt and refusing to let go. "You didn't help him! You wouldn't help him because he's a *seeker!*" Beth drew out the last word like a child and sucked in a noisy breath through her mouth. "You didn't love him enough to help him just because he's a seeker! I'm a seeker too, then! *Daddy!*" Beth tried to fold down to Ted's body again, but this time Kahtar picked her up and held her against his body tightly so she couldn't hit him.

"Listen to me!" he growled into her ear. "I would have for you! You asked and I would have healed him for you no matter the consequences, but it was too late, Beth! Your father's heart was frail as silk web and moth wings! There was nothing I or any Covenant Keeper could have done!"

His words were true, and Beth sobbed against his chest. "I'll die without him!"

Kahtar held her tightly wrapped in both his arms and Beth realized he was sobbing too, feeling all the loss and anguish from her heart. Somehow they were in the kitchen, leaning against the refrigerator. Welcome Palmer was there. Placing both hands on either side of Beth's head he kissed her forehead, his heart saying more than words could.

"I'm going to give her something to make her sleep," she heard him whisper to Kahtar. "Move, let me get her a drink of water."

Kahtar half sat Beth on the granite island in the kitchen.

"I don't want to sleep! I want my dad!" Beth sobbed, knowing she should shove the feelings down, let them out in private, grieve like a grown woman and not a child, but she couldn't do it. She would never hear her dad's voice again. He'd never hug her or sit by her and tell awful jokes. Her gaze slid across all the piles of baby stuff he'd bought for Dianta, most still in their boxes, to the box of huge candy bars he'd bought to give out to their one trick or treater on Halloween. Welcome Palmer, glass in hand, opened the freezer for ice cubes and Beth saw little glass cups of brightly garnished purple halo-halo ice-cream.

The place in her heart where her dad belonged seemed to ice over. The pain traveled, sharp and cold from her chest downward. Unable to breathe she opened her mouth wide. Kahtar put a big hand on either side of her face and bent his close, saying something she couldn't hear. Welcome spun around, dropping the glass as he lunged toward her to the sound of breaking glass. Beth wondered how the glass was cutting through her insides when it was on the floor. The world went black.

"YOU GOOD, KAHTAR?" asked Welcome Palmer.

Kahtar forced his gaze off Beth lying on the table in her blood-stained dress and tried to turn his mind away from all the times in the past year she'd been hurt or hurting or at Cobbson Clinic. Using a large cotton towel, Welcome wiped blood off Kahtar's hands as though he weren't capable of doing it himself. Kahtar let him. Maybe he wasn't. He'd never been so tired in his life.

"We've got the bleeding nearly stopped." Welcome tried to put a positive spin on it, but Kahtar's personal eternity never allowed for self-delusion. Placental abruption meant the baby needed to come, sooner rather than later, and even for one of his children this was far too soon.

Kahtar glanced over at Carole perched on the edge of her seat. He'd almost forgotten the Old Guard had brought her with them. She sat with her head in her hands and her heart broken. Tears welled in Kahtar's eyes and he nabbed the towel from Welcome and walked to her on wooden legs, settling onto the glass footed sofa next to her.

"I'm sorry, Carole," he said. "Your Ted was a good man."

She shifted her position, turning away from him a bit, and the ocean of sorrow emanating from her heart affected his. Placing his hand over his heart he took a deep breath. Carole didn't believe him. Obviously she knew enough about Covenant Keepers to question a compliment they gave a seeker. "I've been around long enough to recognize a good man. It took great strength and love for him to hold onto that intruder like he did. Your husband trusted his heart. I respect that in a man."

Carole didn't say anything.

"If you have any questions, anything, I will answer them honestly."

Raising her head, she looked into his eyes. Kahtar's heart sank at the haunted expression in hers, recognizing regret. He put a hand on her shoulder but she shrugged it away.

"Anything," he said.

"Is Beth going to be okay?" she asked.

"Yes," Welcome answered.

"What about the baby?"

Welcome turned his attention back to Beth without answering.

"You said you'd answer me honestly," said Carole, looking at Kahtar.

Putting his elbows on his knees, he dropped the bloody rag to the floor. "I don't see how, Carole." He kept his voice low, just in case Beth was conscious enough to hear him. "Beth's been through a lot of trauma during this pregnancy. That baby needs to be born by tonight and it's far too early."

"The baby needs to be born within the hour," said Welcome in a tight voice.

"That means Cesarean, and the baby's too small to breathe on her own," said Kahtar.

Carole sat up straight. "So? People have Cesareans every day. The baby can breathe on a ventilator."

Welcome and Kahtar glanced at each other. "You know how I healed you?" Kahtar asked. "You realize when that intruder threw you he broke your back, right?"

"Can you fix the baby's lungs like you did my back?"

"I can fix things that are broken, but my healing skills won't age or mature a baby so it can breathe on its own. It's a great tragedy of my kind."

Carole glanced between the two men, and Kahtar knew she had caught on to what they weren't saying. "Are you telling me Covenant Keepers let premature babies die rather than use ventilators? That's insane!"

Welcome swung a hand toward her, palm up. "Thank you for seeing that for what it is! You've got the situation exactly, Mrs. White! We are actually forbidden from using seeker technology! I do it anyway sometimes because it is a travesty!"

"Why isn't there a ventilator here, then?"

"They're expressly forbidden," said Kahtar. "The punishment would be..." he shook his head. "The Old Guard—those are the men who brought you here, you should understand they're our guardians for want of a better term—The Old Guard are also our enforcers, and they watch Welcome to make sure he doesn't bring in a ventilator."

"Only because the clan told them to," said Welcome. "The Old Guard don't care about ventilators!"

"The clan makes these types of rules in response to their interpretation of our laws," said Kahtar. "I don't know how much you know about Covenant Keepers. Obviously some things?"

"Enough to know your kind are best avoided," said Carole. "I'll get a ventilator. I'm not allowing my granddaughter to die."

Kahtar and Welcome looked at each other.

"That would work," they said together.

"See we're forbidden because we're clan, but you—" began Welcome, but Carole interrupted.

"Would one of those Old Guards take me to a hospital so I can steal one? Right now?"

"That would work!" said Kahtar and Welcome again.

"Don't steal," added Kahtar. "Welcome, do you have any money?"

"There's a drawer full of it over there." He nodded toward a cupboard in the corner. "Take it all because they're expensive."

"A hospital isn't going to sell me a ventilator for a bag of cash."

"Just leave it," said Kahtar.

"Someone will steal it," said Carole.

"Just do it anyway," Kahtar said, and shouted for Old Guard.

WHEN CAROLE RETURNED she had on hospital scrubs and carried one of the clear plastic incubators Kahtar knew seekers used for preemies. Old Guard appeared a beat behind her, carrying boxes of equipment. Welcome immediately tore through them, searching for what he needed.

Kahtar emptied a bottle of antiseptic over his hands and Beth's belly as he scanned into her. The baby needed to come now, no matter the consequences.

"There's no electricity?" Carole searched along the walls for an outlet.

"We don't use it much but when we do, Tesla is more our style," said Welcome as he filled a small machine with water and it began to bubble. "No cords or outlets. I can have all this working in no time. Kahtar, if you'll get the baby?"

No sooner had Kahtar lifted an obsidian scalpel than Carole was there.

"You're not cutting into my daughter."

"There's no time to waste being squeamish. I've done this countless times, but I could use your help. Can you scan inwards?" Kahtar cut right down the middle of Beth's belly.

Carole looked away from it and took a deep breath. "I'll try."

"I'll explain as we go. Mostly I just need extra hands for this," said Kahtar as he pulled Beth's flesh open and sliced the scalpel through a thin layer of fatty tissue before plunging it deeper into reddish muscle.

"Is this something all police chiefs can do? You'd better know what you're doing, Kent Costas!"

"It's something all warriors learn, and my real name is Kahtar Constantine, Carole. After all you've been through today, I think you should know it."

"Don't hurt my daughter."

"I won't even scar your daughter." Mentally whispering healing prayers to kill bacteria, Kahtar separated the thick layer of muscle and slid his knife over membrane.

Carole tentatively pulled the wound further open. "My real name is Cahrul."

Kahtar lifted his brows in surprise but didn't question her. Now wasn't the time. While he had performed this surgery more times than he could recall, this was the first time he'd done it on his wife and while trying to save the life of his own child. Water spurted from the wound. Carole's hands shook. "If this disturbs you to watch, you can assist Welcome."

"It doesn't bother—"

"Then grab your granddaughter," said Kahtar.

Carole obeyed, plunging her hands inside Beth to wrap around the impossibly small baby. "She's far too frail!"

"I know," said Kahtar.

Over his shoulder Welcome commented, "Small but well developed. Cahrul, watch that umbilical cord, it's half around her neck, and try to shield her eyes from the light if you can."

Kahtar ran a finger around the baby, dislodging the cord. Carole held her cupped between both hands as though to protect her. Welcome shoved his head between Kahtar and Carole.

"Do you know how to suction the mouth and nose?" asked Kahtar.

"I'll do it," said Welcome, using a small plastic syringe that had certainly come in Carole's looted equipment. "Cahrul, just set her down on Beth's thighs and grab that plastic tubing on the tray. See those tiny prongs? Yep, stick them right inside her nostrils. Quickly. Do, don't think. Do."

The baby didn't struggle or make a sound. As they worked her ruddy skin seemed to grow lighter and Kahtar mentally timed them as he removed afterbirth and began using his healing skills to repair the damage he'd done to Beth. He glanced toward her face on the other side of a heap of blankets and saw her watching him.

"Welcome!" he said.

The doctor didn't look away from his tiny patient. "Hey, Beth. Wondered when you'd quit pretending to be asleep. Let me know if you feel any pain. The poking and prodding feelings are normal, but you should be numb from the chest down."

Beth's chin wobbled and she kept her eyes locked on Kahtar, probing for truth.

"As expected it's a girl," said Welcome, taping tubes on the limp infant. "Your mother borrowed some equipment from a hospital to give us a hand with this baby. Let me just get everything going here. This little one doesn't look like Dianta at all, though I'm not sure who she does look like!"

Kahtar glanced over and his breathing hitched. It was the frailest baby he'd ever seen. She looked almost white. There was no way it could live.

"I can't feel her heart," whispered Beth. Neither could Kahtar.

"I can," said Carole in a shaky voice.

"I can't feel anything."

"Just breathe," said Kahtar.

"Do you have a name?" asked Carole, stroking the lifeless baby with her pinky as she taped tubes to her face.

Beth shook her head, staring at the ceiling.

"If you don't have a name picked out, I have a suggestion," said Carole, her voice a low whisper.

"It doesn't even matter," said Beth. "Does it?"

With tears in her voice Carole said, "You could name her Teddy, after your father. It's my favorite name in the world."

Beth began to cry at the exact same moment Teddy began breathing.

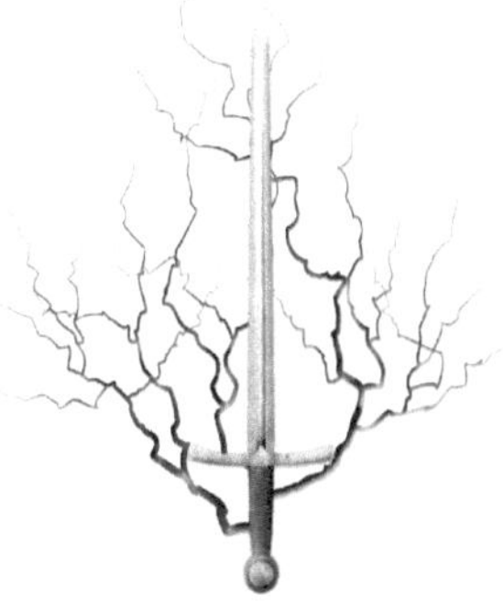

CHAPTER
TWENTY-TWO

Bloody Unexpected—Mongolian Steppes

THIS LATE IN the year light faded inside the big old barn early. Kahtar shrugged out of his suit jacket and lit a lantern, rotating it so the light hit the ring of mirrors circling the middle of the barn.

In the flickering light, Carole shut the rolling door behind her and tossed her long coat onto a bale of hay. Clad in a pair of black trousers and a blouse she'd borrowed from Beth for Ted's funeral, she moved into the open area of the barn. In the lantern light with her short blonde hair slicked back, she looked small and pixyish. Kahtar felt a twinge of remorse for accepting her challenge when she'd just buried her husband. At five feet nine inches and a hundred and fifty pounds, she didn't stand a chance against him. The diameter of one of his biceps was nearly both her thighs.

"I choose the spear." Carole nodded to the iron weapon hanging on a cross beam of the barn, higher than she could reach.

Ironic of course. It was the one weapon Kahtar hated. He'd used it to kill God centuries ago, back when he'd been known as Longinus. Not in the millennia since had he even touched one. He made the plebes clean it.

Rolling his sleeves up, Kahtar looked at the weapon. "What rules of engagement did you have in mind?"

Waves of fury emanated from Carole and she kicked her boots off in the corner, returning barefoot to the same dirt circle where Kahtar battled Old Guard nearly every day.

"No rules," she said, her voice cold.

No rules? Well, if that gives her hope. "I will not fight you to first blood."

"Yes, you will."

"No, I won't, and the winner gets to make a request of the loser. One they must submit to. Will you agree to that, Mother?"

"If you call me that again I will kill you."

"Carole—Cahrul, why are you so angry with me?"

"I hate what you are. Your kind killed my father." Her voice broke and she fought to control the emotion in her face, but Kahtar felt anguish escape the heart she always kept on lockdown from both him and Beth.

"I'm sorry," he said.

"They would have killed Ted too, or even Beth, and she was just a baby. I've spent decades watching over my shoulder to protect them, and then one day you waltzed right into my life—Beth's life—and see what you brought? Death. I know what you thought of Ted. I know you yourself would have killed him if not for Beth."

"Carole, once maybe, but not—"

"I don't care what you have to say! I saw the way you looked at Ted the first day you met him! You thought about killing him! *Deny it!*" Carole screamed.

"I do deny it."

"Liar! I saw your face!"

"You saw my shock. You saw ages of training wrestle with my heart. You saw my duty to my clan argue with my duty to Beth. I would have fallen on my own blade before I'd have hurt Beth's father. My clan—Beth's clan—is different than most."

"They allow you to join with seekers?" It sounded like a challenge.

"Of course not, but we don't travel the world seeking to do harm to those who do."

"Liar!"

"Some clans do that, Carole, but we're different. We try not to judge seekers. In fact we strive to help them. In addition to the laws of being we attempt to follow the teachings of the Christ. It's quite a conundrum at times, but we do try. That's why Cultuelle Khristos welcomed Beth into the fold. They wanted to give her a home. I expect they might make the same offer to you."

"I want nothing from any of your kind."

Trying to disguise a sigh, Kahtar reached up and grabbed the spear. It didn't make him shudder like he expected as he handed it to Carole. He moved to a post where a katar dagger hung. "I will fight you only to first dirt. That means whoever knocks the other first—"

Kahtar never had a chance to finish, because that fast he was on the ground, a jarring impact ringing through his bones as puffs of dirt rose above him. Dim light shone through windows set in the high ceiling and a strange scintillating light filled the domed space high above him. If memory served, that dim light flickering like fireflies in unison was Old Guard laughter.

Carole bent over him. "I win by your rules. My request, the one you can't deny, is to continue this fight to first blood." She vanished from view, but Kahtar sensed her take position, holding the spear ready, one leg stretched out just beyond his reach. There was no way he could stand without taking another blow.

For the briefest moment he was tempted to transport himself into position, but there was no way he'd do anything to seem more other to this woman than he must already be.

Not *this* woman. *My mother. My family.*

Lying flat on his back with his head and the backs of his knees throbbing, Kahtar considered the distance to his dagger on the beam above. He would cut her just enough to draw blood on her cheek. It would infuriate Beth, but it would satisfy Carole's blood lust and the scar would be minimal.

And also memorable. She can wear it and know it could have been her throat.

He blinked, forcing Carole to wait, prepared should she decide to do further harm with that spear. One thing the woman needed to learn, far more important than fear of warriors of ilu, was respect.

For one brief moment Kahtar tensed every muscle in his body, preparing himself for the blow he knew would come. Suddenly he propelled himself to stand, as far from Carole's spear as possible and near his weapon. He nabbed the katar dagger off the peg and spun to face Carole at the same time her spear cracked against his ankles and swept his feet out from under him again. He tried to thread his fingers through the hilt of the weapon but there wasn't time. Catching it with the pinky of his right hand, he grabbed Carole's hair with his left and pulled her down with him.

Kahtar sensed her spear slide across the floor and mentally criticized the small woman for losing her weapon so easily. They hit the floor together, Kahtar holding a handful of Carole's short hair and her riding his torso like a horse. Bracing for impact and planning to roll onto her and claim first blood, Kahtar never expected a brutal knee to his balls.

In battle they were protected by gear, and among warriors it would never happen in a fight unless death was on the line. He'd underestimated untrained fury. Everything in his torso seemed to try to escape the nearest exit; air and bowels felt as though they were going to explode out his penis or worse, if there was worse. Kahtar threw up stomach acid into his mouth. Somewhere in the back of his instinctual brain arose the urge to kill Carole. *As soon as I can move again.*

Both her hands were on his right wrist, wrestling for the katar dagger. Refusing to lose any battle with the dagger he'd been named after in this repeat—this repeat that meant so much to him—Kahtar rolled onto Carole, pinning her down. He landed belly down and Carole grabbed his wrist, forcing him to slash his own blade down his face.

She won.

Kahtar couldn't move. Not because he'd lost to Beth's mother, twice, but because his left gonad seemed to be lodged inside his belly and had certainly been crushed. His head swam from lack of oxygen and pain caused a wave of nausea to shoot through every nerve in his body. He vomited into his mother-in-law's hair.

"You broke my arm," Carole said in a faint voice.

Instinct made Kahtar scan. He'd also dislocated her shoulder, broken her collarbone and the wrist of the hand she'd cut him with.

Her voice sounded pained. "I think I cut your eye. Can someone fix that?"

At that moment he didn't give a shite about his eye. Kahtar wanted to pass out, to hide from the pain and somehow not dirty himself in front of this warrior.

HIDING FROM A man who could scan seemed a waste of time. Hiding from her own mother seemed heartless, but Beth couldn't bear looking into her mother's grief-stricken eyes any longer. Right now she was too angry at both of them to care what either of them would say. If they were going to fight each other like a couple middle school would-be hoodlums, let them. She wasn't going to stick around and watch. *I just buried my father!* Leaving her babies with Welcome Palmer, she ran.

Not once in her life did Beth recall Carole touching her heart like a Covenant Keeper did, but it didn't stop Beth from feeling the pain of her mother's broken heart. Or the anger. Carole wore Ted's death like the weight of a mountain, and her fury against Kahtar like a smoldering volcano. Beth needed a few minutes of peace. Not just from Carole, but from Kahtar's desperate reassurances, and Teddy's eternal crying—and, as shameful as it was—from Dianta's heart endlessly seeking reassurance amidst chaos.

Oddly enough living in the veil again didn't frighten Beth. Kahtar had reassured her that all the monkeys had been relocated, and she felt safe. She hurried along the path past the pond, hoping she'd have at least a few minutes before someone hunted her down. The grass where Tartarus had been looked dead, worse than most of the winter grass.

I died right there. Beth moved past the spot, wondering if she would always feel this numb. Tears blurred her vision as her boots crunched over dead leaves. *No, I will always feel this hole Dad left behind.* Part of her heart felt missing, amputated. Beth sniffled and wiped a cold hand under her icy nose, walking faster. She wanted to run. She wanted to scream. She wanted to rip trees out by the roots and curse at the universe. She settled for a slow jog that wouldn't draw Kahtar's attention right away, and that gave her time to dodge sticks and occasional roots littering the little traveled path into the woods.

Despite her vigilant intentions, less than half a mile down the path Beth tripped over a root and sprawled headfirst, plowing leaves as she slid. Like a child she screamed into the earth. In little more than a year she'd married Kahtar, and had not one but two babies. She'd been shunned by the clan and her husband. She'd died and returned to the world of living by becoming some immortal-like being—something that provided only anxiety for the future, with no benefit day to day. Falling scraped her hands and skinned her knees like every other fall in her mortal life. Beth had discovered her husband was part-demon—though she'd suspected something like it for a while if she was honest with herself. Now she'd watched her father burned alive by a real demon. Something had broken in her heart, something that could never be repaired. That truth was inescapable.

Beth covered her head with her arms. *It's too much. I can't take it.*

The howl of a coyote sounded deeper in the forest and Beth pushed to her knees. Darkness arrived early this time of year and even this early in the afternoon daylight came shadowed so deep in the trees. One of the coyotes made a strange gurgling sound that reminded Beth of Wolves and she jammed the heels of her palms against her eyes and sobbed.

"Hey, girlfriend," interrupted a voice. "You are going to be all right in time. I know this, and you know this too." Beth recognized

Delphine's sing-songy storytelling voice, and her friend's tiny hands squeezed her shoulders. "It's going to take a while, as it should. What I'm wondering is, do you need to get away for a while?"

Beth uncovered her eyes. The pretty brunette crouched on her heels, her scarlet cloak and dark hair making her look like a sexy Red Riding Hood. She nodded in answer to Delphine's question. "I shouldn't though. Do you know what has happened?"

No one had heard from Delphine since she'd offered herself up to Clan Aberdyfi. She couldn't possibly know how much had transpired in such a short amount of time.

Delphine wiped tears off Beth's face with warm fingers. "Yes. I snoop around quite thoroughly. My heart aches for you. You're one tough chica. I am devastated for the loss of your father." Delphine's heart pressed against Beth's, offering comfort unlike any other. There was nothing but love there for the loss, love undiminished by judgement for his being a seeker. Even The Mother had been unable to offer condolences without relief evident in her voice. The clan no longer needed to worry about Beth's meddlesome seeker father.

Delphine leaned forward and kissed her quickly on her blessed spot. "You are so blessed to have had him. I envy you. But you need to get out of here for a bit, Beth. You can't breathe here right now."

"I think the Old Guard are really watching the veil. Kahtar asked them to, even though Tartarus is dead and nothing else has happened here. One of them even pledged himself to me, and I have a feeling he watches me a lot. If you shouldn't be here, you're going to be in trouble because they will notice you."

"All the more reason for us to go now. Let's go somewhere far. Sometimes you just have to run away from the pain, you know?"

"I do know. I guess that's what I was trying to do."

Delphine glanced around the forest path. "This really isn't far enough after the year you've had."

"Kahtar will get mad."

"Oh, pooh. He'll get over it. I'd invite you to Aberdyfi, but I haven't chosen a spouse yet, so that's probably not a good idea. They might decide you need to stay until I do. Where do you want to go, Beth? Do you like beaches? The weather's nice in Australia right now."

Beth shook her head. "I don't know where I want to go. I don't care about beaches."

"Well, what needs done then? Turn your mind to something that needs to be done. You still have the shop. I imagine it's a mess if you haven't been keeping it up. I know where you could score the absolute best chocolates on the planet."

"I don't care about chocolate, Delphine. I don't care about anything. It scares me."

"What needs to be done for your shop most of all?" Delphine asked it in her sing-songy voice and Beth found herself doubly compelled to answer.

"We need brack tea. Despite everything that has happened, people have pestered me about it, including that Old Guard who pledged to me."

Grabbing Beth's hands, Delphine hauled her to stand. The petite woman had some strength. "Where does brack tea come from? You know I've tried to find that stuff myself. You've got mad skills."

Some part of Beth slipped into business mode. "No stealing my source? On your honor?"

"You have my word." Delphine placed a hand over her heart.

"Not that she'd sell to you. You wouldn't believe the negotiating I have to do."

Delphine waved her left hand. In the dimming forest veins of light shot out, forming a tunnel. "China?"

"Mongolia, and you swore. Don't you forget it."

Delphine's tunnel solidified. The storyteller grabbed Beth's hand and tugged her inside it.

"I THINK THERE'S a flaw in our plan," said Delphine as they exited the tesseract to a blast of icy air and darkness "What's the time difference?"

"It's about three o'clock in the morning here right now. That's actually not a problem. Khunbish Cotota is a night owl, or an early bird. I'm not certain which. Is it possible to be so old you don't sleep anymore?"

"I don't think so," said Delphine. "I hate these steppes. This place is wretched. No wonder no one else has come out here looking for brack tea. I'm freezing my hoo-ha off."

"You're vulgar." Beth slipped her arm through Delphine's, feeling oddly comforted to be here despite the darkness and the cold. As her eyes adjusted she could make out Cotota's ger in the distance. The circular tent looked exactly like a yurt. Here on the steppes the portable home seemed to be the only kind. "Since you brought up your hoo-ha though, how're things going with that quester of yours? What's his name?"

"Augustus," Delphine sighed.

Beth squeezed her arm. "Like that, is it?"

"I wish. That's why I haven't been able to pick someone else. I want him."

Beth tried to remember that day in Persia. Her mind hadn't been much on Delphine's quester, but he'd seemed an honorable warrior. "Is he not as interested as you are?"

"Oh, no. He definitely is. He just doesn't know how much yet."

For the first time in weeks Beth chuckled. The poor guy wouldn't know what hit him by the time Delphine finished with him. As they approached the ger her smile faded. "Just be honest with him, Delphine. Don't use your storytelling on him."

"I won't!" Delphine's protest sounded a bit pious, but she added, "I can't. His gifting protects him from it. It's worse than you. At least you'll hear the truth when I speak it. He won't even listen to that. He's as drawn to me as I am to him. I mean, I never thought I'd find someone, you know? And then bam. Out of the blue like that."

"It is surprising, especially since you seemed so dead set on having Kahtar."

"Sorry about that. I think I just wanted who I thought Kahtar was."

"You wanted a father. Just make sure you don't make the same mistake with your quester. Look, she's awake! I told you she's a night owl. See her lamp is lit? Khunbish Cotota is up."

"What kind of name is Khunbish?" said Delphine.

"I don't know. I assume it's Mongolian."

"In Mongolian, Khunbish means something like *not a human being*," said Delphine. "I hope you don't call her that to her face."

"Yipes," said Beth. "Everyone in the village calls her that. I thought it meant wise old woman or something."

"Cheese-whiz, Beth."

Beth scratched on the felt frame of the doorway, speaking in Russian, "Khun—uh—Cotota? It's Beth Constantine—I mean Beth White." It had been some time since Beth had made this trip. "I'm here for brack tea."

"We didn't bring any money," Delphine said, pointing out the obvious.

"Oh, she doesn't accept money. She barters. How do you feel about milking camels?"

Delphine laughed. "I feel like you suck."

Cotota's hoarse, aged voice replied in Russian, "The camels are around back."

BETH WONDERED WHEN the last time Cotota's camels had been milked. Judging by the amount of milk the beasts produced, it could have been a year. The sun had risen by the time Beth and Delphine finished. They pounded lids on the buckets and stacked them inside a shed.

"So they ferment this, right?" asked Delphine. "Man, I smell like a freaking camel now." She'd peppered Beth with questions about camels, brack tea, the shop, and anything else that seemed to pop into her mind for the past few hours—all obviously designed to take Beth's mind off her aching heart.

Delphine had taken off her cloak and wore a pretty red dress beneath it. She'd rolled up her sleeves and wrecked the dress without complaint, and now camel hair and milk stains covered the fabric. "I'm glad that's over with," she said, delicately lifting her arms to sniff beneath them. "This might be the grossest I've ever smelled, and that's saying something."

"The bad news is that isn't the worse part of the bargain."

"Oh, great. Please tell me we don't have to service an outhouse."

"This does involve a compost toilet, and cutting Cotota's toenails. I don't know how old she is, but the poor dear needs diamond blades on her clippers."

Delphine grinned. "I'm never going to forgive you this."

"Liar," said Beth, linking her arm through Delphine's. "You also have to enthuse over her butter tea, which might be the worst part."

"That doesn't sound so bad."

"Maybe not for you, but I can't lie. It's made with brack tea."

"This just gets better and better," said Delphine. She retreated as Beth headed for the compost toilet. "What is that sludge dripping out of that thing?"

"What do you think? We're going to have to clean that for her. The poor thing needs help."

"Fine," said Delphine. "Where does she keep a shovel and wheelbarrow?"

A BOWL OF icy cold water sat on a table outside Khunbish Cotota's front door.

"For all the good this will do," said Delphine. They washed anyway and walked into the ger together. The teapot sat on the table beside three steaming cups of tea. Beth bowed to the tiny woman, who barely came up to Delphine's breast.

Cotota returned the bow and sat on a stool, asking them to tea in Russian.

Delphine flashed her dimples. "Cotota, I'm honored to meet you. I'm Delphine Green."

Cotota ignored pleasantries and verbally reviewed the camel milking process, quizzing them on procedure and bucket placement in the shed.

"Have you ever noticed how no one does things as well as you'd do yourself?" asked Delphine. "If you check and we did anything wrong, next time we're here I'll shovel up your Bactrian camel dung too."

Cotota laughed and waved her hand at Delphine as though telling her to go on.

Beth smiled as she watched the woman with a broad freckled face and grayish white hair flutter around her hut like a tiny bird. In the two years she'd known the woman, she'd never once seen her smile. She had bricks of brack tea stacked on a far table, and absolutely nothing ornamental inside the ger. Everything looked functional; a few dishes were stacked on a shelf, a glass jar of grain and pitcher of water sat on the sideboard, and a pallet to sleep on rested on the floor. Spilled salt coated the floor by the front doorway like a coarse white welcome mat.

"Are you keeping something evil out of your ger with that salt, Cotota?" asked Delphine in a conversational tone. The old woman lifted her hands toward the heavens as though imploring and shivered.

Beth patted her knee and Cotota looked at her. Her eyes widened and she backed away.

"Your eyes," said Delphine.

"I'm sorry," said Beth. "Something bad happened to me and it affected my eyes."

Cotota scooted the chair further away, but leaned forward in her chair and pointed at her own face, widening her own eyes with effort. Wind and time had left her face little more than age spots and wrinkles. She pointed at her eyes and strained to open them wide.

Delphine gasped.

Cotota said, "Something bad happened to me too, a very long time ago. I thought maybe Morning Star no longer troubled the women of the world."

"Oh, dear sweet Lord," said Beth, sliding off her chair to sit on the floor as any regained strength drained from her. The room spun around her at the mention of Morning Star's dreaded name. Worse than that, Cotota's eyes, hidden in the wrinkles of her face, were the exact same steely eyes that Kahtar had first brought to Beth's life.

"Oh, ilu," whispered Delphine, placing her hand over her mouth. "Beth, do you know who she is?"

Shaking her head Beth said, "How many of us are there? How many women have been used like that—I mean, Delphine, your eyes are still your own!"

"It involves heart, Beth. Tartarus wouldn't share his heart with me. Thank God. I have enough problems without living forever."

"Artarus?" said Cotota. "Tartarus? Artarus?"

"Oh no!" said Beth, covering her mouth with both hands. "She knows him!"

"Do you know Kahtar too?" asked Delphine. "Attar?"

"Attar!" said Cotota, slipping into an ancient dialect that Beth barely understood as she beamed. Cotota put her hands over her heart. "My Attar. Kidnapped by a horrible woman."

"Abigail," whispered Beth and Delphine together.

"This isn't possible," said Beth.

"And yet it is," said Delphine. "Good lord, Beth. Do you realize this woman is Kahtar's mother?"

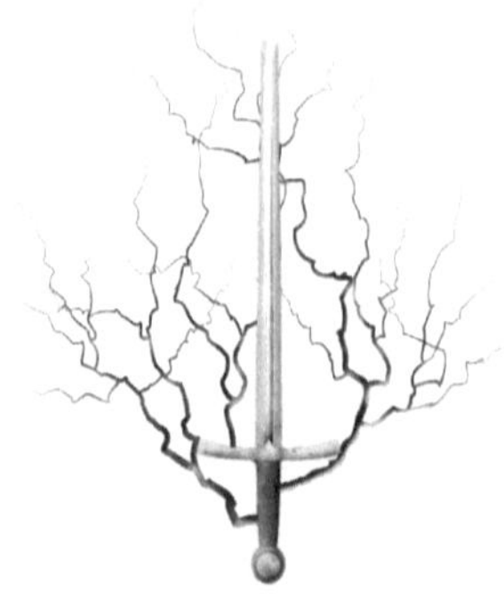

Bloody Ending—Wolf Woods

BETH ROSE TO her feet. "Old Guard!"

"Are you insane?" said Delphine, looking around fearfully.

"I'm close to it I suspect," said Beth. "It has been a hell of a year. But this is bigger than us, bigger than sneaking off to get some brack tea. One of them pledged to me after my father died." Her eyes warmed with tears. "He came to me and said he'd listen for my voice no matter where I was, and call if I needed him. I doubt I'll ever need him more than right now. OLD GUARD!"

"They can't always hear, even when they listen."

"He promised. OLD GUARD!" Beth closed her eyes and tried to focus her second voice, reaching like a prayer. "OLD GUARD I NEED YOU!"

She opened her eyes as the giant man shimmered into being inside the small ger.

"Truth Speaker?"

Beth put her hand over her heart. Poor Cotota had backed herself across the ger and into a wall. "I think that this woman is Kahtar's mother—his first mother."

The Old Guard blinked at her. Until this moment Beth hadn't been certain they had eyelids. "Did you know?" she asked, suspecting it was going too far. Old Guard didn't answer questions, not for her. *If they knew her, they'd have had a source for brack tea.* "Cotota is called Khunbish by the locals. She has Kahtar's eyes."

The Old Guard turned his head to study the woman. Cotota wrapped her arms across her chest, trembling. Her steely eyes were wide and clearly visible.

"She's who I get brack tea from," said Beth, hoping it offered the woman some protection. *Surely they won't hurt her.* "Maybe you could bring Kahtar?"

"Doorway," shouted the Old Guard, but though Beth knew that's what he'd said, it sounded more like music, notes on an unfamiliar instrument sounding strangely from the Old Guard's mouth.

A young woman with long red hair opened the door of the ger and walked in. "Sorry, the doorway is busy. I can get a message to her."

"Does she know the warrior of the ages' mother?"

The woman frowned at Beth's dirty clothes, and looked over at Cotota. "I don't think so. Hold still a moment, I'll ask her." She moved back through the doorway and reappeared almost instantly, chewing her lip. "I mean no disrespect, Old Guard, but the doorway said—I'm only repeating her words—'How am I supposed to keep track of every single thing?' She also said unless the woman is still fertile, she'd be in no further danger from Morning Star." The young woman eyed Cotota shivering against the wall of the ger. "It's good, Mother. No one here will hurt you. He is one of ilu's own." The redhead pointed at the Old Guard and Beth. "She is the woman Kahtar has joined with—his only wife."

Cotota straightened. "My Attar, my Kahtar is a good man?"

"See for yourself," said the redhead.

Kahtar shimmered into view at the side of an Old Guard. A bloody wound cut across his left eye, and Beth felt a twinge of guilt. He'd come looking for her before having an Old Guard heal him. He hurried to her side and wiped smudges from her face, examining her.

"I'm fine," said Beth. "You're not here to see me."

Kahtar glared at Delphine. "We're going to talk, storyteller. You'll not be doing this. Does the quester know you're gone?"

"He's not my keeper," said Delphine.

"Only your new Warrior Chief."

"Kahtar," said Beth. "This is rather important. Do you recognize this woman?" She indicated Cotota with a dip of her head.

Kahtar looked toward the small woman for the briefest moment. "No."

"Look at her eyes. Feel her heart." Beth smiled at him, her heart welling with joy.

Kahtar looked at Cotota for another moment, and his face blanched. "Deda?" he gasped, his voice a hoarse sob.

"Attar, my boy, my Attar." Cotota ran across the small space and burrowed into Kahtar's big waist. "My boy! My boy! Where have you been?"

BETH'S OLD GUARD deposited her back in the woods of Kahtar's veil, almost in the exact same spot Delphine had tessered her from. Beth had a feeling one of the giant men had escorted Delphine back to Aberdyfi and the quester. Kahtar had chosen to visit with his mother.

"Thank you," said Beth, moving a step away from the shimmering Old Guard, hoping he'd leave even if it would leave her in the dark woods alone. She could see the light of the cabin, and she'd rather face her mother's sorrow than time alone with an Old Guard. "You know, thank you for coming when I called."

"The dog," said the Old Guard. "The one who died."

Beth shivered under his black gaze. "Wolves," she said with a trembling voice, and she swallowed.

"We don't want him," said the Old Guard.

Beth stared at him for a moment. "Wolves is alive? I thought he died." *But so did I.*

"He returned after ingesting your blood."

"Wolves drank my blood?"

"Absorbed. It was instinct. He lay across your body as you passed. There is a connection of hearts between some humans and canines. Old Guard do not feel a connection with this canine."

Tears ran out Beth's eyes and down her cheeks, and she felt her face screw up into a quivering mess. *How can I not have run out of tears by now?* "Can I have him back?"

"Certainly," said the Old Guard. He extended his hands in her direction and a dog appeared to drop from thin air. It wasn't Wolves as she'd seen him last. This shaggy, multi-colored canine looked something like Wolves might have once looked, but younger. "It's him," said the Old Guard, and vanished leaving the dog and Beth alone in the dark woods.

The dog looked like a shadow in the night, darker than the forest. He dropped his front end to the ground, his rear playfully humped up like one of the Bactrian Camels from that morning. He barked.

"Wolves?" screamed Beth, running toward him. He jumped into her arms, his tongue consuming her face and hindering her breathing.

"Kahtar is just going to be thrilled about that," said a voice from the trees, and bright veins of a tesseract appeared in the branches like Christmas lights, illuminating the path.

Wolves stopped drowning Beth with his tongue and raced toward Delphine, tail wagging. The dog halted before he reached her, distracted by his own tail. Beth laughed as he attacked it, yelping.

"Delphine, can you believe this? It's Wolves."

Grinning, Delphine shook her head. "I'm really not positive this classifies as a happy ending. That is one messed up dog, even puppy-sized."

Beth hurried to him and tugged his tail out of his jaws. She kissed it to show the animal it was something good. Wolves wagged it, seemed to identify it as a new playmate this time, and chased it into the forest.

"I love him," said Beth. "I don't care if he's not perfect. Neither am I!"

"True dat, and now that you mention imperfection, there's something I wanted to ask you."

"Hmm?" Smiling, Beth watched Wolves' antics through the skeletal trees.

"Would you be able to forgive the clan if they suddenly started to treat you right?"

Beth stopped smiling and turned to look at Delphine. "They've always had my forgiveness. I just don't like them anymore—at least not most of them. But they're never going to treat me right. It's beyond their capability."

"I guess what I meant was—oh, hell—yanno, I could use my gifting to make at least some of them stop treating you like an outsider."

"Are you crazy? Don't you dare! Don't you believe in free will?" said Beth.

"Of course I do! Look, I owe you one. I want you to have a happy ending. A real one."

"Unless you can turn back time that's not going to happen, Delphine. The clan treating me right wouldn't matter to me unless it was the truth. Besides, the only happy ending I want is to feel the touch of my father's heart again. Wait. Why do you owe me one? Are you being nice because I did the naked thing at Cerulean Blue?"

Delphine held her gaze like a deer in the headlights. "Ah, yeah. That's why."

"You do remember I can tell when you're lying, right?"

"Shit. Okay. I'll tell you. Just remember one thing."

Beth crossed her arms, narrowing her eyes at the storyteller.

"I totally love you."

Hot tears warmed Beth's eyes as the truth of those words hit her heart. "You're such a freakin' cheater! What did you do? If you kissed Kahtar, I swear to God I'll hurt you."

"That day in the Arc when you saw Honor kissing me..." Tears formed in Delphine's dark blue eyes.

"Yeah?" Beth tensed.

"You kept pointing at me and talking, remember?"

"Of course I remember!"

"So, the thing is, your truth can override my stories."

Beth remembered Delphine shaking her head, trying to get her to pretend not to see her.

"What did you do, Delphine?"

"Well, I tessered some dogs—nice ones—over by Dianta, and I told Honor they were wolves." Delphine hung her head in shame.

For a moment Beth couldn't speak. If she hadn't fought with Honor, the shunning never would have happened. Tears trickled down her cheeks and her face screwed up as a sob escaped her.

"No!" Delphine launched herself at Beth and wrapped her arms around her. "Please, don't! Please, don't cry! I couldn't allow Honor to see me! If you knew why, you'd forgive me in a heartbeat! I swear on my heart you would! Beth, please don't stop loving me. I'm so sorry!"

Although she heard the truth in Delphine's words, once she started crying, Beth couldn't stop. She wrapped her arms around the smaller woman and hung on, sobbing against her neck until her tears ran dry and her back ached from bending over. Delphine clung to her, patting her back and begging forgiveness the entire time.

"I never thought it would be so awful! I'm sorry, Beth. It's all my fault! If it wasn't for me you never would have fought with Honor!"

That's not true. Beth stopped crying and pulled away.

Delphine's chin quivered and her bottom lip jutted out. Huge tears slipped down her cheeks.

Beth shook her head. "Don't." Her voice came out a dry rasp. "Once Honor saw me, we would have fought."

Delphine shook her head. "Don't try to make me feel better."

"I'm not. I don't do that." Beth sniffled and pressed a hand against her chest. It ached. Everything was too much and her heart couldn't take anymore. "You should go."

Fighting and failing to control the emotion on her face, Delphine nodded.

"Wait!" said Beth, as Delphine stretched out her hand. "I still love you."

Delphine smiled, but her dimples didn't show, and the smile brushed against Beth nearly like a lie did.

"No, I really do," said Beth.

"I know." A few more tears slipped out Delphine's eyes. "But you don't like me."

Beth considered that, and shrugged. "Maybe not today, but maybe in a few days. I don't have very many friends."

A dimple appeared. "I don't understand why. You're pretty amazing."

Reaching out, Beth gave Delphine's shoulder a quick squeeze. "Thank you for telling me the truth, but you'd better go. I'm tired. Besides, my mom can scan and it's lit up like a Christmas tree out here. If she senses you making me cry, well, I guess she's a shieldmaiden."

"I know. I sensed it. I've known other shieldmaidens." Delphine's eyes widened. "There's something else I noticed about your mother, and you."

"What's that?" asked Beth.

"You don't touch each other's hearts."

"Exactly how much snooping have you done, Delphine? I wasn't aware you'd even met my mother."

"Don't change the subject. Why don't you touch your mother's heart, Beth?"

Beth scowled. "It takes two! She's always withheld her heart from me."

"Why do you think that is?"

"I don't know! It's just the way she is, kind of standoffish."

"Pfft," said Delphine. "Think harder, Beth. Why would a mother withhold her heart from her child?"

Beth shrugged. "To protect it maybe? Do you think that's why she did it?"

"I don't mean to brag, but being a storyteller is sometimes akin to being a fortune teller. We see all sometimes, like this time for instance. Your mother joined, for all intents and purposes, with a seeker man. In order to protect you, and him, she had to keep you from Covenant Keepers. What better way to do that than to hide her heart, and give you absolutely no reason to open yours to the world and search for your own people?"

"There's no better way," whispered Beth.

"You could comfort each other through this. She needs you, and apparently she kicked your husband's ass tonight. You might want to give her something else to do besides beating the fluff out of the clan's warriors. I think she has anger issues."

Without another word, Beth spun toward the cabin and ran.

"Enjoy your happy ending," Delphine hollered after her. "You're welcome!"

ACKNOWLEDGMENTS

Does anyone ever acknowledge the muse on this page? That merciless witch who refuses to let me sleep at night, infuses my dreams with scenes from the book, and wakes me with the shouted command, "Must. Finish. Book. Now. Nothing else matters!"

Surely someone has mentioned the muse before. The truth is, no sooner would I say, "Thanks for making my life chaotic, giving me unreasonable deadlines, and making it necessary to talk to myself out loud due to the chronic story happening inside my head," then she'd bellow, "SHUT UP! Why aren't you working on the NEXT BOOK? Time is a-wasting, slave!"

So, never mind about that tyrant.

Besides, the one who really turns a story into a book, and guides an author, is the editor. My GEC editor went over this story with power tools and heavy machinery, magicking it into the story enclosed. For the wisdom, guidance, and patience, I thank you, Oh Editor. You edit my dreams, trim my verbosity, and punctuate my, like, wordage.

Thanks to my beta readers, Kimro and Lindsay. Also a thank-you to Shieldmaiden for Hire's story edits!

For my dearest Dear Hubby: thank you for again enduring, especially my chronic night-writing. Whether reading dialogue aloud in my office at three in the morning, subtlety tap-tap-tapping a scene into my phone as you try to sleep beside me, or zoning out of our world and into another, you've always been my biggest supporter. I love your guts.

ABOUT THE AUTHOR

An entrepreneur, wife, mother, and novelist, S.R. Karfelt enjoys spending time with her muse and living outside her comfort zone. She currently resides in the soaring capital of the world.

Visit her website:
www.srkarfelt.com